Beyond Safe Boundaries

Margaret Sacks

LODESTAR BOOKS   E. P. DUTTON   NEW YORK

ACKNOWLEDGMENTS

my thanks to Tom Russell
and to Rosemary Brosnan

Library of Congress Cataloging-in-Publication Data

Sacks, Margaret.
  Beyond safe boundaries / Margaret Sacks.—1st ed.
    p. cm.
  Summary: Elizabeth comes of age in 1960s South Africa as her
older sister joins a secret group opposed to the country's racial
policies.
  ISBN 0-525-67281-8
  [1. South Africa—Race relations—Fiction.   2. Race relations—
Fiction.   3. Sisters—Fiction.]   I. Title.
PZ7.S1223Be   1989   88-27311
[Fic]—dc19   CIP
                                                           AC

Published in the United States by E. P. Dutton,
a division of Penguin Books USA Inc.

Published simultaneously in Canada by
Fitzhenry & Whiteside Limited, Toronto

Editor: Rosemary Brosnan

Printed in the U.S.A. First Edition
10 9 8 7 6 5 4 3 2

for my mother and in memory of my father
and for
Harold, David, and Wendy

Yesterday, in the recesses of my wardrobe, in an old, lid-less suitcase filled with mementos, I came across my first school notebook, which I had kept over the years for sentimental reasons. It had been carefully covered in brown paper, and in the top right-hand corner, in large print, I had written:

> *Elizabeth Levin*
> *Sub-A*
> *Queen Victoria Junior School for Girls*
> *Port Me*
> *South Africa*
> *World*

The first page was neatly dated *17th January, 1953,* and the *Port Me* on the cover was testament to the fact that at six years old I had been quite convinced that Port Elizabeth, the city we live in, had been named after me.

I stared at those round, meticulous letters touching the

penciled lines at all the correct points of contact until the print became a blur. Over the past nine years, during my rare bouts of spring cleaning, I had avoided discarding the notebook, but this time, without a qualm, I dropped it in the dustbin. I was shedding the past. No longer could I relate to that innocent, self-satisfied six year old. At the age of fifteen I had become a realist. People I loved were dead, and my sister Evie was gone. I knew that so-called friends whispered about her, and the bolder ones solicited tidbits of information, practically begged for confidentialities, which I knew they would then share at their private tea parties.

I tried to recall when my world began to unsettle, when the seeds of change were first sown, and as always, I came up with the same answer: It was that happy-sad day my father arrived home with his bride—my new mother. I was in the standard-four class at Queen Vic, and at eleven years old, wise enough to feel some apprehension, an intuition that nothing would be quite the same again. It was an unfortunate coincidence that the upheaval in our family coincided with the general stirrings of unrest in our country.

1

The rain had stopped and the sun beat down, making everything steamy. The heat came up off the pavement in front of our house where the ants relentlessly tried to drag a dead beetle into a too-narrow crevice. I kept my feet up in the air as I swung slowly back and forth on the wooden gate, careful not to injure the black hordes of ants marching double file as we did at school. Such energy they had in this damp heat! More than the men and women in caps and bright T-shirts playing golf across the road. If I half-closed my eyes and ignored the narrow one-way street in front of our house, the putting green of the ninth hole of the Port Elizabeth Golf Club became an extension of our front garden. I had a whole collection of golf balls to prove what lousy golfers some of the members were.

At last I saw the Salmons' black car crawling over the hill toward our house. Even the ants moved faster than Aunt Rebie drove. She wasn't my real aunt, but Delia, her daughter, was my best friend and had been since the age of six when we both entered that bastion of the British Empire, Queen Victoria Junior School for Girls, which strove, somewhat unsuccessfully, to convert white colonial children into snotty English ladies.

I had told no one at school, other than Delia, that my father was going to remarry. She said she knew—she had heard her mother and father talking about it, but she wished she hadn't known so that I could have been the first to tell her. Although I made her promise not to tell anyone, the word *stepmother* was soon being bandied around at school.

It may have started the day we played Whispers in the playground, a large area of tar-covered concrete where we sat and ate lunch while the burning tar melted stickily into our behinds. Playing Whispers with our hats on was awkward, but the covering did protect us from the sun and from profuse pigeon droppings. Six of us sat in a line and whispered to each other the word chosen by the person at the front of the line. When the last person stood up and gave a garbled rendition of the original word, we would all laugh gleefully.

Sitting next to me that day was Marsha Baum, with her sallow cheeks and perfect ringlets that hung down to her shoulders like shiny, brown sausages. She insisted the curls were natural, but it was rumored that Marsha's mother wrapped her hair in special rags and curlers every night. Even Marsha's sandwiches, made by her doting mother, were circles with layers of color in them—pink anchovy paste and cream cheese—quite exotic compared with my brown bread and jam that Mathilda, our cook, slapped together for me every morning. Perhaps my new mother would know how to make circular sandwiches too, I had thought, watching her take a bite.

When Marsha took her place at the head of the line, I

was at the end, waiting eagerly as the word passed from ear to ear. Finally it was my turn to stand up and deliver. I had heard the word perfectly clearly, and although the others had shouted out their words, I just whispered mine—*stepmother.*

"Is it true? Is it true that you're getting a stepmother, Elizabeth?" Marsha had shouted, her ringlets jumping nastily. "Stepmother, stepmother!" My ears were ringing with the word. "I hope she's not a wicked stepmother," someone said, and then giggled.

I had wanted to tell them that I was getting a new mother, not a stepmother, but their faces were shining with malice and I knew they wouldn't listen to me. Delia stood protectively at my side, but I ran off to the toilets—a separate building containing a maze of unlighted cubicles with damp floors. It must have been the foul-smelling disinfectant that had made me bring up my jam sandwich.

Another brightly dressed foursome was on the putting green of the ninth hole by the time Aunt Rebie drove up in front of our house. Delia jumped out, and her mother waved at me and blew a kiss.

"Be good, you two," she yelled through the open window in her deep, husky voice, which my father said was the result of smoking too many cigarettes. I'd once heard my father joke that, in their younger days, Aunt Rebie used to fancy him. She'd take the last appointment for the day at the surgery to have her teeth cleaned (those were the days when she still had her own teeth), and my father would be expected to give her a ride home. If he'd married her, I thought, I'd still have a mother, but then I would be only half me.

Delia and I swung on the gate together and watched the putters across the road. Little black caddies, hardly bigger than we were, carried the heavy, leather golf bags.

"What d'ya want to do?" I asked.

"Let's stick out our legs and keep them very still and see who can get the most mosquito bites," Delia suggested.

I had been shooing away the mosquitoes, but now we let the big, black, buzzing bloodsuckers have their fill.

Next door the post box creaked and I saw Fiona Frazer staring at us. She was a fat, freckled ten year old, one year younger than Delia and I, and a convenient playmate when Delia wasn't around. Whenever Fiona wanted to know what was going on at our house, she'd pretend to look in the post box and casually wander over.

"What are you doing?" she asked.

"Getting anemic," Delia replied. I loved the way she knew all those big words. My father said if I read as much as she did, I'd know them, too. But I told him that if I were allowed to go to the "bioscope" as often as she did, my vocabulary would improve, too. "*Cinema,* not *bioscope,*" my father corrected, as he always did when I converted Afrikaans words to English slang. Although I wasn't allowed to see many films, I knew them all because Delia loved to tell a story and she remembered every detail of every one she saw. She also had a picture collection of film stars, including a signed photograph of Elizabeth Taylor.

"I'll join you," Fiona said, sitting on the low, stone wall adjacent to the gate and sticking out her legs. There was no more room on the gate, which was already creaking with our weight.

"There's your dad," I said. Mr. Frazer, in his khaki safari suit, was chipping the ball out of the bunker onto the green. My father was also a golf enthusiast, but he wasn't allowed to be a member of the club across the road for the same reason I'd been refused admission to the Port Elizabeth Municipal Tennis Club when I was nine years old: No Jews allowed.

"Let's see if the mosquitoes like Christian or Jewish blood best," I said to Fiona.

"If I were getting a new daughter," Fiona said prissily, "I wouldn't like her to have red bumps all over her legs."

My feet flopped down onto the pavement, squashing an army of ants. No doubt she was right. I should at least try to look my best when my father arrived from Johannesburg with my new mother later in the day. After all, I had waited for this moment long enough.

Fiona's legs were still up in the air enticing the buzzing insects. "My father says your new mother is Irish, so if she were your real mother you'd be half Christian," said Fiona in her know-it-all voice.

"Don't be dumb," I said, "She's Irish-Jewish, not Irish-Christian."

"You're calling my father dumb?" she said.

"Well, my father is older than yours, and he says she's Irish-Jewish, and he should know."

"If your father is older, he's going to die sooner." And with that prediction, Fiona Frazer jumped off the wall and marched off to her house.

The thought of my father dying and my being left an orphan had always been my one greatest, secret fear, but Fiona Frazer wasn't going to know that.

"Sticks and stones may break my bones, but words will never hurt me," I shrieked at her departing back.

"Your neighbor is so puerile," Delia said, plaiting a

piece of hair that fell over her shoulder. "Let's go inside, and I'll give you an Elizabeth Taylor hairstyle that will knock out your new mother."

The house was unusually quiet. Mathilda, the cook, was taking her afternoon rest in her room out in the yard, while Lena, the housemaid and nanny, had the afternoon off, which meant she had gone to visit her family in New Brighton, the African township that my father said must have been named by a cynical Englishman, considering the impoverished housing conditions. My older sister, Evie, was at ballet class. I was very proud of the fact that my sister was a real ballerina and had even refused a scholarship to Sadler's Wells in London, choosing instead to follow an academic career at Witwatersrand University in Johannesburg. As usual, Evie's room was a mess. Clothes and shoes were strewn all over the floor.

"Isn't your sister going to clean up before your dad arrives?" Delia asked. I shrugged, remembering the scene she'd made two years before when my father told us he was going to marry again, and I knew she would do nothing to make our new mother welcome.

"You know, Dele," I said, "two years ago I wanted a mother more than anything, but now I feel kind of scared. What if we don't like each other or what if Evie behaves like a monster?"

"Oh, don't worry," Delia said, pushing me into a chair and draping my bath towel around my shoulders while she snip-snapped the air with the kitchen scissors—the same pair that Mathilda used to clean the Sabbath chickens that still had a showing of feathers.

"Shouldn't we put some newspaper on the floor?" I asked, getting up.

"Yeah, I guess so." Delia was pretty lazy and I knew I'd

have to sweep up the mess. I didn't dare ask Mathilda, whose sole territory was the kitchen.

"Look, this is the style I'm going to give you," Delia said, pointing to a glossy picture in *Stage and Cinema,* a magazine she regularly bought at the bioscope. The cover of this issue showed a back view of Marilyn Monroe from head to toe. Her eyes gazed at us over a raised shoulder and her fingers were spread against her legs, which formed a deep, inverted, fishnet-covered V.

Delia could see I wasn't too interested in the pictures. "Look," she said, "Evie is going to university soon, so even if she and your new mother don't get along, it will only be for a short time." Delia pulled my hair forward. "First I'll cut a fringe, then we'll wet it and twist it into bangs." Snip-snip! I closed my eyes as hair flakes dribbled down my nose.

"Anyway," Delia said with a romantic sigh, "your new mother must really love your dad to have waited so long."

"Yeah, that's what I told Evie, and she said, 'Well, Dad is a jolly good catch for someone who's not exactly a spring chicken.'" I put my hands on my hips like Evie did in a bossy mood and swung my head, mimicking her.

"Goll-ee," Delia said, as a chunk of hair hit the newspaper, leaving a few spikes on my arm en route.

"You sound just like your sister. You should be an actress."

I loved it when people said things like that. I knew I could mimic well and didn't need a great deal of prompting to act out whole scenes. "You should have seen the time my father told us he was going to marry again. That was a scene and a half!" I was flushed with the warmth of her praise.

"Tell me! Tell me!" Delia cried, snipping furiously. She

loved our family dramas. Everything was so calm in her own household.

"Can I look in the mirror yet?"

"Not yet, hold your horses just a few more minutes. So-o your father came home from Johannesburg with the big news—gosh, that seems so long ago."

Two years, but the memory was perfectly clear. My father had looked so happy. He had brought us gifts from himself, and from "someone else" who was going to be our mother. And then Evie had flung a damper on all our joy.

"We don't need a mother," she had said. "We had a mother and she's dead, and no one is going to take her place." Her body had stiffened up like a toy soldier's and her face had paled. She took a step toward me as though we were allies. I felt myself shrivel up inside, and I could see from my father's eyes that he was shriveling too.

"I want a mother, I do want a mother," I said, flinging my arms around my father. Evie gave me a poisonous look.

"What did my new mother send?" I asked. I opened the tiny box, and wrapped in tissue paper was a gold charm bracelet with a heart-shaped locket.

"And she said to tell you that for every birthday you'll get a new charm for the bracelet," my father said.

"Her name isn't 'she.' What is it?"

"Lydia," he said, flushing.

"Lydia!" I liked the name and wondered what she would want me to call her.

My father tried to give Evie her gift, but she held her hands together behind her back. "I don't need any bribes," she said, and turned on her heel. We could hear her bedroom door slam shut.

"Why's she so nasty?" I was close to tears.

"She's not nasty, she's just upset. She remembers her mother, but you were just a baby—too young to remember. And don't forget, Evie's been like a mother to you the past few years." He stroked my hair as he said this. It was true. Evie had played mother for a long time. In fact, she had even chosen my name when I was born—Elizabeth, after the princess of England who had been crowned queen the year I turned five.

"Maybe this is not the right time," my father had said in a low rumble, and my heart sank as low as his voice.

Evie had had her way then, but finally, my father announced that he had put off his marriage long enough. Ever since his decision, Evie had been having fits of crying crocodile tears. She would lie on her stomach on the couch and chant, "Everybody hates me," until I would go and tell her I didn't hate her, though the truth was I was beginning to feel that I did.

All afternoon I kept listening for the sound of my father's car and his key in the latch, but by four o'clock when Mathilda came in from her rest, there was still no sign of my father and new mother.

"*Hayi, hayi, hayi!*" Mathilda clapped her hands when she saw Delia and me. "What you do?" she asked, pulling at my chopped-up hair. "You plucked chicken or what! And Miss Evie, she going to be mad hatter with you." Tilly's vocabulary had become more colorful since I had read her excerpts from *Alice in Wonderland*.

Evie probably would be mad. Delia and I had decided to play Big Ladies, and it wasn't difficult to find what we needed among the clothes spilling out of her wardrobe and strewn across the floor. They smelled of stale deodorant

11

and face powder, but this didn't deter us from strapping her bras around our flat chests and fastening her garter belts around our waists to hold up her nylon stockings. Her dresses didn't hide our lumpy chests, which we had built up with the help of cotton socks. Clomping to the mirror in high-heeled shoes, we applied layers of lipstick and rouged our cheeks. Our eyelids were a rainbow of blues and greens, and Delia had even dared to curl her lashes with a repulsive-looking instrument.

"The master he late," Tilly said. "And the new madam, *yo, yo, yo!* She don't like the way Mathilda is cooking, then Mathilda go *hamba wena.*" Her laugh was an expulsion of air through the gaps between her long, yellow teeth and sounded like the water draining out of our bathtub. I copied her, which I knew she found irritating.

"You'll love my new mother, don't worry," I told her.

"No one take place of old madam," she said with a hiss. "She the best. She best cook—she teaching me. She best tennis player, too."

For as long as I could remember, people had been asking me if I was going to be a tennis champion like my late mother. They asked this in the same tone in which they inquired where I had bought my "big, brown eyes." Both questions I understood to be rhetorical, although I must have inherited the tennis gene because I spent most of my spare time banging balls against the side wall of the house, with no care for the dahlias so carefully planted by Cuthbert, the garden boy, who was really not a boy, but a gray-bearded black man. At the end of every hitting session, there would be a row of pink and yellow dahlia heads hanging from fractured stems.

"How you like me to knock your head off?" Cuthbert

often threatened, but Lena found a way to appease him. She would cut off the dahlia heads and have them swimming in bowls on every table in the house.

Delia and I were singing a duet on the dining room table, still dressed in full regalia, when my father and new mother walked in. We hadn't even heard the car crunch up the drive. We yelped, and Mathilda got up quickly from her comfortable position on the couch where she'd been sitting and clapping our performance. She gave a slight bow in my father's direction and held out a scrawny, calloused hand to my new mother.

"*Molwena,* new madam," she said with a giggle before disappearing into the kitchen. Despite her smile, I knew she was making it clear that my father's wife was the newcomer.

Delia disappeared with her maid, who had arrived to walk her home, and I was alone, aware of my clownish makeup and Evie's clothes dragging round my ankles.

"This is the baby," my father said. I was thankful he hadn't noticed my hair. He looked so happy—his blue, slightly protruding eyes were clear as sunshine, and his smiles and laughter made the vein on his large forehead stand out like the river on a map. He hugged me tight, biting down on his tongue and making a humphing noise, pretending to squeeze much harder than he really did.

He was unaware of my discomfort, but my new mother came to my rescue. "You must have had fun dressing up, Liza, but let me help you change now." No one called me Liza, but I liked the sound of it coming from her. Her voice had a soft Irish lilt, so different from our guttural South African English. She took my hand and stroked it and

13

didn't let go as we walked to my room. She wasn't much taller than I was, and far prettier than the photograph I'd seen, which didn't show her shiny, dark curls and smooth English skin.

"When you've changed, I'd like you to show me the house," she said.

The kitchen scissors still lay on my dressing table with some telltale hairs clinging to the blades. "We'll go to the hairdresser and get your hair shaped," she said. "Cutting hair seems easy, but you have to know how."

"What shall I call you?" I almost choked on the question.

"Goodness, I'm sorry, that's the first thing I should have thought about. Lydia, if you like, but I'd much prefer Mom or Ma."

"Or Mum or Mummy, like they do in England," I said in my most exaggerated British accent, and we both laughed.

"So you are a good mimic," my mother said. "Your daddy told me all about you."

My face heated up. She probably knew I had allergy attacks most nights; that I knocked the heads off the dahlias every day; and that after dinner each night, when I walked down the dark passage to my bedroom, I barked like a dog to scare off any burglars who might be lurking there.

"Well, are you dressed and ready to take me on a tour of the house?" my mother asked. This time I took her hand. I showed her the bathroom with my father's shaving cabinet above the sink, and the antique washing machine, which the washerwoman, Emily, used every Monday for the sheets and towels. Everything else was hand washed by Lena. Through the bedroom window I showed her the

14

washing line where the sheets flapped and the towels dried to a crust. I tried to bypass Evie's room, but she pushed open the door. It swung wide to reveal the mess, which was even worse since Delia and I had created havoc with her makeup.

When we reached the kitchen, my mother asked Mathilda to please tidy Evie's room before she came home. I was about to explain that Tilly only looked after the kitchen, but before I could say anything, Tilly gave her awful grin and said, "Sure, sure thing, madam."

I showed my mother the lounge, my least favorite room, with its stodgy, formal furniture and heavy curtains that kept out the sunlight; and my favorite room, the oval-shaped porch, which jutted out from the house and had windows all around with views of the golf course, our neighbors the Johnsons' house, and of our garden with its giant hedge of hibiscus.

Finally, we moved on to my parents' bedroom. My father and Cuthbert had brought in the suitcases and bags and hat boxes. So many hat boxes! I couldn't wait to help my mother unpack—to see her clothes and jewelry and makeup. I flung open the door of her wardrobe, and we both gasped together. Hanging on the rack inside the wardrobe were three tennis dresses belonging to my dead mother—old-fashioned tennis dresses that someone had stored away for seven years and purposely hung back on the rack to welcome my father's new wife.

By the time she returned from ballet class, one bed and one wardrobe from my parents' room had been exchanged with the spare furniture in Evie's room. Mathilda told me she had warned the new madam not to sleep in the dead madam's bed. My mother, who I discovered was equally superstitious, went one step further and exchanged the wardrobe, too. At dinner, Evie was barely civil, and I could hardly wait to leave the table. I went to bed at the first suggestion—something quite unheard of. Evie retired early, too. As I lay in the dark, I could hear her sniffling in her room. I wondered at her unhappiness. Was she repenting? Maybe she wasn't the culprit at all. It could have been Aunt Phoebe, my father's sister, who seemed rather disapproving of the marriage, or even Tilly, who didn't want a new madam. My father had barely spoken at dinner and he looked old and worried. I thought of Fiona Frazer and her prediction about death and age.

"Good night Dad, good night Mom, good night Evie," I yelled at the top of my lungs. At least if anyone died during the night, I would always remember my last words to them.

"Good night, darling." My mother appeared at my bedside. "Don't worry about anything. Everything is going to be all right," she said in her soft Irish lilt.

2

"Red leather yellow leather red leather yellow leather red yeller leather. . . ." The elocution class snickered as someone failed to master the tongue-twister we each had to say at lightning speed. I knew my performance had been one of the best, and so it should have been. I had been practicing for days in the hope of impressing Miss Godwin sufficiently so that she would give me a part in the school play.

"Now gels," Miss Godwin articulated, "let us try Peter Piper picked a peck of pickled peppers . . . and then at the end of class, those who wish to take part in *A Midsummer Night's Dream* should sign up. But remember, rehearsals will be every evening for six weeks and you must be able to attend."

For a moment my spirits sank. My mother didn't drive a car and my father never came home from work before six o'clock. But then I knew my mother would get me there somehow. The idea of performing on the city hall stage enthralled me. Miss Godwin's plays had been staged there annually for as long as I could remember, and every year the costumes and stage sets were more sumptuous. With

Evie's ability to dance, she had always been a favorite of Miss Godwin, and I wished I had her talent.

"Of course, there are not enough speaking roles to include the standard-four class. The ten who are chosen will be the trees in the forest, so you will have to learn to sway and *whoosh!*"

"No speaking parts!" someone snorted in disgust, yet almost everyone signed up, and I knew that with my height I would stand a good chance of being a tree.

"Old chicken legs here even looks like a tree," said Marsha Baum with a smirk, her fat ringlets writhing like live worms in my direction. A few of her cronies laughed. We all knew Marsha would be given a speaking part even if Miss Godwin had to create it herself without Shakespeare's consent. Marsha was Miss Godwin's favorite. She was a born actress and knew how to manipulate the teachers with her dimpled smile and perfect diction. They didn't know about the Marsha who dug holes in her garden and covered them with newspaper so that when her "enemies" were invited to play at her house they would fall in and perhaps break a leg.

The play was all anyone discussed on the homebound school bus. By the time we approached my stop, the subject had been talked out and a hush had descended. I could see my mother waiting at the bus stop and so could Marsha Baum, who now bounded out of her seat.

"Is that your stepmother, Elizabeth?" she asked in a stage whisper, which reverberated to every corner of the bus. Her captive audience of thirty-five girls bounced out of their seats and peered through the windows.

"Are stepmothers really mean?"

"What's it like having a stepmother?"

"Where's your real mother?"

18

The voices followed me as I jumped off the bus, which had not yet fully stopped. The warm breeze felt cool against my hot cheeks.

"What's upsetting you?" my mother asked, and when I told her she just laughed and said that my friends were ignorant and therefore curious. "We have to tolerate ignorance and spread knowledge," she said. "It's the same with the natives. If they were educated, they wouldn't annoy us by making silly mistakes."

"Like Tilly ruining your best casserole dish on top of the hot stove," I said.

"No. That she did on purpose," my mother said. "There are agitators in the townships who teach the servants these things, and I'm afraid the next time she follows their advice I'm going to ask her to leave."

By the time we reached the house, all thoughts of the play had drained away, and when I thought about it again I decided to keep it a secret from my parents and surprise them when the cast was announced. But I needed to tell someone.

"Evie, can you keep a secret?" I asked. She was sitting on her bed knitting a sweater. *Clickety-clack, clickety-clack,* the needles bounced against each other. She knitted faster than anyone I knew but hated sewing the pieces together, so her garments never looked quite right.

"Who's that for?" I asked.

"For Dad—my parting gift."

"You make it sound like you're never coming back." I laughed anxiously.

"Well, I certainly don't want to come back. What for? I'm not wanted around here any more."

"That's not true. Ma . . . I mean Lydia loves you. She told me and she said that our real mother was a wonderful

19

person and that it must be really hard for us—especially you."

"She knows nothing!" Evie's jaw was beginning to stiffen. "And one of these days you won't be her little darling anymore either. She'll probably have her own baby and you'll just be the stepdaughter around here."

My hands felt clammy. I wished I hadn't walked into Evie's room and couldn't even remember why I had done so.

"So, chump, what's your big secret?" Evie was her old self again, smiling and confidential. These days I had to suffer before she would show friendship.

"I put my name down for Miss Godwin's play. Only ten standard fours get chosen, but I think I have a good chance. I want to be in that play more than anything in the whole world."

"Uh-huh." Evie didn't seem too interested, and I left her mouthing, "Two plain, two perl. . . ."

Lena was drinking tea out of her enamel mug when I walked into the kitchen. She studied my face and said, "Miss Worriedness! You have mother, you have father, you have nice house, nice nanny. You spoilt or what?" I climbed onto her starched lap and was tempted to take a bite out of her thick slab of bread spread with apricot jam, but like any white child, I knew that eating off servants' plates was taboo. Whether this unspoken rule was for hygienic reasons or to prevent white children from depriving the servants of their full ration of food, I never knew.

"Lena, how many children do you have?"

"One boy in Transkei, one boy dead, and one girl adopted who want job here."

"Which one do you love best?"

"I am loving all my children, but the boy he too clever—

top of class in the mission school." Her chest puffed out with pride and she beamed. It was obvious to me that she loved her natural child best.

"D'you think my new mother will have a baby?"

"*Yo, yo, yo!* Who putting ideas in this head? Your mother she got enough on her hands right now."

"But Evie said she would."

"Miss Evie know nothing. She very sad gel and making big trouble round here."

"Maybe she'll be happier when she leaves for university," I suggested.

Lena's brow furrowed and the whites of her eyes seemed to grow menacingly yellow. "Bad thing for unhappy gel to leave her house. She can get in big trouble outside. *Yo, yo, yo!*" Lena shook her head sadly. I waited for her to bite her bread, but she was waiting for me to leave.

I went outside with my tennis racket, and by the time I had finished pounding the ball against the wall, my arm felt like rubber and a row of flower heads hung loosely from their stems.

3

I studied the sheet of names for a second time and tried not to let the tears form, because if they did, I knew they would gush and maybe never stop.

"This is not fair," Delia said, hardly daring to look at my stony face. "That fat slob Irmgard Dietrich is a tree, and Marion Bell—ugh! How could she leave you out? Miss G-win is a twit." Delia would not speak the Lord's name in vain even if it was attached to another word.

"Look here," I croaked, "Marsha Baum is Mustardseed. That's a fairy, isn't it? Doesn't that take the cake!" I could barely squeeze the words through the tightness in my throat.

"Well, we all knew Miss Marsha the Shloop wouldn't want to be a tree like the rest of the plebs. And what M.B. wants, M.B. gets." Delia was so mature and knowledge-able. She knew just what judgment to make about unde-serving people.

I was subdued for the rest of the day and Miss Godwin must have sensed my disappointment. At the end of elocu-tion class, she called me aside. "Elizabeth, you were one of my first choices for the play, but when I called your mother, she felt it would be difficult for you to attend rehearsals every evening. And believe me, she wasn't the only one. Many mothers couldn't or wouldn't commit themselves."

My mother! My mother did this to me. I was stunned. The whole week I had imagined coming home on Friday with the news that I was one of the chosen, and my mother was to have smothered me with hugs and kisses in an excitement that matched my own. I smiled weakly at Miss Godwin.

Lena met me at the bus stop and I gave her the silent treatment. "Mouse got your tongue?" she inquired. "The madam she lie down. She not feel too good today. So you can pretend to be happy gel."

Probably pregnant, I thought, just like Evie said, and already she didn't care about me.

When we reached the house, I marched through the kitchen and into my parents' bedroom and threw down my school case. "How could you do this to me?" I shrieked. "You've ruined everything."

My mother raised herself on her elbows. "What are you talking about? Why are you so hysterical?"

Hysterical! How dare she call me hysterical. "You know what you've done. You wouldn't let me be in the school play. Miss Godwin told me. You thought she wouldn't tell me, didn't you?"

"Liza, calm down. This is ridiculous. You never mentioned a word about the school play. I never dreamed it was so important to you. And I'd even forgotten Miss Godwin called."

"I hate you! I hate you!" I ran out of her room to my own and passed Evie in the passage. She smirked as if to say, "I told you so!"

The tears that had been wanting to gush all day now flowed in a steady stream.

"Crybebbe, cry," Cuthbert taunted, staring through my open window. He had been planting seeds in the flower bed under my window and took delight in my misery. I threw a pillow at his grinning face and continued sobbing.

"Your mother, she want you to come and have tea with her." Lena was in the doorway of my room.

"What mother? I don't have a mother."

"*Yo, yo, yo!*" Lena clucked her tongue. "You sad gel, but you bad gel, too. No respect for Mamma, *unyoko* she love you."

"She doesn't love me."

"She don't tell you whole story. I hear when Miss Teacher phone Madam. The madam she say to Miss Evie, 'What you think? You think Liza want to be tree in play?' Miss Evie say Liza don't care about play because trees not talking, only standing in one place all the time."

I entered Evie's room without knocking.

"Now what's your problem?" she mumbled, her lips closed over hairpins as she practiced twirling her hair into a chignon.

"It's all your fault," I said. "You told her the play wasn't important to me." I wanted to scream at her, but I was too worn out from crying.

"Oh, our father's wife trying to turn you against me, is she?" she spat out, looking as though she were about to stab me with the hairpins now clenched in her fingers.

"No, Lena told me all about it."

"The trustworthy servant with oversized ears! You'd take her word before mine, no doubt. Now please remove yourself from my presence."

24

I went and stood forlornly in my mother's darkened room.

"Come here, darling. I'm so sorry," she apologized before I could. "Come get into bed with me."

I climbed into her warm bed, not even waiting to take off my shoes, and clung to her.

"I'll call Miss Godwin and tell her I've changed my mind. But I also have something else to tell you."

"Are you going to have a baby?" I asked bluntly.

"You're my baby," she said, smiling. "Even if I want to I'll never be able to have a baby, because I have to have an operation called a hysterectomy. That's one reason I couldn't have taken you to rehearsals."

"Are they going to put you to sleep?"

"Yes." Her hand squeezed mine. "You'll have to help me to be brave."

"Could you die?" An octopus was grasping my heart and squeezing it so tight that I could hardly breathe.

"No, silly." She smiled unconvincingly and stretched out her hand to reach the bell at her bedside that rang through to the kitchen and servants' rooms.

Lena stood in the doorway. "Yes, madam."

"Where's Mathilda? Liza and I would like some tea now."

"Mathilda, she is out. I will make tea, madam." Lena seemed more obliging than she ever had.

"Mathilda's not playing the game," my mother said sternly, knowing that the message would be relayed in Tilly's direction in due course.

"Madam, my cousin is here from the Transkei and she is looking for cooking job."

"Lena, you call everyone cousin. What exactly is the relationship?" my mother asked.

"She my adopted daughter, child of my dead sister," Lena said.

"Does she have a pass to work here?" my mother asked.

"When Beauty get job, then her madam will get pass for her."

"Lena, you know it's not that simple."

A while later, Lena returned with a tea tray laden with a steaming pot of tea, two china cups, and a plate of scones.

"Beauty make scones," Lena said, and, as if on cue, Beauty appeared.

"Well, you really do live up to your name," my mother said sweetly, and Beauty whispered a thank you. She was very young and pretty with large, soft, round eyes, but she was nervous and twisted her hands shyly. Certainly, Lena would be able to boss her around as she never could Tilly.

This encounter with Beauty made me acutely uncomfortable, as though we were being disloyal to Tilly, who had been part of our family for years.

"My mother's having an operation," I announced to Lena and Beauty.

"*Hayi!*" Lena's mouth opened in surprise and she touched her cheek.

"A hysterectomy," my mother said. "But I'm not planning to have it right away."

"Madam getting rid of her box. *Hayi, hayi, hayi.*" Lena sounded quite horrified.

"What's a box?" I asked.

"Where baby grow," Lena answered.

I imagined a shoe box in my mother's stomach.

"She means the uterus where the embryo grows into a baby," my mother explained. "Lena, don't say box. It's not very nice."

Lena tilted her head intently.

I wanted to ask how does the baby get there, but I knew she wouldn't say anything more elaborate than the father plants a seed there. I knew that. I wanted to know the secrets.

"I'm glad you're not having any babies," I confided to my mother, and with my finger I wrote an invisible but fervent message on my father's smooth bedspread: *Please, God, don't let my mother die.* Take the planting box, I prayed, but leave my mother.

4

Before she went into the hospital, my mother decided to invite the neighbors for dinner one Saturday evening. To ease her wifely duties, my father had suggested a sundowner rather than a full dinner, but my mother felt she owed them more than a drink and snack as they had welcomed her so warmly into their midst. She also felt that if we needed anything in her absence, they would be more willing to help.

Mathilda was cooking roast beef and chicken in ginger ale and soy sauce, and I was hovering around my mother, who was pouring brandy onto a swiss roll for the base of her spectacular, though seldom-made, trifle. She rarely went into the kitchen, relying mostly on Mathilda, but this was a special occasion. A spoon clattered onto the white enamel tabletop, and I knew my mother was thinking, "Too many cooks. . . ." Her nose started twitching and her scalp seemed to move as though irritated by an itch. "You make me drop things," she said nervously. "Go help Lena set the table."

Lena and I spread the crisp white tablecloth over the

dining room table and my mother came in to see if we were doing it right. "Chinese," she said of her best embroidered cloth. "One day I'll buy you one just like it." She was referring to some nebulous future when I would marry, which to her was the singular most important event in a girl's life. My aunt Phoebe had already started a "bottom drawer" for her daughter Ruthie, but my mother was too superstitious for that. She'd say things like, "Don't cross your bridges . . ." and "Don't count your chickens. . . ." I could have written a whole book on her superstitions, which in her case, may have had a sound basis: She had been single until her thirty-eighth year.

My mother set one place with her best cutlery and crystal glasses. She flicked a finger against one of the glasses so that it made a pinging sound, which she said was how you could identify fine crystal. Knowing those kinds of things was very important to people like my mother and Aunt Phoebe. Lena and I laid out the other places, making sure that the bottom of the silverware was one inch from the edge of the table. I used my thumb as a measuring stick. Then we rolled the linen napkins and stuck them very gently inside the water glasses so that they looked like many pairs of rabbits' ears.

"There's nothing more to be done right now," my mother said, after admiring the elegant table. "I just hope the guests get on well."

The neighbors were not too friendly to the only Afrikaans family on the block, but my mother found them charming and had been determined to include them in the guest list. "Besides," she had said, "having Afrikaans neighbors could be helpful someday." She thought Mr. Van Zyl Smit worked for the government, and he must be quite posh with that double-barreled name. I was quick to remind her that this was not England and that the Van-Zyl-whatevers didn't even speak decent English. Just as quickly, my mother countered that she liked to hear them speak the Afrikaans language, which had evolved from their Dutch and German ancestors, because it reminded her of Yiddish.

"You need to take a rest now, Liza, if you want to stay up tonight," my mother said.

I had no intention of taking a rest. Instead I followed Lena to her room in the backyard—forbidden territory—where I liked to listen to her stories of African devils, including the *tokoloshe*. Her heavy, iron bed frame was raised on bricks so that the little *tokoloshe*, who terrorized women at night, wouldn't be able to reach her in her sleep. The small room, which smelled of mothballs and her magic skin cream, was crowded with her meager belongings. A framed picture of her son stood on an old, wooden dresser. Her clothes hung from a rod behind a curtain, and berets of every color—some made of felt and others she had crocheted herself—dangled from a thin, wooden hat stand. These were for Sundays and her afternoons off, when she would dress up and scarcely wave good-bye as she rushed off to the bus that would take her to the township where she lived—that mysterious place where I was not allowed to go.

Although Lena was an adult, every time she went back to the township my mother would have to sign her pass book, giving her permission to come home after dark. Now I saw her pass book lying on the dresser, and she caught me looking at its yellowing, creased cover. I took a pencil and flipped the cover over, and there was a blurred picture, presumably of her, though it could have been of anyone. I closed the book with the pencil tip.

"That Dr. Firewood, he start all that. He want to treat us like children." Lena's voice rose angrily. I knew who Dr. Firewood was—she meant Dr. Verwoerd, the prime minister, whom all the maids hated and I despised because my father had said he was pro-Nazi during the war.

"Nothing ever change," Lena said. "You go now, *intombazana,* I must wash and dress for tonight." No doubt she wanted to take a bath before the evening chill set in, for her bath was an iron tub that she carried to her room and filled with buckets of hot water from the kitchen. Lena took down her favorite floral overall with its matching apron, and I went off to find the least hideous of my cousin Ruthie's hand-me-down party dresses.

As a spoilt only child, my cousin Ruthie had an extensive wardrobe of outfits that she rarely wore more than once. Thus, while Evie's well-worn clothes were donated to Israel, my aunt Phoebe gave to several charities—including me. My mother was fond of saying that those who give will always receive, and in the case of clothes I believed this to be entirely true.

The Frazers were the first to arrive—their first public appearance since their eldest daughter, Charlotte, had arrived home from college six months pregnant. Of course Lena had been the first to hear of Charlotte Frazer's condition. The so-called bush telegraph that operated in the countryside was even more effective in the city suburbs, where every house had a maid who, more often than not, was a confidant to her madam. Gossip ricocheted between maids' rooms like shrapnel from a cannon. Lena had also been the first to know, even before the papers were signed, that an Afrikaans family was moving into the neighborhood, and that Mrs. Frazer had exclaimed to her maid Agnes, "What is this place coming to?"

My mother had laughed at that. "How quickly people forget their own beginnings," she had commented, referring to the fact that Mrs. Frazer had been a lowly shop girl who had managed to catch the son of a British peer in what my mother described as "a weak moment." But there was no denying that Mrs. Frazer was an adept student of the upper classes, for she soon learned to carry herself like a duchess, and spoke with a hot potato in her mouth.

"Hello, darling heart," she said as I opened the door. I didn't feel any special glow at being thus addressed—she called all children "darling heart" and adults were all "jolly good chaps." Preceding her husband into the lounge, she glanced around. "Well," she said, "I see the *plaasjaaps* haven't arrived yet."

"The what?" my mother asked, not understanding the Afrikaans colloquialism.

"You know, the country bumpkins," Mrs. Frazer explained.

"Now, Doreen," my mother said, "behave yourself. They're no more bumpkins than you or I, and I think he may have government connections."

The Johnsons arrived next, and then the Samuels with their son, Jeremy. Mr. Samuels walked slowly because he had a lot of weight to carry. He smiled and pinched my cheek, then made a joke I didn't understand because he came from the old country and was more fluent in Yiddish than in English. His wife, Sarah, was short and frumpish with fly-away gray hair. Mrs. Frazer didn't approve of her. I had heard her say to my mother, "That woman could buy a farm in Main Street, and she walks around looking like a poor white." The Frazers didn't approve of Jews in general, but, like us, the Samuels were an exception. Mr. Frazer couldn't get over the fact that a man who couldn't read or write had managed to become "stone rich," as he described it, and still lived according to the Bible. The Samuels didn't flaunt their wealth, though they did live in the largest house on the block. Despite its impressive exterior, I never liked the big, dark rooms with their heavy mahogany furniture. Only when Jeremy played the baby grand did the atmosphere change. I would sit next to him on the tapestried piano seat requesting every popular tune I could think of, and magically, his long, pale fingers would press the right notes. I confided in Evie that some day I hoped to marry Jeremy, with his long, silky hair and burning-black eyes, but I realized that it was highly unlikely, as he had won a scholarship to a conservatoire in Paris and told me secretly that he hoped never to return. I dreaded the thought of never seeing him again, but Evie consoled me with the thought that he would at least return to see his parents. Evie agreed that he was quite divine but far too serious. She preferred fun-loving chaps like Harry Pollack, who was taking her out that evening.

My mother begged Jeremy to play "a little tune" on the piano, and Mrs. Frazer insisted that she wanted to see Evie dance. With everyone cajoling her, Evie finally kicked off her shoes, and pirouetted across the floor in an impromptu dance like some elegant bird of paradise. Jeremy watched Evie admiringly as his fingers skimmed the keys. And as the small audience applauded, I had a vision of Jeremy and Evie bowing and curtsying to thunderous applause and shouts of "Bravo!" in the great capitals of Europe.

The sound of Harry Pollack's special ring at the door

buzzed into my thoughts, and Evie quickly pulled on her high heels and grabbed her evening bag. "Bye everyone," she shouted breathlessly.

"Don't stop, Jeremy," my mother said. And his fingers changed rhythm from the delicate notes of Tchaikovsky to a more strident march.

"Do you hear what he's playing?" my mother whispered, as though it were of great significance.

Even I recognized the piece—it was Mendelssohn's wedding march.

When Mr. and Mrs. Van Zyl Smit arrived, the friendly chatter quietened down and everyone became terribly polite. I wondered what Mr. Van, as he said we should call him, thought of the tall, casually clad Jeremy with his longish hair, for the Van Zyl Smits were typical straight-laced Afrikaners, he with his hair cut short in the back and on the sides and his three-piece suit, and she with her homemade frock and sequined angora bolero to dress it up. Her tidy hair had probably been wrapped up like snails into pincurls all afternoon and the waves pinched into place with steel pincers. My mother broke the awkward atmosphere by ushering everyone in to dinner and boasting that I had set the table and folded the serviettes as though this were the greatest achievement of all time.

"My children help all the time," Mrs. Van said. "We don't keep a servant, and I tell the kids they must do things for themselves because one day all the Bantu people will be living in their own homelands."

"How on earth are twenty million Africans supposed to survive on thirteen percent of the most arid land in the country?" Jeremy asked quietly.

Before his question could penetrate, my mother cut in. "Oh dear, I hope they don't send our domestic help away too soon! You should have seen what the women looked like in England—worn-out drudges, the lot of them. Of course it was wartime, so I suppose that had something to do with it."

"Tell us about the bombing," I urged, loving to hear my mother's war stories and sensing that politics was a taboo subject in this company.

"Oh yes, our house was bombed in London and my hair started falling out in clumps. I had to wear hats to work—crocheted them myself because there was no money to buy anything."

Like Lena, I thought.

Soon everyone was listening to my mother talking about her job in the Ministry of Supplies. She was so vivacious that I could see everyone loved her almost as much as I did.

"You know, I always tell Liza how lucky we are to have fresh fruit and vegetables. During the war everything was rationed and, would you believe, all the carrots were kept for pilots in the airforce. So you see, carrots do give you good eyesight . . ." she turned to me to finish her sentence, which I had heard many times.

". . . and curly hair," I filled in.

Everyone laughed as though I had said something terribly funny, and went on to talk about their children's bad eating habits. My mother looked around at the animated company with the satisfaction of a diplomat who had just defused an imminent catastrophe. Jeremy's question remained unanswered and seemingly forgotten.

When everyone had finished the hors d'oeuvres, my mother rang a little crystal bell to inform Lena that it was time to clear the table. Clearing the table and bringing in the hot dishes was Lena's job because Mathilda had worked hard in the kitchen all day. But Lena did not appear. Instead, Mathilda stood in the doorway and said, "Madam, I am needing to talk to you." My mother got up and I followed her into the kitchen.

"Lena is gone," Mathilda said. "She has not been here all evening."

My mother twitched with indignation. "How can she do this to me—tonight of all nights," she said fiercely. "Go look in her room, Elizabeth."

I walked out into the yard and knocked on Lena's door. No one answered so I tried the handle. The door creaked open and the smell of the mothballs and face cream overwhelmed me as I fumbled for the light switch. Everything was the same as it had been earlier—the photograph, the berets, and the pass book lying on the dresser. I went back to the kitchen and reported that Lena's things were in the room and she couldn't possibly have run away, because her pass book was there. I knew she would never have run away, but it was not uncommon for maids to quietly pack their bags and leave their places of employment without notice.

Mathilda said that while we ate the main course she would ask around the neighborhood. "Perhaps Lena out visiting one of the gels and forget the time," Mathilda said grimly, indicating that if this were the case, Lena would get a mouthful from her.

Everyone enjoyed the chicken and beef and asked for recipes, which pleased my mother no end. She was positively glowing when she rang the little crystal bell again. Mathilda appeared in the doorway and my mother told her how much everyone had enjoyed her cooking. Mathilda smiled and dropped her head like a shy child. Then she looked up and made a public announcement. "Madam, three gels they were talking outside an hour ago. They did not have their pass books, and the police took them in the back of their van."

I almost choked with shock. I thought of the hideous pass book on Lena's dresser, and I knew how the police, "those power-hungry, uneducated hoodlums," as my father called them, must have shoved Lena and her friends into their van with the dreadful metal bars. I had seen them roughly rounding up pass book offenders before.

"How could they take them from right outside the house?" I blurted out. My mother gave me a look that shut me up. She looked at the Van Zyl Smits and wailed, "These maids are so unreliable. What am I to do? Just when things were going so well!"

My mother had struck a chord with Mr. Van. "Unreliable, you are so right," he said. "Tell you what, I'll call old Potgieter at the station and he'll fix things up."

My mother drooled her thanks. She gave the others a look that said, See, I told you it was useful having Afrikaans neighbors.

Mr. Van made the phone call, speaking rapidly in Afrikaans. He returned to the table, enjoying the silence and his moment of importance. "They're there all right," he said. "We can fetch them after dinner."

My father and Mr. Van went to fetch Lena and her friends from the police station while my mother served coffee and I handed round After Eight chocolate wafers and truffles. When I heard the car brake in the garage, I ran out to see Lena as she walked through the yard to her room. Her pretty, floral overall was all crumpled. Her shoulders sagged and she didn't look at me. I should have run out to give her a hug and say it was all right, but the truth was I couldn't bear to touch her. She'd been contaminated by being in jail. My mother came into the kitchen and took out the food that had been put away. She piled a plate high and poured a large mug of sweet coffee and took it out to Lena's room.

It was late and I was tired, but I went back into the lounge. I had no intention of going to bed until the last visitor had left. The conversation had dwindled, except for Mr. Van and Jeremy, who were talking about the conservatoire in Paris. "Yes," Jeremy said, "I don't plan to come back. There's no future here. Tonight just proved that."

As my father said later, "You could have heard a mosquito breathe in the ensuing silence," but at the time he had a stricken look on his face as though expecting to have to quell an argument.

Then Mr. Van spoke again. "I agree with you, Jeremy. These kaffirs will never learn their place. Mind you, Verwoerd knows how to put his foot down—if anyone can teach them a thing or two, it's him. Ah, Verwoerd, now there's a man!" He popped a truffle in his mouth and smiled as everyone watched with fascination as he chewed.

5

My mother said that my father carried the whole world on his shoulders. If he wasn't worried about the political situation (his party never won elections), he would worry about the stock market. Or the horse races! The "inside" information gleaned from jockey acquaintances seemed especially fabricated for outsiders. Now, with my mother in the hospital, my father's brow was perpetually furrowed. Sometimes I counted the creases and decided there was one for each problem.

Although my father's concerns had always seemed remote to me, my anxiety about my mother's hospitalization matched or even surpassed his; but Evie, who had previously enjoyed sharing my father's confidences, showed no sympathy for him at this time. She flippantly declared that a lined forehead made him look old, and that marriage obviously disagreed with him. It was hard for me to be around Evie these days since she was so obviously happy to be in charge of the household again. In fact, she had become so tolerable since my mother's hospitalization that her temporarily shelved boyfriend, Harry Pollack, was hanging around again and she sang incessantly, "I'm just crazy 'bout Harry and Harry's just crazy 'bout me," until I was ready to choke her.

In a burst of energy, Evie completed the sweater she'd knitted for my father and presented it to him on a Saturday morning, the third day after my mother's operation. The gift was wrapped in the brown paper that Tilly stored away to drain her fried fish. *For my favorite Pop-sicle,* Evie wrote in her large, round hand, and to please her, Father tried on the sweater right away.

"Daddy, you look so handsome in your new sweater," Evie crooned, straightening the shoulders. She patted his slightly rounded belly. "There, it's a perfect fit. Go look in the mirror."

"Thank you, darling," Father said abstractly, kissing her lightly on the forehead. I could tell he was anxious to leave, to visit my mother in the hospital before seeing his Saturday morning patients at the surgery.

"Come on, Daddy," I nagged. I was eager to leave, too—to see my mother for the first time without her "box."

"Wait, master!" Lena came puffing up with a carrier bag. "This food for Madam. Hospital food too terrible bad."

I wondered how Lena knew about hospital food. Everyone knew that Provincial Hospital was for whites only. And then I remembered that my natural mother must have been in the hospital for a long time, and Lena had experience in such matters.

"And Beauty, she make some biscuits for the madam— in here." Lena pointed.

"But Lena, you made them! I saw you making them

40

yesterday when Tilly was off. Don't give us that Beauty rubbish," Evie exclaimed.

"Miss Evie wrong." Lena frowned at her, then turned and looked me straight in the eye. "*Intombazana,* you tell the madam Beauty make the biscuits for her. And master, please tell the madam she must get better quick. We are missing her too much around this house."

Evie looked at Lena from under half-closed lids, her top lip raised in a sneer. Her look was partly of disgust, but it also contained an element of disbelief. I, too, couldn't help wondering about Lena's sincerity, for since my mother's absence, she had spent the mornings chatting on the telephone to friends, and every afternoon the neighborhood maids had congregated in our yard, where she provided them with tea and slabs of bread with jam. She had even borrowed cups and saucers from our everyday set when there weren't enough enamel mugs to go around. Lena would never dream of insulting her guests by offering them tea in one of Cuthbert's empty jam tins.

Our next-door neighbor, Mrs. Frazer, had called several times about "the jabber" permeating through the fence during her siesta time, but I loved to hear the maids talk. Their loud, vehement voices overlapped in the still afternoon air, the emphatic clicks of the Xhosa language lending great import to every statement. Lena must have given several detailed, gory accounts of my mother's operation, because between the unfamiliar words, I heard "madam" and "box" repeated several times. Her audience sat riveted as her hands slashed the air, wielding an imaginary knife, and her mouth grew ugly with the horror of it. Although every maid appeared to have an anecdote about her madam, Lena's story, received with the loudest cries and clucks, was undoubtedly the hit of these afternoon sessions. How unlike the chatter of my mother and Aunt Phoebe, who drank tea with their pinkies elegantly crooked and spoke in low voices about the latest marriages and divorces and their most recent servant problems.

"Well, are there any more messages for the hospital?" my father asked, turning hopefully to Evie. But she was busy getting his hat out of the hall closet. Either she didn't hear or she pretended not to hear.

"Here's your hat, Dad," she said, perching the gray felt on his head and planting a good-bye kiss on the tip of his nose, just like my mother did every morning.

"Come on, Liza, let's go," my father said, digging for his keys in his jacket pocket. "Do something useful with yourself today, Evelyn," he called over his shoulder.

Outside, the emerald-green kikuyu grass sparkled thickly with dew. I pulled open the sodden, wooden gates to the driveway and thought of my mother lying in a stuffy hospital ward. She loved the early mornings and could stare indefinitely at the trees and sky and even into the heart of a single flower. Nature, she said, contained the essence of honesty and beauty, and she alone understood when I pointed to the faces in the clouds and saw waves crashing in their ever-changing patterns.

My father reversed out of the driveway and I climbed onto the leather seat, which was icy against my bare legs. "I wonder how your mother's feeling. I wish Evie would open up to her more—she's such a good woman and loves you girls."

He didn't expect an answer. It was as if he were talking to himself, but I couldn't resist a little spite.

"Oh, Evie's just jealous," I said, "and by the way, that

42

sweater she knitted looks a little lopsided. I would give it to Cuthbert if I were you."

It was too late. I had said it and I should have bitten my tongue instead.

"You are not me and the sweater is very nice," my father replied sternly. "Besides, it's the thought that counts."

The hospital corridors reminded me .of school, with their lime-green and cream walls and disinfectant smell. I held my breath so that I wouldn't breathe in any germs, and by the time we reached my mother's ward, I was almost in need of resuscitation. I felt suddenly shy and froze in the doorway, wondering how this pale, frail figure lying in bed in a pink nylon bed jacket could be the same person who, until just a few days ago, had been the pillar of strength in our household.

"Liza, how wonderful to see you," the pathetic figure said, extending an arm, but still I didn't move. "Is that parcel for me?" she asked. I was carrying Lena's parcel of food.

"Lena sent this and she said that Beauty made the biscuits, but I know she didn't. Evie and I both saw Lena make them. She just wants you to like Beauty better than Tilly." My voice was shrill with embarrassment and indignation.

"Liza, tell Lena and Beauty thank you, and the rest will be our secret. I assure you that, in any case, the biscuits would not affect my feelings for Beauty or Mathilda." My mother's low, controlled voice made me feel foolish.

"Is that a new sweater, Abie?" she asked.

"Yes, it's the one Evie knitted."

"It's absolutely stunning. Tell her I think she's marvelous with her hands."

"Don't you think it's lopsided?" I muttered, hoping to recruit my mother as an ally, but she apparently didn't hear.

"What else is news?" my mother asked, looking at my father, but I rushed ahead, and she gave him a smile and a look that said, He who hesitates is lost!

"Lena has been talking on the phone nonstop, and Mrs. Frazer has called twice to complain about the noise in the afternoons," I volunteered.

My mother sighed. "Mrs. Frazer doesn't understand like we do, does she?" The natives' loud speech, my mother had once explained to me, was a carryover from the time when they lived in the countryside, where they had no telephones and would shout to one another across great distances.

"These poor people are so controlled as it is, can you imagine if we also tried to control the volume of their speech! Heaven knows what they would do out of frustration!"

I knew that my mother was referring to the national cliché that every white family could expect to be stabbed to death by the next-door maid.

There was a knock at the door and a nun's face appeared.

"Ah, we're disturbing you!" said a voice with an accent just like my mother's.

"No, no, come in and I'll introduce you to my family," my mother said, sounding pleased.

Three nuns filed in, filling the tiny room with their flowing black robes.

"Sister Katherine, Sister Josephine, and Sister Therese—they're also from Ireland"—my mother smiled—"and they've been to visit me every day."

"We're from Dublin, too," Sister Katherine said, and they all nodded happily.

"And they've promised to come and visit us at the house," my mother said, her voice becoming weaker, as though our presence was beginning to tire her.

I groaned inwardly at the thought of the nuns visiting our house. Fiona Frazer would never believe that my mother was Irish-Jewish.

"I have a friend at the Holy Rosary Convent school who plans to be a nun," I said. "Her name is Megan, but she says she's going to be Sister Magdalena. Her mother is so proud, but my mother would die if I didn't get married."

Sister Katherine's wrinkled face creased into a smile. "Ah, but your friend will be married—to the Lord, that is."

"Will she have to shave her head?" I asked, unable to detect any wisps of hair escaping from under the tight, white border of the nuns' black veils.

My father coughed. "We need to be on our way; your mother is tired and I have a lot of work to do." He kissed my mother and whispered something to her. "It's been nice meeting you," he said to the nuns, giving a small bow in their direction and slightly raising his hat.

"Little Liza looks just like you," the youngest nun said to my mother as we were about to leave.

I looked back at my mother with one eyebrow raised in a question mark—a gesture learned from my English teacher to indicate her disapproval of young ladies who spoke out of turn. But my mother just winked at me.

"Thank you, Sister," she said graciously.

6

"Why are people so stupid?" I asked my father. "That nun must know Mom is not my real mother, so how can she say we look alike?"

"She was just trying to be kind, or maybe she really doesn't know. Anyway, I'd rather have people who are stupid and kind than stupid and vindictive like some of my patients."

My father was angry with some of his white patients who had complained about his not having separate surgeries for blacks and whites. At great expense and discomfort, the old house on Caywood Street, where he had practiced for years, had been renovated to accommodate those who favored separate facilities.

"Anyway, the complainers are paying for this renovation nonsense," my father said, grimacing. Then he grinned gleefully so that his eyes popped. "What they don't know is that I have only one instrument sterilizer for all the instruments, and anyway, you can't write *blankes* and *nie-blankes* on stainless steel!"

My father's policy was to charge his patients according

to their means, so that while his wealthier white patients paid according to a semistructured fee scale, his black patients often paid only a few pence.

What my father found interesting, he said, was that no black person ever wanted charity. It was a matter of pride to pay in full, even if it took several months.

"Of course, if I had my life over," my father said, as he often did, "I would be a farmer."

"Maybe I'll be a dentist, then I can help you."

"Heaven forbid!" He looked horrified. "Why would you want to deal with Mrs. Baskind's halitosis, or Uncle Sid's ropy saliva, or Mr. Glazer's shrinking jaw?"

We cruised slowly down Caywood Street, which was steep and curved, and as my father pulled up to the curb in front of the surgery in his shiny, blue Studebaker, I felt like arriving royalty. The verandah surrounding the old house teemed with natives, most of whom were swathed in blankets, and almost all had scarves covering their mouths so that only their dark, enigmatic eyes were visible. They had bussed or walked from the township or the surrounding countryside, and at least one had arrived by donkey, a mangy-looking animal tied to a street lamp in the alley separating the surgery from the next building, which housed *Die Oosterlig,* the Afrikaans newspaper and government mouthpiece. It often occurred to me that my father's black patients never owned cars, shiny or otherwise.

In the back room of the surgery, Popeye, the dental mechanic, was testing the bite on a set of dentures. A row of jaws in various stages of development, from white plaster casts to unnaturally pink gums sprouting pearly white teeth, grinned from the shelves.

"Hello *kleintjie,* you come to help old Popeye?"

We both knew I was no help, but more of a hindrance. I

had my own little corner in the workroom where I kept rubber molds in the shapes of various characters that I would fill with a plaster of paris mixture. When the mixture was dry, Popeye would help me peel off the mold, and presto! I would have an ornament to paint and glaze.

"I think I'll make this ballerina for Evie," I said. "It can be her going-away present."

Although everyone called Popeye by his nickname, because of his puffy cheeks that were like the cartoon character's, my father always called him by his real name, Mr. Coetzee, out of respect. Mr. Coetzee, my father said, was the best dental mechanic in the country, but he caused another furrow in my father's brow because he was unreliable. Like many Colored men, Popeye had a drinking problem that was caused, my father explained, both by a lack of identity and by the unusual circumstances of his personal life. The Colored people, descendents of white settlers and native women, considered themselves to be brown-skinned Afrikaners. Although they spoke the Afrikaans language and bore the names of their white forebears, they were regarded as second-class citizens and had even lost the right to vote. To complicate matters for Popeye, he had been educated in England and had married a white woman overseas.

For many years, the Coetzees had lived in South Kloof, a community of Coloreds, Indians, and Chinese, until the government declared the area for whites only. At that point, the Coetzees were legally divorced, so that Mrs. Coetzee and their son, Willem, who passed for white, could remain in the house. Officially, Mr. Coetzee was said to have moved to a Colored area, but I knew that he lived with his family in secret, because at the end of every month I would drive with my father to the little cottage in South

Kloof to deliver Popeye's wages to his wife. My father explained that this was to ensure that Mr. Coetzee was not tempted to drink away his earnings before his wife had paid the bills.

"So tell me a story, Popeye," I said, pouring the chalky plaster of paris mixture into the mold of a ballerina. Popeye loved to tell stories and I was a good listener.

"Once upon a time, when I was a young boy living in the country, we had an old, old teacher with a long white beard. It was so long that when he sat in a chair behind his desk the beard reached the desk top. In fact, he was so old that he would fall asleep in midsentence. His head would drop to his chest and he would snore till the bell rang at the end of class. Then he would jerk his head up and look around like a wild horse and shout, 'Dismissed!' "

At this point in the story, Popeye reached beneath his chair and took out a brown paper sack. He turned his back to me and took a quick swig from the bottle hidden inside it.

"Telling stories is thirsty work," he joked, in answer to my disapproving look.

I desperately wanted to stop him from drinking, to somehow make him so happy that he would never want to drink again.

"You know, Popeye, my dad says that with your hands, you'd have been the most brilliant dentist."

Popeye turned his slightly bloodshot eyes to me and I realized he'd already had more to drink than I had thought.

"*Ek meneer en jy meneer, wie sal dan die wa smeer?*" he said sarcastically in Afrikaans, and I recognized the expression from the list at the back of my Afrikaans Taal book: If I am sir and you are sir, who will then polish the wagon?

"That's your government's policy," he said, grimacing. "They believe some people are born to do menial work."

49

"You know it's not my government. I'm not a Nat," I said indignantly, not quite sure what exactly the National-ist government stood for, but aware that my parents didn't vote for them.

"Anyway, don't you want to hear the rest of my story, *kleintjie?* OK, so one day when the old man's head fell to his chest and he snored so loudly that a draft blew through the room, we kids took a bottle of glue and stuck his beard to the table." Popeye slapped his leg and wheezed with laughter. "Then, when the bell rang at the end of class, the old man raised his head—*harumph, harumph*—he was stuck there!"

"What did he do, for heaven's sake?" I cried, thrilled at the idea of "getting" a teacher.

"We had to cut off his beard." Popeye turned around and took another swallow from the brown bag.

"We couldn't do that at our school," I said disap-pointedly. "All my teachers are old spinsters, though some do have mustaches."

Popeye pointed his finger at me. "The moral of the story is this: Don't get caught napping! Just like your Pop-eye who must always keep awake so that no one will see him sneaking into his own house or see him working here." His voice was so bitter that my skin tingled.

I knew that the workshop was out of bounds to visitors, and that if anyone were to have come snooping, Popeye always had a broom handy and would pretend to be the cleaning boy. My father said that no one would be happy to know that their dentures were made by a Colored man, and I wasn't even sure if a Colored man was allowed to hold such a responsible job.

"D'you think my ballerina is dry?" I asked, taking the

mold down from the shelf. "I think I'll paint the skirt pink. Evie likes pink—she can put it in her room at the university."

Popeye took the rubber mold from me and ran it under the hot-water tap. Then he gently peeled the rubber from the white figurine, revealing pointed toes, a tutu, and arms crossed in front of the bodice.

"My boy is also at Wits University, you know."

Of course I knew. He'd told me a thousand times about his brilliant son, and I didn't want to hear about him again. All I wanted was for the ballerina to come out in one piece, and the narrow neck was the difficult part.

"He's a real world-shaker," Popeye said, leaning down for another swig from his bottle. He looked around furtively and whispered, "He's in the Movement, you know."

"What's that?" Now I was also whispering, sensing that this was a very secretive exchange.

Popeye took another gulp and started laughing so hard that he had to sit down.

I was growing nervous. Who was this stranger laughing so hard at something I didn't understand? "What's so funny?" I asked, picking up the ballerina and easing the rubber mold over the neck.

"Oh no! The head broke off," I cried, stamping my foot with irritation. "All that work for nothing." As I squeezed the disconnected head from the rubber mold, it rolled onto the floor like a white marble. But instead of showing sympathy, Popeye was laughing so hysterically that he lay down on the floor wheezing.

"So many heads must fall," he gasped.

"You're drunk," I said disgustedly.

He lay crouched pathetically on the floor and openly

raised the bottle to his lips. He was no longer laughing, and his cheeks were wet. With his free hand he waved weakly at me as if to say, Go already! And as I was leaving, I thought I heard him whisper, "Go help your pa."

On the way home from the surgery my father was deep in thought. I stared out the window at the houses, which seemed to grow larger and their gardens more lush the further we drove from North End. Large double-storeys lined Cape Road, the main thoroughfare from the suburbs to the city, and on every block of the wide, busy street, bus stop shelters spilled over on the *nie-blankes* side with African women dressed in their finery for an afternoon off in New Brighton, the black township.

"I wonder if Lena's there," I said, scanning the crowd, which had become an angry, fist-raising mass as yet another full bus passed by. I knew how mad Lena became when the buses were all full and she had to spend her little free time waiting at bus stops. When I was younger, Lena would take me to town by bus and she would say, "Those bus conductors are making me so mad, *intombazana*. You see how empty it is downstairs where the white people sit." But I didn't like to sit where the white people sat. It was so boring. Everyone sat tight lipped and stared at everyone else, while at the top of the narrow, spiral staircase a different world awaited me—a world of sweat and old perfume, where every inch of space was filled by gesticulating bodies and vigorous voices jabbering in Xhosa. Close to the ceiling were signs I used to read aloud, mispronouncing the Afrikaans, which Lena translated for me: *Nie-Blankes,* meaning "nonwhites," and *Moenie spu nie,* meaning "don't spit!"

"*Moenie spu nie,*" I said aloud.

"What's that, Liza?" My father looked puzzled.

"That's what it says in the buses—*moenie spu nie!*" I realized that I had never known my father to ride in a bus. "Maybe you should put one of those signs in your surgery," I said.

"On the contrary, I'm always telling patients to rinse and spit! But you know what I don't understand about these African women? They keep asking to have out a healthy front tooth—just one, mind you—and when I refuse, they say they'll have it done elsewhere."

"Oh, that's a love gap," I said. "Lena has one." Although I spoke like an authority on the subject, I had no idea of the real significance of this strange practice.

My father took his eyes off the road and looked at me in astonishment, as though seeing me as someone other than his "baby" for the first time.

"Dad, what is the Movement?" I lowered my voice as Popeye had done.

My father's eyes narrowed and he sucked on his bottom lip so that the corners of his mouth turned down. "I don't know, and I don't want to know." Then his voice grew a little kinder. "Look, my girl, stay away from Mr. Coetzee. His problem is getting worse . . . *tsk, tsk, tsk.*" He clucked his tongue and shook his head. "I've done what I can for him. Even sent him to Alcoholics Anonymous, but the man is a difficult customer."

"You told me yourself Popeye's problem is not entirely his fault. You're just changing the subject because you want to keep secrets from me. Now what is the stupid Movement?" I badgered.

"It's an illegal organization that opposes the Nationalist

government, and the Nats have ways of dealing with these people. So now we need never discuss this again, since no one in our family is politically inclined and that's the way it's going to remain."

And from the look on his face I knew the conversation was over.

7

Mathilda was retired from her job as cook at the end of January, on the same day that Evie left for Witwatersrand University in Johannesburg. In the general upheaval of getting Evie ready for her new life, my twelfth birthday and new seniority as a standard-five student had gone almost unnoticed by my family.

Mathilda shed tears of joy and sorrow—sorrow at leaving the household, but joyful that my parents had provided for her retirement. "To be sure, this old body will have good rest, *intombazana,* then your Mathilda will be back," she said, grabbing my shoulders with her calloused, eagle hands and shaking me gently.

"Of course, Mathilda, you must pay us a visit any time," my mother said pleasantly on hearing Tilly's plans, but her emphasis on the word *visit* made it quite clear that Tilly should not think of her return as a permanent one.

"You wait, *intombazana,*" Tilly giggled, showing her yellow teeth and making her gurgling bathwater sound. "Your Tilly will be here to bake the next birthday cake—

yo, yo, yo! Not too long now and this little one going to be big teenage gel."

I shuddered at the thought. Already my body was out of my control. Tiny breasts had started to bud, making contours in my shirts, and I was developing round shoulders trying to hide this new phenomenon from the world. "Please God, please don't let my breasts grow until I'm at least fifteen years old," I prayed daily, as I stared in the bathroom mirror in a state of fascinated horror. When no one was watching, I had acquired the habit of pushing my palms against the unwanted buds in the hope of stunting growth. I had even thought of binding my chest as the Chinese did their feet.

To add to my self-consciousness, Evie had given me two parting gifts: A cute pair of frilly tennis underwear and—horror of horrors—a beginner's bra. That's what it said on the box in big, blue letters: BEGINNER'S BRA. I could feel my face flush crimson and rushed to hide the unspeakable thing at the very bottom of my underwear drawer. Never would I wear that thing, especially not with the bra-mania at school, where everyone was running their fingers down everyone else's back to see who was or wasn't wearing one.

"Darling," my mother said at lunch as we ingested Tilly's last overcooked chicken and three lifeless vegetables, "developing is a natural thing." She and Evie exchanged looks, and for the first time since our new mother had arrived, I felt like the outsider. I realized that they were probably in cahoots and had bought the bra together since I had refused to go shopping for one. I swallowed my last bite, shoved away my plate, and ran to my bedroom, hoping that my father hadn't heard all that talk about developing.

On my bed was the cricket set my parents had given me for my birthday. I ran my hand along the smooth wooden bat and thought of Delia's face when she had heard what I'd wanted for a gift. "You're such a tomboy," she'd said despairingly. I envied Delia, who had no problem about developing.

"Come sit on my suitcases," Evie said, standing in the doorway of my room. "Otherwise I'll never get them closed."

We went to her room, where a trunk and two large suitcases gaped open.

"Why d'you need so many clothes?" I asked.

"Oh, it's my university trousseau. Lydia says it's the most important time of a girl's life. She says this is the time to catch a husband." Evie giggled. "She's crazy."

"What about Harry?" I asked.

"Oh, Harry's OK, but he's not for me. Lydia says I should set my sights higher. After all, I'm going to get an education and Harry's going to be working in a jewelry store for the rest of his life."

Since when did Evie listen to our mother? I was amazed.

"Well, to tell you the truth, what Lydia says about Harry doesn't count. It's just that I've found him kind of boring lately."

"But Evie, you're always singing that you're crazy 'bout Harry."

"For heaven's sake, Liz, that's just a song, and anyway, people's feelings change. I'm sure Harry has dates lined up for every day of the week. Here, help me write these suit-case labels, and then I'll be ready to leave."

The train station was crowded with students going off to the university. Evie's friends had just as many suitcases as she did, so I gathered that my mother's philosophy was not unique.

"Look, Dad." I nudged my father. "There's Popeye. I'm going to say hello."

"Elizabeth, you stay with us." But as I ran off, his words were swallowed by the din of excited young people.

"Hello, Miss Liz." Popeye scratched at his cuticles, apparently ill at ease as he stood a little apart from his wife and son. He was cleanly shaven and his wasted frame was enveloped in a dark, funereal suit. "Willem," he said to his son, "this is Dr. Levin's youngest."

Willem held out his hand and gave mine a firm shake. "Just as pretty as Pa said." His eyes pierced my skull and I didn't feel like he was talking about my appearance. If anyone else had made this comment, I would have retorted with Delia's favorite remark: Flattery will get you nowhere. But Willem's manner left no room for coy arguments. His self-assurance amazed me. He was short like his father, but the resemblance ended there, for he was stocky and well built like a rugby player, and his dark hair, sallow skin, and hazel eyes were a striking combination. I had never seen a Colored who looked or acted like him. But why did I think of him as Colored? His mother was white and he passed for white. I blushed at my own thoughts.

"My sister's also going to Wits," I said quickly, covering up the guilt that no one else knew about. "Come say hello." I hesitated then, wondering if my family would want to meet the Coetzees in public. After all, my mother was constantly reminding me that my father was "a somebody" in the community and who we children associated with reflected on the family name.

"That's OK." Popeye hung back as though reading my thoughts.

58

"Sure, I'd like to see the doc again," Willem said, not at all bashful and leading the way toward our group.

"You've grown into a handsome young man," my father said, shaking Willem's hand. "My daughter Evelyn is also going to Wits this year. I hope she does as well as I hear you have."

Willem looked at Evie and then at her luggage. "You going to get an MRS degree?" he asked in his guttural accent, a relic of growing up in the impoverished South Kloof neighborhood.

She blushed at his sarcasm, and I realized it was the first time I had seen Evie speechless. She just stared at him.

"What charisma," Evie breathed, as he left.

As the train belched its first warning, we huddled around Evie.

"Remember, Evelyn, it's always important to look nice, and also, be choosy about your friends," my mother said, cramming in some last-minute advice. "And most importantly, stick to your own kind." My mother's expression was deadly serious. "Otherwise it will kill your father."

Whenever Evie or I did something that my parents disapproved of, my mother would accuse us of "trying to kill your father" or "taking years off his life," at the very least. At first I used to watch my father anxiously to see if he would keel over and die, but later I realized this was merely one of my mother's neuroses. However, I truly believed that our bad behavior would subtract years from his life, and thus I always calculated our misdeeds in terms of months and years.

The train lurched, and Evie and her girlfriends shrieked. My father looked depressed, and my mother's face was grim as she dabbed at her eyes. I wondered if she was still dwelling on her belief that Evie had the power to adversely affect my father's health or whether she was genuinely sad to see Evie depart. I decided it had to be the latter. After all, Evie's power "to kill" my father would surely diminish with the miles between them.

8

Evie had been gone for more than six months, returning only briefly during her midyear vacation. Beauty, meantime, had moved into Tilly's old room—a temporary move, my mother had insisted, until we found a more experienced cook, but it soon appeared that Beauty had become a permanent fixture. I was surprised that Lena hadn't moved into Tilly's lighter, airier room, but she chose to keep her old room, which had a good view of the backyard and, hopefully, of unwanted intruders, who were becoming a problem.

Three clocks had disappeared from the kitchen windowsill over a period of months, and Cuthbert had complained about garden tools missing from the shed in the backyard.

"Look here, Lena, Beauty will have to go." My mother's voice was agitated. "She's attracting all the riffraff of the neighborhood. We just can't have these *tsotsis* coming into the back yard like this."

"Madam, Beauty is a good gel. You know I tell these *tsotsis* to *hamba voetsek!*"

"I know you do your best, but you can't be a policeman either," my mother argued. "Maybe we'll just have to put in a gate, then the only way to Beauty's room will be through the garden, and no *tsotsi* will want to risk being seen by one of the family and reported to the police."

Beauty shuddered at the mention of the police, as she still didn't own a pass book, which would allow her to work in the city legitimately, and even on her afternoons off she would often stay in her room.

"It's a pathetic situation," my mother said. "That young girl is like a caged animal, and she's only seventeen." But, at the same time, I wasn't sure just how hard my mother was trying to get her a pass.

Although I felt vaguely sorry for Beauty, my emotions were concentrated in another direction—Brian Johnson, our fourteen-year-old neighbor, who barely knew I was alive before my parents bought me the cricket set. Most of my waking hours were spent thinking about Brian's sandy hair, freckled nose, and lean, brown legs, and my school books were covered with his initials.

Because Brian loved cricket, I became an even more ardent fan of the game, and an afternoon game of cricket on our lawn soon became a tradition among the neighborhood crowd. At halftime, Beauty would bring out glasses of Oros and a plate of Marie biscuits, and often she would watch the game from the sidelines until, one day, as captain of a team, I invited her to play. There was a short moment of discomfort as everyone looked at everyone else, but from then on, Beauty was accepted as one of the players.

Beauty was a good batsman. She had more strength than any of the other girls, who were much younger, and sometimes she would swipe the ball across the fence and into the golf course, automatically clocking up six runs for her team. Her "sixes" made up for her rather slow gait at other times as she ran from base to wicket and back again in an effort to make as many runs as possible before the wicket keeper could receive the ball and catch her out of position. When Beauty ran, Brian didn't do much good as a fielder. He watched her as earnestly as I watched him, his eyes mesmerized by her heavy, swaying breasts and buttocks that rose and fell in a rhythm special only to African women, and that no amount of practice would ever enable me to reproduce.

We were in the middle of a game one afternoon when Delia rode up on her bike and sat with one leg planted on our front wall. "Hello there, yoo-hoo," she shouted. She pointed to Brian behind his back, then folded her hands over her heart and threw back her head in a mock swoon.

"Come and play," I yelled.

"Thanks, I prefer to be a spectator." Delia was still disgusted at my owning a cricket set, which she declared to be decidedly unfeminine. "Anyway, it's going to rain soon." As she spoke, the first few drops fell.

"I'll wait for you inside," she said.

"Yes, you may melt," I called out, wanting Brian to notice how sturdy I was and that a few drops of rain were not going to deter me. But as the sky grew darker, the rain began to pelt down.

"Our team to bat first next time," Brian shouted as everyone took flight.

I ran inside to join Delia, while Beauty hurried to the washing line to collect laundry before it got soaked.

"You'd better change your shirt," Delia said, "or your mother will have a cow. You know how she is about your catching cold."

"My mother's not here, but OK, just wait for me." I

was far too shy to let even my closest friend see me undress; although, at some point after noticing Beauty's charms, I had stopped praying to God for delayed upper-chest development, and I had finally removed the beginner's bra from its secret hiding place in my tallboy.

When I returned to the porch, Delia was listening to the radio and Beauty was dumping a basket of damp laundry in the corner next to the clotheshorse. My skin prickled almost to a blush when I realized that I had run for shelter without a thought about helping Beauty. She was drenched and her clothes were plastered to the voluptuous curves of her body. I expected her to be sullen, but she still smiled, accepting her duties without question or expectations.

"Go and change, for heaven's sake!" My voice sounded imperious.

"Wait, wait! Beauty, teach us the dance you showed us the other day," Delia cried.

Beauty smiled and began to sing what sounded like, "*Asisi noma thetha, hayi ya geza. . . .*" Her body swayed with the rhythm of the song and her head jerked back and forth like an inquisitive chicken's. Grabbing my hand, Delia sprang to her feet, dragging me with her. Beauty's hips gyrated and her shoulders heaved sensuously, but however hard we tried, we couldn't duplicate the flowing movements of Beauty's body. Delia and I were a mass of knobbly knees and jerky shoulder blades.

"Hoo, hoo, hoo," Delia hooted, stamping her feet like a spear-bearing warrior in the introduction to British Movietone News. "Come on, Beauty, show us how they dance in the tribal lands. I've seen them in films—the women are bare on top."

"Show us your titties, Beauty!" Delia and I were pulling at Beauty's wet shirt. But she was laughing and needed

64

little encouragement, and I was thrilled and disbelieving that anyone could be so natural and unreserved about her body. Her smooth brown breasts were large and firm and had a damp sheen either from her sodden clothes or from the exertion of the dance. The porch had grown steamy from our energy and the earlier sunlight that had been trapped in the many-windowed room.

Beauty rolled her bare shoulders and her body vibrated to the words that came from deep in her throat. For a moment she looked up and broke her rhythm. Delia and I caught our breath, but with eyes downcast, Beauty resumed her gyrations in a wonder of sensuality and muscle control.

As Beauty reached the end of her tribal dance, our dance also came to an end. Delia twirled me around, and in that instant I caught sight of a face in the misty window. It was a human fish with bulging eyes and open mouth. Sandy hair clung like seaweed to the startled face of Brian Johnson.

"Oh Dele!" I whispered, "I think I'm going to die. Brian saw us and he's going to think I'm absolutely crazy and disgusting."

"There's nothing wrong with dancing." Delia smirked.

"But what about Beauty—she'll be so embarrassed."

"I think she knew he was there all the time," Delia whispered. "In fact, I think she was dancing for him." She giggled. "You saw him watch her outside, didn't you?"

I squirmed. "You are quite revolting," I whispered indignantly. Sometimes I really wondered about the grotesque thoughts that crowded Delia's head.

Our cricket games gradually fizzled out after that afternoon. Beauty was becoming overweight and sluggish and I even heard my mother telling Lena not to overfeed that young girl—it was unhealthy. Lena laughed and said that *indoda* liked their women with some meat on their bones and that Beauty would soon be ripe for marriage. When I knocked on Beauty's door in the afternoons, she smiled, revealing a newly acquired love gap in her front teeth. Her voice sounded sleepy and she often made the excuse that she was resting. Eventually I didn't bother her anymore.

9

Like Noah's animals about to enter the ark, the standard-five class stood in line, two by two, ready to march to assembly for the last time. Next year we would be entering Queen Victoria High School, situated in a formidable building across the street, but for the moment, we still had to endure our last day as juniors. From across the courtyard we could usually hear the strains of "We Are Marching to Pretoria" or "Onward Christian Soldiers," but today the chatter was so intense that it all but blocked out Miss Henshaw's voice booming, "Come come now, girls! You can talk about your plans for the summer holidays later on."

"Six weeks of bliss," Delia squealed, taking absolutely no notice of Miss Henshaw's admonition.

How Delia had changed in the seven years at Queen Vic, I thought. When we had first entered the sub-A class at the age of six, Aunt Rebie had driven us to school every day in her long, black limousine, which she drove as regally and slowly as the queen's carriage. Inevitably late, Delia would start blubbering as soon as we turned onto

Bird Street and came to a stop outside the school building. My feelings for my closest friend were ambivalent. Although I wanted to comfort her, the urge to be on time was greater. Perhaps, at this time, I was more compelled than most to do the right thing, since many of the teachers knew who I was. To them I was Evelyn Levin's little sister, or "Levintjie," as the Afrikaans teacher called me, using the Afrikaans diminutive attached to my last name. They often asked after my sister Evie, but before I could ever reply, they would purse their lips or suck in their cheeks and say things like, "That was a character for you" or "What a little devil she was." Although these remarks were said with affection, I was careful not to live up to Evie's reputation.

Now, as in years past, we marched to assembly with our backs upright, our shapeless, pleated, navy tunics tied neatly round our middles with a girdle and our navy and white striped bowties pinned to our white shirts. "Left, left, left-right-left," we whispered to ourselves out of habit, but no longer dreading that we would "wrong-foot" and feel Miss Pelham's ruler at the backs of our knees, for surely at this stage we were impervious to her wrath.

Miss Pelham, the headmistress, was short and trim, with a voice that could fill the city hall without a microphone. Her enormous, red-veined eyes were terrifying and missed nothing. In assembly we stood in rows staring up at the podium, where she sang loud and clear, drowning out our rendition of "The Lord Is My Shepherd" and turning it into an aria. When our lungs had been duly aired, Miss Pelham regaled us with reminders to wear hats and blazers in public places—even on the last day of school—and to remove school colors and emblems from old uniforms passed down to the children of "African employees."Miss Pelham would never use anything as indelicate as "servants." Finally, she wished us a happy holiday, and the entire school responded by shouting as they did every year, "No more pencils, no more books, no more teachers' dirty looks!"

On the bus home from school, Delia asked if she could come over for the afternoon, but I quickly made an excuse. "I have a tennis game," I lied, not wanting her to meet Evie's new friend, who was spending an inordinate amount of time at our house.

Evie had already been home a week for her summer vacation, and she was a very different person from the one who had left home almost a year before. Her interests had changed from boys and clothes to a passion for politics. She and my father argued incessantly, so it was a relief when she made plans to go out in the evenings.

On the way home from the bus stop, I stopped several times to lay down my heavy school case. Besides, the longer the walk took, the longer I would be away from the situation at home. As soon as I reached the corner of Allen Street and Westview Drive and saw Mrs. Johnson's pinched smile and heard her curt "Good afternoon," I knew that Willem Coetzee—Popeye's son—was visiting Evie again.

My father had forbidden Evie to see Willem, but she retorted that she refused to have him choose her friends for her, and if he didn't want Willem in the house because he happened to have Colored blood in him, that was fine because she would go to his home in South Kloof instead. My father was silenced and my mother turned a blind eye when Willem visited in the afternoons, never mentioning to my father how much time Willem was still spending at our house.

As I walked up our driveway, my suspicions were confirmed. Willem's bike rested against the hedge. I went to my room, changed into shorts, and laced up my *takkies* to practice tennis outside against the wall. I could hear Willem and Evie talking and laughing in the porch. They always talked incessantly, especially Willem, who seemed to me like a teacher exploding with knowledge and wanting to teach his favorite pupil everything he knew in as short a time as possible.

I had been hitting the ball against the wall for a while and was concentrating on a backhand when I heard Willem's voice. He and Evie were out on the lawn, and I realized they had probably been watching me from the porch window.

"I hear you're playing in a tournament in two weeks."

"Uh huh."

"Look *kleintjie,* I don't want to interfere, but if you want to win, you got to do more than *bloop* the ball back and forth. Tennis is like life—you got to go after what you want." If he hadn't given me a dimpled grin and said it with a twinkle in his eye, I might have told him to take his advice elsewhere.

"You see, if you go *bloop,*" Willem continued, arcing his finger through the air, "there's a ninety percent chance your opponent will also go *bloop*"—another arc—"so you must cut off her *bloop* at the net with a *pow!* Here, let me show you."

Willem took my racket and hit the ball against the wall. As it rebounded, he ran forward and smashed away a volley.

Evie smiled and clapped, but I remained sullen, determined to show no sign of friendship. "I can't do that!"

"You can do anything you set your mind to," Willem said severely. "If we can find a tennis court, I'll be your

70

coach for the next two weeks, and just see if you don't win that tourney."

His enthusiasm was contagious. In spite of myself, I could feel a sudden charge of adrenaline. "The Queen's Club is down the road, and no one plays there during the week. You can borrow Evie's racket and we can ride down to the courts now." I hoped I didn't sound too keen.

"Ride!" Willem scoffed. "Your sister can ride; we're going to run. Don't think I'm going to be easy on you—tennis is not just hitting the ball; it's moving fast and having the stamina to stay out there as long as it takes."

Willem ran at a leisurely pace, but I sped off down the road as fast as I could, determined to show off my agility. After a few minutes, I was gasping for breath and had a fearful pain in my side.

"That's your first lesson," Willem said, slowing down to walk with me. "You have to pace yourself, otherwise you won't last out a match."

We worked for an hour on volleys until my muscles ached and sweat dripped onto the court. He had worked as hard as I had, but wasn't even breathing hard.

"When did you first start playing tennis?" I asked.

Willem looked at his watch and frowned. "Since about an hour ago." Then he laughed delightedly at my look of astonishment.

Every afternoon for two weeks I practiced with Willem. I no longer cared about the looks from the neighbors or the nasty comment from Mrs. Frazer, who said she thought Evie's friend looked like he had more than a touch of the tar brush. My parents were delighted that I was keeping Willem away from Evie, and she, having grown bored with the tennis scene, spent more time with her "normal" friends, as my mother called them.

My first match of the tournament was on a Tuesday afternoon, and on Monday, after practice, Willem asked what my plans were for the following day.

"I guess I'll go to the beach in the morning with Lucy," I said. My cousin Lucy was visiting from Vereeniging and we went to the beach every morning with the driver my mother had employed for the summer.

"Tell me, Miss Levin, how do you usually feel when you come home from the beach?" Willem spoke as though he were a doctor questioning a sick patient.

I thought for a moment. "Thirsty, I guess."

"What else?"

"Pretty lazy. Ready for a nap."

"And this is how you want to feel when you go into your match tomorrow?" There was a slight edge to Willem's voice.

"You have made your point. I will stay home and do nothing."

"Not nothing. You can hit against the wall. If I weren't working I would hit with you in the morning, but I hope to get off in time to see the match."

He must have seen the horror register on my face. "Please don't watch—it'll make me nervous. I don't even let my parents watch my matches." This latter remark was true, but it wasn't the reason I didn't want him to come. I couldn't bear the embarrassment of Evie and Willem being seen together in front of the tennis crowd at the Davies Stadium. And there would be a crowd—all the top stars in the country would be playing in the open division.

"You're a nice one," Evie said to me later. "You're willing to take what you can from Willem, but not to give him the pleasure of seeing how much he's helped you."

72

"Oh girls," my mother interjected, "don't bicker. Your aunt Phoebe called and asked us over for Shabbat dinner on Friday night. She's having a large crowd and says it's important that we all come."

The anticipation of a large family gathering washed away my guilt about Willem. I loved family get-togethers, perhaps because I was the youngest and rarely had a chance to spend time with my older cousins. But, by the time Friday evening arrived, I had changed my mind about Aunt Phoebe's dinner.

"Mom, I'm not going tonight," I said, as I watched her brush her hair and dab cologne behind each ear.

"Is that so? And why not?" I saw her eyes widen in the dressing table mirror.

"The final is tomorrow afternoon and it's just too important. I must have an early night."

I had won four matches in the girls' fourteen-and-under division to reach my first final in a major tournament.

"Darling, you can sleep late tomorrow! Tennis is wonderful for fresh air and exercise, but you don't want to get so serious about it."

"I am serious, and I cannot go," I said firmly, irritated that my mother could never understand my passion for the sport.

"That Willem must be some motivator," my mother said, shaking her head.

Before everyone left for the evening, my mother, Evie, and I lit the Sabbath candles and said the Hebrew prayer, but I silently added one of my own: God, please let me win tomorrow.

I sat in the darkened dining room in the flickering candle-light. Friday night was always my favorite time to sit and dream until the Sabbath candles burned themselves out, but tonight my mind was a tennis court where I played out every point of a two-set match, winning by the amazing score of 6–0, 6–0. Even as I sat in the dark, I could feel the smile of victory touch my lips, but it quickly faded as I realized how lonely it was with no one to share my success.

The house was so quiet I could hear the silence, broken only by the ventriloquists of the night—crickets shrilling outdoors. I went to the telephone in the hall.

"Willem? This is Elizabeth Levin."

"What's the matter, *kleintjie?*"

"I'm in the final. It's at two o'clock tomorrow."

"I know, *kleintjie,* I went to the stadium and looked at the draw and also saw your opponent play."

"What do you think?"

"Man, I think that girl's as big as an ox—strong, but can't move. You just move her all over the place and do your *pow* shots and she'll be a dead ox!"

"D'you think I'll win?" My voice sounded childish, even to my own ears.

"*Kleintjie,* remember I told you you can do anything you want?"

"Yes, I remember." My voice was stronger now. "I just beat her in my head in two love sets."

Willem laughed. "You see, it's a fait accompli!"

"A what?"

"Forget it. Is your sister there?"

"No, she's gone to a family dinner."

"You didn't go?"

Maybe he didn't believe me that Evie was out.

"No, I wanted an early night before my match."

"*Kleintjie,* if that's your attitude, you've already won in

74

my book." Willem sounded as delighted as if I had given him a gift.

"Willem?" I took a deep breath. "Will you come to my match tomorrow? I'd like you to be there."

"Huh? You think I'd miss the match of the season?" He spoke without hesitation, as though he'd been planning to come all along. "Listen, if you get there early, I'll warm you up."

"It's a deal!" I said.

When I replaced the receiver, I felt a sense of calm. The clashing crosscurrents of my mind were all flowing in one direction, and sleep came easily to me.

Sometime during the night, I was wakened by a babble of voices and smothered laughter. My mother was whispering to Evie and Cousin Lucy to hush, then she tiptoed into my room and peered at me in the dark.

"I'm awake," I said croakily. "What happened?"

"Such excitement," my mother whispered, as though she didn't quite believe I was awake. "Your cousin Ruthie is engaged to be married."

"What! To that drip she's been dating?"

"Selwyn's a nice boy, in spite of a bad accent, and your aunt Phoebe says his family 'knows how to live.' "

"Does that mean he's rich?"

"They're in the underwear business," my mother said, as though that would surely answer my question. "Everyone has to wear underwear!"

My father stood in the doorway. "Lydia, couldn't the news wait till tomorrow?"

"I was awake, Dad, really."

"It could be Evie getting engaged if she just showed some interest," my mother said with a sigh.

"Please, Lydia, you want her married at the age of nineteen to some schlemiel with no education?" My father's voice was sharp. "Come, let's leave Elizabeth to sleep before her big day tomorrow."

Saturday afternoon was blustery, and only the center courts were shielded from the wind by the grandstand seats rising to a deceptively calm, blue summer sky. Our match was relegated to an outer court exposed to the elements. After almost two hours of battling both the wind and my opponent, the score was one set each. We stopped for a short break, and I paused at the fence where Willem sat watching.

"It's impossible," I panted. "She kills me when I serve into the wind. I've got no energy left."

"You sure as heck got more than she does. Just take a look."

My opponent was sitting down next to her parents with her shoulders hunched and her legs splayed out, and her face was a steaming red.

"You got to lob to her backhand," Willem said, "especially when she's against the wind. Then you come in with the volley. Also do your ugly little drop shots when you're against the wind."

All these things to remember! I started off badly, but then my opponent went into a slump and I caught up. We battled back and forth until the score was four games all. My opponent was serving badly now, and choking on easy shots. We changed sides at five games to four in my favor. Again I was serving into the wind—this time for the match. We patted the ball back and forth, each waiting for the other to make an error. "Deuce," I called out, as I finally hit the ball in the net. Maybe it was my turn to go into a slump! As

I returned to the baseline to serve, I saw Willem's hand shielding his eyes as though he had a headache.

Gosh, this must be so boring for him to watch, I thought, as the cheering from the center court arena filtered through. I knew that at this point in a match a great player would take charge, and I decided to do just that. The very next point I followed my serve to the net and so startled my opponent that she made a weak return and I was set up for an easy winning volley. I looked at Willem and he gave me the thumbs-up sign.

"Add in," I shouted, buoyed by my latest tactic. I served to the add court, planning to come to the net again, but my ball was several inches out. My opponent returned the serve into the net and began to walk toward me with her hand outstretched. She obviously thought the serve was good and that she had lost the match.

"My serve was out," I shouted to her.

"You sure?" she asked.

I nodded.

"Take two," she said.

I served again, and she went for a winner down the line, but it landed a few inches out.

Willem clapped and congratulated us both, and when the other girl left he stood looking at me with his hands on his hips and his dimple just visible in his cheek. "Interesting finale!"

I knew he was referring to the last point. "You know we were out there for three hours?"

"Don't tell me: I should have brought a sun hat."

"I couldn't just take that last point; I had to win it."

Willem patted me on the back and looked up at the sea of white faces watching the match on center court. "If everyone had a conscience like yours, this country would be a darnsight better place," he said. "Maybe tennis will eventually be your passport to get out of this godforsaken land."

Why did he and Evie have to relate everything to politics, I wondered. Why couldn't they be lighthearted like everyone else?

"You go phone home while I watch center court," he said. "Your folks must be on tenterhooks to hear the result."

My parents arrived with Evie and Cousin Lucy in time for the awards ceremony at six o'clock. When my name was called out, I walked up to the podium, remembering not to grab the silver cup before shaking hands, just as they had taught us at Queen Vic. As I returned to my seat, I could see my family smiling and cheering, and I thought how little they actually had to do with my victory. The one person who should have been there to share the credit was nowhere to be seen.

I didn't see Willem again during the remaining weeks of the summer holiday. On a trip to my father's surgery, Popeye mentioned that his son was working full time during the day and studying at night. I couldn't help but wonder whether my father and Popeye had something to do with his busy schedule.

10

Evie was back in Johannesburg, and peace once again reigned in our household. She never wrote to us about boys or dates, only about the terrible regime under which we were living. Then, as if to prove her point, at the end of March, hundreds of African protesters were killed or wounded during a peaceful demonstration outside the Sharpeville police station. A note of hysteria crept into her letters and she declared her conviction that only the Movement could save the country.

Our family in Johannesburg seemed to take delight in reporting to us that Evie was looking a mess these days and no one could discuss anything rational with her. These tidings added to my father's already overflowing bag of worries. He sighed heavily at the mere mention of Evie's name, but my mother made light of the matter, pretending that there was nothing to worry about. To me she confided that Evie was "killing her father," but all the while she reassured him that it was just a phase and to be expected.

She wrote letters to Evie about the dinner parties she and my father had attended, the latest news of Cousin

Ruthie's wedding plans, and tea-party gossip Aunt Phoebe had told her (and everyone else) in the strictest confidence. She referred to Aunt Phoebe as the CNA (short for the Central News Agency), which she knew would evoke a chuckle from Evie. She also told Evie not to spare any expense to look nice. She needed to make regular trips to the hairdresser and to treat herself to a manicure every now and then. And how was she enjoying the gorgeous clothes they'd bought together? I loved to read my mother's letters, which ran on without punctuation, just the way she spoke.

Evie ignored the questions, but she did say that she would appreciate the extra money offered to keep herself looking well groomed. She also wrote that living in residence was despicable and that she and her best friend, Sara, had found a house to rent that would cost my father no more than the residence fees. It would also be a place for the family to stay if and when they came to Johannesburg. *My entire happiness depends on this move,* Evie wrote dramatically, and after endless discussions at the dinner table, my father reluctantly agreed, although my mother called him a softie.

"Oh, well, Sara Kahn sounds like a nice girl and probably comes from a nice Jewish family," my mother said, sighing and acknowledging defeat.

A house in Johannesburg sounded wonderful to me. A few of my very wealthy school friends (whose mothers wore long gowns to dinner every night) had summer houses in Plettenberg Bay, and now we would have a second house in Johannesburg.

"Please, please let me stay with Evie when I visit Lucy in Vereeniging," I begged. Every winter vacation I visited my Levin relatives on their farm outside Vereeniging, about an hour's drive from Johannesburg. "I could stay with the Levins for two weeks instead of three."

My father smiled at me indulgently as if at a week-old infant. "You're my baby," he said. "I'm not letting you go to Johannesburg with no one to look after you."

"But Evie will—I promise, I promise!"

"You know, Abie," my mother said, "it might be a good idea. Liza could tell us firsthand what's going on there, and it would give Evie a sense of responsibility. Maybe that's what she needs."

My father's expression was not happy, but I could see that he would reconsider.

"So it's settled. I'm going, I'm going, oh boy!" I ran outside and hit a tennis ball against the wall until I was exhausted. Throwing the racket down on the grass, I sprawled out on my back under the winter sunshine. The grass was prickly and alive with a world of activity beneath my skin. Maybe the bugs beneath me had a city—a city like Johannesburg that hummed along at a breathless pace. The sky floated above in shades of clear blue with wisps of white clouds smoothly merging and falling apart like partners executing a familiar dance. But when I closed my eyes, there were no shades of color, just plain orange. I wondered whether blind people also saw orange when the sun shone down on their eyelids, and what about black people. Maybe I would ask Beauty or Lena. I thought how Lena used to scare me when I was little by rolling her eyes back in her head so that only the blood vessels showed. I heard myself say "Ugh!" But another faint sound made me sit up.

Getting up so quickly made me momentarily dizzy and the garden looked dark and secretive.

"Brian, Brian, is that you?" I could make out his

stooped figure at the hibiscus hedge that separated our two houses. I hadn't seen him for ages and my heart was pounding unnaturally. I walked over to him. "Gosh, I didn't know there was a hole in the hedge."

He turned red.

"Did you want to play cricket?" I asked, trying not to sound too eager.

"Nah!" He hesitated a moment. "Thought you may want to fly my plane at the pond on the golf course."

Brian was a whiz at making model boats and planes he could sail and fly by remote control, and I was overwhelmed by the unexpected invitation. He climbed through the hedge and I followed. As I glanced back, I saw Beauty standing at the window of her room.

"Maybe we should ask Beauty to come with us," I said, knowing that I would be in serious trouble if my mother knew I'd been on the golf course without an adult or at least a group of children, and Beauty seemed the perfect solution to this problem.

"Nah, forget it," Brian said sharply, and I didn't argue or he'd think me a scaredy-cat.

Brian's room was a gallery of model boats and airplanes. We stopped long enough to pick up the equipment and then crossed the street into forbidden territory—a forest of long grass and pine trees riddled with mosquitoes and other flying insects. The pond was in a clearing quite a distance from the fairway, but not far from a tin shanty where the caddies lived.

I watched and admired Brian maneuvering his boat through the water and his plane through the air, but after a while I became bored and nervous. Not for a moment could I stand still without slapping at another mosquito biting my leg or a dragonfly diving past my head, and I wondered if Brian noticed how my glance kept straying toward the tin shanty.

"Please could I have a turn," I begged for the umpteenth time.

"OK, I guess," he said grudgingly, handing me the controls.

For a while I forgot the insects as the plane rose and dived and undulated under my direction.

"That's far enough. Bring it back now," Brian demanded. The plane was close to the tin shanty, and a few dark faces appeared in the distance, watching the puppet plane.

"How do I do it?" I was losing control.

"That knob to the left, silly." Brian was shouting now.

When the plane nosedived to the ground, I knew I had pushed the wrong button. Brian's face was white and then flushed red with anger as he screamed, "You allowed the plane to crash! How could you do that?"

"Allow! Gosh, I'm sorry. I didn't do it on purpose." I was whimpering like a baby and hated myself.

"Go get it. Get it right now!"

"I'm not going to get it. You know I can't go over there."

"You're afraid of *tsotsis*," he said, sneering.

"You're just as afraid, that's why you won't go yourself," I shouted, turning in the direction of home and trying not to run like a baby. I felt a sharp jab at the back of my head and heard something hit the ground. My hand went to the painful spot and I could feel blood oozing onto my fingers. Now he was pelting me with stones and I ran in terror through the tall stinging nettles and the dark shadows of the trees.

The half-mile walk stretched to infinity, and when at

last the row of familiar houses came into sight, I climbed through the wire fence without the slightest caution and into the full view of my mother, who was pruning shrubs in the front garden.

"Look at your face and legs scratched to pieces!" she yelled. "What happened?"

As soon as she was reassured that nothing serious had happened, she admonished me that terrible things could happen to young girls, and that next time the *tsotsis* would be waiting for me, and it would serve me right. And how could I expect to go to Johannesburg if I had no sense of responsibility.

Lena came out to see what the commotion was about, and I flung my arms around her. But she wasn't sympathetic.

"You listen to your mother very good, *intombazana*. Those *tsotsis* making big trouble. They supposed to be in school, but what do they do—they caddy on the golf course, they drinking and smoking and just looking for nonsense."

I buried my head in her starched white apron and mumbled, "But I wasn't alone, I was with Brian."

"Un–un–un," Lena said, shaking her head. "That young fella no match for *skollie* boys. *Tsotsis.*" Then she flicked an imaginary knife in front of my nose to show how the *tsotsis* dealt with intruders.

But I was no longer paying attention to Lena's dramatics. I had seen a movement behind the hibiscus—a flash of gray hair and the curve of Mrs. Johnson's tightly pulled-back bun. If she had been listening, I knew Brian would be in trouble. She took every opportunity to castigate him, and more than once I had seen her chase him around the garden, flailing his wooden cricket bat.

That night, after dinner, the doorbell rang, and I ran to answer it, thinking Brian had come to apologize. The front verandah was alive with flames. I slammed the door shut and streaked into the dining room where my parents sat, unaware that the house was about to burn. My mother followed me to the door and I stood back as she opened it.

"It's a paraffin fire—the kind that night watchmen use to keep themselves warm," she said calmly. "It's a prank, and you're not to play with that boy again," she warned. "His tricks are getting out of hand."

I could imagine Brian smirking behind the garden hedge. He must have received a mouthful from his mother, and this was his way of paying me back for blurting everything out. "Just like a stupid girl" was his usual accusation when I did something he didn't approve of. Perhaps he thought I told that he had struck me, and that may be why he never spoke to me again.

11

My mother arranged for me to travel to Johannesburg with Aunt Phoebe and Uncle Cyril, who were going up north to shop for Cousin Ruthie's rapidly expanding trousseau. Evie wrote that she was thrilled that I would be staying with her for a week.

The Colored driver from Uncle Cyril's secondhand furniture store took us to the station in the van because Aunt Phoebe had so much luggage. I was perfectly happy with the arrangement because it meant that not only would my parents be able to see us off, but Lena and Delia could come too. Lena had brought a bright red scarf and promised to wave it until the train was out of sight.

When Uncle Cy saw that Lena and Delia were coming with us, he muttered to my parents, "She's already a teenager. Can't she go anywhere without the nanny?" My parents ignored him. To me he said, "So y'shoulda brought the whole neighborhood."

Uncle Cy was not the sort of person you'd want to claim as a relative, but he had married Aunt Phoebe, who was my father's sister, so I had no choice but to call him Uncle. Now I wondered how I could possibly tolerate them both as my chaperones on the long trip to Johannesburg.

When we reached the station, Uncle Cyril jumped out of the van and struck a pose like the conductor of an orchestra until a porter ambled over to help with the luggage—a thin, sour-faced man in a black uniform and black, peaked cap. I guess anyone would have looked sour at the sight of Aunt Phoebe's profusion of suitcases and hatboxes.

Aunt Phoebe batted her eyelids at him and said in her soft, whispery voice, "You dear man, I've really overdone it, haven't I?"

"She's going to model for *Vogue*," Uncle Cy muttered to us.

"What's that, dear?" Aunt Phoebe asked in her you-dare-repeat-that voice. Delia and I exchanged looks and stifled a giggle.

Although a slow fifty, as my mother described her, Aunt Phoebe wore a girlish, pink floral frock with earrings to match. Her newly blonde hair was combed back in a chignon with just a few loose tendrils framing her lined face, and on top of this perched a pink straw hat, the brim of which appeared to be weighed down by a fruit salad. My aunt Phoebe liked nothing better than to be told that she and Ruthie looked just like sisters, and she did her utmost to maintain this youthful image. I had gleaned from family conversations that Phoebe was a good bit older than Cyril and she had married beneath her, but when you're a spinster and getting on in years, as so many hinted, marriage to Cy Saunders was apparently preferable to being left on the shelf. I had my doubts about this, though I had to admit Uncle Cy was a looker in his way.

His black hair was slicked back from his handsome, jowly face, and a thin, black mustache à la Clark Gable accentuated an Americanized accent adopted from films. His voice reminded me of the sea—kind of husky, and his *S*'s seemed to whistle. Even for the dusty train journey his clothes were up-to-the-minute—plaid trousers, a double-breasted jacket, and a white panama hat.

"Let's find the compartment," Aunt Phoebe said. Her lips were always rounded as though she were sucking on an invisible straw, and her eyes darted back and forth to the porter lest he leave behind any of her paraphernalia.

"On the turn," Uncle Cy replied.

The train stood at the platform like an impatient animal, snorting and belching steam. The engine drivers, their skin blackened with soot, shoveled coal into the engine. The cavernous station building was a hub of activity as vacationers started to crowd the platforms.

"Look at the talent," Delia whispered, nudging me in the ribs as a group of boys passed by. "Gosh, you're so lucky!" Delia was boy crazy and fell passionately in love with someone different every other week. I, on the other hand, was more steadfast, and still pined over the fact that Brian Johnson had turned out to be what Delia described as an "infantile pyromaniac."

The porter's trolley was stacked so high with Aunt Phoebe's luggage that Lena offered to carry my suitcase. I thought my father should carry it, but Lena had insisted, as though she needed an excuse to be there. I carried my school satchel, in which I'd packed books and a deck of cards to play solitaire on the trip, but I knew that most of the time I would stare out the window at the passing scenery or walk up and down the corridors peering in at other compartments and making temporary friendships.

I had packed my warmest winter clothes because the mornings and evenings in Johannesburg were frosty, and my aunt Rhoda was not one to turn on heaters. My mother had insisted I pack her own cashmere sweater, which had seen better days.

"If you slip your legs through the sleeves at night," she said, "you'll be warm as toast." That was a carryover from my mother's growing-up years in England and Ireland. She approved of whatever the English did. In fact, when the government expressed the desire to gain independence from Britain, her greatest concern was that English imports would be stopped. She had a horror of wearing locally made clothes. Whenever we went shopping she would look at the label first, and if it said MADE IN GREAT BRITAIN, she'd like it immediately even if it was quite hideous.

We found the compartment, and I swung myself up the tall iron steps and ran along the narrow corridor. The compartment was all shiny wood with green leather upholstery.

"I dabs the top bunk," I said.

"Of course, sweetheart, Uncle Cyril and I are too old to go climbing," Aunt Phoebe said.

"Speak for yourself," her husband shot back.

"Let's find the bedding boy," she said, ignoring him.

The bedding boy was a middle-aged Colored man who expertly flung sheets and heavy army blankets across the bunks, tucking the edges neatly away.

I loved my top bunk with its smooth, polished wood and glassed-in pictures of proteas and springbok. But best of all was the reading lamp, flush with the wall, which meant that I could read as late as I wanted without disturbing anyone.

The porter was still passing the luggage through the window, and Uncle Cyril was storing it under the lower bunks, on the luggage rack, and on the unused fourth bunk. I saw my father dig in his pockets to give the porter a tip, and I wondered why he would tip for the Saunders' luggage. Then I remembered my mother's description of Uncle Cy as thrifty beyond belief, but then she had added that maybe he had to be miserly to make up for what Phoebe spent on their daughter.

The train lurched and creaked. I leaned out of the window to kiss my parents. My mother dabbed at her eyes with a perfume-soaked handkerchief. "Do you have your spending money, darling? Buy whatever you want." I patted my jacket pocket containing the small purse of money I planned to spend on sweets and magazines sold at almost every stop. I held Delia's hand through the window as the train slid slowly out of the station.

"Have a *lekker* time," she said.

"Give love to Miss Evie," Lena called out, "and you be good gel."

Then the train was moving faster and Lena, Delia, and my parents grew smaller and smaller, and the red scarf became an almost invisible speck. Suddenly the world consisted of a maze of railway tracks and open space. Factories on the outskirts of the city gave way to fields lined with tangled acacia bushes. Clumps of yellow-orange aloes stood tall and bright in the winter sunshine.

The dinner gong sounded in the corridor as the "bedding boy" walked through the carriages from one end of the train to the other, knocking out a tune on the xylophone he carried.

"Da-da dee-dee tea and cof-fee," Aunt Phoebe sang as

the tune crescendoed outside our compartment door and then faded into the distance.

"Cy, dear, I have everything we need for dinner except tea. Please, could you order some from the dining car."

"The kid can go," he said. He always called me the kid.

"Thank you, Elizabeth." Aunt Phoebe smiled. "I'll lay out the dinner meantime."

To reciprocate for the Saunders' chaperoning duties, my mother had provided a dinner—chicken and cold meats, a variety of sandwiches, and fruit—that was sufficient to feed the entire train. Aunt Phoebe contributed one of her famous cakes that she always kept in case of guests. The cakes would grow moldy in their tins, but that wouldn't deter my aunt, who, when guests did arrive, would cut away the mold and serve the rest.

I lurched with the rhythm of the train to the dining car to order tea. Jumping across the narrow join from one carriage to the next was both exhilarating and terrifying. For an instant my hair blew in the wind created by the speed of the train, and down below, the tracks appeared like never-ending quicksilver.

"Hey chick, howzit? Where you going?" It was the group of three boys Delia had noticed at the station. I recognized two of them, Howie Bernstein and Morris Shapiro, from my trips to synagogue on Friday nights when Delia and I would dress in our finery and stare down past the edges of our prayer books and over the ladies' hats to view the "talent" downstairs. Because men and women sat separately, and because it was traditional for the women to sit upstairs, the boys would hold their prayer books up high, and occasionally we would notice someone gaze heavenward, pausing en route at our pew.

"So Lizbeth, come visit us later." I stared blankly at the third fellow who spoke. I had never seen him, yet he knew my name. "You don't recognize me," he said. "I live on Cape Road behind your house—Barry Kaliff."

My eyes opened wide. This gorgeous specimen with a shock of brown curls, high cheekbones, and a giant Star of David dangling around his sexy neck was the same person who, just a few years ago, Lena predicted would grow up to be rubbish because his wild behavior caused every nanny to pack her bags and leave within the first week of employment.

"Sorry," I gasped. "I haven't seen you in a while."

"Yeah, well, I guess we don't hang around with the same crowd," he said. His friends laughed as though they knew something that I didn't, and I blushed, wishing Delia were there. She would have known exactly what to say.

When I returned to the compartment, Aunt Phoebe had unfolded the table from the wall, and Uncle Cy sat with a napkin tucked into the neck of his shirt, filling his mouth with chicken. When he had gnawed every last morsel from its bone, Aunt Phoebe said, "Cy, dear, would you like a corned beef or egg sandwich?"

"Double or nothing," he replied.

She gave him one of each and I wondered at her ability to understand him. "Is there anything more you want, dear, before I clear away?" Aunt Phoebe asked.

"Potatis," Uncle Cy replied, and I gathered it meant he'd had his fill, because she started to wrap up the leftovers.

The adults retired early, and I wondered how they could sleep so easily. I could hear them snoring, and if I sat up in my bunk, I could see the glass of water containing Uncle Cy's dentures. Without teeth, he looked older than Aunt

Phoebe, his face all crumpled and his mustache crowding his chin.

I lay in my bunk reading, enjoying the beat of the wheels throbbing against the steel rails. The tune was constant, changing to a crescendo when the train crossed a bridge, and a muffled roar as it sped through a tunnel. The tunnels were scary, especially during the day, when we would be thrust into sudden darkness. At night the engine's shrill whistle would echo through the tunnel and the lights from the villages and farmhouses were shut out. Everyone would scramble to shut the windows, or else the entire compartment would be covered in soot.

I slept fitfully, waking whenever the train stopped at country stations. I could hear the babble and laughter of people and the creaking of luggage being passed through the windows and stowed away.

In the morning I awoke as the orange sun lit the landscape, which had changed overnight from green to gold. The lush vegetation of the Eastern Cape had given way to the dry grasses of the Orange Free State, still sparkling with frost. The farmlands formed a quilt of yellow wheat and brown soil. Sheep and cattle grazed peacefully, and clumps of mud huts with their thatched roofs broke the monotony of the fields. African children raced toward the tracks, raising cupped hands for food or a few pennies. The older children were dressed in tattered shorts and dresses, but the little ones ran naked on their skinny legs, which looked too fragile to hold up their empty but distended bellies.

I hurried to get some packages of fruit and sandwiches out of the cool bag and flung them out the window. I stuck my head out and could see the little African children flocking for the food like a flurry of pigeons scrambling for bread crumbs.

"Imagine living in a mud hut without a bathroom or electricity," I said aloud.

"That's what the natives are used to. They're happy as they are," Aunt Phoebe said.

"Evie says we shouldn't call them natives. They prefer to be called Africans. Anyway, how do you know they're happy as they are?"

"Gawd, the kid's becoming a commie," Uncle Cy interjected.

Aunt Phoebe gave him a look that stifled him. To me she said patiently, "They're not a sophisticated people." And her tone indicated that I had had no business asking her to explain.

"Here, next time give them the cake," Uncle Cyril said, "or there'll be nothing left for lunch."

After breakfast the train stopped at a dusty siding. Again the children came with their hands outstretched, the older ones with their flashing smiles and the little ones with their solemn eyes and runny noses. An old man, his skin wrinkled like the cracks at the bottom of a dry riverbed, held up some animal carvings he had fashioned from pieces of driftwood.

"Oh, Cy, isn't that delightful," said Aunt Phoebe, pointing to the image of a deer that had sprung to life under the old man's guidance.

"Five shillings, madam," the old fellow called out.

"Let me see it," Aunt Phoebe said, extending her arm through the window. He handed her the statue and she caressed the smooth wood with her manicured hands. "Just delightful," she said, "but on second thought, what would I do with it?" She held it out to him.

"You keep, you keep," the old man chanted, revealing his crooked, yellow teeth. "I give you for three and six-pence."

"No, no, I don't want it." Aunt Phoebe's voice had become shrill. "Give it back to him, Cyril." She sat down with her lips pursed.

Uncle Cy studied the wooden deer. "Hey, *indoda,*" (he prided himself on knowing some Xhosa words) "you haven't signed your name on it."

"You're not in a city gallery, Uncle Cy," I said. "He probably doesn't even know how to sign his name."

"Well, I'm not paying three and six for this," Uncle Cyril said. He reached inside the compartment for Aunt Phoebe's moldy cake wrapped in tinfoil. He handed it to the old man, who beamed and bowed his thanks, probably thinking it was a hunk of meat to feed his hungry family.

The train lurched, its segments jarring against each other like an uncoordinated caterpillar, and slowly glided forward. I couldn't believe it. There was the deer frozen in flight on the lid of the washbasin in the compartment. Uncle Cyril was sitting down. "You gave him an old piece of cake for this?" I was aghast.

"He needs it more than we do," Uncle Cy said, while Aunt Phoebe looked away, her face unusually pink.

I leaned out of the window and saw the children clamoring around the old man, wanting to pry open his silver gift shimmering in the sunlight. Filled with shame, I reached into the purse for the emergency money my parents had given me.

"Here," I shouted. "Here." I waved wildly and flung the coins through the window onto the receding platform. Clinging to the windowsill, I leaned out as far as possible into the wind, but the old man was already an imperceptible dot, almost indistinguishable in the dry landscape.

I left the compartment and went to the dining car, where I ordered a cream soda. The only other people there were a young Afrikaans family with six children under the age of eight, slobbering tea and cake all over the place. The mother didn't look the least bit anxious about the mess.

"The Afrikaners have children one after the other, like steps," Evie had explained to the family on her return trip from the university, "so they can swell the numbers of the white Nationalist population."

"Maybe they got the idea from the African people who do the same thing," my father had said.

"Well, if the African people weren't deprived of an education by the government," Evie shrieked, "maybe they'd know more about birth control."

I covered my ears at the memory of that awful visit, of Evie constantly arguing and crying and my father gradually withdrawing into a mute person I scarcely recognized.

"Hey babe, move over. What you looking so cheezed off about?" Barry Kaliff nudged me over and slid onto the seat next to me, while Morris and Howie sat opposite us.

"So what you got under that jacket you wearing?" Morris snickered.

I blushed, remembering that he had also been the one to scratch my palm when shaking hands and wishing me "Good Shabbos" after synagogue one Friday night. Delia had interpreted the sign in a whisper. "He's asking if you want to do it," she explained, almost spitting out the word *it*."

"Take no notice," Barry said now, not laughing with the others. "The guy's got zat culture. You hear that, Morris—

zat!" He got up and looked at the other two, giving them some kind of signal. "Listen," he said. "Me and this chick are going to take a walk. We'll see you later on."

I wondered if we were going to walk up and down the corridors all afternoon. That would be fine. I already had an overwhelming crush on this tall, handsome, assertive, newly found neighbor, so that all previous loves seemed as inconsequential as a raindrop in an ocean.

Barry didn't plan to do much walking. He opened his compartment door and said, "Come sit down." I obeyed and he locked the door and pulled down the shutters overlooking the corridor. I wondered whether I should lunge for the door, but instead sat nervously scrunched up on the green bunk.

"Listen, babe, get comfortable. I'm not going to bite." He spread his arms in a gesture of innocence. "You want a biscuit?—My ma baked 'em. My ma and pa are getting divorced, and I'm going to live in Jo'burg with my uncle for a while."

I gulped and almost choked on biscuit crumbs. Pictures of my wedding to Barry Kaliff, with Delia as bridesmaid, had flashed through my mind with prophetic clarity, and although my parents would be disapproving at first, they would finally come to love their son-in-law once he had had the tattoo removed from his arm. Now my dreams were shattered with this piece of information.

My expression told all, which is why my mother said she always knew how I felt without my telling her.

Barry seemed pleased at the effect of his news. "You gonna miss me?" he asked, as though we'd been seeing each other every day for years. "Listen, we can write, and I'll be coming back in the summers. We can go to the beach together and take some walks up Happy Valley."

Everyone knew what went on in Happy Valley, a park across the road from Humewood Beach.

"Why d'you have this tattoo?" I asked, pointing to a small, blue picture of a skull and crossbones on his forearm.

"That's my gang's symbol."

"What gang?"

"Duke's gang."

"Duke! You mean the king of the Ducktails?" Everyone knew about Duke, who was rumored to gate-crash parties and wear knuckle-dusters, which he would use if anyone got in his way.

"Sure, I hang around with those guys sometimes. Not all the time."

"You don't even have a duck's tail," I said, looking at his hair.

"Just takes a little Brylcreem," he swaggered, and took a comb out of his sock and scraped it through his thick hair. He edged a little closer.

"You got pretty eyes," he said, touching my lashes. "They'd be good for a butterfly kiss. You want me to give you a butterfly kiss?" He leaned over and fluttered his eyelashes against my cheek. I stopped breathing. All I could hear was a loud thumping coming from inside my chest, and I wondered if he could hear it too. Then he crushed his lips over mine like a wet suction. My mouth was shut tight and my eyes were wide open. Barry's eyes were closed, which made me think he'd done this before. In fact, he must have if he hung around with Duke's gang.

"Hey, babe, don't you French kiss?"

"Sure," I said, relieved. Finally I was on familiar territory. I had seen the French kiss in films and it certainly wasn't disgusting like all this wet, slobbery stuff. The

French knew how to kiss. They started with the back of the hand and went all the way up to the elbow. I held out my arm, but he ignored it. He was at my mouth again, shoving his tongue between my lips. I felt his spit cold around my mouth as his tongue darted inside. Then his whole tongue was rolling around inside my mouth and I had a strange, pleasurable sensation between my legs, as though I were starting to wet my pants after holding in too long.

"You a virgin?" he asked, coming up for breath, and I wondered if it would look bad to dry off my mouth.

"No, of course not!" Virgins did it, didn't they? My mind was in a state of confusion from the kissing and the insult implied by his question.

"You wanna do it? Then we can go steady and I'll give you this." He held the Star of David in his hand and pulled it back and forth along its chain.

"No, I don't want to do anything, thank you." I spoke coldly now, remembering my mother's advice that a boy will offer you anything in exchange for your favors.

"You a little cocktease, you know that?"

"What's that mean?" I asked, but he didn't answer, lunging instead for my mouth. This time I enjoyed the sensation until I felt his hand creeping over my shoulder towards my breast. I caught his hand and withdrew from him.

"I belong to the WHS," he said, sitting back with a toothy grin and chewing on a piece of gum that I realized must have been hidden in his mouth all the time he was kissing me.

"What's the WHS?" I asked, feeling ignorant and out of my depth again.

"The Wandering Hand Society. You want to become a

member?" He was still grinning when there was a rap on the door.

"I must be going," I said, guiltily patting my mussed hair.

Howie and Morris were at the door and stared at me as though I were a complete stranger. I wondered what Barry would tell them. I could have quite a reputation by the time I got back to Port Elizabeth.

"See you this evening," Barry said.

After dinner I wrote to Delia in the privacy of my top bunk: *Dear Dele, Boy have I got news for you. I am madly in love. . . .*

"Elizabeth, come have some coffee in the dining car with us," Aunt Phoebe cooed.

I put down the letter and combed my hair carefully. He could be in the dining car.

He was. He sat with his back to me, across from Morris and Howie, who grinned sheepishly when they saw me. Next to Barry sat a girl with hair teased into a beehive. He and the girl got up and I saw Barry give his friends the same signal he had given them earlier. The girl was at least sixteen, heavily made up with dark eyeliner and pale lipstick. She walked with small steps in her too-tight skirt.

"That's the Kaliff boy," my aunt said. "Has quite a reputation from what I hear. Not surprising with parents like that."

I hated her for saying that, and I hated Howie and Morris for sitting there like two accomplices. But most of all I hated myself for hoping that it was a big mistake and that Barry would return in a few moments.

That night I felt as though I had a large cavern inside me filled with the painful feelings of rejection, and, even worse, a loss of self-esteem, but the feelings dissipated as I expressed them in a new letter to Delia. Besides, with the excitement of our impending arrival in Johannesburg after breakfast, I had no room left for bitter thoughts.

Beach-colored dunes from the gold mines flashed by the corridor windows as we reached the outskirts of the city. And a few windows down, I heard a young girl call to her brothers and sisters to "come look see the gold." It was Barry's girl with the beehive and she wore a large Star of David around her neck.

"Stick to your own kind," my mother had once warned Evie. I supposed it was good advice, but I wondered how exactly you could know who your own kind were.

12

Evie and her friend Sara met me at the Johannesburg train station. I saw them first through the compartment window. Evie had put on weight and her hair was unkempt. Her blouse hung loosely over her slacks as though she were trying to hide the added inches, and it occurred to me that the extra money my mother was sending her was not being used for its original purpose—grooming. Her friend Saraswathi Khanna was not Sarah Kahn of Jewish descent as my parents had thought. She was an Indian girl, very pretty with her long, thick black hair and black-fringed dark eyes.

When Evie caught sight of me leaning out of the window, she waved wildly and shouted, "Liz, Liz!" I returned her wave with less vigor because I was dreading the moment that Evie would bring over her friend and introduce her to Uncle Cyril and Aunt Phoebe.

"Look Phoebe, the kid's with a blooming curry-muncher," Uncle Cy said incredulously as he saw Evie hurrying along the platform to our carriage, and I knew that the news would be all over Port Elizabeth as soon as

Aunt Phoebe returned and had the undivided attention of her tea-party companions.

Sara shook hands with me and smiled with very white teeth when we were introduced, and she nodded politely at the Saunders, instinctively knowing not to offer her hand. I covered up the awkward moment by profusely thanking my relatives for taking care of me on the trip. Uncle Cy still looked positively stunned, so that my aunt had to remind him to give me a hand with my suitcase.

"Sara's car is parked outside," Evie said. "We can manage the suitcase ourselves." The old Evie would never have dreamed of carrying a heavy suitcase when she could have had a porter do it for her.

Sara had a little Austin, which she wound in and out of the heavy city traffic, past tall buildings and pavements thronging with people.

"We're coming into Hillbrow," Evie announced as we neared her house. Hillbrow was a maze of shops and foreign restaurants with names like Tony's Pizzeria and Venezia, and everyone on the streets looked Greek or Italian.

"Is this still South Africa?" I joked.

"It's exciting, isn't it? Very cosmopolitan," Evie said.

Her house was on a street of large, ugly, old houses with a thin strip of yard separating them. Inside was dark and gloomy and almost empty of furniture except for the beds in every room.

"I thought just you and Sara lived here," I said. "Why are there so many beds?"

"Oh, sometimes we have meetings here and they finish late, so people just stay the night. And we do have one or two semipermanent residents, like Sara's aunt, Mrs. Patel. Here, come and meet her."

Mrs. Patel nodded a silent greeting with her large,

round head. She sat immobile on a chair in the gloom, her brown sari exposing a tire of fat around her waist.

In her room, Evie had her old trunk and a narrow wardrobe that couldn't possibly have held the trousseau my parents had bought her.

"Surely all your clothes can't fit in this wardrobe," I said incredulously, yanking at the door and wondering why it wasn't open and spilling out Evie's usual mess. It was not only closed, but locked.

"Leave it alone. You'll unpack later," Evie said sharply. "My clothes fit in the trunk. I don't have many anymore. I gave a lot away to people who really needed them." She ignored my surprise and talked on. "We have to be at a meeting on campus in a little while, and it will be interesting for you to come along."

What else was I supposed to do, I thought. Stay alone in this mausoleum? So much for our holiday house in Johannesburg—it was the creepiest place I had ever been in.

Wits University was like a separate city of large, old buildings. Students were jammed together in the main hall, and the noise was like a wave that never fell. The boys were dressed casually in jeans, but the girls were neatly dressed in skirts and blouses, their hair teased to just the right height and their makeup carefully applied. They looked as I thought my mother would want Evie to look. A row of young men entered the front platform and a familiar figure stepped forward and raised his hand. A hush descended and I looked at the figure on the podium dressed in a blazer and tie. Although I had never seen him dressed so smartly, I knew instantly that it was Willem.

"You remember Willem Coetzee?" Evie whispered. "He's head of the student body."

"Of course," I whispered back. No wonder Popeye was

so proud of his son—a young man who could command attention by just raising his hand.

"Before we proceed with this meeting, I would first like to welcome our honored guests." Willem's voice was filled with sarcasm. "Sergeant Van Tonder and Sergeant Kleinhans of the Special Branch have honored us with their presence once again."

"Boo, boo! Kick them out, kick them out!" the students jeered.

"They come to every meeting," Evie whispered, pointing out two men older than the rest and dressed in sports jackets. "That Van Tonder is a real bastard."

I looked at the man with the stony, pock-marked face and greasy, blond hair. "Why don't they camouflage themselves by dressing like the students?" I asked.

"What do they care! They have the power behind them, and they think we'll be careful what we say if they're in the audience."

The jeers died down and Willem continued.

"Your student council has called this meeting to protest the banning of Professor Eksteen for reasons not given by the government. Professor Eksteen is being detained illegally without recourse to a fair trial." Willem's voice had grown stronger with that final sentence and he delivered each syllable like a retort from a gun.

A roar rose from the students. "We want justice, we want justice!" They chanted on and on as though they would never stop.

Finally, Willem raised his hand and again there was quiet. "Perhaps Sergeant Van Tonder and Sergeant Kleinhans will come away from this meeting with some knowledge of the rule of law, which they can then pass on to a government that denies its existence."

The students applauded their approval and Willem continued. His words floated over my head as I looked around me. The students were listening with rapt attention, and Evie, too, was under Willem's spell. But the two Special Branch sergeants fidgeted and looked at their wristwatches. Van Tonder opened his mouth in a wide yawn like a crocodile about to swallow its prey.

Then it was over. I stood with Evie and Sara as the students filed out of the hall. Willem came up to us. "So the Port Elizabeth contingent is here," he said, smiling at me. "See, you're never too young to protest." Then he gently squeezed the muscle in my forearm and exclaimed, "Hm, *kleintjie,* I can tell you're still slaying them on the tennis court!" I grinned shyly, overwhelmed by seeing Willem in his capacity as a student leader. He turned to Evie and patted her on the behind. "See you girls tonight. The meeting's at nine, and have something good to graze. I'm sure everyone will be hungry."

He spoke to Evie with such familiarity that I gathered she was still seeing Willem against our parents' wishes. "What's Willem talking about?" I asked her.

"Oh, there's a meeting at our place tonight. It will be quite late, so you can just go to bed."

"It's not a school night," I huffed.

"Yes, well, I'll introduce you to everyone and then you can go to bed." Evie was quite firm. She turned to Sara. "What shall we make for them?"

"Curry and rice, maybe?" Sara said, shrugging.

I had no idea my sister could cook. She had certainly never lifted a finger to help in our kitchen at home.

Sara found parking in Hillbrow and we walked to a grocery store with a sign that said Q. L. Son Hing above the door. The store was dark and smelled of old wood and exotic spices. A Chinese girl named Venus served us and took us to a back room where the wooden floor creaked with the weight of large barrels filled with grains, dried legumes, and spices. Venus measured a little of this and a little of that on a scale, according to Sara's instructions. Evie paid what Venus described as wholesale price, and she included a strip of licorice, "for the little sister," from one of the glass jars filled with sweets on the front counter.

We stood outside the store for a moment, blinking in the unexpected sunlight.

"Hello girls, what you doing here?"

"Oh, hello Chandra, we could ask you the same question," Evie said. "By the way, this is my baby sister, Elizabeth. Liz, this is Ramachandra."

Chandra was a tall, handsome Indian fellow. He shook my hand vigorously and introduced us to his friend Asan, who nodded deferentially as if he were not used to meeting white people socially. I knew how he felt. People around us were staring.

Chandra spoke again in his typically Indian accent, emphasizing the consonants and slightly slurring his vowels. "Up the road, I saw a car parked and I recognized it as belonging to the one I intend to marry." He looked innocently at Sara.

Sara had been standing slightly behind Evie and me, and I noticed that she had not uttered a word, but stood with her eyes downcast, her long lashes shadowing her cheeks.

When they were gone, she turned to us with her eyes dancing. "Isn't he just too handsome and wonderful!" she cried.

I looked at her in amazement. "But you didn't show the slightest interest in him," I said.

107

"Oh, but I couldn't. Things are different in the Indian community. If you look at a boy straight in the eye, people think you are flirting and you get a bad name."

"Well, we wouldn't have told anyone, would we?" I looked at Evie.

"Yes, but what about Chandra's friend," Sara said, "or even someone passing by on the street. That kind of news spreads like wildfire in the Indian community. Everyone knows everyone else's business. And it would bring dishonor to my family, especially to my father, who is very highly respected in that community."

I couldn't help smiling at the similarity between her community and ours, despite the difference in color. Listening to her talk was almost like hearing my mother say, "And always remember your father is a somebody in the community."

Sara took my smile for mirth. "You shouldn't laugh at another person's beliefs," she said. "You European girls are too forward."

I blushed at the thought of Barry Kaliff—of his wet kisses and how he had ignored me later.

"Yes, and what have you been doing?" Evie asked, my shame apparently glaring her in the face.

"I smooched with someone on the train." The words came out in a rush before I could stop them. I'd been wanting to tell Evie all day—to hear her say that I wasn't a harlot. But now, looking at Sara's shocked expression, I thought how lucky the Catholics were that they could confess privately and anonymously.

"You are only thirteen," Sara mumbled.

"Almost fourteen. But I could just die," I said. "I'm so disgusting. I'll never do that again."

"Yeah, till the next time," Evie mocked. "Look, don't

be silly," she added, "you're normal. Just so long as you don't go any further than kissing."

"Oh, I wouldn't! I won't!" I said, relieved that she knew of my infamy and had set boundaries within which I could conduct myself.

"Have you ever kissed Chandra?" I asked Sara.

"No, we have only met in the presence of a chaperone, but we have held hands. Oh, but the desire is so strong!" She winced at the thought of it, and then laughed at herself when she saw the empathy on our faces.

We had been walking all this time and now we entered the butcher shop, where Evie took charge and ordered what she needed. Sawdust covered the floors and carcasses hung from the ceiling on wire hooks.

"I think I'll wait outside," I said.

"Not in Hillbrow, you won't," Evie retorted.

"I'll stay with her," Sara said. And to me she said, "I don't eat meat, so to look at it raw makes me ill."

We stood outside on the pavement watching the shoppers pass by, but it soon became apparent that Sara and I were objects of curiosity. A European girl standing together with a sari-clad Indian girl was obviously a strange combination even in Hillbrow. If I had been with an older black girl, everyone would have accepted that I was out shopping with the maid. Sara was sensitive to my discomfort, and we were both relieved when Evie finally appeared.

At the house we helped Sara's aunt in the kitchen. As an antidote to the hot curry, we filled side dishes with sliced bananas, mangos, coconut, and chutney.

"Mrs. Patel, this curry is wonderful," Evie raved, taking a spoonful. The old lady smiled for the first time. "Go on, try some," she said, handing me a spoon.

I dug out a spoonful of the aromatic vegetable curry, and as soon as it was in my mouth I knew I had made a mistake. Tears poured from my eyes and flames enveloped my tongue and palate. Even my aunt Phoebe's homemade horseradish on Passover, to remind us of the bitterness of the Jews' slavery in Egypt, was like manna compared with Mrs. Patel's curry.

I looked at my sister, who hadn't shed a tear, and I wondered how it was possible that we should both have been raised on Tilly's bland diet of overcooked meat and vegetables. Evie had changed both inside and out, and I wasn't sure if it was for better or for worse. Even her voice had become louder and more strident, as though she were emulating her African friends. When she had been in Port Elizabeth on her last vacation, she had sat cross-legged on her bed for hours at a time studying Sotho, pronouncing the words over and over again, but when she had tried to communicate with Lena and Beauty in that language, they had understood little because the language of the Transvaal was different from that of the Eastern Cape. However, they were delighted that Evie was taking the trouble to learn an African language and rewarded her with breakfast in bed every day.

"Don't worry, little sister," Evie said. "The meat is made without curry for those who can't handle the heat!"

"Funny," I said. "When can we eat? I'm about to expire."

"You and Mrs. Patel can have dinner now if you like. Sara and I will wait till later."

Mrs. Patel dished up for us both and she sat opposite me at the kitchen table immersed in her plate of food. Whenever I looked up, I caught sight of the red dot on her forehead and the jewel at the side of her nose. I wondered what Uncle Cy would say if he could see me now.

Port Elizabeth and the safe boundaries of my world had receded into a haze. I had promised to telephone my parents, but I would do that later. I was weary; it had been a long day and it wasn't over yet.

13

Whenever my parents entertained in the evenings, they left the front lights on to welcome the guests, so at 8:30 P.M. I did the same thing in Evie's house. Besides, it was creepy walking around in the dim light from two feeble lamps.

"What do you think you're doing?" Evie asked.

"Shedding a little light on the matter. You're having guests, aren't you?"

"D'you want the whole police force converging on this place?" Evie asked. "They don't like multiracial gatherings. You don't know what they'll accuse us of."

"What could they accuse you of?"

"The Immorality Act for one. They've used that before."

I was aghast. "Was it true? Were you doing *it* with a nonwhite?"

"Don't be ridiculous! I don't do *it* with anyone, whether they're pink, white, green, or purple. But they concoct any rubbish just to harass us."

By 9:15, I was reading in bed and dozing, and I wondered if Evie's meeting had been postponed until another evening. I had heard no one enter the house. But then there were voices coming from a back room and the clink of knives and forks.

I put on my dressing gown and crept down the passage. The door was slightly ajar and I could hear Willem's voice. "Evie will distribute the pamphlets that she's duplicated. It's important that you hand them out at the bus stops in the townships when the workers get off the buses tomorrow evening. We must urge them to boycott their jobs on Thursday and Friday. We will not only be striking a blow at the white supremacists, but also presenting ourselves as a unified force."

There was a rumble of agreement from the few people gathered in the room.

"Furthermore," Willem continued, "on Saturday, Sampson and I have something big planned, something that does not involve the rest of you. I would suggest that each of you plan an alibi for that day. The scheme we are involved in has been organized at a much higher level of the organization, and there is some risk involved. Sampson and I will also have an alibi, but I want you to know that if I am caught, I will have nothing to tell the police because I honestly don't know where my orders are coming from. I value my life above all things, and if any damage is done to me, you must believe it is the work of the police."

A black man, whom I presumed to be Sampson, stood up. "I too will not hang myself in a jail cell, nor will I jump out of any interrogation room window. They will have to push me," he said.

Everyone was silent for a moment, thinking private thoughts.

"I'll make coffee now," Evie said. She swung the door wide, startling me. "What the hell are you doing here?"

"I came to meet your friends." She couldn't see my crimson face in the dark passage.

"Come inside then. Everyone, this is my sister Liz. This is Sampson and Irene Sobetwa and Joshua and Miriam Makala, and you've already met Chandra."

I had never been introduced to black people by their first and surnames. The only black people I'd met were servants, and it never occurred to me that they even had surnames.

The company was polite but obviously preoccupied. I slipped out, remembering that I still hadn't phoned my parents. I dialed the operator and heard a click, then my mother was on the line.

"Darling, where have you been? We called you earlier, but we thought you'd be asleep by now. How was your trip? We miss you already." She rambled on and finally my father came to the phone.

"How are you, darling? How is Evie? Can I talk to her?"

"Evie's fine," I said. "We cooked dinner and now there's a meeting going on."

The telephone clicked. "Dad, are you still there?"

"Yes, baby, we'll talk again. Go to bed now."

Evie came out of the kitchen with a coffee tray and a packet of rusks. "What are you doing?" she asked.

"I just called the folks. They send love and Dad wanted to talk to you, but I said you were busy with a meeting."

"You did what?" She flung open the door of the back room. "Leave, everyone! Now! Go right now!"

No one asked any questions, but they left as silently as they had arrived. Only Willem sat drinking coffee at the kitchen table with Sara.

Evie unlocked the wardrobe in her room, took out a pile of pamphlets, dumped them at the bottom of my suitcase, and covered them with clothes.

Someone was knocking viciously on the front door.

"Let those bastards sweat," Evie said.

Finally she opened the door when I thought they would tear it down. Three plainclothes policemen pushed her aside and strode from room to room. When they reached her bedroom, they threw everything out of her trunk and kicked at the door of her wardrobe till it splintered and burst open. They found the duplicating machine and smashed it against the wall. Then they tore out the drawers but found nothing there.

"You got it coming to you, you kaffir-loving bitch," one man said, and I recognized his pock-marked face and greasy, blond hair from the university meeting earlier that day.

"You too, you *wit-kaffir*," he said to Willem, smashing his fist on the kitchen table so that the saucers jumped. Willem continued drinking his coffee, his face a mask, but Sara's eyes were large with terror and I realized that my eyes, too, were twice their normal size.

When they left, Evie had tears in her eyes, though she had shown no fear in their presence. Willem stood up and held her against him until she relaxed. "Please be careful on Saturday," she whispered. "If anything happened to you I couldn't bear it." She wiped her eyes with the back of her hand and then smiled at me reassuringly. "It's OK, kid. Just watch what you say on the phone next time."

14

At Willem's suggestion, Evie agreed to come to Vereeniging with me on Saturday, and my parents were delighted at her apparently renewed interest in the family. Sara, too, decided to take a trip out of town to visit her relatives in Vanderbijlpark, which was a short drive from Vereeniging across the Vaal River. She and Mrs. Patel offered to drop us off on the way to save the Levins a trip into the city.

The small Austin chugged along at a slow pace, weighted down by the luggage and by Mrs. Patel, who sat as large and silent as a sphinx filling the back seat. It was still early morning and the streets were relatively quiet. Outside the city we stopped for petrol.

"I need to go to the toilet," I said.

"So go and hurry up," Evie said. She had been in a bad mood all morning, obviously worried about Willem. They had spoken in whispers for hours the night before, and when Evie had finally come to bed I had listened to her tossing and turning for what seemed like an eternity.

"There's no need to rush, Elizabeth. I need to go, too," Sara said.

"Ugh, it's pretty disgusting. I hate public toilets," I said, coming out of the tiny cubicle at the side of the service station.

Sara emerged a few minutes later holding out her wet hands. "There's nothing to even dry one's hands with."

I was offering her the hem of my skirt when an obese, florid-faced man emerged from the front of the petrol station.

"Hey you, coolie girl, can't you read what the sign says?" His eyes bulged with rage as he raised his arm to a faded EUROPEANS ONLY sign above the toilet door. I thought he would smash his fist down on Sara's head and crack open her skull. She must have had a similar vision, for she cowered and fled to the car. Sara hugged the steering wheel to gain control of herself. She was shaking so much that she could barely start the car.

"You fat pig," I screamed at the man from the safety of the back seat as we finally pulled onto the road.

"Don't waste your breath," Evie said. "He's beyond help."

It was a gray day and the dry grass matched the sky. We drove in silence past fields of bearded mealies and pastures of thickly coated curly-haired sheep. Sara took a detour to the Levins' farmhouse along gravel roads that cut through private farms separated from one another by barbed wire fences and wide gates. Emerging from nowhere, little black urchins ran out to open the gates for us, swinging on the iron bars with hands outstretched for a few pennies.

Aunt Rhoda answered the door as soon as I rang and she hugged me with delight. "I'll send the boy out for the luggage," she said, squinting out at the parked car. "And tell Evie to bring her friends in for something to drink. They must be tired. It's no joke traveling on the bumpy country roads in a car that size."

I ran to the car and invited Sara and her aunt to come inside.

"Come on, you look like an exhausted wreck," Evie cajoled. And after a little further nagging, Sara agreed.

Evie introduced her friends to Aunt Rhoda, who tried to smother her surprise. "Why not go in the kitchen and I'll tell Eunice to give you some tea."

I had never known my aunt or my cousin Lucy to entertain their friends in the kitchen, but I was at least thankful that she didn't tell Sara and Mrs. Patel to use the back door.

Evie watched Eunice take down two enamel mugs and two china cups and saucers for tea and she immediately got up and took down two more china cups and saucers. "You can put these away, Eunice," she said, picking up the mugs.

We didn't see my aunt again until our guests had left, and she wasn't quite as friendly as she had been. "Evelyn, you mustn't interfere with the servants. Eunice is quite upset."

"Eunice is either brainwashed or brainless," Evie said, and I sighed at the thought of what was yet to come, particularly when Evie remet our cousin Lucy, who she said had popcorn between her ears.

Lucy had spent the summer with us when Evie was home from university. While Evie studied the Sotho language at the top of her lungs, Cousin Lucy, only two years my senior, quietly practiced the language of love. And while Evie argued with my father about government policy, Lucy taught me her policies on how to catch the opposite sex. Admirers called constantly begging her for dates, which proved to me that her methods were tried and true.

"I wish Evie would take some tips from her cousin Lucy," my mother had said with a sigh. "That girl has what it takes." I guess I understood what she meant. Lucy was blonde and dimpled and had an enviable chest, and her allure had not escaped a single member of the male population of the summer crowd who flocked to Humewood Beach in search of suntans and female flesh. Nor had her appeal escaped our Aunt Phoebe, who was wont to mumble, "That girl never misses an opportunity to slap her gender in everyone's face."

Lucy had not changed at all since the summer. She bounded into the house in time for lunch, her gender charmingly accentuated by a short tennis skirt. She hugged Evie and me and introduced us to her latest beau, Joey Bloch, who stood in the hallway perspiring from his tennis game. His horn-rimmed spectacles were all steamed up, either from exertion or, possibly, I thought, from the proximity to bare-legged Lucy.

"Well, fair maidens, I shall see you anon," Joey said, finally taking his leave.

"Joey played Hamlet in the school play," Lucy giggled, by way of explaining his dramatic speech. "When the English teacher, Mr. Tubbs, whom we call Tubby 'cos he's so fat, asked Joey to recite Hamlet's soliloquy to the class, Joey stood up, and with a very serious expression on his face, he recited, 'Tubby or not tubby, That is the question.' " She giggled again. "He's really a scream."

Joey was rather plain and thick set, not at all typical of Lucy's boyfriends, but he had apparently won her through persistence and a rare comic ability. But I wondered how long the attraction would last. No one had ever held her interest for more than two weeks at a stretch, although she declared that she and Joey had been going steady for a month.

"Lucy's going to a dance tonight. Can't we arrange a date for you with one of her friends?" Aunt Rhoda asked Evie.

"No thanks," Evie replied with an amused smile. "I'm not in the habit of cradle-snatching. I'm going to walk to the stables and maybe take a ride around the farm."

"Oh well!" Aunt Rhoda sighed, and I knew she was thinking she could tell my mother she had at least tried.

Evie went off to the stables and I stayed with Lucy. We were in the bathroom admiring the grit she had washed out of her hair from the sandy tennis court when the phone rang.

"The phone's ringing," I said.

"Hm, answer it," she said, swishing the basin clean.

"You know it's for you," I said.

"My hair's wet, and anyway, it's not my policy." I knew her policy perfectly well: Keep 'em waiting and don't let them think you're hanging around waiting for calls.

When I heard Joey's distinctive voice on the phone, I said, "I'll call her."

"No, no," he said. " 'Tis your ladyship with whom I wish to converse. What dost thou this eve?"

"Why?" I answered suspiciously, knowing that Joey was taking Lucy to the dance at the country club.

"Well, I have this handsome, brilliant cousin who has just arrived and needs a date. He's going to medical school next year and he's a grandiose tennis player." Joey had adopted his best salesman-of-the-year voice.

"Thanks anyway, but I'm busy tonight." I blushed at the lie and wondered if Joey could detect it. "Tell you what," I added brightly, "I'll ask Lucy to call around and ask if any of her friends are available."

I replaced the receiver, disappointed at the missed opportunity, but I knew Lucy would approve of the way I had handled the situation. "Never accept a last-minute date," she always said. "It's bad policy."

"Who was it?" Lucy asked with concentrated indifference. She had a towel twirled round her wet locks and was studying herself in the long mirror in the bedroom we shared. She would probably spend the rest of the afternoon dabbing stuff on her face and trying out new hairstyles.

"Just Joey trying to fix me up with his gorgeous cousin."

"Good, you'll join us then." She sounded as though she knew all about it.

"No, I told him that I was busy and that you'd call around to see if anyone else was available."

"Are you crazy?" Lucy exploded. "Keep him for yourself."

"I thought you always said I was too young for your crowd," I reminded her.

"So you are. But I told Joey that you were fifteen because I knew his cousin might arrive."

"Well, it's too late now," I said, surprised at her vehemence.

"No it's not. I'll phone Joey myself and tell him you can come."

Lucy's decision was final. She returned from the telephone triumphantly. "It's all arranged. Now sit down and let's see what we can do to make you look a little older."

Changing a snub-nosed, freckle-faced teenager into a sophisticate was a formidable task, and the transformation never quite succeeded. Somehow my freckles would work their way through the camouflage of powder, their presence even more pronounced against the artificially pale background, and my eyes took on a rosy hue as we discovered that I had an allergy to the bright blue eyeliner. But Lucy never gave up. She teased my mousy brown hair into a bird's nest that seemed to grow from my forehead, cheeks, and chin.

"Go wash that muck off your face," Evie said, when she returned later. I noticed that she said nothing to Lucy, who had so subtly enhanced her features that her make-up was barely visible.

"Well, well, quite a beauty treatment," my aunt exclaimed, her voice pitched a little higher than usual. "What are you going to wear, Elizabeth?" I wished I could wear jeans or shorts. I still hated the expensive creations passed down from my cousin Ruthie, who was six feet tall and had constructed an hourglass figure for herself by means of a waist cinch and padded bras. Wearing Ruthie's dresses was always a reminder of the dreaded trips to the cat-filled house of Mrs. Summers, the dressmaker, where I would sneeze and weep allergically as she tucked in the bodice here, let out the waist there, or lopped off a gallon of hem, later to be made into a headband. I must have had a never-to-be-worn sash or headband for every one of Ruthie's dresses.

"Secondhand Rose." I grimaced, as I enviously watched Lucy lay out her new dress at the end of her bed.

"I think the white one with the silver beads round the waist would look great on you," Lucy suggested.

I tried it on, and every other dress that I'd brought, eventually returning to the white one, which made me look like a zeppelin with silver hieroglyphics round the middle. The bodice sagged, so I stuffed my bra with cotton socks. If my mother hadn't spent a fortune on Evie's clothes, which were now distributed throughout the Johannesburg township, perhaps I would have some decent dresses, I thought bitterly. And so much for her grooming money, which was spent on duplicating machines and the like.

"You look sensational," Lucy commented, as she lifted my ridiculous beehive hairdo with the handle of her comb. I couldn't return the compliment because she hadn't slipped into her dress yet. She never did, until the doorbell rang. "Always keep them waiting," she'd say with a half smile, her lashes lowered as though she were hiding a big secret. "It's good policy."

On Lucy's instructions, I answered the door after the second ring. Joey stood there very dapper in his navy suit and horn-rimmed spectacles. "Well, fair maiden," he said, in what my aunt called his gift-of-the-gab voice, "meet my cousin Hotspur, better known as Lester Schwartz."

My eyes traveled up Lester's tall, broad, cream-clad presence, and my expression must have said Wow! because he smiled, revealing flashing white teeth against his perennial tan. The scent of Brilliantine from his pitch-black, slicked-back hair mingled with Old Spice after-shave, and his nostrils flared as he spoke. We went into the lounge, where my uncle and Evie were reading and my aunt was pretending to read. By the time Lucy entered the room, my aunt knew practically all Lester's life story, what his father did for a living, and what his mother's maiden name was. My back was to the door, but I knew when Lucy arrived because Lester started to say something, but no sound emerged. His long, narrow eyes were no longer on my aunt, but had slid sideways to take in a stunning vision in green chiffon. I heard a sigh from Joey and wondered if it was one of admiration or resignation.

"You must be Lester," Lucy said breathily, not removing her large eyes from his face. Then she turned to Joey.

"Sorry if I'm a little late, but I was so engrossed in this medical article I was reading." I looked at Evie and rolled my eyes. Lucy had obviously been preparing to meet Lester, the medical student. The only time she read anything other than *True Romances* was before a date when she wanted to impress. "Doing your homework before a date is good policy," she'd say. But she needn't have bothered this time—Lester was already too distracted for intelligent conversation. In my mind's eye, I could see Lucy and Lester floating through the evening, oblivious even to Joey's halfhearted clowning. He would hold her delicately on the dance floor, like he might a cream bun, not wanting any of the delicious center to escape, while Joey wept on my shoulder, deciding whether to be or not to be!

"Let me know all the details," my aunt insisted as we were leaving. "You'll have to tell us what everyone was wearing and what you had for dinner." Dinner! I was so excited that the thought of food made me ill.

"Have a good time," Evie said quietly to me, pushing a stray hair behind my ear. "Joey will be good company." Her mouth smiled, but her eyes looked so sad that I wondered if she missed the flossy kind of life she'd once had—the parties and dating people like the handsome, suave Lester—or was she just anxious about Willem and his mystery mission?

"I'll see you later. And I'll tell you all about it," I whispered to her with tongue in cheek, letting her know that I knew what to expect.

I never did tell Evie about that evening. She wasn't at the house when we returned. The lights were on in every room, which was quite unlike my aunt Rhoda, who believed in conserving electricity and anything else that cost money, except where her only child was concerned.

My aunt was walking around in her dressing gown, quite hysterical. The Special Branch had come for Evie—God knows why—she'd been at the house all day. And what would the neighbors think, and their friends, if Evie were put in jail? After all, it wasn't like we were distant relatives. And the stigma for her poor parents! On and on she rambled. She had telephoned my father with the news and he was flying to Johannesburg the next day.

The following morning, the Sunday *Times* headlines read JOHANNESBURG-PRETORIA RAILWAY LINES SABOTAGED. In the body of the article was a list of suspects taken into custody. Among the accused held in solitary confinement were the names Willem Coetzee and Sampson Sobetwa. And among those placed under house arrest was Evelyn Ann Levin.

15

Evie was back in Port Elizabeth when I returned. My mother told me that my father had persuaded the Special Branch, in his fluent Afrikaans, to please let Evie remain at home with him where he could keep an eye on her. And he had also explained to them that her interest in politics stemmed from her unhappy past, as she had lost her mother at a tender age. The head of the Special Branch had been quite sympathetic, my mother said, and had offered to lift the ban altogether if Evie would act as an informer for them. My mother, who never swore, would not repeat what Evie had replied to Colonel Prinsloo, but it was something most unladylike. Prinsloo had given my father his private number in case Evie changed her mind at any time. After all, he knew that for a young girl to be confined to her home and to be allowed only one visitor at a time—that is, if anyone would want to visit a political prisoner—was not very pleasant.

"Evie may have had good intentions," my mother said bitterly, "but she's destroyed this family." And I understood that the stigma would always remain and that my father would no longer be quite such "a somebody" in the community.

The fabric of life had changed in other ways in the three weeks I had been gone. Beauty was no longer in the kitchen. She was pregnant by a mysterious stranger whose name she would divulge to no one, although my mother thought she had finally told Lena after Lena had beaten her mercilessly about the face. "You should have heard the caterwauling in the backyard," my mother said. "Like animals. It was a disgrace! I threatened to call the police but Lena knew I wouldn't because Beauty still doesn't have a pass."

Beauty had returned to the Transkei to marry a man who needed a fertile wife. She had been replaced by Florence, an excellent cook, who unfortunately, my mother soon discovered, ran a shebeen in our backyard, supplying her special brew to the *tsotsis* from the golf course. As soon as she could be replaced, Florence would also have to go.

Evie grew thin and pale as she languished in her room from day to day, her only outing a weekly obligatory trip to report to the local police station, and we were constantly aware that our house was under surveillance from a car parked across the street close to the fence of the golf course. Delia and I devised a special code for the telephone, which was undoubtedly bugged, an idea she found thrilling. But Delia didn't have to deal with the day-to-day reality of arriving home from school to the sight of that old Pontiac with its tinted windows that represented our lack of freedom. It was the first sight that greeted me as I turned into Westview Drive when I walked home from the bus stop each day, and today was no different.

I threw down my school case and perched on the window ledge in the porch, still dressed in my navy school uniform, a book lying idly on my lap. Lena was sitting in a wicker chair darning socks. Outside the sky hung like a yellow-gray prairie, washing the flowers and shrubs in an eerie light and illuminating their colors against the dark backdrop of pine trees that edged the golf course. I could smell the sweet, cloying yesterday-today-and-tomorrow shrub with its confetti of tiny flowers, some violet, some purple, and others pure white, and I wondered, as I often had before, which color was meant to represent which moment in time.

"You dreaming again, Miss Liz, 'stead of doing your homework," Lena reprimanded. As I turned to look at her, I caught the smell of freshly ironed laundry airing on the clotheshorse. Tuesday afternoon was her time for mending, and on the table lay an old school case containing threads, needles, and pins. She had thrust a light bulb into the toe of a sock to expose a hole that her nimble fingers were covering with tiny, invisible stitches. I noticed that she had begun to attach "Miss" to my name, as though I were one step away from being "madam."

For a while I went back to my book until the quiet was broken by the rumble of a Pickford's removal truck that stopped next door, outside the Johnsons' house. When I'd first heard the Johnsons were moving away, I had felt uneasy, a temporary remorse that something else was about to change. Only one family had moved from our block since I was born, and I knew every house, both inside and out, and the idiosyncrasies of the people who lived in them. But if I had been told that one family out of the six on our block had to leave and the choice was mine, I probably would have chosen the Johnsons. Brian Johnson still ignored me, and his grown-up sister Elise, with her blonde, wavy hair and flat face, would practice her operatics whenever I tried to study. The high notes would pierce through the hedge of hibiscus, and I would watch the windowpanes to see if they would shatter. The only respite from Elise's singing was when she accidentally swallowed a needle while altering the hem on her white dress for her debut in Handel's *The Messiah*. I imagined she must have held the needle between her lips, and then in a forgetful moment probably broke into song. I never could put a needle or pin near my lips without my mother reminding me about the cotton-wool sandwich that the doctor had made Elise swallow.

No one was there to wish the Johnsons a final farewell. The street was deserted except for the Pickford's men loading furniture, heavy stinkwood tables and chairs, and velvet-upholstered sofas haphazardly draped with protective sheets. The men were tall and strong with sullen faces, and they were not too gentle with the furniture. Mr. Johnson followed them in and out of the house gesticulating anxiously, but the men ignored him. One bent to pick a long stem of grass, which he chewed and then left hanging from the side of his mouth.

"The street is so empty, no one wants to be caught in the storm," I said to Lena, who had stood up to stretch her legs.

She jabbed me and nodded toward the trees. "Some people not worried about the weather, Miss Liz."

Only then did I notice three *tsotsis* almost blending into the dark pines. How long had they been there? One sucked on a cigarette "stompie," and another whipped a nettle against the fence in a slow, rhythmic motion. I hadn't seen them before.

"The Johnsons better take everything they got or those *skollies* going to take it for sure," Lena said.

I could picture a swarm of *skollies* darting like lizards across the road to the Johnsons' house, easing their slender, unwashed bodies through the narrow windows and burglar bars, taking a warm blanket or some clothing to their tin shanty on the golf course. Worse still, I imagined them living in the house secretly until the new neighbors arrived.

A gust of wind came up and Mr. Johnson looked forlorn, his too-wide trousers flapping against his skinny legs.

"I wonder why Mrs. Johnson isn't running the show," I said.

"She probably in the hospital with Miss Elise. Beside, she never want to see this house again."

"Did Elise swallow another needle?" I snickered, knowing full well I was not to ask the servants about this. My mother had said that all I needed to know was that because of Elise's illness, the Johnsons were moving to a flat on a brightly lit street always streaming with noisy traffic. I had begged to hear what else the grown-ups were whispering about behind closed doors. But now, as Lena suddenly said, "You big gel now, you should know." I wanted to withdraw to safety, to put my hands over my ears and remind her of my mother's wishes.

"Miss Elise been attacked," Lena said.

Attacked! It was such a strange word. The only attack I'd witnessed had been in the game reserve, where we'd watched a lion kill a buck just a few feet from our car. Everyone had said how lucky we were to witness the attack and kill, but I had felt sick to my stomach at the sight of gushing blood and the terror in the eyes of the buck. But I knew Elise's attack must have been different.

"You mean the *tsotsis* got her, don't you?"

"One evening Miss Elise she alone at the house. A man, a man in a clean suit, he knock at the door and he say, 'Please madam, I want something to eat, just a loaf of bread, I am out of a job.' She close the door, but she not lock it while she go to the kitchen for bread. When she come back, the man is inside the door."

So it wasn't even a *tsotsi,* I thought. A wolf in sheep's clothing came to mind—my mother was always saying those kinds of things. "Wasn't Lettie there?" I asked.

"She was in her room in the yard. But Lettie is a new gel. You know *that* madam, she cannot keep a gel for very long."

"But didn't Lettie hear her . . . hear anything?" I asked.

Lena shrugged. "Mebbe. Mebbe not." She seemed unconcerned. And then I thought of Brian and of Beauty pregnant. And through my mind flashed a phrase: An eye for an eye. . . .

The wind was getting stronger now and I could see blood-red petals falling from the poinsettia bush beneath the window. They blew around on the grass. I closed the window and hugged my knees to my chest. I noticed that the *tsotsi* boys had vanished from the golf course.

"Maybe I heard her scream," I whispered. "Maybe I thought it was just another high note."

"Un–un–un." Lena shook her head. "That poor gel, she not going to be singing around here any more." Her face was impassive.

16

Not only were our household and neighborhood in transition, but the school atmosphere had subtly changed as well. Delia was more distant since she had acquired a steady boyfriend who she admitted had *vreyed* her. At the look of shock on my face, she immediately said that she was just teasing, that she would never let anyone touch her boobs. But I knew she had, and to me she began to look more and more like the girl on the train to whom Barry Kaliff had given his Star of David.

Since Evie had made headlines in the local newspaper, the other girls at school had stood around in groups, tittering behind my back. But all the snickering stopped when Irmgard Dietrich stuck her forefinger into my nipple, twisting her hand around like a dagger. "You commie Jew!" she spat out. I knew she spoke for the rest of the students at Queen Victoria High School who held me responsible for my sister's convictions—the kind of convictions that could unsettle their charmed lives.

The assault took place under the gnarled, old oak tree in the playground as we waited to march back to class after a game of volleyball. Thoughts of permanent deformity flashed through my mind as I instinctively hit Irmgard's offending arm, causing her hand to shoot upward and dislodge her glasses, which smashed on the asphalt. Her thick, protruding lower lip quivered for an instant before she yelled to the teacher on duty. "Miss Cox!"

It must have been the note of hysteria that brought Miss Cox running. Miss Cox never ran, and under normal circumstances she would have given the insolent girl fifty lines to write—something ridiculous like, *I must not shout out a teacher's name in vain*—to cure her of her rudeness. Miss Cox's stern eyes took in the smashed lenses and Irmgard's accusing finger pointed at me.

"Elizabeth," she said, "go immediately to the principal's office."

That very morning in history class, after we had read about Germany's part in the Second World War, Miss Cox had looked at us with her owl eyes and said, "One outstanding trait of the Jews that we can all learn from is that they never fight back. History has shown them to be a passive and forgiving people." I had proved her wrong, and she took my retaliation as a personal affront.

Instead of going to the principal's office, I went to my classroom and packed my case, then walked out of the school's gates with the intention of never returning. I expected voices to call me back, to reprimand me for leaving without permission, but no one even noticed.

I also had no intention of returning home to the sinister parked car with its anonymous driver and to Evie listlessly knitting while my mother chirped away in an effort to keep up everyone's spirits. Secretly she told me that this whole business was killing my father, and it would be best for everyone if Evie could leave the country and start a new life for herself away from the influence of that Coetzee boy. My mother's younger brother and his family, who lived in England, were also bleeding-heart liberals and would be happy to have Evie stay with them. But she would have to wait till her banning order was over, and then there was no guarantee that they wouldn't renew it. Also, it was highly unlikely that the government would ever give her a passport. Whenever my mother was in one of her confiding moods, she would turn up the radio and speak in a whisper, in case the walls had ears.

I walked past the school bus stop, crossed Western Road, and hesitated at the edge of the Donkin Reserve, a deserted common that curved like a parabola to the edge of town, serving as a shortcut and a favorite haunt for hobos and drunks who hung around the bar of the nearby Palmerston Hotel.

Queen Vic girls were forbidden to walk on the Donkin alone, and my heart pounded as I heard footsteps behind me. Glancing back, I saw a Colored man running toward me. I panicked and ran, too, wondering if I should throw down my suitcase, which was hindering my speed. I thought of Elise, who had been attacked in her home, which somehow seemed preferable to being found ravaged in a public place.

"Miss Liz, Miss Liz!" I turned to look back, and now I recognized Popeye. He was out of breath, running with a limp, and in his hand was a bottle that he held out in front of him as though offering me a drink. He no longer worked for my father on a regular basis, but came and went as he pleased, preferring that my father pay him by the hour.

Popeye sat down on a wooden bench, out of breath. "I heard from my boy, you know. He managed to get out a note to his mother, and this one's for your sister." He took a dirty, crumpled envelope from his pocket. It wasn't sealed. "I put it in the envelope," he said. "You can read it."

The scruffy note with its torn edges was written in pencil and could fit in the palm of my hand.

"But this was written a month ago," I said.

Popeye shrugged. "It came about three weeks ago. I was going to bring it to the house, but that blerry car's outside all the time and I didn't want to give it to your pa. You read what he says. Those bastards must be making him pay. You can be sure they're torturing him good and proper." Popeye raised his hand to his face and stuck his thumb and forefinger into his closed eyelids. I thought he was going to cry, but then I could hear him praying.

"I have to go now," I said, seeing someone in a navy uniform approaching. Soon, groups of Queen Vic girls would be walking into town and I wanted to avoid them. Popeye didn't hear me. He was in another world, mumbling to his God in a drunken incantation.

"That Colored bothering you?" Sybil Carter came up to me.

"No, he just works for my dad."

"You walking into town? Want to come to the Willowtree?"

Sybil Carter had the worst reputation at Queen Vic, and I knew that the Willowtree was where she hung out in the afternoons with her boyfriend, Duke, and his gang—the gang of which Barry Kaliff had been a proud member.

"Sure, why not!" I already had a reputation for being a commie; I might just as well have one for being a "sheila."

First we went to the rest room in Garlicks department store, where Sybil shoved her school hat into her satchel, which contained no books. She never did homework. She teased her hair around her face, applied lipstick and false eyelashes, raised the collar of her blazer, and pushed the sleeves up to three-quarter length. Finally, she puckered up her uniform at the waist so that the hem displayed more leg.

We strolled into the Willowtree, where a greasy-haired, leather-jacketed group played pinball and fed coins into a jukebox. Elvis's voice vibrated through the room. Duke dislodged himself from the rest and, without a word, walked up to Sybil, put his hand on her behind, and crushed her to him. He kissed her on the mouth, then walked away, ignoring her for a while. Then he came back. "Who's this?" he asked, looking at me.

"Jus' a school friend. Name's Elizabeth," Sybil said, pouting.

"She stuck up or something?"

"Ag, Duke, jus' leave her alone, man!"

Sybil and I shared our problems over a float. Her life was simple compared with mine. Maybe God was punishing me, I told her. It had occurred to me many times that none of this would have happened if I hadn't introduced Willem to Evie at the station.

"Ag, that's not true," Sybil said. "If it wasn't this Willem guy, it would have been someone else. It's like me and Duke. If I wasn't doing it with him, I'd be doing it with someone else."

I was so startled by her admission that it took me a while to figure out her logic. I'd always wondered whether she'd really done it, or whether it was just talk. Somehow it seemed all right for girls like her, and at the same time I realized that I wasn't going to make the grade as a sheila.

A small, blue Anglia was parked outside our house when I finally got home, and I recognized it as belonging to the nuns. Since my mother's hysterectomy, the nuns had visited at least once a month, and since Evie's house arrest they had come more often, to give moral support, my mother said.

Chopin was playing loudly on the record player, which meant that my mother must be discussing something private. The nuns sat like three ravens, their heads perked forward, listening to my mother. When she saw me she roared, "Where have you been? I've been so worried. I called Delia and she said you may have had detention, and I called the school but no one had seen you. Don't I have enough troubles already?"

"I was in town," I said quietly.

"Next time you phone me, do you hear?"

The nuns surveyed me. "Listen to your mother and you'll never go wrong," Sister Katherine intoned.

I left them to their private discussion and went to Evie's room. She was asleep, so I sat in the porch and contemplated Willem's note over a glass of milk and Marie biscuits. I could be sitting in the very chair that Willem had sat in more than a year ago when he had watched me play tennis against the wall, I thought.

"What's that, Liza?" My mother's voice startled me. I hadn't noticed the nuns leaving the house, and now my mother was nodding at the note in my hand.

"I bumped into Popeye and he gave me this note from Willem to give to Evie."

My mother read the note softly.

"Darling, this is going to upset your sister terribly. Wait until after Ruthie's wedding on Sunday before you give it to her. She's been so looking forward to her first social event for so long, and you know what trouble Daddy went to to get permission for her to attend the wedding."

My mother's request sounded quite reasonable. I would give Evie the note after the wedding, which was only three days away. Meantime I would keep it safely hidden between the pages of my diary in my bedside drawer.

17

Aunt Phoebe wanted her daughter's wedding to be like no other celebration. Nothing was left to chance, for she didn't want to give the gossips an opportunity to make a single disparaging remark about *the* coming event of the year, as she so boldly named it. My mother crossed her fingers and said, "Please God," every time Aunt Phoebe spoke about the wedding because she still didn't believe one should cross one's bridges . . . or count one's chickens.

Ruth had wanted Evie to be her maid of honor, but whether Evie could even attend the wedding was too uncertain at that time. Thus Lucy, the next eldest cousin, was selected, and I was to be one of the bridesmaids.

Several months before the event, Aunt Phoebe had arrived with a swatch of pale yellow *broderie anglaise* material and a bridesmaid's pattern. I looked at my mother and she knew my thoughts immediately—yellow was not my color. I would look thoroughly insipid, and in fact, so would everyone else in the retinue.

"Ruthie chose the bridesmaid's material and pattern herself," Aunt Phoebe boasted.

"I'm sure she did," I said.

Aunt Phoebe looked at me sharply, but I just smiled sunnily, to my mother's relief. I wasn't going to tell my aunt that her beloved Ruthie was making sure that none of the members of her retinue would outshine her at the altar on her momentous day.

"Now I'm going to tell you a secret," my aunt had whispered through the side of her mouth as if she were about to divulge a juicy piece of gossip. "Her name is Winnie."

"Who is Winnie?" my mother asked, bewildered.

"The dressmaker, of course. The best."

"What about Mrs. Summers?" I asked.

"Oh, she's fine for alterations, but Winnie is an artist—and don't you go telling a living soul about her."

"She must charge a fortune," my mother said dubiously.

"No, she's even cheaper than Mrs. S. She's a Colored woman," my aunt explained.

When Aunt Phoebe had driven away, I asked my mother why she had never mentioned Winnie before.

"Oh, you know your aunt and her crowd. They don't want anyone to know who sews for them, otherwise their dressmakers might get too busy and too independent."

Winnie came to the house for fittings, and with her expertise, my bridesmaid's dress turned out to be far prettier than I had imagined. My mother had also bought yards of deep blue chiffon for a dress for Evie, in the hope that she would be allowed to attend the wedding.

Evie enjoyed the fittings, which were salted by Winnie's unsubtle brand of humor. "Ag, Miss Eve, you's going to get your Adam one of these days!" Winnie would exclaim. And one afternoon, when Winnie met Jeremy Samuels, who was home for a vacation, she winked conspiratorially and grinned, baring a gummy space where her two front teeth should have been. "Ag, Miss Eve, you catch the boket at the wedding and you sure to be next," Winnie predicted. As the dresses came close to completion, Lena, too, never missed a fitting. She would stand in the doorway, stomping her feet and clapping ecstatically. "My gels going to be the best," she would say. But, when the dresses were finally hanging in the wardrobe, draped in tissue paper, the excitement died down until the weekend of the wedding.

Traditionally, the bride and groom were not allowed to see each other on the day of the wedding, so Selwyn spent his last night as a bachelor at our house. Early on Sunday morning, I walked into the porch and found Selwyn sitting there, enunciating over and over again, "H-ow n-ow brown c-ow."

He looked sheepish when he saw me.

"What on earth are you doing?" I asked in a voice that said, Now I've seen everything!

"Ruthie's been giving me speech lessons so I won't make a fool of myself at the wedding. That was one of her exercises. Can I practice my speech in front of you now?" he asked, nervously clutching a sheet of paper.

"Of course," I said, and then added sweetly, "but if Cousin Ruthie prefers her own accent to yours, perhaps you should have told her to make the speech."

Later on in the day, Evie and I were dressing when Lucy arrived with her parents from the hotel where they were staying. She carried her dress covered in plastic—no doubt she would only slip it on at the last minute. We were ready to leave for the synagogue when Lucy finally appeared. I knew she had entered the room because Selwyn stood riveted with his jaw open in midspeech—a reminder of the late Lester, as Lucy named her ex-beau, Lester Schwartz, since discarding him for someone else.

My father nudged Selwyn out of his daze, and I heard him whisper in an amused tone, "My boy, at this stage you can only look and long."

Lucy had used neither the pattern nor the material given to her by Aunt Phoebe. She wore a deep yellow, tight-fitting, Spanish-style dress with a frill around the shoulders and another around the hem that was long at the back and curved upward in front to display her knees.

"Aunt Phoebe's going to have a cadenza," I said to Lucy.

"Good, I like to give people cadenzas." She giggled.

We all hovered around Lucy at the synagogue, waiting for Aunt Phoebe's reaction, which was surprisingly restrained. "My girl, I think you forgot your castanets" was all she said, and when I saw Cousin Ruthie looking like a goddess in white lace, I understood Aunt Phoebe's calm, for no one could eclipse the bride on her wedding day.

The ceremony and reception went without a hitch. My parents sat at the main table with the bride and groom and aunts and uncles, while Evie and I sat at the table reserved for the retinue. She invited Jeremy Samuels to sit with her. As the band struck up, Ruthie and Selwyn took the floor for the first waltz, which I was sure she had made him practice ad nauseam. Then Evie and Jeremy floated away, and she seemed to sparkle as she hadn't done in months. It had occurred to me during the evening that no one at our table spoke to Evie, as though they were scared to spark off a conversation that might lead to a political discussion.

At one point, the band took a break and Jeremy, who had been discussing Evie's future with her, turned to me

142

and said, "And you, Liz, what are you planning to do when you leave school?"

The general conversation at the table had waned, and everyone was looking at me expectantly. "I'd like to be a lawyer."

"Uh-huh. Where do you want to study?"

"At Cape Town University." I didn't add that my father had said he would never allow me to go to Wits.

"You know if you study law in South Africa you won't be able to practice anywhere else, because none of the other English-speaking countries uses Roman-Dutch law."

"I wasn't planning to go anywhere else," I said.

"Always keep your options open," Jeremy said.

"Why would you want to do law?" someone asked.

"Maybe I'll be able to do some good—like defending political prisoners."

"I'm afraid you won't get much work in that line," Evie said drily. "In case you haven't noticed, political prisoners rarely get tried."

Someone coughed uncomfortably, and everyone looked relieved as the band began playing again.

Later in the evening, in the midst of the revelry, I noticed Evie staring into space. Her face was white and she shivered as though blasted by an icy wind. "I have to go," she said. "I feel strange."

Jeremy willingly offered to take her home, and I wondered if the earlier conversation had upset her. As they left the hall, a man slipped out after them. I walked to the door and saw Jeremy's car being trailed. Even tonight Evie was being watched.

When I returned home with my parents after midnight, Evie was fast asleep under a pile of blankets, despite the warmth of the night. I was still in my bridesmaid's dress, brushing out my unnaturally teased hair when I heard a low wail, like that of an animal in pain, coming from the backyard. My mother must have heard it, too, for we met at the back door and agreed that the sound was coming from Lena's room. We knocked on the door and pushed it open. On a chair sat Beauty, a thinner version of her formerly plump self, and tied to her back with a blanket was a chubby, sleeping infant. Lena lay on the bed, her eyes like slits in her swollen face.

"They taking my boy," she cried over and over. "Those *tsotsi* soldiers they threatening to kill my boy if he don't come with them. Then they sending him to another country to become fighter. When he come back he will not be knowing his mother. He will be like a dead son to me."

My mother clucked sympathetically and explained that this was something Lena had been afraid of for some time, that young militants were threatening to kill school boys in the homelands if they didn't follow their orders to be trained as guerilla soldiers. The older Africans, like Lena, she said, also wanted change, but not through violent means.

"You must be telling no one," Lena said fearfully. "Otherwise the police they will be after me to find my son."

"We know nothing," my mother said, and I nodded in agreement. Then she looked at Beauty, the bearer of bad tidings. "Why don't you sleep in your old room tonight, Beauty, and let Lena get some rest."

With the excitement of the wedding, and the trauma of Lena's personal drama, Willem's note lay forgotten between the pages of my diary until two days after the wedding. Evie was in the bathroom taking a shower when I found the note.

"It's midafternoon," I shouted next to the curtain. "Why are you showering now?"

"It's all the same to me," Evie replied. "Day is night, night is day." She had been sounding depressed again since the wedding was over.

"Keep the water running. I have something to tell you," I whispered, as she emerged from the shower cubicle.

Evie held up the dirty piece of paper as though it were fragile, then she mouthed the words I had already seen: *Be strong. I can bear the pain knowing we'll be together someday. john.*

"Why does he sign it John, and how do you know it's from him?"

"It's his writing, and John is a private joke. His initials are W. C., which stands for 'water closet,' or the john!"

Evie covered her face with her hands. "Oh God, they must be torturing him. I'm not waiting any longer. I'm going to phone that Colonel Prinsloo and pretend I'll be an informer. Maybe that way I can bargain for Willem."

"You're crazy," I said. "Those Special Branch types aren't stupid."

"I've been thinking about this for a while now," she said, with a determined look on her face.

Evie went to my father's room in her dressing gown, her hair still dripping wet. Colonel Prinsloo's number was under the glass next to the telephone on his bedside table.

"I'm going to listen on the hall phone," I said, but I don't think she even heard. She sat strumming her fingers on the bed, staring at the number. It took a while to get through to Colonel Prinsloo, and then he was on the line. "*Ja,* Prinsloo here."

"Yes, this is Evelyn Levin." Evie's voice shook and then she gained control. "I've been thinking about your offer, and I'm willing to help you in exchange for the release of a friend of mine."

"And who might that be?" Prinsloo sounded quite friendly.

"Willem. Willem Coetzee."

"Ag, but you're a little late, young lady. You see I got word a little while ago about our prisoner Coetzee. Seems he couldn't handle solitary. Some of them can't, especially ones like Coetzee who are used to being on stage all the time."

"What's happened to him?" Evie's voice was low and trembling.

"Like I said, Coetzee couldn't take it. Jumped from the interrogation room window Sunday evening."

There was a pause as the news sank in, and a picture flashed through my mind of Evie pale and shivering at the wedding on Sunday evening.

"Murderer!" Evie screamed. "You bloody murderers, you pushed him!"

I heard the phone crash against the table. When I ran to my parents' room, the mouthpiece dangled an inch from the floor and Evie was crouched on the bed sobbing, her wet hair spreading a dark halo on the white pillowcase.

18

Evie cried for three days following that phone call. In desperation my mother called the family doctor, who gave her a sedative. Dr. Gelbart and my mother spoke in whispers for a long time, and when he finally left, she had a look of determination on her face that I hadn't seen there before.

At Mrs. Coetzee's request, Willem's body was shipped to Port Elizabeth, and several days after the doctor's visit, the funeral was to take place at the South Kloof cemetery. None of our family planned to be there. In accordance with her banning order, Evie was not allowed to attend gatherings of any sort, and my father chose not to go. He decided it would not be a good move politically, and I thought how cautious he had become, and how the spunk had gone out of him since the start of this business with Evie. In the space of months, he had grown stooped and his eyes had lost their mischievous light. He had even bought a new sterilizer for his "white" surgery, but only, he said, because his growing practice required it.

On the day of Willem's funeral, Lena asked for the afternoon off. I watched as she walked through the yard in her black church-choir dress with its white collar and cuffs.

"I didn't know you had church in the middle of the week," I called.

"Not chech," Lena said. "Funeral. Going to funeral for man who die for our cause. The whole of New Brighton going to be there." She made a dramatic arc with her arm.

"It's Willem's funeral. You know Evie's friend—the one who used to come to the house."

"*Hayi kona!*" Lena was shocked.

"I want to come," I said on the spur of the moment, a certainty welling up inside me that I ought to be there.

"You cannot come," Lena said firmly. "Fest of all, you still in school uniform. Second of all, the madam she give me off till Monday night, so I cannot bring you home."

"For heaven's sake, I'm not a baby. I can catch the bus on my own."

"Two buses," she said.

"And my school uniform is perfect for a funeral!" Contrary to my vow never to set foot in Queen Vic ever again, I had returned with my head held high, determined to ignore the groups of whispering girls who had eyed me while talking behind their cupped palms. Surprisingly, no one seemed to snicker anymore. The incident with Irmgard had cleared the air.

"Ma, I'm going to a friend's house," I yelled. "I'll be back later."

"Be careful," she shouted back, but she didn't sound overly concerned. She had been busy these past few days plotting and planning, as she called it, though for what I did not know.

The bus into town was relatively empty, but from the town to South Kloof we were squashed together into a single body, dangerously spilling out onto the platform.

148

The cemetery stood atop a hill overlooking a disused rail yard on the outer edge of the harbor. The wind blew in from the sea as if to tear the thorn bushes and long, limp strands of grass from their roots in the sandy soil. Grit from the gravel path edged inside my shoes, and Lena had to stop several times to catch her breath. Below us, like swarms of ants, people converged from all directions as though the wind had blown them to the edge of the steep path—black people in dark dresses, Indians in saris, poor Coloreds and well-dressed Coloreds, a few Chinese, and a smattering of white faces.

Among the gray, granite tombstones decorated with benevolent figurines of winged angels and elaborate crosses, the mourners stood still and sullen, and it seemed to me, for an instant, that they were the dead risen from the graves. I could see nothing of the ceremony from where I stood, so I left Lena and wound my way forward in time to see the plain, wooden coffin being lowered into the gaping ground. And then I heard the dull thud of earth as it fell on the coffin. "Dust to dust . . ." the minister intoned, and it didn't seem possible that Willem was in that box—Willem with his animated, intelligent face and his charisma that had kept an entire hall of students spellbound and had swept Evie off her feet the first time she'd met him; Willem who had motivated me to my first major tennis victory. Now he was being mourned by hundreds of people who didn't even know him, but knew what he stood for. His mother stood alone, grasping a balled handkerchief in her tight fist. I couldn't see Popeye but I imagined he was there somewhere.

The minister's speech was over and suddenly the voices of hundreds of mourners rose into the wind. "*Nkosi Sikelel'i Afrika. . . .*" With their right arms raised, they sang the

African national anthem, and their voices were so pure that tears stung my eyes and I could feel goose bumps rising on my arms. I wished that the wind, blowing inland, would carry the sound all the way to our house for Evie to hear.

An Indian couple was standing on either side of Mrs. Coetzee and I ran over to them. "Sara! Chandra!" People were shaking Mrs. Coetzee by the hand, and then it was my turn. She put her hands on my shoulders, drawing me close. My hands hung awkwardly, and I didn't know what to say. "I wish you long life," I said, remembering what people had said to my father when he was sitting *shiva* for my grandfather.

Mrs. Coetzee was unaware of my discomfort. She spoke to me urgently. "Mr. Coetzee left the house when we got the news and he hasn't returned since." She tried to blink back her tears. "Tell your daddy to find him, please my girlie." I wanted to apologize that my father wasn't there, but I kept quiet.

Sara and Chandra had driven down from Johannesburg for the funeral and to see Evie before they left for England. They no longer needed a chaperone. Three months earlier, Evie had received a wedding invitation rudely opened and left unsealed by those anonymous people who opened her letters.

"How was your wedding?" I asked, noting how Sara had filled out and looked more beautiful than ever.

"The wedding was a family affair, which meant that the entire community was there because everyone is directly or indirectly related to everyone else! We brought photographs to show you."

"You here alone?" Chandra asked.

"Uh huh."

"We'll take you home, so you can show us the way."

"Evie's expecting us," Sara said, noticing my hesitation. "I phoned earlier and, of course, I stated quite clearly, for anyone listening, that we would see her one at a time."

"She doesn't look too good," I warned them.

"That's to be expected, but soon everything is going to change. Your mother has been in touch with us."

I wanted to ask what she meant, but Chandra gave her a look and changed the subject.

At the house, Sara brought out her wedding photos, and my mother exclaimed how wonderful that Evie's friends would be in England. I thought how insincere my mother could be at times, since she always said she would hate to leave the South African way of life and return to cold, clammy England.

"I can't wait," Evie said, and her eyes looked brighter than I had seen them in a long time.

"For what?" I asked.

My mother put her fingers to her lips. "It's all arranged," she whispered, while the radio blared. "But!"—she drew a finger across her mouth—"you keep *shtum,* understand!"

The following day was Friday. My mother made breakfast, and my father took Evie to report to the local police station as he did every Friday before he went to work. When he dropped her back at the house, he looked haggard, and hugged her as though he would never see her again. "It's OK, Popsicle," she said, "I'm going to be fine."

At ten o'clock, two of the nuns arrived for morning tea. Sister Katherine carried a large bag. They went into Evie's room, and while the kettle boiled, my mother scraped back Evie's thick hair and pinned it down. Sister Katherine placed the firm, white edge of the black veil against my sister's forehead.

151

Two nuns and a "novice" had tea on the porch with my mother. Then Evie came into my room, where I lay in bed with stomach cramps. My mother hadn't believed that I felt too ill to go to school. "You just don't want to miss out on anything," she had said. And then when I had winced, she had said it was probably just the excitement.

"So this is it, little sister." Evie took in a deep breath, as though filling her lungs with the sweet air of a home she might never see again. "Just remember to always keep fighting."

"For what?" I asked. "I don't want to end up like you or Willem."

"There are other ways," she said. "You're smarter than I am. You'll find your own way. I know you'll fight for what is right." Her eyes shone and her cheeks were flushed. She made a very pretty nun.

"I'm not even sure what's right."

"Yes you are! Just take a look around you."

I looked around my room, at the wooden furniture and flowered curtains faded from the sunlight. I knew that was not what she meant. But these were the things that she was having to sacrifice, and I didn't ever want to be forced to leave everything that was familiar.

I got out of bed to give her a hug in her strange garb. At the door she turned and looked back at me. "Oh my God," she said. "You finally have your period!"

I looked down at my blood-stained pajama pants. I was almost fifteen years old and still hadn't had "the curse." I had been to the doctor, who pronounced me a late bloomer, but my mother thought I should keep it to myself, just in case. No man would take seriously a woman who couldn't bear children. And I had thought of

Beauty, whose proven fertility had made her an acceptable wife.

"I'll get Mom," Evie said. I noticed she didn't call her Lydia.

Later, my mother said it was a good omen that I had reached womanhood on the day that Evie left, and I accused her of creating her own superstitions. But she may have been right. On Monday, three tense days after Evie's departure, a telegram arrived from her brother in England: *Thank you for the precious gift. Arrived intact. We will cherish.*

On Tuesday morning, Lena, having returned from her extended weekend off, took breakfast to Evie's room and found it empty. "Madam, madam. Miss Evie gone!"

My mother threw up her hands and gasped. "Don't worry, Lena," she said. "I'll deal with it." She found Colonel Prinsloo's number and dialed carefully. Her voice quavered when she finally got through. "This is Mrs. Levin, Evelyn Levin's mother. I'm afraid I have to report her missing. When the maid took her breakfast this morning, she wasn't there." Then my mother began to sob and I watched with fascination her realistic performance, until I realized she was shedding real tears into her Irish linen handkerchief.

That day, my father returned home from work earlier than usual and I found him sitting lifelessly on the bed in her empty room. He looked around and then he said, "The police found Mr. Coetzee out at Swartkops. His car was in the brush above the sea. He'd used gas. God, how he loved that boy!" He let out a bark that I thought must have been a laugh, but I saw his crumpled face and realized it was a sob. I had never seen my father cry, and I knew his tears weren't just for Popeye.

"This country is a one-way street, and God help you if you ignore the signs and go the wrong way," he said, shaking his head.

"Daddy," I said, no longer able to contain the burden of guilt I'd been harboring since hearing Colonel Prinsloo's terrible pronouncement to Evie on the telephone. "I'm the one who killed Willem, and now Popeye!" My eyes brimmed with tears. "If I'd given Willem's note to Evie on the day I got it, she could have saved his life."

"Ah, my girl!" My father held me close. "You can't blame yourself. Your sister was naïve to think she could make a deal with Prinsloo. You have to understand that those people would never let someone like Willem live. He was a remarkable leader, and nothing terrifies the government more than charismatic leaders with liberal ideals. Popeye knew, and Willem knew too, that it was just a matter of time. The boy was prepared to be a martyr."

I shivered. "I don't ever want to die like that."

"God forbid! But if you don't know it yet, you will eventually realize that you have too much heart to stay here. There is room in this country for only two types of people: Those who believe in the system, and those who passively abide by it."

"But what about those who are willing to fight?" I ventured, thinking of Evie's parting exhortation.

"Haven't you seen enough to know the answer to that question?" My father's voice was bitter. "Dying or being imprisoned for your ideals won't change a thing, and the black man won't even thank you for it. One day, when Lena's son returns like a mindless fighting machine and you are standing in his path, he's not going to know that you are the white girl his mother loves like her own daughter. Nor is he going to stop and think, Ah, let's spare this one, she truly has a good heart."

I closed my eyes against the picture he was creating. "You paint a brutal picture, Daddy."

"A realistic one, my baby, but believe me, I hope I'm wrong."

"Dad?" My chest was constricted with fear. "I don't want to leave yet."

"Of course not, sweetheart, I'm talking about the future. The time will come when you will want to leave, and as much as I dread that day, I won't stop you." He gave a defeated sigh, and the lines of his face were valleys of sadness. "There'll come a time when all our children will want to leave."

I knew, then, that he meant not only his own children, but the country's young people. And I had a vision of parents growing old, alone, and brothers and sisters scattered across the globe, wherever they could find refuge.

I was crying softly now in the dark room. Evie could never again return, and I hoped I would never be in her shoes. "I always want to be able to come back."

"Of course," my father said. "Always."

First Willem, then Jeremy, and now my father! They had all foreseen a future for me someplace else, a future I had refused to contemplate. But perhaps Evie knew me best. She knew that I could not leave without a fight. She had said I would find my own way. Others could wield sticks and stones, but I knew the weapon I would use: Words! I could always fight with words. "Sticks and stones may break my bones, but words will never hurt me," I had long ago shrieked at Fiona Frazer when her words, like arrows, had pierced me to the very core.

155

As I dried my eyes in the darkening room, my path suddenly seemed perfectly clear, and wherever Evie was at that moment, thousands of miles away, struggling to find refuge, I felt closer to her than I had in a long time.

She poured herself a second cup, threw her head back and swallowed it in one gulp like a shot of cognac. Then she bent over, lifted the sculpture off the floor and dusted it off with her sleeve. She rubbed the nostrils and ears roughly with a turpentine rag, as if to humiliate the model in absentia, took off her glasses and held the bust right in front of her near-sighted eyes, almost touching it with her nose.

"Yes," she said. "The forehead was good. Very high, very broad. Almost as if she were intelligent."

"She wasn't?"

"No. She had intuition—that's already a good deal. I'd have recognized her by the mouth, myself."

"Really?"

"Tight-mouthed. A mean mouth."

"Anabel wasn't mean," I said firmly.

"No?" She put her glasses back on and studied me. "When did *you* know her?"

"Before the war."

"When, before the war?"

I thought back, forced myself to make an effort and get things straight.

"Two or three years before."

"I'd lost touch with her by then," said the painter, putting the head back on the floor. I couldn't stop myself from picking it up, turning it this way and that. I felt that she was watching me and put it down again.

"You can take it home with you—on loan."

"What would I do with it?" I said hastily, got up and looked at my watch. Although I studied both hands intently, I couldn't make out what time it was. I just stood there foolishly in the middle of the room. The painter watched me in silence and waited. I took two steps away from her, then turned back again.

"When did you know her?"

"When her name was still Anabel Beauregard. We lived together."

"Lived together . . ." I repeated, staring at her. She nodded. I walked slowly back to the hassock, playing for time, sitting down carefully, smoothing my skirt, clasping my hands around my knees.

"What do you mean, you lived together?"

"In my studio in Paris, Rue Vineuse," she said quietly.

"I never knew that Anabel was . . ."

"Yes, she was. She played it both ways. I've always stuck to women myself. But that's a matter of taste, not virtue."

Slowly, casually, and without any special intention—I thought—I folded my arms across my chest. She watched me and laughed.

"Go ahead and cross your legs too! What a prissy little thing you are! How old are you, for God's sake? Thirty? You're not in any danger. You ought to know that."

I got up, looked toward the door, looked at my watch once again, murmured.

"And—you did this head?"

"Who else? It's not very good, but it's like her."

"Very like her," I said.

She was still studying me through her glasses, neutrally, without smiling.

"I think that's enough for today. You're sure you don't want to take it home with you?"

"Quite sure."

"All right. Eleven o'clock on Friday."

2

Did I say it all began in the painter's studio? Mistake. That's where it ended. My discovery of the bronze head was the epilogue.

In one of my suitcases was a cardboard box tied up with string. It stayed there permanently, in the same corner, right down at the bottom. I never left it behind, but I never unpacked it either. I just needed to know it was there, first, so that nobody could open it—this was the only suitcase I always kept locked—and second, in case some day I decided to undo the string.

I knew what was in the box: a diary and a letter. I had never opened either of them. I didn't want to. I couldn't. Whenever I opened the suitcase to pack and saw the box in the bottom corner, looking more ominous and threatening every year, I would pile underwear and sweaters over it. But I never left it behind.

•

The incident with the bronze head occurred toward the end of 1947. I'm sure of that because I happened to be in London at the time, although we had already been living in Hollywood for two years. In 1947 my former husband was filming on location in England and I found myself living in a hotel; I was neither actress nor housewife and woke up in the morning without a schedule to meet, feeling free but lazy. So I was quite pleased to be posing for a painter; it gave me something definite to do twice a week.

I hadn't known her long. Someone had taken me to a gallery where she had a one-woman show. The exhibition had been on for weeks, and nearly all the paintings had little red "Sold" labels stuck to the bottom right-hand corner of the frame. Twenty or thirty people, catalogues in hand, were wandering about the two large rooms, in the usual solemn, vaguely embarrassed way.

Suddenly the street door burst open. In the entrance stood a small, stocky woman of about fifty in trousers and poncho, a sort of Venetian Doge's cap on her head. A flat, angular face, a child's turned-up nose, and a wide, thin-lipped mouth —the painter, no doubt, although there was only a slight resemblance to the photograph in the catalogue. She stood still for a moment, as though refueling, then marched diagonally across the room toward the office door, closing it behind her. A second later it flew open and she reappeared, flanked by the owner of the gallery, a bespectacled bald-headed giant, and a young man, flapping helplessly around both of them.

"This one and that one over there," she said in a loud voice, pointing to two paintings with red dots on the frames.

"Out of the question. They're sold." The giant's voice was brusque though subdued, yet people in both rooms began to gather around; no one wanted to miss what was going on. Neither the giant nor the painter, engrossed in their anger, saw or heard us.

"Take them down," said the painter curtly. "I have to

make some changes. I told you to hold them in reserve, not to hang them. You can have them back by the end of the week."

The gallery owner glared at her over the top of his glasses as we waited expectantly, then turned and went back to his office without a word.

The painter pursed her child's mouth, folded her arms and watched the young man struggle with the hooks on the wall. Looking around, she noticed us for the first time. As she glanced at me, something caught her eye and she stared fixedly, without embarrassment.

The young man stood panting, waiting and silently beseeching, balancing the two paintings in their heavy carved frames.

"Put them into my station wagon."

She marched to the door, held it open for him, then turned back. Planting herself in front of me, she said, "I'd like to do a sketch of you. Maybe even a portrait. How about it?"

•

At the first sitting she put the charcoal down after ten minutes.

"Take that thing off. Here!" She walked over to a chest and took out a light poncho with a fringe of llama hair.

"From Cuzco. Genuine."

"Did you paint in Peru?"

"For many years. I was going to stay there."

"Why didn't you?"

"I'm too old. Or not old enough." She laughed and pointed to a chest of drawers in the corner on which stood a grinning mummified Peruvian head with shaggy black hair, the Venetian Doge's cap perched on top. It looked not unlike her.

In the gypsy-camp bathroom where she washed her brushes and which stank of turpentine, I changed into the poncho. I didn't think it suited me, but she gave a satisfied nod, made three or four sketches and started to paint. That was three weeks ago. We never spoke, just listened to music, drank coffee and said, "Goodbye then."

I had tried to find out something about her at the gallery. "A difficult person. Tricky." That didn't bother me; it applied to most people who wanted to achieve something. No one knew her personally. I didn't either, although I spent an hour and a half in her studio twice a week.

Slowly the colors on the canvas began to merge into a dense texture. Not that she ever said, "Would you like to look at it?" She probably guessed that I did anyway during breaks, as soon as she disappeared into the kitchen.

•

On that ominous day—a foggy, wet, English afternoon—I had walked all the way from her studio back to my hotel. I needed time. I couldn't get rid of a tingling, prickly feeling, the kind you get from an electric shock, although it was over an hour since I had held the bronze head in my hands, Anabel's head, shrunken, the way the Jivaro Indians preserve the heads of their enemies.

I knew perfectly well what I had to do as soon as I got back to my hotel room. It wasn't to be put off any longer.

Upstairs, I stood by the window for a while. The fog outside did me good, it left no view to look at, just a gently drifting, shapeless mass. From time to time it parted and for a moment there was a glimpse of the Thames far below, slate-gray and sullen-looking. Then the river disappeared again behind the quilt of fog.

Not that I wanted to put it off one last time. On the contrary, now that the time had come, I felt almost impatient. But I refused to comply right away with this sudden urge. A few minutes of torturous suspense was the least I deserved after so many years of procrastination and excuses. Besides, I wanted to make sure that I knew what I was going to let myself in for, once I descended to the hotel's luggage room.

Slowly I walked down the long corridor, spent some time chatting with the porter, forbade the page to accompany me, selected the suitcase and lugged it all the way back to my room.

I set it on the bed and looked at it. It had been light enough to carry; it was empty, after all. Except for the cardboard box.

My keys. A light, tentative touch, and the locks snapped open almost of their own accord. There it was.

I took a pair of scissors, cut the heavy string and lifted the lid. The diary. Brown leather with an elaborate lock, probably real gold. Lying beside it, the key, also gold. Everything Anabel owned was real. And the letter.

I opened the book. On the blank title page was a scrap of torn-off paper with a message printed in pencil in capital letters: "NO! FIRST THE LETTER!"

I tore up the scrap of paper. No, first the diary.

The careful, round, even handwriting was as familiar to me as my own. And yet there had been few letters from her; we had nearly always been in the same city, in London. Obviously this diary was one of a series, because it didn't explain anything but started right in the middle of a Mediterranean trip in the summer of 1935. That was before I knew her.

But, judging by what the painter had said, I didn't know her later either. I had no idea she kept a diary, and a pitiless, hate-filled one too, as a glance at the first page told me.

Hatred for her husband Bill, for her daughter Nina, most of all for herself. So she had hated herself even in those days, before she ever met Jerome and me.

The first entry was dated October 10:

> I always leave the lunch table now before B. helps himself to fruit. I can't stand the way he bites into an apple, making the juice spurt in all directions.

Right hook at her husband, Bill Maclean. Bill. Slowly he came into view, in a tweed jacket, deliberately and expensively old-fashioned with two nineteenth-century slits at the back, a stiff very high shirt collar, his wavy hair and freckles. Once—when could it have been?—I watched him holding Anabel's fur coat for her, but, instead of letting go, he threw both his arms around her from behind, pressing his face into her hair and murmuring: "Oh, that feels good!" He had forgotten I was there. She held still, but I was glad he couldn't see her face.

Next entry, October 11. A slap in the face for her daughter Nina, who must have been fourteen at the time:

> We finally arrived in Genoa yesterday and I put her on the train. She took it for motherly solicitude.

I stopped reading and thought: Never! Never at any time did Nina credit her mother with solicitude toward her.

> Actually I just wanted to make sure I'm rid of her until the Christmas holidays. As the train pulled out, I blew a kiss after it. What I really felt like doing was throwing myself on the tracks in front of it. Like Anna Karenina. Tolstoy knew. This longing to be annihilated, crushed to a pulp . . .

It had grown even darker. I was having trouble deciphering the words. I went back over that last phrase: ". . . annihilated, crushed to a pulp . . ." The writing was careful, relaxed and rounded, the dots meticulously placed above the *i*'s.

I closed the book.

3

I lay in the dark for a long time, trying to get my mind off the diary, but it clung like a tarantula. In the end, dead tired but still wide awake, I remembered my old childhood remedy. "Think of Charlemagne," my father used to say when I was too excited to fall asleep the night before some great event. Why Charlemagne? My father would smile mysteriously and say, "You'll see. It helps." Charlemagne under his jagged crown never failed me. It always took some initial effort to make him appear—he was so very gray—but once I got him into focus he stopped the merry-go-round in my brain, even if he only stayed enthroned in my mind for a few seconds.

Okay, Charlemagne. Bring him on! There he was, carved in stone, sitting large and squat on a very small horse—face like a pancake—nose worn off—gone again. But I could hear surging, splashing sounds all around me, as though I were surrounded by water. Whenever I thought myself back into the past, I would "go under," faces and events would come swimming toward me, others lay darkly at the bottom or drifted about like seaweed, eluding capture.

Except for anything to do with Jerome. All that was lying just below the surface, crystal-clear, outlines and background floodlit. I could hear his voice and those of the people around him, and my own voice too, as distinctly as if I had taped them.

•

We first met Anabel just after we moved into our little apartment in Hampstead. That was the end of our nightly sneaking into the house in Parsifal Road, where I lived with my mother and my two sisters. If my mother ever heard us, she never let me know it. The house was also home to a few boarders, whose private lives were strictly their own affair, and in this respect my mother treated her grown-up daughters as boarders.

Up to that time, during the day, if I wasn't filming or rehearsing and if it wasn't pouring rain, we used to wander about in Hyde Park. We loved Hyde Park. It had brought us luck; ever since the afternoon when I first laid eyes on Jerome, it had been our refuge.

April 2, 1936! That was the right date, the day it all began. Lyon's Corner House at Marble Arch. Not very chic, but at the time I was only playing small parts and had to look twice at every shilling. Early afternoon, the café was empty. I was waiting for my agent, who was supposed to bring me a film script—unless they'd decided once again that they wanted an English girl for the part.

The agent hadn't shown up. I'd give him another ten minutes, then take the bus home. My mother would guess by my face what had happened. By tomorrow I'd have forgotten all about it and be off eagerly pursuing other possibilities. As I turned the pages of my newspaper I suddenly felt a pair of eyes on me, burning through my beret and my mop of hair. Diagonally across from me sat a young man, drinking his tea. The chair next to him was tipped against the table to show that it was reserved. Somebody had stood him up too. Dark complexion, dark hair, dark eyes that quickly frisked me—obviously not an Englishman. When I looked at him, the eyes stopped investigating and he smiled. I turned back to my newspaper but remained conscious of his gaze, which never left my yellow mane. At that time I was a flaxen blonde, convinced that this would help me become a film star. A few minutes later he deposited his cup of cold tea beside mine, sat down on the empty chair and suggested that we might go for a walk, since it had stopped raining.

Crossing Oxford Street, he put his hand under my elbow, a touch that has always ignited a response in me, out of all proportion to the purpose intended. (I once happened to glance through the window of my taxicab and see a man I loved accompany a strange woman down the road. I bade my driver to stop for a moment. I wanted to see if he would put his hand under her elbow while crossing the street. He did. I drove on.)

As if prearranged, we walked briskly into Hyde Park. He knew a corner, he said, where one could get a deck chair without paying sixpence an hour. I knew all about that corner. The summer before—my first summer in London—it had been my luncheon restaurant. Day after day, I had sat there eating my unbuttered crispbread and slice of ham that was supposed to shrink my stomach and end its craving for milk chocolate, for on camera I looked like a full moon. That was a year before. In the meantime I had lost ten pounds as well as my fond belief in an immediate and meteoric career in England.

Way ahead, not far from the Serpentine, there was a stretch of grass so remote that the park keeper hardly ever came around to collect the money for the chairs. We walked in silence. Now and then I glanced at him surreptitiously. He sensed it every time and smiled back at me. Out in the daylight his complexion and hair looked darker than ever, the upper part of the face almost sinister, with a low forehead and heavy eyebrows which nearly met above the nose, and slanting eyes, set a little too close together. The lower part, the nose, mouth and chin, were so delicately chiseled that they might have belonged to a girl.

I noticed of course that he, too, was taking an occasional glance at me, appraising, perhaps even approving, though I wasn't quite sure about that. I wasn't very sure of myself at all, didn't know how much of the odor of sensible shoes, bobby sox, and ink-stained fingers still clung to me from the happy years I'd spent—not that long ago!—hiking under a heavy rucksack along the Rhine and the Mosel rivers together with my classmates, boys and girls. Aggressively healthy, noisy and indefatigable, we climbed trees, walked twenty miles a day and slept in youth hostels or barns, closely supervised by our teachers. No hanky-panky of any sort.

The result was that I displayed a hearty jocularity toward boys or, even worse, my behavior would be that of a possible competitor on any project they might propose. I knew I had to get rid of that penetrating girl-scout smell but found for a couple of years nothing to replace it with except embarrassed silence. Gradually a sort of tentative flirtatiousness developed, awkward and immature and at first quite ineffective. My girl friends seemed to have no difficulties in changing texture, but I remained strangely retarded in some areas.

Take dancing, for example. Mortified, I watched other girls executing the most complicated steps and turns in their partner's arms. How on earth did they guess what the fellow was going to do next?

I confessed to my mother that if a boy asked me to dance I would always plead a terrible headache. So one day at lunch my father surprised me by announcing, straightfaced, that he had arranged for me to take private lessons in the foxtrot, the English waltz and the tango. A young lady of good family would be my teacher.

The young lady of good family was called Fraulein Wassermann. She was about twenty, four years older than I. She had a wind-up phonograph, a stack of records, and a huge bust. The latter was a drawback because it got in the way when she clasped me tight (for purely pedagogical purposes), especially in the tango with its convulsive movements. She would hold me elegantly by one hand as we swayed leg to leg in dips and kneebends, but a second later, when she clutched me to her with a typical tango jerk, I would bounce against those huge boobs, out of breath and out of step.

The first time I came up against a hard masculine chest instead of those bouncy boobs turned out to be an anticlimax, for the owner of the hard masculine chest wasn't nearly as proficient in the steps as I was. I therefore clutched him in an iron vise and manipulated him back and forth and up and down, the way Fraulein Wassermann had ordered.

I still remember the expression on his face as he hurriedly escorted me back to my table.

·

The young man and I found two deck chairs under an ancient beech tree, pulled them close together and stretched out. In the distance children played and their nannies on the benches watched them, chatting and knitting. Occasionally a dog came and sniffed at us but soon went off again in response to a whistle from an invisible master.

I decided to put order into the situation.

"What is your name?" I asked severely.

The young man hastily came up with his personal data. His name was Jerome. His father's name was Simon Lorrimer, his mother's Garibalda Pampanini.

I heard no more. Garibalda Pampanini! Twice I had stood in line for the third gallery at Covent Garden to hear her in *Turandot* and *Carmen*. Pampanini's son! His mother was from Sardinia, wasn't she? Yes, from Olbia. The youngest of fourteen children. "My grandfather was in jail at the time. He worshipped Garibaldi. My mother was the second daughter he named after him; the elder one was already married and he had to have someone at home who would answer whenever he yelled, 'Garibalda!'" From early childhood on she had sung the solo parts in the local church choir until, inevitably, somebody heard her and had her trained by somebody else. The rest followed just as inevitably: The great soprano Adelina Patti found herself indisposed one evening, and eighteen-year-old Garibalda made her début at the Paris Opéra as Aïda. The tenor's name was Caruso.

"And your father?"

Jerome plucked two blades of grass, pressed them flat between his thumbs and blew, producing a strident sound.

"My father? He's away at the moment."

"Where is he?"

"Somewhere. My parents have been separated for years. They may even be divorced for all I know. My mother paid for new uniforms for the Papal Guards year after year, trying to get a civil divorce recognized. You see, she's a good Catholic. On Catholic holidays we have a procession through the apartment, Mamma in front, I follow with the incense, then the cook, then the chauffeur—he doesn't like it, he is Church of England—and finally Benito, the dachshund. Every corner of every room has to be cleansed and sanctified with incense. That's how good a Catholic she is."

I dropped any semblance of polite restraint, and asked eagerly for more information on Garibalda—what she was like to live with ("Not exactly dull"), whether one could talk to her ("Sometimes—then she sounds like a wise old peasant woman"), whether she was a good mother.

"A good mother? She's a singer. I was one of her least remunerative guest appearances."

"*Was*? You're not anymore?"

"The other day she tried to auction me off. She had a suitable candidate in mind, so she looked me critically up and down and decided my body was too long for my legs and I'd have to propose sitting down. But I didn't want to get married, either sitting down or standing up. So she cut the cord."

"You must have had a hard time when you were a child."

"Only when I came home from boarding school at the beginning of the holidays. She would draw me a bath and give me a spoonful of castor oil before she would let me embrace her, 'because a son must be clean inside and outside to greet his mother.' "

I stared at him. He laughed.

"She was much more amusing than other mothers, I can assure you. Now what about you? Where are you from? What do you do?"

"I'm from Berlin."

"Refugee. I knew it. You live in Hampstead."

"How did you know?"

"All refugees live in Hampstead."

True. The first German émigrés chose the suburb of Hampstead because the solid Victorian houses with the maple trees in front reminded them of respectable German streets.

"I'm an actress."

"I know."

"How could you know?"

"By the color of your hair. Do you have a lover?"

Outraged, I stared at him without answering. What a cocky little bastard! He took my hand.

"Chapped," he said, stroking it. I snatched it away and hid it in my sleeve, yet could not stop myself in time from explaining, even apologizing.

"The water at home is hard. I always forget to buy hand lotion."

"Glycerine jelly," he said. "The best and the cheapest. Everything else is scented trash. I know—I'm a painter, the turpentine lacerates my skin. I'll bring you some tomorrow. Where do you live?"

That's how it began. With glycerine jelly for chapped hands.

The grass in Hyde Park began to flicker . . . our deck chairs floated away . . . I tried to bring Jerome back into focus . . . there he was . . . next day, at our garden gate in Hampstead, carrying a package . . . I was watching him from the window . . . the picture grew blurred and fuzzy . . . dissolved and faded out.

4

Next day the telephone woke me up.

"Where are you?" The painter's voice.

Where was I? I had to switch on the light before I knew. "At the hotel. Why?"

"It's eleven o'clock," she snarled and hung up.

Half an hour later, when I arrived at her studio, panting and without breakfast, she was sitting at the easel muttering something without looking up, absorbed in background shading. I hastily pulled on the poncho and assumed the pose, hands clasped, head turned to the left, toward the mantelpiece.

There it was, the little head, slightly more forward, in full view now. Perhaps she had been looking at it again.

She turned her eyes, those concentrated, absent, painter's eyes, on me.

"You look tense. Think about something."

"For instance?"

"It doesn't matter. But think about something definite, an experience of some kind. It will show in your face, but that doesn't bother me because I'm working on your knee. Your body will relax and you won't be conscious of holding a pose."

Think about something definite. My mother waved in the distance . . . Charlemagne galloped past without a word . . . Jerome appeared . . . and stayed. Jerome. That first beautiful year, when neither of us had a penny, when we could afford a movie only every second Saturday, upstairs in the balcony.

One memorable Saturday we were sitting up there, though not for the sake of the movie.

"You've got to meet my mother," Jerome had said several times. "Then I won't always have to be explaining things to you."

Why couldn't I go to her place and say hello? Out of the question. Garibalda didn't allow her son to bring a girl to the apartment. Why not? Garibalda never gave reasons.

Well then, how could it be arranged? "By accident," said Jerome, and that's why we happened to be at the Carlton Cinema for a movie premiere. Garibalda had promised to appear.

Jerome had the use of her Bentley for the evening. She would occasionally lend it to him, without chauffeur, of course. And without gas. Garibalda felt "the girl" should contribute that, a full tank if possible. The inside of the car smelled of tuberoses. I was wearing a new dress; Jerome for the first time was in a dark suit.

From the balcony we watched the theater fill up. "There she is," said Jerome. Quite unnecessarily, because no one could have failed to notice her entrance. White ermine from head to toe, diamond earrings, orchids in her hand—a bird of paradise followed by three penguins, immaculately attired gentlemen of suitable age. She walked slowly down the center aisle, smiling right and left, displaying two rows of very white teeth. She was recognized, there was some restrained applause, and she sat down.

Having seen her on the Covent Garden stage, I knew what was underneath the ermine: the ample body of an Italian prima donna crammed into a corset, but saved by an unexpectedly long neck which supported the dark head with the splendid blackberry eyes like the stem of an exotic jungle fruit. When the lights went out, I could still see the gleam of the white fur and the sparkle of the diamonds.

After the movie we fought our way into the foyer and watched Garibalda slowly and regally descending the wide staircase. Jerome pushed me forward, and the lady in white stopped in surprise.

"*Mio figlio,*" she explained to her penguin escort; it sounded like a Verdi recitative. Jerome nudged me another step toward her and she extended a white kid glove, which I held gingerly while making my curtsy. "Ah," she said graciously, "so this is the little girl. Charrrming." Turning to Jerome, she added something in Italian, smiling like a Christmas angel. Jerome translated it for me later. What she'd said was: "If I find one scratch on the Bentley, I'll beat the living Jesus out of you."

"*Naturalmente,* Mamma," said Jerome gratefully, kissing the white glove. Then she glided away from us.

·

"Break," said the painter and disappeared into the kitchen.

When the first swallow of hot coffee had gone down, I made a bold decision.

"Couldn't you move that head?"

"Which head? Oh yes, of course. If it bothers you."

But she didn't get up. She kept right on drinking and smoking and looking at me with a smile.

"Does it upset you?"

I didn't answer. She got up and hid the sculpture behind a book on the shelves.

"I need a quiet, relaxed model," she said, sitting down again.

"Sorry."

"If I were Cézanne, I'd send you home and say, come back tomorrow. But I'm not Cézanne."

"Maybe I wouldn't come back."

"Quite. I can't afford to take a chance, with a painting half finished. Okay, no more work today. Tell me about it."

"About what?"

"About Anabel. All I know is that she went to England and got married. What happened to her?"

I poured myself a second cup of coffee but remained unable to answer. I decided to go over to the attack.

"You tell *me* about Anabel."

She leaned back in her chair and took off her glasses, stretched like an old tomcat and replied in a surprisingly civil tone, "What would you like to know?"

"What was it like, living with Anabel?"

"Just as bad as living with a man."

"Was she your model?"

"No, but she would have liked to be. I had advertised for one and already interviewed a few. Too thin, all of them. It was soon after the war and there wasn't much to eat. Then the doorbell rang and there she stood. In a raincoat, belted too tight to show off her waist. I didn't give a damn about her waist—"

"What were you looking for?"

"The right proportions, of course, and hers were all wrong. Shoulders too wide, legs too long and too thin. But I liked her. I liked her enough to make coffee. She slithered about among my canvases like a canned sardine, a cup of coffee in her hand, smacking her lips, and said all in one breath: 'I don't enjoy coffee if I can't make a noise—I like it here.' Then she put her cup down and started to take her clothes off, unhurriedly, relaxed, exactly as if she were about to take a bath at home. She folded each piece of clothing neatly and laid it on the hassock, the one you're sitting on now—"

I jumped up. She stopped speaking and tilted her head sideways as if I'd said something she hadn't quite understood.

I sat down again. Quietly she resumed, " . . . laid it neatly on the hassock and stood up. 'Well?' she said. 'Beautiful?' 'No,' I said. 'Like a picked chicken bone. Try a fashion magazine. Maybe they can use you.' 'Are you sure you can't use me?' she asked. And stayed. That's how it began."

She stopped speaking and reached for a Gauloise. "I made a big mistake, and I should have known better. After all, I was ten years older and a hundred years wiser. But I fell for her, and when I realized it, it was too late."

She lighted the new cigarette from the old one. "I mistook her passion for warmth, had to pay a pretty stiff price— considering my resources."

"What were your resources?"

"A skin as thick as a rhinoceros's. You needed that in Paris in those days if you came from the provinces. I didn't know a soul when I arrived but I knew I had talent. And I knew that men weren't attracted to me. Probably because I wasn't attracted to them. Sometimes I got fond of a woman, but most of the time I lived alone. Anabel was an exception. She got under my skin, perhaps because she was both lover and child to me. She couldn't have been more than eighteen. I educated her, taught her, she knew absolutely nothing and was proud of it. But she gradually caught on to a thing or two."

So this woman with her glasses and her paint-stained smock, sitting there in a cloud of smoke, had lived with

Anabel when I was still at school! Anabel at eighteen, too fragile even then, callow, and shameless. And the other one, the painter, what was she like at that time? She had been much closer to Anabel than I had ever been. Had she been able to get rid of her without getting hurt?

"How did you break with her?"

"Drastically," she said grimly. "I couldn't afford her any longer. Not on account of the money, though that part of it was pretty rough, but because I couldn't paint anymore. I used to stand at the window looking down at the Avenue Kléber instead of sitting at my easel. I'd watch for a taxi stopping in front of the house. Sometimes I'd listen half the night. One evening I caught myself staring down into the dark and wringing my hands like Lillian Gish in a silent film. That's when I realized I had to do something. So I packed her things into three suitcases, tossed them in any old way and threw a few paint rags in between her evening clothes for good measure. You can never completely get rid of that smell. I even topped it off with a few drops of turpentine. Finally I took my big scissors—that pair over there—cut her fur coat into little pieces and arranged them neatly on top. I closed the suitcases and placed them on the landing outside the front door and went to bed. Without a sleeping pill. At some point the door bell rang. I woke up—and remembered. I was afraid I'd back down, so I said to myself in a loud voice, 'Are you a doormat or a painter?' She shouted at me through the door, 'What did you say? Open the door.' I got up and opened it. 'What does this mean?' she asked, pointing to the suitcases. 'It means that I'm a painter,' I said, slapping her face as hard as I could. Then I closed the door."

I sat quite still. This woman had slapped Anabel in the face as hard as she could. She read my eyes and said calmly, "I never regretted it. It had to end like that. It was the only way of breaking with her."

"Was that the end?"

"Just about." She laughed, as if she enjoyed the memory, shook her head (over herself or over Anabel?) and reached for another Gauloise, exhaling the first puff of smoke together with her next words. "A few months later I was sitting in a chair at a vernissage when someone put her hands over my eyes from behind and said, 'Guess who.' I tried to free myself because I'd recognized the voice, of course, but she hung on tooth and nail. 'Smell this,' she said, pressing her hands hard against my nose until I thought I'd suffocate. 'Turpentine!' Then she let go and pushed her way quickly through the crowd and out the door."

"And the bronze head? You said Anabel never . . ."

"She didn't. I modeled the head much later, I don't know why. I'd forgotten all about it until you dug it out yesterday. I'd forgotten Anabel too. I don't even know whether she's still alive."

5

The minute I stepped out of the door I was swallowed up in thick, blackish-green fog. The famous London pea-soup fog. It would suddenly appear out of the blue and envelop the whole city in less than an hour. There would be no more buses or cars; only the streetcars would keep running, slowly, as in a dream. No traffic lights, instead policemen in white coats waving torches or flashlights at major intersections. Even if you knew your way inside out, you got lost. I stopped several pedestrians who loomed up suddenly like ghosts to ask where I was, but they didn't know either. At last I made out a great *U* flickering in the distance, an entrance to the Underground. I groped my way down a few steps and saw a faint beam of light shining hesitantly at first, then more convincingly, and suddenly, instead of drifting helplessly around in the black of night, I had found my bearings and was safely back in civilization.

My hotel was within sight of an Underground station. I swam through the pea soup the few hundred yards to the entrance and let the revolving door swing me back into the security of its warmth and bright lights.

As I entered my room, the telephone rang. "Are you there?" growled the painter's voice. "Good. That's all I wanted to know." And she hung up.

On days like this, everyone in London either stayed home or stayed put until the fog lifted. Not a soul would expect me or come to see me today. Dead silence outside. Now and then a foghorn on the Thames.

I had intended to visit my mother in Hampstead and return to the hotel late, tired out, too tired to open the diary.

There it was, lying in wait for me, not letting me out of its sight, spying on me. "I don't want to know," I had said at the time. "I don't want to hear her confession." But perhaps it wasn't a confession.

•

Diary. October 1935. Return to London.

Naiveté. It would disarm me if I didn't have such a bad
character. After I'd switched the light out in the sleeping car
B. confessed that he was terribly disappointed about something
but hadn't been able to tell me until now, in the dark, on our
way home. Paul Mildman had raised his hopes that "everything
would be all right again" once we got away from that old
double bed at home. "Get into another landscape," he had
advised, preferably on board ship. M. may be a good friend,
even a good doctor, but he's an idiot. Did he think the rocking
of the waves would throw us on top of each other?

Poor Bill Maclean. Run aground. Still thinking he could win Anabel back by his hungry serfdom. It never dawned on him that he had married Diana the huntress and had long ago become her prey, not even her trophy.

Was he present when we met her for the first time? A vernissage at the Lafarge Gallery. Was that really the first time? Strange that I wasn't quite sure, that the day wasn't etched on my memory. Did the owner of the gallery introduce us? Probably. I remember a man with a mustache, standing beside us. The painter. Anabel had bought a painting, the most expensive one in the whole show. He kissed her hand. The gallery owner was sticking the little red "Sold" dot on the frame. I also remember Jerome's expression while he watched. No one had so far offered him a show, not even one of the crummy little galleries in Chelsea.

There she stood. In a red coat. Alone, so Bill couldn't have been there. She turned away from the painting she'd just bought without even glancing at it. She was looking at us, at Jerome and me. I think she even exchanged a few words with us. Later, as we walked down the narrow staircase, she was behind us and tripped, and Jerome caught her and said something that made her laugh. Then we all went into the Berkeley Bar next door. She must have invited us, for we didn't have the money for such things.

Now at last the whole picture emerged, persons and background stood out, like a photograph under the developing solution, growing more distinct by the minute. Anabel was sitting on a stool at the far end of the bar, wearing something sheer and sleeveless, her coat draped around her shoulders like a red frame. Everything about her was elongated and delicate as eggshell, even the head and straight black hair hanging down over her forehead, hiding part of her face. Thick straight eyelashes strung over her dark eyes like an awning, the nose a bit too long and narrow. She looked like a beautiful sad raven.

That must have been sometime in the summer or fall of 1936, because I could see my white dress with the black dots that I'd bought out of the proceeds of my late lamented play.

Impatiently, I turned the pages. I wanted to know what she

had written about me. It must be there somewhere, she couldn't have left that out. I riffled quickly through the winter of 1935–36 . . . the spring . . . the summer . . . wait now, slowly now! July . . . nothing . . . August . . . there it was:

> Vernissage at Lafarge. Bought a painting. It'll go into the attic, but the painter looked hungry. That's why I was invited, after all. Met two young people. Refugees. She, at any rate, he perhaps not.

Was that all? Then why did she invite us to dinner? There must have been something about us that she liked.

•

First evening at the Macleans' home. What food! Served by a butler, followed by a maid in a white cap with the sauces, three different kinds. I didn't know which one to take and got no hint from her expressionless eyes.

Afterward we sat in the drawing room. Eighteenth-century walnut tables, deep armchairs, large modern paintings, flowers everywhere in gigantic pots. And now at last there was Bill, the way I would often see him from then on, shadow-boxing in the farthest corner of the room with his back to me, feinting and ducking and hitting the air to the low murmuring of a radio next to him broadcasting a match. Anabel paid no attention.

The first of countless meals at the Macleans', of countless hours spent in that room. I plunged in headlong, hadn't been aware of how much I needed it. I quickly got used to the weird paintings, stopped praising the flower arrangements and poured out my anxieties, my presumptions, my self-deceptions, my stratagems, my disguises as well as my comforts and my exaltations to Anabel, who sat facing me in a yellow wing chair, her thin fingers spread out on the arm, always on the alert, always passionately involved. Afterward, when I climbed into my little car to drive home, I always felt restored and safe and armed to the teeth. I had a girl friend again.

In my childhood "the girl friends" played an important role. There were quite a lot of them, five at least, including one "best friend," and over the years I was absolutely loyal to them. They were of special importance to me because even as a child I was obsessed by an urgent need to confide and share. I simply had to communicate everything I thought and felt to somebody, preferably to several people at once. Nothing seemed to me worth doing if I couldn't tell someone about it. Unlike Oscar Wilde, according to whom even the dullest thing becomes exciting if one makes a secret of it. Not to me.

It was different when other people confided in me. Then I could keep a secret. After all, it wasn't *my* secret, so it wasn't important and was soon forgotten.

When emigration separated me from my friends, some of them left behind in Germany, others scattered to the four corners of the earth, I was forced to keep to myself, something the English appreciate anyway. My need to communicate dried up. Now at last it could blossom again.

Anabel's diary began to mention me right after that first dinner at her house, first in monosyllables, then, all of a sudden, possessively.

L. for lunch.

And a week later:

L. for supper.

Then, soon after that:

L. all afternoon, until Nina came home. She refuses to go to her room when L.'s here. Won't leave her alone. Hangs around, always wants to "listen," sticks like glue. Spoils everything for me.

So it had become important to her. *I* had become important to her.

The only thing that rubbed me the wrong way was her manner of bringing Nina up. But I kept my mouth shut, I didn't feel sure enough of myself to raise objections. At the Macleans' things were not the way they were at home, and "at home" was my only guideline. We had been kept on a short, tight rein held by such careful, loving hands that they maintained their grip even when the walls came crashing down. At the Macleans' they used reins of a different kind. Some of them were slack and worn out, and the one they kept Nina on seemed to be hopelessly twisted, probably right from the start, because, according to Anabel, Nina had come into the world "by mistake." She was short-necked, plump and—perhaps because of that—resentful.

"She has pimples on her face," said Anabel. "Why does she have pimples? I never did."

Nina was being brought up in the "modern" fashion. By the time she was ten, Anabel was reading Shakespeare aloud to her. She said the child preferred it to *Babar* and *Peter Rabbit*. Nina was not supposed to be afraid of anything, so from time to time her parents would go out at night on their couple's day off, leaving Nina alone in the house. Sometimes, when I got home from the theater, my telephone would ring and a piping, childish voice would say, "I can't sleep—I'm scared—don't tell Mother." Then I would remind her of Georgie, the German shepherd, keeping guard in the hall, ". . . and if you can't sleep, recite very slowly 'The quality of mercy is not strained . . .' And if you're still awake, try 'O, what a rogue and peasant slave am I . . .' And if that doesn't work either—call me back."

She never called back.

Who knows, it may have been good for Nina to confront life unafraid and well versed in Shakespeare. Although Anabel had been educated in France, she was a walking Shakespeare lexicon. And lion-hearted. One night there was a fire next door. While the house's owners stood in the street wringing their hands and counting the treasures they had thrown out of the windows, Anabel tied a wet cloth around her mouth, forced her way through the back door and into the smoke-filled kitchen and rescued the cat.

It was Nina who told me that, not Anabel.

•

Throughout the first year of our friendship I was appearing either in bad plays on the legitimate stage or in bad films in the movie studios. I remained, however, obstinate and blind, confidently expecting the big breakthrough, telling myself at the mere sight of a new script: this is it! In all my hopes, forebodings and inevitable catastrophes, Anabel was with me every step of the way:

> L. for tea after her matinee. Told me all about the bloody mess. They are all on half-salary since yesterday! If the producer were not such a crook, I'd pump some money into the thing to see if it doesn't catch on. Behind her back, of course.

She hardly ever spoke about herself. All I knew was that she had been born in Paris, that her mother had died early on, that she hated her father and stepmother and had used her first passport to get out of France. But why had she married Bill? Bill, of all people? Because he reminded her of her father, she said once. Of the father she hated! (But who had left his considerable fortune to her, not to her step-mother.) Like Bill, he had been a stockbroker, an occupation she detested. Then why? "To get my own back." (On whom? On her father? On Bill?) "I'm a vindictive person. Didn't you know that?"

No, I didn't know that, and it wasn't true. She said it because she liked to see me baffled, chewing my fingernails. Then she would laugh and say I shouldn't believe everything she said. But what was I to believe? Gradually I gave up asking questions and hardly noticed that I was the one who did all the talking, while she listened. And what a listener she was! I could even tell her everything about Jerome, all the things I didn't tell my mother. Though my mother too, and no less intensely, shared all my daily triumphs and de-feats, everything except my "private life." There she was strangely embarrassed. So was I. I told her only what was strictly necessary.

Diary:

L. has a mother. A mother who is important to her. Odd! The whole relationship is odd. At home L. is the head of the family—and at the same time "the child." The mother speaks bad English, smiling disarmingly. Still has all her own teeth.

Her own teeth! Of course. That was something unusual in England. "No one should have teeth. Teeth are unhealthy," people used to say, and even young girls and boys would grin cheerfully at you with chalk-white china choppers.

The mother rents rooms to other refugees. This is a help to L. All the same, L. ought to get away. She shouldn't keep on being Mummy's goldilocks forever. But she can't bring herself to do it. At present she's living half with J. in a tatty little apartment, and half at her mother's, eating her dinner with meat and vegetables and pudding like a good girl. And next morning, at the studio, she's supposed to ooze sex appeal. Makeup alone won't do it.

On the nose!

The mother was an actress before she married. You'd never guess. Or maybe you would. Sometimes, when she gives you a searching glance, she looks anything but bourgeois. I don't think she likes me. Doesn't trust me. Maybe she's jealous.

Way off the mark! My mother wasn't jealous. She was watchful.

Yesterday I called for L. at her house. J. was there too. He loves that mother. He'd move right in if she'd let him.

But she wouldn't let him. After my father's death she had accepted the fact that her three daughters had boy friends, something unknown in her day. She invited the young men to the house, offered them tea and was glad to bid them goodbye again. If asked, she'd give her opinion. She found Jerome "interesting" but still not the right man for me. She wanted her three future sons-in-law to be like my father. She wanted three replicas of the man who had made her a happy woman for twenty-four years until the day he died.

•

Jerome accompanied me only rarely when I went to the Macleans'. Now and then he would come to supper. With the help of a glass of wine and a good cigar he could even get along with Bill. He wasn't particularly interested in Anabel; he said she was too thin, she ought to wear a brooch to show which was the front.

The diary rarely mentions him.

L. and J. for supper. L. follows him with her eyes wherever he goes.

Did I?

J. is a mixture of decadent gypsy and randy intellectual.

And:

If J. ever pats me on the head as if I were a dog again, I'm going to tell him I know he's a shit.

When was that? When was Jerome a shit? In November 1936, pretty early on. No, they didn't like each other, argued a lot. Anabel would get nasty when she thought he wasn't sufficiently attentive or affectionate with me. I was both the link and the buffer, so I was sometimes quite glad not to have Jerome around. "You're spoiled," I used to tell Anabel. "Bill spoils you because you don't love him. That's the difference."

When I talked to Jerome about her, I didn't get very far. "Stop singing her praises. And stop being so eternally grateful. We don't owe her anything. We give her as much as she gives us."

"What do we give her?"

"Color. That's worth more than good food."

I saw it differently. Anabel gave *us* color, exquisite, expensive color, something I was very keen on. When I wasn't working, we used to go to concerts with her, sit in her box at the opera, go driving in her Rolls Royce on Sundays. Once we went to *Così fan tutte* at Glyndebourne. That time Bill came along too, sitting in front next to the chauffeur, fumbling with the car radio in order to catch a boxing match somewhere. After that we gave up music and concentrated on old towns, castles and churches, leaving Bill to his Sunday golf. Until then all I had seen of England was the film studios and the stage doors; now I began to get to know it for the first time. Jerome would sit next to me, hand on my knee, the Rolls would glide soundlessly along, through Tudor villages with thatched roofs and duck ponds. Those were the best Sundays; I was sitting between the man I loved and the friend I loved.

Anabel's diary reads like a Baedeker:

Chester. Bought Sheraton table for the guest room. Restored, of course. L. doesn't have a clue about such things. Showed her where it had been repaired. She's learning. Found a bracelet for her, old paste, very beautifully set. She didn't really appreciate it, but she acted pleased so as not to hurt my feelings.

Or:

Winchester. L. sat in the cathedral for hours in rapt silence. I froze. How she can enjoy herself!

That I could. Right from the start. If I concentrate, I can even now capture a tiny whiff of the physical joy I experienced when, at the age of about twelve, I'd bring my bicycle up from the cellar on a warm summer morning and climb on the saddle, my head high, my eyes half closed, my feet so full of pent-up energy that they barely needed to touch the pedals—and I'm off, on my way to school again, past the Reichskanzlerplatz, down the gentle slope of the Heerstrasse, where you could take your hands off the handlebars and raise both arms sideways, not just to show off but to expose as much of your body as possible to the rush of warm air—and so I would streak along in the sunshine, perfectly and deliriously happy.

Years later, when I tried to imagine what it must be like to lie in a man's arms, I would always think of those summer-morning bicycle rides as the very essence of bliss and of ultimate rapture.

6

When I rang the studio doorbell at twelve o'clock, she made me wait a long time before she opened the door. In spite of the warm weather, she was wrapped up in something thick and shapeless ending in trousers tucked in galoshes.

"Got a cold," she croaked. "Can't work today. You can go home."

I hung my coat on the hook.

"Shall I make you some hot tea with lemon?"

"I hate tea," she muttered, waddling into the studio ahead of me. "I'll make coffee."

Strange silence in the studio. For the first time there was no music. The painter appeared with the tray, panting and wheezing behind the thermos and the cups. We drank without talking.

"Isn't there anybody in your life . . ." I ventured, surprised at my courage.

"What do you mean?"

"Somebody to look after you?"

"Can't stand being looked after. I can doctor myself. I

41

studied medicine for a few terms." She coughed and clutched her throat.

"You shouldn't talk," I said.

"All right. *You* talk."

She looked at me expectantly, having set the trap. My turn now.

"What would you like to hear?"

"About Anabel. What else?"

"There's not much to tell. We were friends, just . . . friends."

She grinned.

"You don't have to spell it out."

"Well, we were friends."

"I know that already. Anything else?"

She coughed violently, almost choked. I poured her some more hot coffee. When the spasm had passed, she opened her mouth like a bird, perhaps because she couldn't breathe or because she wanted to be fed.

"It just occurred to me that I first met Anabel in the same setting in which you saw her for the last time, at a vernissage. Strange, isn't it?"

She showed no surprise, muttered, "What were you doing there? Buying?"

"No. We had no money."

"Who's *we*?"

"My boy friend and I. He was a painter."

"Here in London? What was his name?"

"Jerome Lorrimer."

"Lorrimer? Graphics?"

"No, a painter."

"He does graphics now," she whispered. "Quite good ones. Didn't you know?"

I shook my head. She gave me a serious, almost shocked look.

"Did Anabel break it up?"

"No."

Under her gaze, I stared out of the window.

"When she was living with me," she whispered hoarsely, "she was still practically a child. Innocent, with a sort of animal meanness, the way children are."

"Anabel wasn't mean."

"You said that before. Maybe she grew tamer over the years, that's all. It wasn't a question of being immoral, she *had* no morals. Helped herself and never paid up. She was a tramp. And a predator."

I stared stubbornly at her.

"I know a different side of her."

"Which side?"

"She was my friend."

"Not anymore?"

"No."

"Why not?"

"Circumstances. I live in America."

She looked cross and coughed hoarsely.

"You were going to tell me something, but it's like getting blood out of a stone. Go on home. I'll call you when we can work again."

I left.

7

A diary entry in September 1936 says:

J.'s father is back.

That's all.

Yes, he was back, but he remained invisible. And my acquaintance with Garibalda hadn't grown any closer since the Carlton Cinema. I had seen her once more, but only from a distance: at Covent Garden as Tosca. She had given Jerome two tickets, a rare treat, and we sat in the stage box.

Garibalda was slightly past her prime. She carried herself more majestically than ever, but it was obvious that she was making a great effort. Jerome, in the chair next to me, lived with her through every sound she made. Before a high note he ducked, as if somebody were about to hit him. During the third act, when she reached the dreaded *"Vissi d'arte . . . ,"* he closed his eyes, slid deeper and deeper into his seat and whimpered soundlessly until she landed—not altogether victoriously—on the high C. After which she relaxed, resting lovingly though a little too long on the following lower notes. Jerome relaxed too. He sat up straight and dabbed at his face with his handkerchief. Gently, because he'd had a hard day. On days when she was going to sing at night, Garibalda used to throw things. That day she'd thrown a jar of her special face cream at him, which may have contributed to her beauty but not to his, for it left him with a large blue bump on his forehead.

And now his father was back.

"Can you remember the time when your parents were still living together?"

"Vaguely. The only thing I remember clearly is one day hearing a loud bang. A very loud bang. In fact, that may be my earliest memory." He frowned, knitting his thick eyebrows into an unbroken black stripe. "It was early in the morning, the sun was shining and I was wearing a sailor suit—for the first time, I think. That's why I was so excited. I was hopping about the apartment on one leg, and finally I hopped into the living room, where my father was sitting. Probably working on his mathematical problems even then. Anyway I refused to stop hopping, although he firmly told me to. I remember him trying to grab my collar, which I thought was a lot of fun, and I crept under the piano and crowed like a cockerel. Whereupon he fired his pistol at me. He was in uniform, so he had it handy. That was the bang I remember. The bullet lodged in La Pampanini's piano, which was unfortunate."

"For your father?"

"No, for the piano."

•

He rarely spoke about his father. All I knew was that he was a physicist and lived in Chelsea. Jerome lived there too, part of the time. Or he slept at Garibalda's. A Bohemian existence. I put an end to it when I found the two rooms in Hampstead, but his most precious possession, his easel, remained at his father's place. This made me jealous. But there was "more atmosphere" at his father's.

"Perhaps it would be a good idea for you to meet him," said Jerome hesitantly.

"Aren't you allowed to take me to his place either?"

"On the contrary, I'll have to."

It was a Sunday and Jerome was still in bed, although it was already twelve o'clock. Sometimes he didn't even get dressed on Sunday. I disapproved. (My father would have, too.) Either one was up and dressed or one was sick.

I tidied up the room, hung his things in the closet. He sat up, caught hold of me and pulled me down beside him on the bed. Stroking my arm, he looked at me dubiously.

"I'll have to," he repeated.

"Have to what?"

"Take you to his apartment. It's really only one big room. He's there now and he won't go out again until next May."

"Why not?"

"Because during the months with an *r* in them he stays home. He's done it for years. He hasn't even got a winter coat."

"Why not?"

He let go of my arm and took my hand instead. He stroked it—it wasn't chapped anymore—remembered, laughed and kissed it, then turned it over and began to study my palm.

"Hardly any lines at all. Barely the major ones," he said, wrinkling his forehead. "Like a chimpanzee. How can I explain my father to a chimpanzee?"

He sighed and shook his head. "You see, everybody—you and me included—is always worrying about what we are. My father decided to concentrate on what he's *not*. And there he found his vocation. Do you understand what I mean?"

"No."

He smiled patiently.

"Think of shellfish, oysters for instance. You don't eat oysters in months without an *r* in them, do you?"

"Does your father think he's an oyster? Is he afraid of being caught and eaten?"

"It's not quite as bad as that. He knows he's not an oyster, but he loves them and the *r* business suits him nicely. He is available between September 1 and April 30. Then a four-month closed season. He's not completely normal, of course, but what does 'normal' mean anyway? The people Simon works for at Kodak—"

"You call your father Simon?"

"That's his name. The Kodak people consider him completely normal. They gave him a job here in England years ago. He developed two camera lenses for them, which bring in a lot of money. Not that they ever offered to raise his salary. Neither did he ask them to. He's always broke, but as long as he has his eyric and as long as no one makes any demands on him, he's quite happy."

"And he just sits there in one room for months? Like in prison?"

"Prison wouldn't worry him as long as he could have his books. You'll see, the walls are lined with books on math and physics. Nothing else interests him. No, that's not quite true, food interests him—and sex."

"You talk about him as if he weren't your father."

"He's not. Or only by accident. You'll know from the physical resemblance that he sired me, but that's the extent of his fatherhood. He only lived with Garibalda for a few years."

"How did they ever get together?"

"By mistake, I suppose. She was quite famous already and he was a lieutenant. In those days he was very good-looking. Now he's like a barrel. Some time ago I was rummaging in old suitcases in the attic and I found his uniform. I couldn't button the tunic! She must have been in love with him, because apart from the uniform he had nothing to offer. He belonged to a distinguished regiment, though. If it hadn't been for that business with the horse . . ."

"What horse?"

"His horse. He could never remember which was his horse, and that won't do in a cavalry regiment, where horse and rider are supposed to be indivisible. Simon's problem was that he couldn't distinguish one horse from another. Finally he tied a red ribbon to the tail of his horse. That worked for a time. But then came the day of the parade, general on the grandstand, military band, dress uniforms, medals, rows and rows of black horses' noses, and black horses' tails—and one red ribbon rippling in the breeze. The general was not amused. End of a military career."

"And of Garibalda too?"

"I wonder." He leaned back, clasped his hands behind his head and considered the question as if it had never occurred to him before.

"It's still not entirely at an end between those two. I think they just happened to wake up in separate places one day. From the very start he had affairs with her girl friends, because it was more restful that way, he didn't have to go hunting around. But absentmindedly—he has been absentminded all his life—he would call Garibalda by one of her girl friends' names, and she didn't like that one bit. Once he even escorted the wrong woman home after a party. That did it, I believe. Maybe they would have stayed together longer if he'd tied a red ribbon in Garibalda's hair."

A few days later, on a Sunday evening, we took the bus to Chelsea, the part of London that's been the favorite haunt of artists, scholars and madmen for centuries. I was given some last-minute instructions.

"We musn't stay long. When the boy brings his dinner, we must leave at once. He has room service like in a hotel. His—his current female sends it up. He keeps some kind of emotional life going, and he's very choosy. He confines himself exclusively to restaurant owners. During the months without an *r*, he systematically works his way through all the restaurants in the neighborhood, and he has an eagle eye for sex-starved restaurant owners. There are hundreds of eating places in Chelsea, so he's never at a loss and gets first-class meals sent up to his room. He must have some very special aces up his sleeve, for he always gets away with two conditions: First, an affair is strictly limited to one season, for by the end he is sick of the menu; second, she is not allowed to bring the food up herself. He eats alone. He only enjoys his meals if he can concentrate on every bite, without having to talk. I'm not allowed to be there either. Except occasionally when he happens to be "between restaurant owners" and no one is feeding him. Then he lets me stay and share his dry bread."

We were hanging on to the straps in a crowded bus and I gave him a quick kiss, without anyone noticing.

"Literally dry bread?"

"He's quite fond of dry bread. It's indispensable to fill his stomach, otherwise the red wine doesn't taste good."

The bus stopped. We jumped off.

"That's where he lives, up there on the fifth floor. Let's take it slowly."

There was no elevator in the house, one of the many tall eighteenth-century buildings that line the banks of the Thames. Slowly we climbed the narrow, dark stairs, switching the electric light on again at every landing. When we reached the fourth floor, Jerome said, "Let's sit down. There's something else I must tell you."

We sat down on the stairs, panting.

"I would like it if you two—" He broke off. "Well, anyway—don't be surprised at the entrance ritual. Simon has a pet fly which he loves and which he doesn't want to escape." A look at my face, and he continued hastily, "He's always loved flies, and you'd be surprised how long they last with him. He gives them names, usually after popes. He's had whole dynasties of them. The present one's called Leo. Leo VII. You'll see little bowls of sugar water all over the place. And when the fly settles on his bald head and buzzes, he's happy."

"Jerome—he's nuts!"

"Why is it all right to like a goldfish but not a fly? Just wait. You've never seen such a fine black specimen."

"Is it some special kind?"

"No, just a regular fly. But his are always extra-fat and black."

We climbed the last flight and Jerome knocked: one knock, then three rapid ones. From inside a deep voice called, "Okay," at which Jerome sat down again on the top step, pulling me with him.

"He said 'Okay,' " I whispered.

"That means he's looking for it, on the lamp, on the table, under the table, on the bookshelves . . . "

"But it takes hours to find a fly."

"No, it doesn't. He has his own methods, he knows where they hang out. For the books he uses a feather duster."

A gruff voice from inside the room growled, "Now!"

The door opened a crack. Jerome sprang to his feet, jumped across the threshold, pulling me after him, and slammed the door behind us.

At first I saw nothing but a broad back making for the desk and paying no attention to us.

"Come, take your coat off," said Jerome casually. "Give it to me. The chap over there behind the desk is Simon. Simon, this is the girl I've been telling you about."

"Evening," said the fat man, putting on his glasses. "Watch out, son, he's on your sleeve."

"Is it the same one as last week?"

"You have no eye for detail. Strange in a painter, I must say. Leo VII died on Monday night. I found him on the windowsill, all rolled up and shriveled. This is Leo VIII. Much smaller. Bluish wings. Can't you tell?"

"Let me take a closer look," said Jerome, picking up a ruler from the table.

"Don't you dare!" exclaimed the fat man. "You wouldn't get him in any case—he's far too intelligent for you. In a single morning I taught him where all his sugar-water bowls are, and he buzzes like a lawnmower."

"Well, kindly teach him to buzz strictly in your domain," said Jerome, taking me over to the other side of the room. There stood the easel, in front of a big slanted window offering a view of treetops and, below them, the Thames. It certainly had more atmosphere than our flat in Hampstead, whose window looked out at the back of a warehouse.

"This is my studio. Up to that white chalk mark. When Simon is here I remain strictly within my borders while I'm working and pay him ten bob a week."

Each side had an armchair, a big table and a couch. Simon's walls were hidden by bookshelves, Jerome's were covered with canvases and drawings. The white chalkline on the floor ran diagonally through the middle of the room.

"Won't you sit down?" said the fat man, beckoning.

I moved over to his side. Jerome sat down on the floor

beside me. Above us hung a birdcage with the door wide open. Inside cowered a moth-eaten old canary.

"Does the bird fly around in the room too?" I asked.

"Several times a day," said Jerome, "as you can see from the white splotches on my canvases. Sometimes I just leave them. That damned bird has a good feeling for composition."

"And what happens when it sees the fly?"

"Nothing happens," growled the old man. "They're scared of each other."

I took my first close look at him. He was fat but not flabby, the face was round, the features sharp as if carved with a chisel. Wide, dark eyes, without bags or wrinkles, the eyes of a young man. Two fleshy cheeks pressed from each side against a small, delicately carved nose and a pointed mouth. All of it framed by an ample double chin at least two inches in depth, like a separate, folded white collar.

"I'm sorry I can't offer you a drink," he said. "I haven't stocked up yet. I only just got back. But perhaps Jerome . . ."

Jerome laughed, got up and strolled over to his side. In one corner stood a small refrigerator and a stove. He opened the refrigerator with a key he took out of his pocket and removed half a bottle of white wine and the remains of a loaf of bread. Two glasses appeared from somewhere and a third from the bathroom. Simon began to look very cheerful and promptly reached for the bread, then for the bottle.

"Cheers, little lady," he said, emptying his glass. "So you're an actress. What are you appearing in right now? Do I have to come and see it?"

"No," I said hastily. "It's not a good play."

"Are you well paid?"

"No, she isn't," said Jerome darkly, knitting his eyebrows. "There's no point in getting your hopes up."

"Pity. I wouldn't mind being kept by a young actress. I'd

even be prepared to do something for her in return. Oh well. Cheers! Better luck next time. Speaking of money, I hear your mother's getting married again."

"First I've heard of it," said Jerome, "but it's possible. She narrowed it down to two candidates some time ago."

"Which one's got more money?"

"The one she'll be bringing to see you." Jerome turned to me and added, "She always drags her candidates up here to be looked over by Simon first. That's her Italian family sense."

"Up to now I've always talked her out of it. After all, she's still doing all right on her own. But perhaps the time has come. How old is she exactly?"

"How should I know? Can't you remember?"

Simon shook his head.

"Even in the old days you couldn't believe a word she said."

He extended his head gently toward the lamp and Leo VIII actually emerged from his dark hiding place and settled on the bald surface, buzzing contentedly. Simon closed his eyes.

"Is he rubbing his forelegs together?" he asked, as if in a trance.

"Yes," I exclaimed. "He's rubbing them. Look, Jerome."

But Jerome, who was standing by the window, was unimpressed and went to get my coat.

"They all rub their legs together. Rub and buzz, that's all they do. We must be off. Here comes the boy, Simon, with a huge tray."

"Time to go, children, time to go. Now's the moment. When he's grooming he doesn't like to interrupt himself to take off. Still—be careful!"

The last thing I glimpsed from the doorway was a motionless shape at the desk, a bulky colossus, its eyes closed like the Golem, on the softly gleaming bald head a black speck, gorged and glossy.

•

Hard to imagine that this man, with his papal flies, and Dame Garibalda had ever dropped anchor next to each other long enough to bring my Jerome into the world!

I glanced stealthily at Garibalda, lying in a deck chair under a big umbrella. We were in Eastbourne, an expensive old-fashioned seaside resort on the English Channel. In a second deck chair next to her, a young man with a bronze tan lay asleep: Federigo, a pilot in an Italian air force unit. I was glad he was asleep. When he was awake, his black eyes glowed too fiercely and the tips of his mustache twitched with desire.

Garibalda was a health fetishist. Cold seawater, uncooked fruit and vegetables and morning exercises were indispensable for good skin, teeth and vocal cords. She went to Eastbourne twice a year and swam in the sea every day. Usually she was accompanied by a Scottish laird of ancient family who had worshipped her all his life. When he couldn't be at her side—he had a bony, stern wife at his ancestral seat—she received a letter from him every day. This daily letter was important to her; it was her rod and staff, even— or especially—when she was being unfaithful to her Scotsman, which happened occasionally.

Early October 1936 was one of those occasions. Her saltwater cure was due, but the laird, to his chagrin, could not get away. On the spur of the moment Garibalda yielded to the passionate entreaties of a young Italian, who until then had been spending his leave in vain on his knees in her dressing room at Covent Garden. He had a lot to offer. He was young and handsome and he was there. Unfortunately he was pathologically jealous and apt to be savage. Garibalda was reduced to tipping a bellboy in order to smuggle her daily letter from the post office into her bedroom.

She had ordered Jerome to Eastbourne for a week, possibly to protect her from physical assault by her passionate troubadour. Jerome, however, declared that he didn't want to be away from me for so long, and so she lowered her Sardinian eyelids in resignation and announced that I was included in the order. But we were not to stay at the Grand Hotel with her and her flying ace but would have to make do with a modest boardinghouse outside Eastbourne. It didn't matter to me. I was used to modest boardinghouses, and the thought of finally getting to know Garibalda, perhaps even making friends with her, was exciting.

The first two days offered little opportunity to remind her of my presence. She ignored me in the friendliest possible way. Early in the morning Jerome and I would already be out on the beach, lying in the two deck chairs she had rented for herself and Federigo. We would jump up respectfully when she approached, wearing an enormous straw hat and a chiffon beach wrap over a bathing suit with pleated shirt.

The bronzed pilot in his white trunks was displayed to full advantage at her side. They would smile graciously in our direction and stretch out in the chairs. "The children" sat beside them on the cold sand.

We were glum. The modest boardinghouse was modest indeed. For the first time in my life I discovered that a mattress can be important. Mine felt as if it were stuffed with potatoes. The food was inedible and the sea was icy. Instead of swimming, Jerome and I jumped and splashed around and turned blue after five minutes. Garibalda and her escort, however, seemed to find a warm Gulf Stream current and swam with graceful, leisurely strokes.

After the second "modest" dinner we decided to leave the next day, whatever happened. We packed our things and spent a better night on the potatoes for knowing that it was the last one. The next morning we marched to the beach to await the right moment for telling Garibalda we were off.

She was already lying in her deck chair, wrapped in chiffon scarfs. Federigo said the air was cool and he was going swimming right away.

"I'll be right with you," said Garibalda amiably, following him with her eyes as he trudged down to the water.

As soon as he had disappeared into the surf, she extracted a letter from her handbag and immersed herself.

We exchanged glances. Was this the right moment? Yes, Jerome signaled, as soon as she stopped reading.

It was a long letter, four closely written pages. She took her time, oblivious of our presence, occasionally chuckling to herself with her eyes closed, like a young girl.

Suddenly a shadow fell on the page. The troubadour was standing before her, dripping and threatening.

"Who's that letter from?"

Garibalda batted her eyelashes.

"This letter?" She stared at the pages as if she couldn't imagine how they had gotten into her fingers. Federigo's hand shot out to grab it, but she was even faster and tossed it boldly into my lap. "This letter is from her dear mother," she said, smiling gently into his blazing black eyes, and turning to me she added tenderly, "Thank you, my child, for letting me read it."

I automatically picked up the letter and clutched it in a daze. The blackberry eyes were still fixed on mine, but the smile was no longer tender, it was imperious. I hastily stuffed the letter into our beach bag.

Federigo, forsaking his role of troubadour in favor of Othello, looked suspiciously from one to the other, the damp tips of his mustache twitching ominously. He took a step toward me, but didn't quite dare to grab my beach bag, so he remained standing in front of us, glowering and covered in goose pimples from the cold.

"I'm ready to go swimming with you now, dearest. Come along," announced Garibalda, peeling off the chiffon and pulling the reluctant Federigo toward the water.

"Well," said Jerome, "let's see what your dear mother has to say," and retrieved the letter from the depths of the beach bag.

Dear mother had an ardent love letter from Scotland. Jerome grew happier with every page. Finally he folded it up small and stuck it under the sole of his right sandal.

"We're going to make a little deal with Garibalda. She'll get the letter back only if she lets us move into the Grand Hotel. Otherwise your dear mother's letter will be handed over to Federigo. Go back to the boardinghouse and wait for me. You're not up to the kind of storm that's about to break."

I left in a hurry.

Half an hour later Jerome appeared in our room, disheveled but cheerful. He reported that Garibalda had cut short her health-giving dip, leaving her Othello to brave the waves alone. She had returned to the deck chairs, out of breath and hand outstretched.

Jerome, still squatting in the sand, had looked up politely and attentively.

"Where's the letter?" she began majestically, every inch Aïda, and the battle began. It had to be fought with restraint on account of the neighboring deck chairs, but the sand flew in all directions. Jerome proved himself a worthy son of his mother, squatting stolidly in his sandals, fending off his mother's slaps and pinches and smiling inscrutably, his strongest weapon.

Not until she saw Federigo heading for shore did Garibalda give up. Gnashing her teeth, she signed a check, which her son held up to the light before putting it away.

Then he took off his right sandal.

At noon that day, we were standing with our suitcases in the Grand Hotel lobby when Garibalda and Federigo returned from the beach.

"Mamma," announced Jerome happily, "imagine! We've got a double room exactly like yours on the same floor."

While Federigo was getting the keys from the desk, Garibalda turned on Jerome. "Haven't you got any shame, you misbegotten pup? Appearing publicly in the Grand Hotel with a girl you're not married to!"

"But Mamma," said Jerome innocently, "you and Frederigo—isn't that the same thing?"

Garibalda raised her right hand in a solemn gesture of benediction *cum* traffic policeman and turned her blackberry eyes heavenward. "Leave your sacred mother out of this," she intoned and disappeared into the elevator.

We never found out how she explained our sudden presence to Federigo. But from then on both behaved as if they didn't know us.

We didn't mind. Restored by soft mattresses and splendid meals, we spent four unforgettable days at the Grand Hotel in Eastbourne.

8

No sign of life from the painter. I called the studio. No answer. Strange—she hardly ever went out.

I went over and rang the doorbell long and stubbornly until, finally, I heard footsteps. "It's me." Silence. Obviously she was making up her mind. Then the door opened a crack and she pointed to her throat without speaking.

"I thought so," I said and pushed the door open. She looked like an old Eskimo woman left out in the snow to die. A woolen scarf covered her head, two sweaters full of paint stains and moth holes were tucked into crumpled pajama pants. On top was an old sheepskin rug tied up with string.

"You can't talk?" No answer. I pushed her aside and marched to the telephone.

There was plenty to do while we waited for my doctor. The heater in her bedroom wasn't working, hence her extraordinary outfit. I dragged her mattress and bedclothes, covered with coffee stains, into the warm studio, while she sat silently on the hassock, watching, sweat pouring down her face.

"You ought to be ashamed of yourself," I yelled, as I ran

back and forth looking for clean sheets and not finding any, putting water on to boil and turning the pantry upside down in a vain search for tea and lemons.

I pulled her up from the hassock and untied the string. The sheepskin fell to the floor and I pushed her ahead of me and then down on the mattress. She put up no resistance when I dragged the two sweaters over her head, taking the scarf with them, and bundled her up under the blanket. She lay quite still, staring straight ahead. Maybe she wanted to die.

"Do you want to die?"

She shook her head.

"Well then."

•

My doctor came—a pasty-faced, overworked, impatient young man with bitten fingernails. He wasn't happy in his profession, and his patients got on his nerves. Sometimes his eyes would narrow as if he couldn't take anymore, and he would start talking about his own stomach symptoms. But he was a good doctor. No professional bedside manner, no miracle worker, but prepared, if necessary, to make a house call at three o'clock in the morning.

While he was examining her, I went into the kitchen and tidied up and washed some dishes. Then he called me in. The best thing would be to take her at once to the hospital. A glance and a gesture from her cut him short. Well, then, could I take care of her? I heaved a deep sigh, making sure she heard it. Cheerful self-sacrifice would have been the last thing she needed.

He left, leaving prescriptions and instructions. I got my coat, took the key out of the lock and departed.

When I returned a little while later with fresh linen and medicines, she was lying there on the mattress as if she were dead. I pulled her up by the hair—she offered no resistance —held the pills and then a glass of water to her lips, and burst out laughing. That furious face under my fistful of hair! She glared at me and for a moment there was murder in the air. Then her face crumpled up as if she were about to burst out laughing herself, but all she could produce was a hoarse, barking growl. She drank and swallowed painfully. I let go of her hair and she dropped back on the pillow and immediately fell asleep.

I left again to find an electrician to repair the bedroom heater, had to be satisfied with vague promises, and returned. She was still asleep. I wandered quietly about the studio, examining the canvases, looking over her books— and suddenly came face to face with the bronze head again. A glance at the mattress—she was sleeping quietly, her mouth neatly closed.

I carried the little bust to the window. At last I was able to examine it at leisure. The narrow, Egyptian-looking skull, the hair around neck and cheeks like a thin silk scarf, the "mean mouth"—a sullen mouth, a taciturn mouth, but mean? Never. I'd often seen her sitting by the window with exactly that expression on her face, severe, concentrated, turned off. She worked several hours a day, brailling books and delivering them to the home of the blind. Dozens of its rooms were fitted out with armchairs and radios she had supplied, and she liked to spend whole afternoons there talking to the residents, many of whom she knew well. Sometimes she would make Nina accompany her. Not a good idea. Nina would stand by in silence while the blind people crowded around her mother. Nina had nothing to contribute, remained literally invisible.

The painter hadn't moved, but I felt her eyes on me. She was watching me with apparent indifference, as I stood by the window with the bronze head in my hand.

I put the sculpture down on the windowsill. Time for her pill. I refilled the glass and held it threateningly under her nose. She struggled upright by herself, swallowed and took a drink of water. Victory.

Before lying down again, she made a sign that she wanted something to write with. Maybe she was in pain and had decided to go to the hospital after all. I found a sketchbook and a piece of charcoal by the easel. And her glasses. Slowly and painfully she wrote something, tossed it over to me and watched with indifference as I picked up the charcoal and angrily rubbed at the black mark on my fresh white sheet. Impatiently she pointed to the sketchbook and closed her eyes. I deciphered the shaky, smudged letters printed in charcoal: "YOU CAN HAVE IT."

I seized the charcoal and printed underneath: "NO THANKS"—and realized that I was behaving like most of Beethoven's visitors, who used to push a notebook under his nose expecting him to write an answer to their written questions. Which made him angry every time.

"No thanks," I said in a loud voice. She opened her eyes and barked—or perhaps it was a laugh—until she choked.

I stuck a throat lozenge in her mouth. "Don't forget to take your pills, every three hours. The lozenges are to stop the coughing. Try to sleep. If you feel bad, call me. You don't have to speak—I'll know. I'll be back tomorrow to get your breakfast."

She stared at me, nodded imperceptibly and closed her eyes.

9

On the way back to the hotel I thought about Nina, couldn't get her out of my head. Plump little Nina, who had inherited nothing from her mother except her black eyes, those watchful black raven's eyes that missed nothing. Those eyes had watched her mother leave the door of that house in St. James's Street, hail a taxi and drive away. Those eyes, those raven eyes, obeying some raven instinct, had continued to watch that same door until they were rewarded by the sight of a man coming out into the street: Jerome.

What date was that? (Why was I so keen on getting the dates straight? What did it matter exactly when it all happened? It did matter. Once I had finally decided to open those locked doors I might as well let it all stream out in the right order, like a parade, events following events according to their marching orders. I might even feel some sort of painful satisfaction at having to rethink and relive methodically through the memories of those years, one by one, continually coming to a stop and exclaiming: Ah! So *that* is why we did this or that! Or: Ah! *That* explains why such and such took place! And in spite of the pain there was the clean surgical satisfaction of "knowing at long last" and a feeling of liberation.)

Years later, when Nina told me about it, she couldn't remember exactly what date it had been. All she knew was that the tulips were in bloom because that afternoon her class had taken a course in botany in St. James's Park.

If the tulips were blooming, it must have been April or May. And it was probably a Thursday. On Thursdays I had a matinee. Who had made the first move? One or the other always takes the initiative, gives the first signal. Which of them had it been? Jerome?

The diary hardly mentions him in January 1937; in February it ignores him altogether. She wrote only about me, about my interminable, tiresome worries which never seemed to tire her, my pipe dreams, my new winter coat. Then suddenly in March:

Called J.

So it was Anabel. Yet, who knows, perhaps in response to a word or a look from Jerome . . .

No entry in the diary for three days. On the fourth day, at last, the whole story.

Called J. again. Asked for L. He laughed and said didn't I know she was at the theater. I told him I had to talk to him. Important. For all three of us. He laughed again. I said, "Three o'clock at the boat house in Regent's Park," and hung up. He kept me waiting but he came. Strolled up as if he were out for a walk. I was wearing my red coat. He told me I looked like a red raven. Too cold to hire a boat. We walked over the little bridge into Queen Mary's rose garden. Nobody about, the benches still wet. We wandered around. I told him

everything. Of course he knew but he was surprised that it
dated back to the Berkeley Bar. I went too far and told him I
had felt an electric shock as I sat next to him and our knees
touched for a split second. He laughed again. Probably thinks
I'm crazy. Am I? I don't think so. I've never felt like this
before. But I shouldn't have told him, you don't tell things like
that. But that's why I've ever since avoided all physical
contact with him, as far as I possibly could.

I never mentioned L. Neither did he. Gave me a few sidelong
glances. Why is he always smiling? Self-defense? Then he
said he wouldn't mind stepping out of line a bit, but not too
far and with small steps only. He wasn't geared for "passion."
As he said that, he even dropped that damned smile. Then he
strolled calmly out of the rose garden, toward a taxi rank.
With me beside him. He gave the address of his apartment,
opened the door, got in and didn't seem to notice that I got in
too.

I had to stop reading for a moment, although only the
details were news to me. But I hadn't known before—and it
brought back at once all the old hurt, all the old feeling of
impoverishment—that it had been in our apartment, our
cheap little apartment, in the cheap little bed with the cheap
chenille bedspread . . .

Wouldn't it be wiser to skip a couple of pages? Did I
really have to know the details? And the details are always
the things that get stuck in one's mind. Could it be that I was
actually enjoying them? No, goddammit, it was plain
necessity to read every line or I would once again invent a
taboo-territory around which my thoughts would circle and
snarl.

It was exactly as I had imagined it hundreds of times. But
exactly. My eyes were closed tight. I was functioning only

inside myself. At one point the telephone rang. J. let it ring but finally picked it up. We both knew who it was. L.'s matinee was over. She just wanted to say hello before lying down for her hour's nap in the dressing room. She didn't notice anything.

Correct. I have no memory of that conversation.

I quickly left. J. made no effort to stop me or to see me home or get me a taxi. It was raining. I got soaked, had to walk a long way before I found one. I rolled down the window to let the rain continue wetting my face. I needed the rain. I needed to come to my senses.

The next day she wrote only one sentence:

No word from J.

Same thing on the following day. On the third day:

Is he doing it on purpose? Surely he knows that one needs some word—some sign. Every time the doorbell rings, I think: Here it is. Perhaps a single rose! How corny can you get? I can't see her now. Don't know what excuse to make. She thinks I'm sick and insists on coming over. Why doesn't he call? Bad conscience? Was he bored? Or—on the contrary— did I take him too far out of line? Anything's possible. I need some word from him. He'll *have* to let me hear from him. He owes me that much. At least *that* much.

Next day:

I would like to kill myself. In some repulsive way. Cut my throat. With Bill's razor. I'm ashamed of myself. Ashamed. Ashamed. Ashamed.

No entry for two days. Then:

L. came bringing flowers. She thinks I'm upset about something
she has said or done. She stayed for ages, is convinced I'm
sick. She's right in thinking she's done something to upset me.
I hate her for knowing nothing. She has no right not to be
suspicious, not to sense anything. She has no antenna to tell
her what's going on inside the people she loves. She has no
right to trust J., and if she trusts me, she's a blockhead. If
she'd given me one suspicious look, I'd have hugged her like a
sister. But she's a cow. I threw her flowers into the garbage
can.

I had to get up, I had to move my head from side to side,
up and down, around and around. My neck was rigid, it felt
as if it might break off. It had to get unstuck before I could
read any more. Perhaps I would then get some more air into
my lungs and breathe normally. In and out. And in and
out.
The next day:

A ray of hope. Next Monday is J.'s birthday. Bill wants to
celebrate at the Savoy Grill. I'll see him! I'll be able to tell
from his face why I haven't heard from him. I'm eating again,
I'm stuffing myself. Bought a white evening dress. White
makes you look fatter.

I can still see that white evening dress. She looked like a
calla lily. I was happy because it was Jerome's birthday,
because we were at the Savoy, drinking champagne, and
because Anabel was her old self. Or almost. She tried to light
a cigarette with Jerome's lighter, but her hand was shaking
so hard that he placed his hand over hers to steady it.

"You're trembling," I exclaimed anxiously.

"It's the champagne," said Jerome. "It sometimes affects me that way too."

Why do I remember that? His hand on hers . . . Was the cow beginning to catch on after all? Not perhaps in the top layer of my conscious mind but somewhere in the one right underneath.

He placed his hand over mine, otherwise I could never have lighted my cigarette. In full view of everybody he placed his hand over mine. I knew then I could call him up again. Had to wait until the next evening, until L. was at the theater.

"Jerome," I said, "I'm sorry. I wish it had never happened. I must have lost my mind. Forgive me. Help me!"

"Of course," he said. "How?"

"I must explain to you. Come to the boat house on Saturday afternoon. That will be the last time."

On Saturday I had another matinee. And it wasn't the last time. But at least she never went to our apartment again. She rented one in St. James's Street under a false name. Nobody knew about it, nobody recognized her. Except Nina.

•

The entries for the next two months record happiness, intact, flawless, no hint of even a faint shadow of guilt feelings. One short sentence brought back a long-forgotten incident. Immediately after the evening at the Savoy, Anabel told me she was going to order an evening dress for me, from her own couturier—Hartnell! Hartnell dressed the royal family! I had never owned a couture evening dress. I was to choose it myself. Mannequins paraded for me alone, presenting models, turning this way and that, smiling a sterile smile and withdrawing. Anabel selected the most beautiful dress of all, probably the most expensive one too. I threw my arms around her neck. Nobody had ever given me such a present.

All the diary says is:

Ordered an evening dress for L.

.

They were leading a separate, independent life, those two, but it was I who called their tune. As long as I was working, they had nothing to fear, it was child's play. But if my film came to an end or my play closed, I cut their lifeline and the apartment in St. James's Street remained unused.

In the summer of 1937 it stood empty for two months.

On July 1 he's going away. With L. To stay with friends in the south of France. Vacation. Only one more week and he'll be gone. Two months! How am I to live through those two months? I'm making all kinds of plans, all dangerous. Like taking Nina to some place nearby. But she doesn't want to go and it's too risky without her. Two months! I'll have to talk her into it.

But apparently Nina wasn't to be talked into it, because Jerome and I left on July 1—it was a real wrench for me to leave Anabel behind—and we didn't see her again until the end of August.

10

July 1, 1937. My first vacation since I left school, the very first with Jerome. Our final destination was Grasse, where Jerome's friend Peter Gurnemantz owned a peach farm. But first we were going to Paris; we had saved enough money to be able to stop over for a day. At the Hotel de la Muette, for old time's sake.

The Hotel de la Muette had been my first harbor when I arrived in Paris late in 1933 at the age of eighteen, ready to remake my life in French, to conquer the film studios and the legitimate stage and start a "world career." I didn't even get my nose inside a film studio and had to admit total defeat one year later.

That was a bad year, 1934. In January my father had died in Berlin and the two of us who had managed to get out, my sister Irene and I, knew that we must get the rest of the family, our mother and younger sister Hilde, out of Berlin as quickly as possible. We sold everything we possessed. With the proceeds I went to London in January 1935 to try my luck in English. Slowly, very slowly, I gained a foothold and at the end of that year a shout of joy: a contract with a London film company. Irene came over from Paris, my mother and Hilde and some furniture from Berlin. We were a family again.

And now Paris, for the first time after three years. Three years is a long time when you're twenty-one. An eternity since I'd boarded the London train at the Gare du Nord, grimly determined, nodding an indifferent goodbye to the city rushing past outside my compartment. It was a completely different person who now sat in the taxi, looking out the window at the familiar streets, squares and buildings. Now I asked nothing of the city, didn't want to belong to it, struggle with it, conquer it. I was a tourist, I belonged somewhere else and had a return ticket in my purse. Thus for the first time I appreciated Paris and cried out with delight at the sight of the Champs Elysées and the Arc de Triomphe.

"I thought you'd lived here," said Jerome. "You act as if you were seeing it for the first time."

"I am seeing it for the first time."

Arrival at the Hotel de la Muette.

I recognized the concierge; he did not recognize me. I shook his reluctant hand just the same.

"Don't you remember the two sisters who lived here three years ago? Up on the top floor? The ones who always saved German stamps for you. Remember?"

Something began to dawn on the walrus face with the stiff, bristly mustache.

"The ones who always kept salami and cheese on the window ledge?"

"That's right. They send their regards."

"*Merci,*" he said in bewilderment and escorted us to the elevator.

A nice room, even a private bath, very different from the hole Irene and I had lived in. I stepped out onto the terrace and looked down over the treetops at the Bois de Boulogne, the same treetops that had so often comforted me, except that now, from the elegant balcony on the first floor, they were closer and even more friendly. For the first time in my life I felt a sense of achievement and the span as well as the end of an era.

·

While I was meditating, Jerome was speaking into the telephone. He was calling Babs, so I quickly stepped back into the room. Babs, Babs Siodmak. High time I introduced her—after all, she played a role in the story, wove a few essential threads and decisively though unintentionally influenced the course of events.

Babs had once been my "predecessor." One day Jerome happened to mention her name and was surprised and amused by my reaction. "But I know her!" I exclaimed excitedly. "I knew her in Paris! That is—well, I saw her once through the window of the Café Colisée," I concluded lamely.

"You sound like the poor little girl with the matches," said Jerome. "Why through the window?"

"I didn't go to cafés in those days."

"Pity. Yes, the Colisée, that's where she still holds court. She has to have a regular café in every city, where she holds her levees. When we were living together in Berlin while I was studying at the academy, it was the Continental on the Kurfürstendamm. It has to be a café, there have to be masses of people coming and going, getting up, sitting down, waiters rushing around, and it has to have the smell of cigarette smoke, coffee and coats. Only there does she feel really comfortable. Once I dreamed that she had died and been buried, but I dug her up again and she opened her eyes and sat up in her coffin. 'Come along, Babs,' I said. 'Go on home and lie down and rest.' 'I've rested enough,' she said, putting on her hat. 'I'm going to the Continental!' "

She was so much talked about in refugee circles in those desperate days in Paris that she became a kind of mythological figure in my imagination, floating about in delicate colors and fluttering her famous hands, "which Botticelli might have painted." And then, one day, on the Champs Elysées, somebody pointed her out to me through the window. There she sat, enthroned inside her Café Colisée, serene and elegant, dressed, however, not in delicate colors, but strictly in black and white, Paris fashion. Thereafter she stopped floating about in my mind and remained firmly anchored inside the Colisée—but still way beyond my reach.

Now, however, via Jerome, I felt myself suddenly catapulted through the window and sitting right next to her, one of the family, so to speak. She was a good ten years older than Jerome but that was an advantage, he said, he was always eager to learn. When Robert Siodmak, the director, appeared on the scene in Berlin, he yielded gracefully to him, and they parted on the most affectionate terms. Robert and Babs emigrated to Paris, but she and Jerome still kept in touch by letter.

And now he was actually talking to my mythological figure on the telephone, laughing and making a date. Six o'clock at the Café Colisée. Where else?

Babs, in black and white, tanned, beaming, and surrounded by her court, recognized Jerome as soon as he came through the door and called out, as if she were in her own living room:

"Sherome! Feins ici!"

My Botticelli came from Stuttgart and had a Swabian accent!

"Carçon, teux chaises!" The others were drinking coffee, but they ordered ice cream for me as if I were a child and gave me an extra-large spoon and a waffle to keep me quiet. I was excluded from their conversation, which dwelt on memories of Berlin, and was tempted to bang my spoon against the plate. Once she did turn to me, gave me a candid, friendly look and said that Jerome and I made a charming young couple.

"You talk as if you were my aunt," said Jerome.

"That's the way I feel," she replied, stroking my cheek.

·

That night the sleeping car left for Nice and our destination —the "Gurnemantz holiday."

The transformation of the German sculptor Peter Gurnemantz into a French fruit farmer had taken place in 1934. In pre-Hitler days he had married the eldest daughter of a Jewish banker in Berlin and had refused to divorce her despite considerable pressure from Goebbels's Ministry of Propaganda. Instead he emigrated, along with his whole clan, his wife Ursula, his five-year-old son, and Ursula's younger sister, Eva.

Gurnemantz, a burly, blond fellow from Schleswig-Holstein, had little to say during the day; at night, after two glasses of Pernod, he became a bit more talkative, but not much. He lived chiefly through his downward-slanting eyes, which seemed unwilling to leave whatever they were resting on at the moment. Nervousness, not to speak of panic, was outside his experience. When, for the first time in his life, he had to say to someone in Paris, "Could you lend me a hundred francs?" he realized as the words came out of his mouth that his career as a sculptor was over. At that very moment he made up his mind to start a new life, preferably one in which he could use his huge, square peasant hands.

His banker father-in-law appeared on the train from Berlin, a small, gray and nervous man. He carefully took his pajamas, slippers and a heavy woolen dressing gown out of his meticulously packed suitcase. Equally carefully he removed from inside the lining of his dressing gown a canvas whose ecstatic colors sparkled with glee over the inefficiency of the German customs officials: a Renoir landscape which had once hung in a magnificent golden frame in his dining room.

The next day he boarded the train back to Berlin. He had no intention of emigrating. "I'll be on the last train to leave Germany," he told his two daughters as they stood on the platform in tears. And he was. Destination: Auschwitz.

•

Gurnemantz sold the Renoir and with the proceeds bought a hillside in the south of France. On the sunny side he planted hundreds of peach trees. On the very top he built a house, built it with his own hands and without ever having learned how. During the day he planted and watered his young trees, and in the evening he studied textbooks to learn how to mix cement and control tree diseases.

Now, three years later, he had invited us to visit him in Grasse and help with the harvest. Our first Gurnemantz vacation.

11

Ten years later, while I was sitting for the painter, Peter Gurnemantz the sculptor popped up out of the past.

She was up and about again, though still a bit shaky. Her voice had come back. Every day I brought her a fresh vegetable soup, which she could warm up. She wouldn't accept any help. "This is *my* kitchen. Out!"

I wandered around the studio, stopped in front of the bookshelf and took out a large art book, *Twentieth Century Sculpture*.

She carried the tray in from the kitchen and set it down on the table, breathing heavily, glancing over my shoulder at the massive bronze figure of a woman I was studying.

"Maillol," she said. "I worked in his studio in Marly-le-Roi for a few months. There were no fine tools—he had deliberately blunted them all because he thought he was getting too persnickety, too wrapped up in detail. That gave me something to think about. I blunted myself too, concentrated on the large issues, on the essential way things hang together. Helped me a lot. Very important."

"Did you happen to know a pupil of his by the name of Gurnemantz?"

"Peter? He was just a beginner at that time. I lost trace of him, but I remember his work. Talented. I don't know what became of him."

"A fruit farmer."

"What?" She laughed, reaching for her Gauloises and her glasses. "Why?"

"Hitler."

"Pity. He'd have made it. Did he give it up entirely?"

"Just about," I replied. "When I knew him, just before the war, he'd done one last sculpture fifteen feet high and sixty feet long."

"There's no such thing," she said crossly.

"Well, it's there, and as far as I know, it's still standing. It's a house! He built himself a house like a huge sculpture, like a human body resting on its side."

"A house like a sculpture! Have you seen it?"

"I've even lived in it, three times, for three summer vacations. It was built on a hillside, not far from Grasse, strung out and undulating in large curves. The belly was the living room, the head the library, the two guest rooms the thighs. Around the belly, like an apron, a wide terrace. The rain-water cistern was also the swimming pool, shaped like a peanut and icy-cold. The whole thing stood amid olive trees, and there were olive trees right in the middle of the living room; Gurnemantz had built the walls around them."

The painter stared at me with her mouth open, yapping softly like a bloodhound.

"Actually it was very practical. It didn't collapse in storms or leak when it poured with rain. It was also ridiculously cheap. That was the main thing. He had planted peach trees and had to wait three years for his first crop. We lived in one of the thighs and helped with the harvesting. The only other help he could afford was Aesculapius, the donkey, who carried the baskets back to the house when they were full."

She stretched out in her armchair and stared at the ceiling, as she always did when she wanted to get a clear picture of something.

"A donkey carried the fruit back to the house," she repeated slowly. "Paradise! Picking peaches . . ."

"Not till the sun started to go down—otherwise it was too hot. We all slept all morning, Gurnemantz, his wife, Ursula, her sister, Eva, their little son, Jean-Pierre, and Jerome and I."

"How do you pick peaches? With a knife? With clippers?"

"By hand. It's not as easy as it sounds. You have to take them by surprise. Peaches are tricky, they know that you have to handle them like Christmas-tree decorations. If you press too hard, you leave bruises. The trick is to give them a quick twist and snap them off before they have time to adjust to the new position."

"Tricky fruit!" she said pensively. "I'm not surprised, they're so round and smooth and sweet. Tell me more about the donkey."

"When you'd filled two baskets, you whistled, and he'd come trotting up, God knows where from. A beautiful animal, light-gray and very intelligent. First you gave him a bruised peach and then he trotted up the hill to the terrace. There Ursula would be waiting with the most important job of all, the sorting. On the terrace wall stood the wooden crates and stacks of green pleated paper cups. There were three grades. Number one: large peaches with rosy cheeks. Number two: small peaches with rosy cheeks. Aesculapius used to hang around while we were sorting. Number three belonged to him. He nodded his head and opened his mouth whenever a scruffy one turned up."

"Paradise!" murmured the painter with her eyes closed. "And then?"

"Then we fitted the peaches into the paper cups, packed them, marked the price on them, loaded the crates into an ancient pickup truck . . . ."

"Paradise!" she repeated almost inaudibly.

"We ate supper late, trying to stay awake as long as possible because we had to leave at three in the morning. We sneaked out of the house, trying not to wake up the little boy, crowded into the truck and roared down to Nice."

"Nice!" she exclaimed, sitting up straight. "To the market? I've been there to buy flowers many a time."

"We sold our peaches there twice a week. At four o'clock in the morning."

She stood up and paced excitedly about the studio, smoking.

"And you helped sell them? Shouting and haggling?"

I laughed. "I'd have liked to, but the men wouldn't let us. 'Women bring the price down,' they said. We had to sit in the truck and watch, but that was fun too."

"I bet it was," she exclaimed, combing her shaggy black hair with her fingers. "I always got there too late, about eight o'clock, and by that time everything was calm and orderly, the fun was all over. But sometimes my friends would get up early, or stay up. They said at four o'clock it was exciting, a real witches' sabbath."

"Yes, the entire square was in an uproar. Booths were erected, roofed with sheet metal or tarpaulins. A primitive little village would spring up before our eyes, with fancy 'buildings' or slum ones. And the noise! The yelling would even drown out the hammering. Everyone shouted at the top of his voice to no one in particular until finally the hammering and the pushing and shoving came to an end and fruit, vegetables and flowers were all neatly arranged and everybody would collapse behind his counter, exhausted and silent. Then they'd make coffee and eat pancakes."

The painter sat down again and looked at me, fascinated.

"And you watched it all? Jesus! I made up my mind to see it hundreds of times, but I was always either too drunk or too disorganized. I always overslept."

I patted her hard painter's hand and poured her another cup of coffee.

"And then? You waited until the cafés opened and ate breakfast?"

"No, something much better. When the men came back with their empty crates and full purses, smelling of Pernod—"

"Pernod!" she cried and her eyes were suddenly full of tears.

"—we'd roar off in the old truck to the Hotel Negresco. In those days that was the most elegant beach on the coast, but at five o'clock in the morning there wasn't a soul around. We'd always find a couple of cabins open and we'd change into our swim suits and run into the warm sea. An hour later we'd be on our way back to Grasse in the early-morning light, so sleepy that we had to take turns driving, because no one could stay awake longer than fifteen minutes."

She sat there in silence, smoking and brooding.

"Anabel?" she finally asked. "Was Anabel ever with you?"

"Twice."

"Did she pick peaches?"

I nodded.

"And swim in the sea?"

I nodded again.

"Strange," she said.

12

Diary, November 1937:

Catastrophe. I was sitting on the floor in the living room, wrapping Christmas presents. Suddenly I began to cry. Couldn't stop. A real crying jag. Sat there among piles of shiny paper, sprigs of fir and gold ribbons, and howled. Don't know why it hit me just then, why among the pretty Christmas paper and packages, why at all. Was it because there was so much heavenly blue about me, with little gold angels? Lately I've been unusually touchy, as if someone had peeled off the top layer of skin. Can't listen to music, can't bear Bill anywhere near me. Told him so. He didn't say anything but now he does his boxing in his bedroom. I'm ruining his life, that's crystal-clear. But I don't care. I've lost all touch with myself, have hidden myself somewhere and mopped up all traces. Perhaps that's why I cried. Lovely floods of tears. I felt relaxed and quite happy crying away—when suddenly L. walked into the room. I hadn't heard the bell, I wasn't expecting anyone. I was simply exercising my privilege of sobbing contentedly in my own living room. And she had to burst in! Fell upon me, took me completely by surprise. Catastrophe.

It certainly was. She was sitting on the floor amid rolls of paper, ribbons and packages. I had to kick it all out of the way to get to her—after all, I couldn't just stand there and watch her sitting on the floor, crying. The least I could do was sit down beside her, ask questions, take her hand, comfort her. Although I felt more like getting out as quickly as possible. When grown-ups cry, I've always wanted to run and hide, but never before so urgently. Anabel in tears! There was something obscene about it. She cried without making a sound, the tears streaming quietly down her face, but her whole body shook with her sobs. It must have come on quite suddenly; she didn't even have a handkerchief.

Sure enough, she wanted me to "tell her all about it." I cried into her handkerchief, stalling, trying desperately to invent something. Couldn't think of anything to save my life. I kept repeating stupidly: "Nothing—it's nothing—really, there's nothing the matter with me—" but she said no one sits on the floor alone crying over nothing. She wasn't going to leave until I told her. Told her what?

I forced myself to sit down beside her on the floor and put my arm around her shoulders. I don't know why it was so hard for me to do it. Her shoulders jerked convulsively when I touched her. I stroked her hair, wet with tears, made soothing noises to show I loved her. Finally I asked her quite sternly what in God's name was the matter. She kept on shaking her head, as if flies were bothering her.

Finally I gave up. Simply let things take their course. Told her point-blank I have a lover. She wasn't as surprised as I'd expected. Nor shocked.

I stopped reading for a moment. Shocked? Was I a prude in those days?

She probably has a pretty good idea of what goes on, as far as Bill and I are concerned.

Naturally. The only thing I didn't know was that there actually was somebody else.

Of course she wanted to know who it is. And I suddenly came to my senses. Could have kicked myself. From one minute to the next I became completely clear-headed and stopped crying. Invented all sorts of reasons why I couldn't tell her who it is. None of them made sense and she wouldn't buy them. Then it occurred to me to give my "lover" a name, at least a first name. I'd been reading Molnar, so I named him Ferencsi. I could read her eyes as she racked her brain, trying to remember if she'd ever met anyone by the name of Ferencsi. And all the time she was patting my hand or stroking my head, smiling and eager to show me that she didn't disapprove. I suddenly felt like hugging her. Instead, I babbled on and invented all kinds of rubbish about Ferencsi. What if I don't remember it all? I think I said he's half French, half Hungarian, Catholic, married, two children—that's important so that she won't drive me insane with bright suggestions about divorcing Bill and living happily ever after with Ferencsi. He lives in Paris and I knew him "way back." Very plausible. He only occasionally comes to London on business. A good touch, it explains why she never meets him. And so—sob—the situation is completely hopeless. She nodded sympathetically and then came out with the inevitable question: "Does he love you?" "I don't know," I replied. "I don't see him often enough." At that she protested indignantly, "What does that fellow think he's doing? He's cheating on his wife and he's making you unhappy. Where's this going to get you? Are you sure you can't tear him out—by the roots?"

She gave me a long look. Her eyes were still red and her eyelashes damp and stuck together. I thought she was never going to answer, but finally she whispered: "I was trying to. When you came in, I was trying to."

·

That was all I could get out of her. She wouldn't say any more. Did Bill suspect anything? I only saw him at meals now; he didn't do his shadow-boxing in the living room anymore. And Nina? Maybe she knew, maybe that's why she hunched her shoulders whenever she caught sight of her mother, as if to protect herself from something. Perhaps she knew Ferencsi.

I sat in my car in front of the house for a while before I felt able to drive off. What a mess. I could still feel her shoulders shaking in my arms. How strange. This was a new Anabel. Gone the aristocratic, splendid bearing, the unshakable poise. In their place a fragile, trembling little heap of misery, sitting there among the Christmas wrappings. Ferencsi. What sort of fellow could that be, what did he look like, how on earth had he managed to . . . ?

I started up the car and drove slowly away in the direction of Chelsea. One didn't visit Jerome in his "studio" at Simon's except in an emergency, and they had no telephone. Today was an emergency, Anabel needed help. Immediately. I wasn't free, I had to be at the theater by seven at the latest. But there was Jerome, after all. Unsentimental, unprejudiced, discreet, wise, accustomed to shipwreck and disaster since early childhood, he'd probably just smile. The only hurdle was that he didn't really like her.

Simon muttered something uncomplimentary when I came in. Jerome, paintbrush in his mouth, palette in one hand, closed the door behind me, signaling something. Pius III was dying on the windowsill; his successor had not yet been named. Silence in the studio except for the frantic buzzing of the fly's death rattle. Simon rose, walked over to the window and watched the six legs twitching convulsively. Pius was already on his back, yet his twitching managed to propel him sideways for a fraction of an inch. Abrupt silence. Pius lay still and started gently to shrivel up. Simon went back to his desk in silence.

Jerome raised his eyebrows inquiringly. I motioned to him to step into the tiny bathroom. We closed the door. In a whisper I told him, a bit too excitedly, what had just happened at the Macleans'.

He showed no surprise, kept chewing the end of his paintbrush thoughtfully but didn't speak. I hesitated, sensing his resistance. "Jerome—won't you call her up? Take her to a movie. She needs it, she shouldn't be alone today, she's canceled all invitations, doesn't want to see anyone. But she mustn't stay home with just Bill and Nina. I could meet you somewhere after the show, when your movie is over. Take care of her a bit, will you?"

Jerome considered, then nodded. All right, he'd take care of her, but only this once. No permanent caretaking. "She gets on my nerves."

·

Diary:

Now I've really done it. Missed my chance. For months I've been putting it off from one day to the next. And yet I knew all the time it was urgent!

What prevented me from saying to her yesterday: "I'm crying because I hate myself. I hate myself because day in and day out I'm deceiving you, because I love you and betray you every second. It's no good telling myself that I'm not robbing you of anything that belongs to you. You wouldn't understand. You'd see nothing but theft and treachery. You only recognize black and white and you think you can distinguish between right and wrong. I have some kind of cancer. I've always had it. Perhaps something could have been done about it when Maman died. She would often put her arms around me and say, "It's not enough for us to love you, you must love us in return!" She knew about those bad cells inside me. It was probably frightening to her, a child that can't love, a child that doesn't really want anything. And yet I did love her, but I never knew it until she died. Died so quickly that I was hardly aware of it. How old was I? Twelve. Old enough. But I had paid no attention, never asked why she was getting so thin. She had cancer too. A different kind.

A few weeks after her death I was sitting on my swing in the garden and swung so wildly and so high that the posts shook. But now there was no voice calling from the window, "Anabel! Not so high, child, you'll go right over!"

I let the swing die down. My arms and legs went limp with the first and overwhelming feeling of loneliness. How I had resented that voice! And how desperately I wished I could hear it again. When the swing stopped, I didn't jump off, I sat there, hating my dead mother for abandoning me.

Yesterday, when L. sat down beside me on the floor and stared at me with her large round cow's eyes, I felt I was back on the swing and I could hear the voice from the window calling, "Anabel! Not so high, child, you'll go right over!" So I howled a bit longer to gain time, let the swing die down—and invented Ferencsi.

Suppose I'd told her the truth, how would those big cow's

eyes have looked at me? I've imagined it hundreds of times. And not without a certain amount of pleasure. It's a pleasure to feel that you can destroy someone, especially when you're the weaker one. Because she's the stronger. Only she doesn't know it yet.

13

How very kind of Jerome to take Anabel out twice a week while I was at the theater. I was deeply touched. He seemed a bit restless at the time, possibly an early symptom of the hepatitis which put him out of action for six weeks a little while later. It wasn't only Anabel who got on his nerves—I did too, though only once, but it upset and confused me for days.

It happened while he was sick and had to remain in bed at our apartment, jaundiced and bloated-looking. I nursed him and spent every free minute away from the theater sitting by his bed. On matinee days I would have liked to ask Anabel to take my place, but he wouldn't let me. She sent her chauffeur over every day with special food, fruit, flowers and magazines, but she never came to see him.

Ours was a two-room apartment, with bath and small kitchen. Only the bedroom was furnished—the bed, bedside table, two chairs and a wardrobe. The second room served as a studio when Simon was being difficult, and as a store-room for Jerome's finished paintings, for Simon might have been tempted to pawn them occasionally. "If only I could get a few of them framed," Jerome used to say from time to time. "They'd look quite different framed. Then I could show them to a gallery."

I had just made an extra fifty pounds posing for photographs advertising nightgowns and nylon stockings (then brand-new) and felt the moment was propitious. While Jerome was asleep, I sneaked out to a frame shop, carrying three of his largest canvases.

"What kind of frame would you like?"

What kind? At home in Berlin all the pictures had been in carved and curly gold frames, but Jerome hated curls as well as gold. What to do? Helplessly I stared at hundreds of samples, row after row, wide ones, narrow ones, in all colors, materials and profiles.

"Something simple," I said hesitantly. Then, remembering the gallery owners, I added hastily, "But—imposing."

The salesman gave me a look. "I see," he said and selected one. It was certainly simple, and imposing too. It was made of iron and so heavy that I could hardly lift it. I bought three of them, and it took me half an hour to lug them upstairs one by one and stealthily set them up in the studio.

Then, sweating and excited, I sat down on Jerome's bed and confessed what I'd done. He was very touched, eager to see them, and asked me to bring them in right away. Panting, I dragged *Gypsy Mother and Child* into the bedroom. He stared at it, speechless, while I went for the second one, *Foreign Legionnaire*, and then the third, *Olive Trees in Grasse*. I stood the three of them, locked in an iron embrace, at the foot of the bed. Simple but imposing.

Jerome's silence lasted too long for me.

"Don't tell me you don't like them," I bristled. "They cost forty-five pounds."

"Forty-five pounds!" he shouted, and his swollen, jaundiced face turned a dull red. "Are you out of your mind? Are you really blind and dumb? Those aren't frames, they're horseshoes!"

I was already in tears and didn't hear any more, except an order to take "those goddam things" off his canvases immediately because they were suffocating.

"Can't you see that they're not framed? They're murdered."

Sobbing, I carted them back down the stairs. One of them fell on my thumb and squashed it. I drove back to the frame shop and was happy to get twenty pounds back, probably on the strength of my tear-stained face and swollen thumb.

•

Why had he shouted at me? He had been so patient otherwise, all through his long and depressing illness. As if something that had been brewing inside him for a long time had suddenly erupted.

On my return from the frame shop, I found him flat on his back, staring at the ceiling. No music, no book, and his temperature had gone up. I wanted to call the doctor but he wouldn't let me, caught my hand as I reached for the telephone and silently covered his eyes with it.

That was the only quarrel we ever had. Generally his arms were around me. Whenever we were alone somewhere, he'd automatically put his arm around my shoulder, asserting his rights and offering protection. It didn't bother me that other girls always looked at him a bit too long when we went out together; he only had eyes for me. When I had time, he painted me, tenderly, making me look more beautiful. "That's not me," I would say, waiting for the inevitable reply: "Yes, it is. That's you. In my eyes, at least."

•

One afternoon I picked him up at Simon's. The hepatitis was over but he was still too thin and a bit shaky.

I was helping him on with his coat when there was a loud, peremptory knock at the door. A female voice called fortissimo:

"Open the door, Simon, or aren't you alone?"

Simon turned to his son. "Your mother," he said reproachfully. "Wait," he muttered, searching for the fly. Garibalda's powerful voice came through the keyhole: "The hell with your damned flies or mice or frogs or whatever you've got now, we're freezing out here."

Simon had located the fly and was on his way to the door.

"We?" he exclaimed, appalled, dragging Garibalda into the room, accompanied by a tall, thin man wearing tweeds and a red checkered vest. "Who's this?"

Garibalda acted as though she had had no part in the undignified entrance and made the necessary introductions with a gesture straight out of *Turandot*.

"My ex-husband, my ex-son, his girl friend—Lord Springwell."

"How d'you do," said the thin man, with a slight movement of his head in the appropriate directions.

"Sit down," she continued, taking Jerome's armchair. His lordship sat down cautiously on a hassock, shooing away the fly, which was trying to make friends with him.

"Don't flap at him," warned Simon. "This is Clemens II. He's only one day old and still a little jumpy."

"How d'you do," said Springwell.

Simon picked up a little bowl of sugar water and approached them.

"Here, Clemens, here! There's a good boy. Isn't he incredible?"

Triumphantly he carried the bowl with the small black speck perched on it over to the windowsill.

"Garibalda, you look marvelous. To what do I owe the pleasure—"

"Hugh and I want to get married, and I'd like you to get to know each other."

I looked at Jerome questioningly. The pilot had obviously taken off, but what about her faithful Scotsman? In place of an answer, Jerome drew me down beside him on the floor. No one was paying any attention to us, but we had front-row seats.

"Well, well," said Simon, withdrawing behind his desk. "That certainly is good news—that is, provided . . ."

"Go ahead and ask him," said Garibalda, lighting a cigarette. She was one of the few singers who smoked. On stage too. I'd seen her in *Carmen,* singing the *"Habañera"* with a cigarette dangling from the corner of her mouth. A gasp had run through the house like a gentle breeze; everybody was whispering to his neighbor, "It's lighted!"

"Go ahead and ask," she repeated. "He's prepared."

"Well, well," drawled Simon thoughtfully. "Where do you buy your vests?"

"Fisher and Clogwell," said the thin man. "Thirteen Hanover Square, second floor left. Mr. Whittle."

Simon jotted down something on a scratch pad. He hated vests.

"But watch the back—they never make them long enough to suit me."

"Back," said Simon and scribbled some more. "I'm glad you warned me. Do you pay cash?"

"Of course not," said Springwell, shocked. "He bills me once a year."

"And one pays promptly?"

Springwell looked bewildered. Garibalda may have prepared him for the pet fly but not for such manifest lack of breeding.

"That would be a shock to him," he said icily. "One only pays when one changes tailors."

Simon, blithely unaware of the rebuke, nodded approval. "Garibalda, you have fallen into the hands of a gentleman. Have you any family?"

"A daughter from my first marriage."

"Pretty?"

"No."

"Then she'll need money."

"Don't worry. Garibalda will be well taken care of."

"How well?"

"Fifty thousand."

Simon stared pensively ahead. "Not good enough. Let's say seventy-five thousand and I'll give my consent."

A pause. Garibalda inhaled, rounded her lips and projected a perfectly rounded capital O into the room.

"Agreed," drawled Springwell.

"Where will you be living?"

"In Canada."

"Good Lord! Garibalda, you're giving up singing?"

"From now on she'll be singing for me alone—in the bathtub," cried the thin chap, bursting into surprisingly noisy laughter.

Garibalda remained silent and continued filling the room with those splendid smoke rings.

"Excellent," said Simon, standing up. "I herewith bestow my blessing on the happy pair. Er, Jerome—do you happen to have—get a bottle from your refrigerator."

"Very civil of you," said his lordship, visibly moved. "Let's have a drink."

"God forbid!" exclaimed Garibalda, pulling her husband-to-be to his feet. "You don't know the kind of wine he drinks, you'd never survive it. Now that you're friends, we can go. That's really all I wanted. Simon, we're leaving."

"Just a minute!" cried Simon. Then: "Okay, he's still sitting on his bowl. Quick now! All good wishes and *bon voyage!*"

"Goodbye, Mr. Lorrimer, it was a pleasure . . ." said Springwell, trying to shake hands with his host in spite of Garibalda steering him toward the door. She waved in our direction, blew a kiss to Simon and pulled Springwell, who was offering only token resistance, over the threshold. Exit.

"No one could say that you and your mother exactly dote on one another," said Simon after a short pause. "Can't you forgive and forget?"

"I'd be glad to forget her but she keeps getting into my field of vision. And as for forgiving, it's easy enough for you to talk, you only had to put up with her for a few years."

"As far as I remember, you too were parked out fairly early with the hired help."

"Best thing that ever happened to me," said Jerome, opening his refrigerator and taking out a bottle of red wine, ice-cold, but better ice-cold than missing.

Simon was watching him with the eyes of a greedy child, and Jerome smiled and filled two glasses. He handed one to his father and continued his train of thought.

"The going only got rough when she'd suddenly reappear and assert her rightful motherly demands. In her case, quite peculiar ones. For instance, whenever she sang Aïda, I had to appear promptly and shave her armpits. 'One expects a steady hand from a painter. What else is he good for?' she said, threatening me with the razor."

Simon laughed, his double chin wobbling up and down.

"She never wanted you, let's face it. You were a traffic accident. Cheers!"

"She was caught in a trap—she never really wanted a

husband, let alone a child. Can you blame her if she's not particularly attached to either of us?"

"You're mellow today because she's going to increase your allowance," said Jerome. And turning to me: "She has now finally received a papal annulment, solemnly proclaiming that her marriage never existed. Yet she knows something the Pope doesn't know, because she's a Sardinian peasant. Simon is and will always be her husband, and if she wants to marry again, she thinks she needs *his* gracious permission."

"And you?" I asked. "Where do you come in? Are you also annulled?"

"No," he said and kissed me. "I'm very much in existence, but I don't 'come in,' I'm not part of the show, I'm kept somewhere in the wings. Occasionally she lets me watch and applaud. The trouble is, I'm getting older as she gets younger. That's hard for her. And yet I know that tonight, for instance, the telephone will ring sometime, summoning me to her apartment. And she'll hug me and kiss me and for an hour she'll be 'Mamma.' That's the hardest part."

Simon stared at his son, but before he could say anything there was a single knock followed by three rapid ones. A hurried fly ritual, then he called, "Now!" and opened his desk drawer and extracted a huge, stained napkin, which he tucked into his collar below the double chin.

The door was kicked open, and a boy appeared with a tray, panting, his nose red with cold. He was balancing a steaming chafing dish set on a brass food warmer.

"Lobster thermidor," said Simon. "Jerome, do you happen to have . . ."

Jerome fished in his pocket for a sixpence for the boy, who disappeared in a flash. We too were already at the door.

"Goodbye, children," called Simon. "I deserve your deepest sympathy."

"Whatever for?" I asked, stopping in surprise.

"Because I'm going to have to drink chilled red wine with my lobster," said Simon, waving us on our way.

•

Diary, January 1938:

I look dreadful. I've lost five pounds. My hair's like straw and it's falling out. My face is so narrow, I could kiss a goat between its horns. My body's as thin as a sliver of soap. J. hates skinny women. "I'm thin myself," he says. "I want something I can get hold of. My ideal is a woman who would engulf me like a wave. Eat!"

That was yesterday afternoon. He was lying in bed, smoking. He's not really supposed to since the hepatitis but I didn't want to make a fuss. Alone with him again at last after six endless weeks! The flat was shining like a new pin—not that he'd ever notice! (I've got a new cleaning woman, Mrs. Cook, fat old broad, wheezing and snorting, but thorough. And fresh! When she passed J. on the stairs, she tapped him on the chest with her forefinger and said, "Have a good time, son.")

Afterward we talked about L., usually taboo. "I'm not the faithful type," he said. "I'm not a good friend or a good son either. My father thinks faithfulness is either lethargy or lack of imagination. Fidelity is plain pigheadedness, he used to tell me, it only means that you wear blinkers. Be a Renaissance man, he used to urge me when I was a child, keep your eyes open, be aware of everything that's going on around you, don't miss anything, and above all, never worry about consequences, just go ahead and do what you want. There'll always be somebody to clean up the mess after you're gone."

I was lying quite still next to him. It's rare for him to talk about himself. Who knows, there might be some sort of loophole in his stronghold where I might slip through—and stay!

"But . . ." And then came a long pause. My heart was pounding so hard in my throat and we were lying so close together that I was sure he'd feel it. "But what?" I finally asked. He turned toward me and looked at me in surprise as though he had waked up to find a stranger in bed with him. And at once he smiled that awful, sly, conspiratorial smile of his. "But what?" I insisted. He stroked my head and looked for a long time straight into my eyes. Then he said slowly and deliberately, "But I'd like to grow old with L. I'd like to die in her arms. What am I to do to make sure of that?" He asked *me* that! He expected an answer. Wanted *my* advice. To grow old with L.! The words crackled and banged around in my brain, wouldn't settle. To grow old with L. Is that a devastating criticism or is it love?

Both, if you ask me.

I couldn't contain myself any longer or I'd have suffocated. "And what about me? What's my place in your design for living?" "You? You have a very important place, you represent everything I don't like—and that's what I do like about myself. Do you understand what I'm getting at? If you were a cozy buxom Rubens with four breasts—like the one in the Louvre I love—instead of the highly charged electric eel that you are, it would all be quite commonplace, plain ordinary wish fulfilment. But the fact that I'm lying here beside *you* is a triumph for you. Besides, you're my guardian angel, my skinny guardian angel. I need you. You know I do."

The crackling inside my brain sounded as though a pile of plates had crashed to the floor. No loophole! Yet: "I need you." That's all I can hold on to. I pulled myself together and said, "Guardian angel is right. I protect you from other women.

And I protect L. too." "Against what?" he asked in surprise
and sat up. "Against you," I said. He lay down again, and
after a while he put his arms around me.

Guardian angel! Did I need a guardian angel? What I
needed was glasses!

My mother noticed something, even without glasses. One
day she was in the garden of our house in Hampstead watering the wallflowers I had planted to hide the fence.

"What's wrong with your friend Anabel?" she asked,
handing me the empty watering can.

"What do you mean, what's wrong with her?" I trotted
over to the spigot.

"Something's wrong," she called after me. "Haven't you
noticed how ill she looks?"

"She's—thin," I said, letting the water overflow.

"She's thin because some man's making her thin," said my
mother with quiet conviction.

I carted the full watering can over to the flower bed, full
of admiration for her intuition. When I tried to hand it over
to her she didn't take it from me.

"I know who it is, too," she said, folding her arms over
her chest. All of a sudden the watering can weighed a ton. I
had to set it down. Did my mother know Ferencsi?

"Can't you guess?" she asked, looking me straight in the
eye. I consulted my watch, picked up the watering can and
waved it back and forth over the wallflowers until it felt
lighter.

"You're wrong," I said, handing it to her. "Believe me,
you're absolutely wrong. I've got to go or I'll be late to the
theater."

"Drive carefully," she said and began to water the wallflowers.

·

Bill noticed something too. Once, after my performance, the four of us had met at the Four Hundred, a nightclub in Leicester Square. He had asked me for a dance, something he didn't often do. He danced well, but always with Anabel.

"Do you happen to know why my wife's so depressed?" he asked as we shuffled about on the tiny, overcrowded floor.

"Is she depressed?"

"Well, look at her." He jerked his chin in the direction of our table. Jerome and Anabel were sitting side by side in silence. Jerome, cigarette in mouth, was a hundred miles away; Anabel was supporting her head on her hand, staring over the heads of the dancing couples with unseeing eyes.

"Is she ill? She doesn't tell me anything. Does she talk to you?"

"Perhaps she's tired," I said. "Maybe she needs a vacation. She ought to come to Grasse with us and stay with our friends the Gurnemantzes at their peach farm. It would be a change for her, out of doors, working in the orchard, swimming in the sea . . ."

•

Take Anabel with us to the Gurnemantzes'! Bill had no objection, made plans to go sailing, and Nina wanted to spend her vacation with friends anyway. Jerome, however, was not enthusiastic. "She won't fit in," he said. "Can you imagine her sorting peaches and trekking to the market at night in that decrepit old buggy? Anabel?"

"You underestimate her," I said. "She's not a hothouse flower. I don't think you really know her."

And so in the summer of 1938 she went with us to Grasse. Peter put her to work without further ado, she was detailed picking peaches, learned to sort them and pack them, waited with us in the truck at the market, loved it all and swam with us in the sea.

Actually it was a good thing she was there, for something was brewing in the Gurnemantz household. Outwardly nothing had changed except that Peter was frantically building a garage (but why? For that ancient truck?), working at it until late at night. Ursula lay under an olive tree, glancing every now and again under half-closed eyelids at the peach orchard, where Eva was picking peaches all alone. In the daytime? In the hot sun?

We speculated about it in our guest room in the "thigh." Something was up—but what, exactly? It was all the more mysterious since there was no tension. On the contrary, the three of them were always throwing an arm around each other's shoulders, making affectionate noises.

Until, a week after our arrival, Ursula summoned us all to a "council meeting." That very evening, please, after supper. Was Anabel to come too? Yes.

We solemnly carried coffee, Pernod and fresh almonds out onto the terrace and lay down on our air mattresses. Ursula blew out the storm lanterns, then jumped up and crouched on the terrace wall, her lean, long body silhouetted jet-black against the star-studded night sky.

We waited, flat on our backs, staring up into the flickering chiaroscuro of the summer night until our tension and expectancy gradually melted away. We dozed. Silence, soft black silence. I fell asleep.

Suddenly somebody was gently tugging my sleeve. Anabel. And from far away, though gradually coming closer, I could hear Ursula's voice.

" . . . probably been wondering why I'm loafing around like this. Well, unfortunately I have no other choice. The doctor in Nice says it may take as long as a year to get completely well. Imagine! A full year! He told me something else, too—" She broke off. Then, speaking into the darkness: "My glass is empty."

A large black shape got up—Peter. A gurgling sound from the Pernod bottle, and he lay down again on his mattress.

After a brief pause Ursula's voice resumed, cool and factual. "I've got to give up what the silly old clot referred to as 'marital pleasures,' I'm supposed to rest. *Rester tranquille.* 'Are you out of your mind?' I asked him. 'Okay, suppose I manage to *rester tranquille*, what about my husband? Is he supposed to be *tranquille* for a whole year?' He was embarrassed, said this really wasn't his domain, and—well, there was a certain district in Nice to take care of things of that sort, '*Vous comprenez?*' 'Thanks so much, Doctor, how much do I owe you?' That didn't embarrass him at all, that was his domain all right. Well, Peter tried out the certain district. One morning, after the market, he dropped us off at the Negresco and drove on. To a different market. An hour later he picked us up at the beach. We were all pretty grim on the way home, and the first thing Peter did was jump into the water cistern."

She paused. No one said a word.

"That's when I thought of Eva. It's important that you remember that *I* was the one who thought of Eva, no one else. She's always been a part of us, right from the beginning. She's shared everything with us except—well, you know. So why not close the gap? I don't believe anything will change radically. Peter agrees. Tell them, Peter."

Out of the darkness came his deep voice: "I agree."

"It's important to me that you all hear this, so that nobody could later on—" She broke off, couldn't keep up the matter-of-factness, sounded suddenly defenseless, even imploring. After a few seconds she regained control and concluded briefly: "Eva has some reservations. Tell them, Eva."

From the farthest corner of the terrace Eva's chirpy little voice piped up promptly. She had just celebrated her twen-

tieth birthday and greatly enjoyed being the center of atten-
ton.

"I have reservations because it's immoral."

"Why?" Jerome's voice, obviously interested.

"Why? Because Peter's my sister's husband. Otherwise I
wouldn't have any objection. I'm no virgin, I'm experienced."

Jerome cleared his throat.

"Under ancient Jewish law," said Ursula quietly, "such a
thing wouldn't have been immoral at all. In fact, the husband
had a sort of first option on the younger sister—"

"Only after his wife was dead," Eva cried heatedly.

"I *am* dead," said Ursula calmly. "And I'll remain dead
for a whole year. Then I'll rise again." Silence. "I called you
together for a council meeting. You two know us, and that's
an advantage. Anabel doesn't know us, and that's an advantage too. What do you think of my proposal?"

Jerome's voice was the first to break through the darkness.

"The most important thing is that Peter shouldn't have to
jump into the water cistern anymore. Every situation spells
out its morality. Why did the ancient Jews give the widower
an option on the sister? Because sisters are often alike, they
often have the same kind of skin, similar hair, a similar
smell. So if the husband's got himself acclimatized to one
sister, he might as well have a go at the other."

"Nonsense," said Ursula. "It was to keep the dowry in the
family."

"Both," muttered Peter. "Both solid reasoning."

"Wait a minute!" I exclaimed, sitting up because I
couldn't stay down any longer. "Are you all insane? What's
going to happen afterward, when Ursula's well again? How
can you ever undo that sort of thing?"

"Undo it?" repeated Jerome, trying unsuccessfully to pull
me down onto my mattress. "Why on earth should they

want to undo it? All this could be a marvelous new source of experience, enrichment . . . "

"Very dangerous!" I shouted a bit too loudly; the darkness intensified every sound.

"Why always play safe?"

Silence again. Sounds of one or the other sitting up. The Pernod bottle gurgled again, and the silhouette on the wall moved too.

"What does our guest have to say?"

Anabel, next to me, had remained quite still on her mattress. Without any hesitation or embarrassment she said quietly, "Playing it safe is never any good. 'Afterward' will bring its own solution. The problem is 'now.' As I see it, the decisive factor is that it's Ursula's idea. You three will never lose each other."

"Cheers!" said Peter.

Ursula climbed down from the wall and lay down by his side. He put his arm around her and gave her a drink of Pernod from his glass.

The council meeting adjourned.

14

She didn't take the diary with her to Grasse. Too dangerous. There were no entries until after we returned.

First entry, September 1938:

Played at being a peasant for six weeks. Close to the soil, the smell of leaves in my nostrils, dirt under my fingernails, my brain gummed up with resin. Gained five pounds. Picking peaches. For hours at a time, until that silly animal came trotting up, gaping at me reproachfully with its big donkey eyes. I'd stick my best peach in his mouth and he'd look amazed and trot off and then I could keep watch through the tangle of branches trying to get a glimpse of Jerome, way off in the distance. Now and then I'd catch sight of a black patch of hair or the tanned arm I knew so well. Meant a great deal to me. Just to feel him close by, to sit opposite him at meals. Better than staying home, crying, like last year. Not once did he come anywhere near me alone. Selected his blasted peach trees rows and rows away from mine.

L. on the other hand would often come and visit with me while we were picking. Helped me fill my baskets. Showed me time and again how to twist the damned things off, declaring passionately, "Just feel how hot they are. You can smell the sun!"

The Gurnemantz threesome—quite interesting! Especially one of the girls, the older one. She is Electra; mourning distinctly becomes her. No fool. Senses everything, catches on at once. I had to watch my step. Had the feeling that she had sniffed the air a couple of times in my direction—and guessed! Was therefore doubly careful with J. The younger sister is nothing much. Just young. Bursting with health. Iphigenia. Even though she is very proud of not being a virgin anymore. That won't save her from being sacrificed, though. First to her dear brother-in-law. Later on—catastrophe. They'll end up loathing each other, all three of them. Of course, what I said aloud was just the opposite. Proclaimed in Delphic tones, "You three will never lose each other." And I have a feeling the process has already begun. Soon they'll be snarling at each other. Perfect harmony *à trois*, the harmony they so bravely dream about, just doesn't hold for any length of time in the cold light of day. Nor in secrecy either—like L. and J. and me.

And now, at long long last, back in London and back in the old groove. Apartment sparkling clean. Mrs. Cook a jewel.

L. rehearsing a new play. As enthusiastic as ever. Could be this time with some justification. What a blessing a long run would be! For her as well as for us.

The blessing came to pass. My first real success. The play was called *Little Ladyship*. It presented me with a juicy role —and a dislocated shoulder. During the tryout in Edinburgh. On stage. I was running down a flight of stairs, slipped halfway down and banged my elbow against the banister. I didn't fall but remained stiffly upright where I was. My right arm hung limply somewhere behind me, twisted slightly sideways, and refused to obey my command to get back into place forthwith. It seemed to have declared its independence. This surprising fact was the last coherent thought in my mind before I was enveloped in whirling darkness.

When I came to in my dressing room, yelling vigorously, they were cutting my dress off my body and a gentleman I had never seen before was bending over me. Apparently the curtain had been rung down in a hurry and three separate physicians had responded to the stage manager's anxious appeal: "Is there a doctor in the house?" As soon as the strange gentleman had diagnosed a dislocated shoulder, I was rushed to the hospital, put to sleep, and my recalcitrant arm encased in a plaster cast.

Sometimes it popped out again—and back in, and I learned to handle it. Once when I was standing on a chair in the painter's studio, reaching for a bottle of turpentine on a shelf, I fell with the chair and the bottle on top of me. To her astonishment I rolled over on my stomach, howling, and pressed my right shoulder hard against the floor. Crrrack—and it was back in place again.

•

Strange weeks. The same schedule almost every day, as if I were back at school. Now there were daily and regular hours at the painter's to make sure that she took her medicine, to shop for her and see that she ate something. The doctor had made it clear that such were my duties for the time being. She was the only patient he enjoyed, he told me. Actually she was well again, but he kept finding excuses to visit her, though he never sent her a bill. She saw through his "solicitude," went along with it, and gave him a water color.

And every single evening I would reach for the diary,

even on the rare occasions when I came home late. I couldn't go to bed until I'd read at least one entry. It had become part of the daily schedule, and I couldn't make up my mind if it was now a sacred duty or a compulsion or even an addiction. At any rate it forced me to relive those three years almost day by day and thus uproot and then liquidate all my previous (and deliberately blinkered) memories of that time. Turning the pages I was either silently nodding in reluctant agreement or shaking my head in furious and belated recognition, until I would close the book for the night and slink off to bed shaken and undone—and always enslaved. I led a double life during those weeks, my daily prosaic existence and my former one, the diary one. That one appeared to me somewhat suspended in midair, dislocated, and quite independent of my will. Like my shoulder. And as with my shoulder, the first impact had been devastating, too agonizing to bear without some kind of painkiller, but gradually I had gotten used to it, the bits and pieces fell into place—and now I even had a nightly craving for it.

Every now and again I still felt a twinge of pain. Then I'd close the book, switch off the light and have it out with Anabel, with Jerome and with myself.

•

The painter was sitting at the easel studying my portrait when I came in with my shopping bag. "I'm still not up to it," she said, without turning around. "I don't know why. I'm quite well, but nothing clicks inside."

I took off my coat.

"Shall I take the pose? It might do it."

"I don't think so. I can't see anything except colors and lines. No patterns, no plan, all running wild."

"Mozart?"

"I'm sick of Mozart."

I took the pot of soup out of the shopping bag, set it down and reached for my coat. She turned around.

"I'll make coffee." In other words: I don't want to be alone.

The kitchen was spotless now, the bedroom heated, and the bedding back on the bed. I had engaged a Spanish cleaning woman who came for two hours a day and cheerfully put up with the painter's grumbling and growling since she couldn't understand her polemics. The only place she wasn't allowed to touch was the studio, and the dust accumulated on the canvases. "That's good, it gives them patina," said the painter.

While she was heating the soup, I took a half-bottle of red wine, a corkscrew and a napkin out of the shopping bag, collected her glass from the bathroom, cleaned it, drew the cork and set the table. Today she needed some wine, no matter what the doctor said.

She appeared in the doorway with the tray and stopped in surprise when she saw the bottle. I took the tray from her and pulled her down on the chair, using force to spread a napkin on her lap.

"Napkin," she said contemptuously. "Reminds me of my mother. All that damned ritual. You think I don't know about that? I was brought up as a precious jewel soaked in loving affection, the real article, you know, no phony stuff. Plus splendid examples set by my father and mother of the right kind of behavior and the right kind of manners. They did a good job, it certainly took with me, and I had a hell of a time getting rid of them—the good behavior and the manners, I mean. They cling to one like a permanent illness. When things go wrong, you run to your good manners and you think you find solace by 'behaving well.' A drastic withdrawal cure was the only thing that saved me. After that my work began at last to buzz and to crackle."

This unexpected outburst contained more words than all the ones strung together that she had ever addressed to me since I first met her.

"Eat. It's getting cold." I sat down in the corner on my hassock.

She ate. "It takes a great effort to go to pot when you've been well brought up. At home everything was so—so right, so solid. No cheating, no flimflam, no false facades. Everything was the genuine article. My father, my mother—they were genuine too."

"Were you the only child?"

"Yes. That was the trouble."

She ate her soup in silence, drank the wine and grunted contentedly.

"Is there any more? I know, I'm not supposed to, but . . ."

I brought the bottle and she filled her glass and drained it slowly.

"And you, too, you'll never amount to anything if you don't learn to be less level-headed. You are level-headed—I can smell it, and it's death. Death to anything connected with art. And you are an artist, after all."

"I'm not sure. I have to labor for everything."

"Nothing wrong with that." She poured the rest of the wine. "Labor is always good, even if you're a genius. Genius is mostly hard labor. Did you know that? Obsessive hard labor. Are you obsessed?"

"Sometimes."

"That's not enough. You ought to be obsessed *all* the time."

The wine had taken effect quickly. All that medication had made her vulnerable.

"I'll try," I said and stood up to take her plate back to the kitchen. "Dirty plates stink."

"There you go again," she said fiercely. "What's wrong with stink? You're squeamish and orderly, like my mother. Her last request, on her deathbed, five minutes before she died, was for a toothbrush to clean her teeth."

I put the plate down and moved my hassock close to her chair. She leaned back and took off her glasses and I could see quite clearly how she must have looked when she first arrived in Paris, young, sturdy, but thin-skinned and lonely. She felt with her hand for the familiar pack of Gauloises, remembered that she wasn't allowed to smoke, fidgeted, and finally folded her hands to keep them still.

I waited until her gaze came to rest on me, then took a chance.

"How was it with you? Congenital? Didn't you like boys even when you were a child?"

"I certainly did. I liked them a lot."

"When did you change? In Paris?"

"No. Long before. In Rouen. I was still at school." Silence. After a while she spoke again, more to herself than to me. "I can't be absolutely sure, of course. Who knows how it might have turned out if it hadn't been for that?"

"For what?"

She settled even farther back into her chair, lying rather than sitting, staring at the ceiling without moving. "For what?" I asked again. She took her time.

"I'd just been confirmed. He was sitting on a bench in the park."

"Who was?"

"He was. That was the first time I ever saw him. The day after my confirmation, on the way home from school. There was a little lake, with ducks and weeping willows. A bench. Usually empty because it was so damp there. I used to catch frogs there when I was small. He was sitting on the bench, feeding the ducks. They came waddling out of the lake and quacked around him. He was talking to them, and now and again he'd try to stroke one of them. Then they'd squawk and run away, but they soon came waddling back again. We stopped and watched, two girl friends and I—we always walked part of the way home together. Next day there he was again, feeding the ducks. He waved to us. The day after, he wasn't there, but the following week we saw him from a distance and ran up to him. He was very tall and his hair was white at the temples. At school we could talk of nothing else, and we combed our hair and tied each other's ribbons before we set out for home. He let us sit by him on the bench and talked to us, calling us *'kleines Fräulein'* and using the grown-up *Sie* rather than the childish *du*. He asked about our parents, about school, wanted to know what we were studying and how old we were. I was the oldest, almost sixteen, the others a few months younger. He was particularly nice to me, and they noticed it, of course. One day they told me they weren't walking through the park anymore and I could have him all to myself. From then on I went home alone. Every day I prayed that he'd be sitting on the bench. Two or three times a week he'd be there and I did have him to myself for ten minutes—no longer or they'd have asked questions at home. He told me he was a retired army officer. He looked like one too, distinguished, and very elegant and precise in his movements, and polite and reserved. I hadn't mentioned him to my parents, and my girl friends weren't speaking to me. I didn't care. Things went on that way for about a month and then one day I told him tomorrow would be my sixteenth birthday—a great day, I would legally be an adult then, and my parents were planning a little party for our relatives and friends. 'What time?' he asked. 'About six. Why?' Did he want to come too? No, he had something else in mind, he would like to give me a birthday party too. His mother would bake me a cake and there would be a special surprise. He wrote down his address. I knew the house, not far from ours. He lived with his mother, they'd be expecting me for coffee and birthday cake at five o'clock."

She got up abruptly, searching for her Gauloises. I didn't dare to protest, because she looked as though she needed one. She inhaled deeply, returned to her chair, stretched out and stared at the ceiling.

"What a night I spent, the night before my birthday! Only a child can get into such a state! Juliet's age. Shakespeare wrote about other lovers too, but never again about another fourteen-year-old. For good reason. Of course I wasn't an Italian girl, I was really only a child. All I dreamed of was to be allowed to sit beside him and look at him. Maybe hold his hand. Maybe—maybe kiss him. But that was going almost too far. The idea of meeting his mother, being allowed into his house, his living room—I stayed awake half the night.

"Early next morning there was a birthday celebration at home before I left for school. My father made a little speech, he had tears in his eyes as he hung my great-grandmother's pearls around my neck. My mother brought in her present, holding it carefully over her arm: a white batiste dress trimmed with lace and white satin bows, the sort of thing girls wore in those days, delicate as a soap bubble. At school, the class sang "Happy Birthday" and in honor of the occasion I made up with my two girl friends. Today, we decided, we'd all three walk through the park like old times and say hello to him—but the bench was empty. We hung around for a while, as disappointed as the ducks quacking around us. I didn't say a word about the invitation—they might have wanted to accompany me.

"At five o'clock sharp I was at his house, one of the city's seventeenth-century buildings. I was wearing my new dress, hadn't even dared to sit down at home for fear of wrinkling it. White shoes and stockings. I had told my parents some tale about a birthday party a friend was giving for me and had promised I'd be back in time for the family celebration.

"I let two minutes pass for the sake of good manners, then I rang the bell. I could hear it ringing inside the house. Silence. Good God—he couldn't have forgotten, could he? At last I heard steps and breathed again. The massive old door opened and there he stood, smiling at me, kissed my hand 'in honor of my sixteenth birthday' and led the way through the front hall and into the living room. A large, dark room full of heavy oak furniture. I couldn't see it very clearly, since the curtains were drawn, although it was still daylight outside. 'It's more festive that way,' he explained in answer to my question, pointing to the table. And there, on a white tablecloth, stood a magnificent cake with sixteen candles, the only source of light in the room.

" 'How kind of your mother!' I exclaimed. 'Where is she? I must thank her.'

" 'She'll be here in a minute,' he said. 'She's in the kitchen making coffee—it's the cook's day off. Come along now, make a wish and then you must blow out all sixteen candles in one breath and your wish will come true.' He took my hand and led me to the table. My head swam. What could I possibly wish for when my heart had everything it desired? Dimly my brain formulated something like an absurd wish to remain for the rest of my life as blissfully happy as I was at that moment. Then I took a deep breath and blew out all the candles. Suddenly it was pitch dark. 'Please turn the lights on!' I called out. 'Where's the switch?' 'Here,' he said in a voice I'd never heard before. 'Give me your hand.' I groped blindly in his direction and felt his hand close over mine. With one shove he threw me down on the floor. I screamed with fright, thinking it was an accident, and tried to get up.

But he was already on top of me, pinning my shoulders against the floor with his full weight. My dress! I thought. My dress! On the dirty floor! 'What are you doing?' I shouted. 'Let me get up. Let go of me!' And all at once I realized what was going to happen, because I could feel his hands tearing at my skirt. 'Help!' I screamed. 'Mother! Mother!' I was calling his mother as well as mine.

"And then something frightening occurred. He relaxed his grip for a moment. I could feel his breath on my face and heard his hoarse voice quite close to my ear, tough and vicious. Nobody had ever spoken to me in such a voice before. 'Shut up, you stupid cow. There's no mother here.'

"From then on I offered no resistance, it was as if I were paralyzed. I screamed. I don't know for how long. Suddenly he was gone, but I can't remember hearing him leave. I was alone in the pitch darkness. I tried to get on my feet, but I fell down again, bumping into a piece of furniture. I didn't dare make a sound for fear he'd come back. I groped around until I found a wall, then a door. The hallway was dimly lighted. I saw a large mirror but turned my head away; I couldn't bear to see my hair in a mess and my white dress crushed and torn. All I wanted was to get away, out of the house, quickly, quickly, before he could grab me again.

"I had some trouble opening the heavy door. There wasn't a sound from inside the house. And suddenly I was standing outside in the street in bright sunlight. Fortunately there were not many people about. I ran, pressing myself close to the buildings, until I came to the corner, when I heard someone behind me calling: 'Whatever's the matter, child?' I ran all the faster, crossed the road right in front of a street-car and heard another voice: 'What on earth has happened to you?' I ran and ran and ran and finally I got to our house.

"I didn't wait for the elevator, I climbed the stairs to our apartment step by step. Every step hurt. But I made it, and I finally stood in front of our door and heard voices and laughter and the chinking of plates. I waited. Inside, a door closed and the voices grew fainter. I rang—I still had no key of my own. And then I realized that our maid would be serving the coffee and that my mother would open the door herself.

"Too late. There she was, her eyes laughing and welcoming, her mouth open and ready to say: 'Well, here you are at last, we've all been waiting for you . . .'

"Then she saw me and turned pale.

" 'What in God's name . . .' she gasped.

"I walked past her and made it to my bedroom door, hoping to get to the bed, but the carpet came up to meet me.

"I was out for a few minutes only, because, when I came to, my mother was kneeling on the carpet beside me, holding a bowl of cold water. 'Have you been run over?' she gasped, her eyes wide open in terror. I struggled to get up. She unbuttoned my dress and gave a loud cry. She'd seen the bloodstains."

•

Her voice had grown more and more husky, and I couldn't quite catch everything she said. Suddenly she stood up, extended both arms sideways as if she were doing her morning exercises and yawned loudly.

"Are you still awake?" she asked. "I've almost talked myself to sleep."

I was wide awake, I said, and I simply had to know what happened to the man. Jail?

"Jail, hell," she said, looking for her throat spray. She opened her mouth wide and sprayed. "Grrr. I was legally of age as of that day. That's what he'd been waiting for. Grrr.

Grrrrr. All the same, my father wanted to kill him. It's a good thing he wasn't to be found. Of course, the house didn't belong to him—he was the caretaker and the owners had left their keys with him while they were on vacation. Grrr . . ." She shook the spray. "Empty."

"Did it take you a long time to—to get back to normal?"

"To normal? A lot of people would tell you I'm not normal even now. My parents took me on a long trip to Italy and Greece, everybody who 'knew' spoke to me in a soft voice as if I might break apart, but by the time we got back to Rouen, I was really in pretty good shape. I could laugh again and I'd even gained some weight. Though three or four years later—my father had died in the meantime—when my girl friends were having their first love affairs or getting married, I simply couldn't go along with it all. Couldn't stand looking every day at my mother's unhappy face. So I dropped out of medical school and took off for Paris. Other people had worse things happen to them. That's my life, and that's all there is to it. Tomorrow we'll start work again, ten o'clock sharp."

15

My first portrait sitting in three weeks, and the painter was too nervous even to say hello. She sat in front of the easel like a clod, stared and stared, jumped up, put on a Mozart record, stared again, and at long last turned toward me, though her imploring eyes didn't really take *me* in, they were firmly embedded in her own and purely arbitrary guidebook to my face. She was hunting for traces of the path she'd been pursuing before her illness, and she was terrified that she might not recognize the signposts.

I sat completely still, intent on helping her by concentrating on "something definite." That was easy nowadays—so many scenes emerged, unbidden, from the past that the problem was rather to get rid of them. There appeared, for instance, a view of Jerome and me in our tiny kitchen, getting breakfast ready. I was piling plates and cups on a tray, my mind on Anabel. Since I had found her crying on the floor, everything was changed; now it was she who needed my protection and solicitude. Protection against outside interference and possible suspicion and solicitude for her state of mind.

"He's torturing her," I said, thinking aloud. "The son of a bitch has a guilty conscience toward his wife and children and he's taking it out on Anabel. I have a feeling he's the type of man who doesn't mind tormenting people."

"Maybe that's what she likes," said Jerome, carrying the tray into the studio. Since my success in *Little Ladyship*, it now boasted a table and two chairs.

"She says he's in London right now. I wouldn't mind telling him a thing or two."

"What would you say to him?" Jerome spread butter and honey on his roll.

"I'd tell him to leave her in peace. I'd tell him that he's ruining her life."

"What makes you so sure he's ruining it? Was she any happier before she met him?"

I stared deeply into my coffee cup as if it could provide the answer to this difficult question. Happier? With Bill and Nina? Jerome lighted a cigarette, watching me without his customary smile, his narrow black eyes deeper than ever under the heavy brows, and an unshaven hollow under the sharp edge of the cheekbones. That's what he'll look like when he's old, I thought to myself. Not like his father or his mother, both conspicuously and oppressively manifest, but like a nomad, inscrutable, shadowy, unsmiling.

"Well?" he insisted. "Was she happier before?"

"Probably not. All the same, I'd like a word with him. He doesn't have to make her suffer, does he? Why can't he be—well, nicer to her?"

"Like Bill, you mean?"

I piled the plates on the tray and carried them back to the kitchen, calling through the open door, "Maybe one day I'll tail her."

Jerome appeared in the doorway, cigarette in mouth, and

watched me washing the dishes. He took a towel and started to dry them.

"Don't," he said calmly. "One shouldn't poke one's nose into other people's secrets."

"Even when it's a friend you love?"

"Particularly then."

•

"Break," said the painter, heaving a deep sigh. She got up and wiped her sweaty brow with her sleeve. "Not bad," she said. "Not at all bad."

I stretched. I hadn't noticed that fifteen minutes had elapsed. I was still standing in our little kitchen, handing the dripping plates to Jerome.

The painter brought in the coffee, found her Gauloises and gave me a look that was almost affectionate.

"I 'm back. Right back. It's crackling again."

She poured herself a cup of coffee, held it in front of her eyes and contemplated her shaking hand and paint-stained fingers.

"That's enough for today, or I might ruin it. But it's still all there, that's all I wanted to know. Ten o'clock tomorrow, okay?"

•

Diary, March 23:

L.'s filming during the day. In the evening she's at the theater. She's so tired that she prefers to sleep at her mother's in her old room, in what I call the nursery. She says her mother looks after her, leaves a dish of applesauce by her bed at night, gets breakfast for her at six a.m. She couldn't ask that of Jerome. True. No one can ask anything of Jerome. He gives what he thinks he should give. But that doesn't mean that he gives what one needs. L. knows this. Never demands anything of him. Wise! Whereas I demand. I demand that he make an effort to come to our apartment even when it doesn't suit him. Because *I* need it. He doesn't respond to that, remains deaf. Today, for instance. Today I needed to be with him, to lie beside him, his arms around me, my arms around him. Today's our anniversary. Two years ago today—by the boathouse in Regent's Park. Two years! The other day I added up all the hours we've spent alone together and it comes to no more than five hundred. A little over twenty days. Haven't had him to myself even for one single month. Can one live like this?

I called him up and said, "Happy birthday!" He said not to bother him with crap like that while he's working. I hung up. Nina happened to come into the room just at that moment. Didn't ask any questions, just looked at me and went out again. So what.

Tried to think of something, anything, some way to celebrate. Hit on a crazy idea. Went to see Simon.

What? I read the sentence again:

Went to see Simon.

So she did meet Simon! I had no idea. She knew Simon! That explained a lot of things.

Just dropped in. Knew he'd be home. Had to be near something that belongs to J. In any case, have been wanting to meet him for a long time. J. always refused point-blank. Knocked cautiously at the door and waited. That business with the fly. But he called out right away, "Come in!"—doesn't have a fly at the moment. Instead he has a creature called an axolotl, a

kind of pink lizard with a flat head, as if somebody had stepped
on it. Keeps it in a goldfish bowl.

When I introduced myself, he was first surprised and then
delighted. Apparently he knew all about me. J. has told him,
he said. I wonder why? J. always says Simon's not to be
trusted. More likely he hasn't told him anything and Simon
just put two and two together. I'd brought him a bottle of
brandy and he couldn't wait to open it. I kept up with him for
a couple of glasses, I needed encouraging—or company, or
some sort of trampoline. Something to stop me spinning around
my own axis like a top. He knew right away why I'd come,
so didn't have to explain anything. He's not very fond of L.
Said she's not his type, and that he's surprised at his son. L.
doesn't fit into the family. But she's useful, he said, let her
keep on being useful. Her matinees are useful too—"Aren't
they, Anabel? I may call you Anabel, mayn't I?" Suddenly he
looked like a crocodile. "No," I said. "You may not." He
laughed as innocently and naturally as a small boy, took my
hand with *grandezza* and kissed it respectfully. I didn't know
anymore where I stood with him. He poured us both another
cognac. Fool that I am, I drank it, and much too quickly.
Suddenly I banged my fist on his desk and said, "Stop making
trouble between L. and Jerome, will you?" He burst out
laughing again until he choked, and his eyes watered. "And
what about you, dear?" he said. "What are you making?" I
stood up and leaned across the desk until my face was quite
close to his. I really wanted to spit in his face. But I couldn't.
My mouth was too dry. Realized I was about to burst into
tears. So I began to yell at the top of my voice—can't
remember what exactly, very longwinded, not very coherent,
something about being well aware that I meant nothing to J.,
that I was on the receiving end of all that was bad in him while
he was the beneficiary of all that was good in me, that I felt it
would soon be over, that it was two years ago today, that I

had never tried to take him away from L.—on the contrary,
that I knew I was exactly what J. needed in order to be happy
with L., and if it weren't for me, they'd be in trouble all right.
That did it. I was exhausted all of a sudden, and deflated, and
sat down.

All through my screaming, that fat barrel organ of a man
kept staring at me openmouthed while his double chin
wobbled up and down like other people's Adam's apples.
"You're the only *woman* I've ever met who knows
where she stands," he said at last. "Take me, for instance. I'm
a bastard; I know it and I take pleasure in it. But I'm an
absolutely honest man and I decline all responsibilities that
don't fit into my life style. My flies fit in, one-day flies, four- or
five-day flies at most. But marriage, fatherhood, friendship,
possessions—they're only impediments. They all entail
obligations, and that's a dirty word in my vocabulary. Thank
God, there are hordes of people around who vie with one
another in order to be responsible for somebody or something.
Only then do they feel grown up. Now, where would all those
people be if it weren't for me? I allow them to be concerned
about me, to boost their moral ego at my expense. I could
furnish a *raison d'être* for an entire Salvation Army."

"You're dripping with brotherly love," I said, getting up.

"Oh, don't go, Anabel!" he exclaimed. "Will you stop
calling me Anabel!" I said.

He pretended not to have heard. "My son doesn't know
what a treasure he has in you, he's still wet behind the ears, no
backbone, no line of his own . . ." And all the while he was
trying to push me toward the sofa, that great colossus—and
me not too steady on my pins, though still faster than he was. I
grabbed the table lamp and he let go of me and laughed—
reminding me suddenly of J., for the first time—and
retreated behind his desk. Said it was all in fun. Only then did
I put the lamp down. Must have been pretty plastered, because

I remember asking if he could recollect the last time he had cried. He thought very seriously but couldn't remember. Said he thought it must have been when he was about ten and lost his first watch.

I picked up my coat and stopped on my way to look at the bowl with the axolotl in it. It was floating motionless, midway between the surface and the bottom, its hands, minute human hands, spread out, ogling me out of its round eyes. On its flat, bald head was a little ring of red spikes, like a crown. "He looks as if he's been dead for a long time," I said, at which Simon hurriedly ambled over. "Doesn't he, though? That's what I love about him. He may be dead for all I know, or he may be in the pink. I feed him regularly—that is, I dangle a tiny bit of meat in front of him as if it were alive, but he never snaps at it, just lets it sink gently to the bottom. Sometimes it gets caught in his crown but he doesn't deign to notice. He never eats in my presence. He's either a snob—or he's dead."

I feel a certain resemblance to that animal.

That was the last entry until May 1939. Inexplicably, for six long months she hadn't written a word. Suddenly, on May 25:

For Christ's sake, I can't be . . .

On June 1:

I am.

.

So it must have been early in June that she showed up in my dressing room between the matinee and the evening performance. She would do this occasionally when I was too tired to drive to her house during the interval, for I was filming at the same time. That meant that except on matinee days, I spent the day at the studio and the evening at the theater. I raced back and forth, changing costume in the car, tearing my wigs off, nervously looking at the time, arriving everywhere at the last minute, and getting dirty looks from everyone. There was no choice, though. "Strike your neighbor while he's hot," we used to say at school. Well, at long last it looked as if my neighbor was hot and waiting to be struck. It was only a question of holding on for another month and then—vacation, Gurnemantz vacation, with Jerome and Anabel. During the last few weeks I didn't even have the time to see the people I loved. No more Sunday drives with Anabel—I spent my Sundays sleeping and got up only for an occasional dinner at her house, accompanied by Jerome. And every time I thought Anabel looked pale and thin. Bill was thin too, even Nina was thinner. Maybe it was my imagination, or something wrong with my eyesight. Like El Greco.

On that June day she sat on the visitor's chair in my dressing room and watched in silence as Maudie, my dresser, helped me out of my costume and into the old makeup bathrobe, and covered the tray of sandwiches and orange juice with a napkin. "Go to sleep," she said, significantly wagging her finger at Anabel as she left the room.

"I'm going," said Anabel. She stood up and switched off the light. I made no effort to stop her; I simply had to get some sleep before the evening performance. "Bye-bye, darling," I said with a yawn and turned my face to the wall. Silence. No sound of a door opening or closing. I turned around again and peered through the darkness. There was the outline of a limp hand hanging over the back of the visitor's chair.

"What's the matter?" I cried, sitting up and groping for the light switch. She looked green in the face, there was sweat on her forehead and her eyes were closed; her breath came convulsively through tightly compressed lips.

"Anabel! What on earth's the matter?"

"I feel sick," she whispered.

"Do you want a glass of water?"

She shook her head. "Give me a minute—I feel terribly sick—yesterday too—and the day before."

Wide awake, I knelt beside her chair.

"Something you've eaten? Think back. Do you have a pain in your stomach?"

She opened her eyes, twisted her face into a faint smile.

"For a doctor's daughter—you're pretty dense."

I understood and involuntarily drew back.

"Ferencsi?"

She didn't consider it worth the effort to answer.

"Oh, my God! What on earth—do you want to keep it?"

The raven eyes turned slowly toward me. They had never looked so diabolically black before.

"Do I want to?" The eyes searched my face, as if seeking a solution there. I met them helplessly, tried to muster a cheerful smile to make sure she knew that she had my support no matter what she was going to do. Her eyes grew dull, as if she had switched off the light.

"Do I want to?" she repeated again. "That isn't the point."

I didn't have to ask what the point was. Ferencsi was married in the Catholic church; a divorce was out of the question, she had told me that right at the start. Should she leave Bill and Nina and have Ferencsi's child somewhere in secret? And then what? As if in answer to my thoughts, she said, "Of course, he doesn't know about it. If he did, he'd never see me again. In any case I have a feeling it's only a matter of time."

"So you want to get rid of it?"

"Yesterday I went to see Mildman, our doctor. He confirmed it. He also made it clear that he has no sympathy whatever for the situation."

"How does he know—"

"That it's not Bill's? He knows I haven't slept with Bill for years. Bill once asked his advice. They went to school together."

I got up.

"Do you feel a bit better? Can you walk?"

She managed to stand up by holding onto the dressing table, but she still looked very white.

"Come on, we're going to see *my* doctor. He's a refugee, used to practice in Berlin, where he was official doctor for the British Embassy women. He knew my father, although he's younger. I think—I can't promise—but I think he'll help you. In the first place, he doesn't know you, and I'll introduce you as Miss So and So and say you haven't got the money to bring up a child and you'd lose your job. In the second place, he has a sense of humor. I once went to see him and told him about Jerome and he asked me in a fatherly way if I was 'being careful.' 'Well, I'm trying,' I said, 'but it takes a while to get used to driving on the left.' He laughed so much he couldn't speak for a while and just patted my head. He's had a soft spot for me ever since. Come on. Let's see if he's still at his consulting room."

·

Dr. Lauter's Harley Street waiting room was full, but his receptionist said she'd "squeeze me in" since I only wanted to ask him a question and had to rush back to the theater. Anabel had remained outside in the taxi.

Lauter, washing his hands, greeted me with the usual inquiry as to how I was making out with driving on the left. I laughed heartily for Anabel's sake and came straight to the point: I had a friend, my one and only girl friend. In trouble. I'd pay all the expenses. This idea came to me spontaneously as I was speaking, and I felt sure it would sound more convincing and perhaps more appealing and noble on my part. The doctor stopped laughing. He sat down behind his desk, rested his chin on his hand and sighed.

"I never thought that *you* would come to me for that. Every day people pester me with exactly the same story. And I refuse them all. Categorically. Every time. Why should I jeopardize my existence and that of my family just because some silly kid can't—"

He broke off, so I took the risk of finishing his sentence with: ". . . can't get used to driving on the left?" And he couldn't help grinning, his anger gone.

"Unmarried, you say? And the man won't—the old story. And no money either."

"She's—a kindergarten teacher."

"That too! And you're being noble and offering to pay for it? Out of the question. You're not exactly affluent all of a sudden, are you?" I felt neither appealing nor noble anymore. "So if I do it—mind you, I'm saying *if*—it won't be at the hospital but here in my office. After six. She'll have to take a taxi home. And it won't be any fun for her, I can tell you that. Call me tomorrow evening. At home. I want to think it over."

"Dr. Lauter—thank you!"

"Nothing to thank me for yet," he snapped. "I haven't promised anything."

I walked toward the door.

"How's what's-his-name—your boy friend?"

"Jerome. He's fine."

Some time before we had happened to be sitting next to each other at a movie and he'd had a long conversation with Jerome afterward and seemed to like him.

Anger suddenly flared again behind his glasses.

"Let me tell you one thing, so you won't ever come here to ask. You've used up all your credit with me. I'm not going to abort any child of what's-his-name's—eh, Jerome's. Let's get that clear."

•

In the evening I called Dr. Lauter from the theater. Might "Miss Shelling" come and see him after office hours? "Yes— for an examination," said a testy voice. "And then perhaps— next Friday. I'll see. And if . . . then you'll have to wait in the waiting room and take her home. She can't go alone."

"But Doctor, I have to be at the theater at seven."

"Then you'll be late," he snapped and hung up.

He knew perfectly well one couldn't be late for a performance! And yet the call "Curtain going up" was so trivial compared to an ever-looming medical disaster. As ill luck would have it, I appeared in the very opening scene—in fact, when the curtain went up I was already on stage, alone, in bed. A lucky thing that I wasn't needed at the studio on that Friday. I decided to take my stage makeup home with me the night before and to wait in Lauter's waiting room already fully made up. That would save me half an hour. The curtain went up at eight, but before that I had to take Anabel home in a taxi. Everything depended on how long "Miss Shelling" would have to spend in the doctor's consulting room.

Anabel had been strangely monosyllabic when I told her,

radiantly, that Lauter had agreed to see her. She seemed neither grateful nor relieved.

"Have you changed your mind? Do tell me! Maybe you want to have it after all? Or at least talk it over with Ferencsi first?"

"No. Never."

16

Diary, June 1939:

She asked if I maybe wanted to have the child after all.
"Maybe!" Never in my life have I wanted anything so much.
Up to now I can't remember ever wanting a particular thing
very much. (Except Jerome, and I realized right away that no
one can "have" him.) It was only when I did *not* want
something that I'd blow my top. "Wildcat!" my stepmother
would scream, before she slapped me.

    Now I want this child. At night I spread my hands on my
belly, trying to persuade myself that I can feel it.

    At the same time—grotesque, of course—I tell myself that
it doesn't belong to me, that it's only on loan. I'm just a
deputy. L.'s deputy. The other day she told me she never
allows herself to look into baby carriages because it makes her
feel envious. She knows there's no place for "all that" in her
life, she said, not now at any rate. Maybe later. Maybe never.
Said she knows J. doesn't want a child. The idea scares him.
He knows he's not cut out to be a father. He once said

something to the same effect to me: "What will I use for flies
when I'm old?"

I lie awake at night, stroking my belly, imagining how it
would be if I could have the baby and place it in L.'s arms.
"It's *our* child," I'd say. "Yours and mine. From now on you'll
never have to look for work anymore, I'll make all my money
over to you—and to our child." I believe—I truly believe—I
could then manage to live without J. I would never even need
to see him again because we'd have the child, she and I
together. I know, I know. Pregnant women are often quite
unhinged.

At six-fifteen on Friday evening I was sitting in the waiting room. "Miss Shelling" had disappeared into the consulting room after her knock had been answered by a brusque
"Come in!" Lauter hadn't even said hello to me.

That was more than twenty minutes ago. Almost a quar-
ter of seven. I went over to the window. How long did this
sort of thing take? Did they have to make all kinds of prep-
arations? Injections? How long would the effect of the
anesthetic last?

It hadn't been too easy at home either, for my mother had
suddenly appeared in my room.

"Isn't that Anabel out there in the car—" She broke off
when she saw the heavy stage makeup on my face. "Why are
you making up at home?"

I stared fixedly into the mirror. She'd been an actress herself; I couldn't fob her off with any pseudo-professional de-
vice. No credible explanation occurred to me however fever-
ishly I racked my brain. My mother sat down and broke her
iron rule of never interfering in her daughters' affairs un-
asked.

"What's going on? What are you up to?"

"Don't ask. I can't tell you."

I reached for the powder puff, upset the box, and a cloud of white powder streamed across the table, settled on the makeup mirror and hid my face.

"I have something to tell you," said my mother. "I hoped I'd get away without having to, but now I think you ought to know."

"Go ahead, go ahead," I snapped, polishing my mirror.

"The other day, when you were all in the garden drinking coffee, you went back to the house to get something. I happened to be looking out of the upstairs window . . ."

"And?"

"Jerome bent forward and put his hand on Anabel's knee and said something I didn't hear . . ."

"And?"

"She didn't answer, but the way she looked at him . . ."

I turned and looked her straight in the eye.

"I've asked Jerome—for good reasons of my own—I've asked Jerome to take care of her."

"He's taking care of her, believe me."

"Oh, for God's sake!" I had to laugh, out of sheer despair. "You're on the wrong track altogether."

She sat there for a moment and watched while I hastily put mascara on my eyelashes and dark-red stage lipstick on mouth, then she got up without a word and left.

•

Anabel was waiting outside in a rented car with chauffeur. She didn't want to use her own. When I opened the door, she was sitting huddled in one corner.

"Are you in pain?"

She straightened up and shook her head. The car drove off. I looked out the window.

It was some time before I noticed that she was crying,

soundlessly, the way she had cried among the Christmas wrappings. I took her limp, icy hand, couldn't think of anything to say. She pulled her hand away and threw her arms around my neck, holding on to me as if she were drowning. I tried to stroke her head—unsuccessfully, for she kept thrusting it in mute despair from side to side—and then her face, bathed in floods of tears. She stopped throwing her head about and allowed my hand to rest on her cheek, and then she began to kiss my hand as if she were in love with me. I tried to pull it away but she wouldn't let go, burying her face in it and kissing it over and over again.

Gradually she calmed down. The tears dried up and the wordless sobbing stopped. She sat there so rigidly, her face still buried in my hand, that I wondered if she had fallen asleep.

Harley Street. I waited in the car while she combed her hair and rummaged for powder and lipstick, then I opened the door. Remote and impassive, she walked up the steps beside me. The car waited.

That had been forty-five minutes ago. The lazy-busy tick-tock of the clock on the mantel. Seven o'clock already, only one more hour until curtain time. It was raining outside. Suppose there were complications? Suppose she didn't wake up from the anesthetic? Things like that did happen—anesthetic shock. The door would open, Dr. Lauter would appear and say hoarsely, "Miss Shelling is dead—"

At that the door did open and the doctor appeared. "All right. You can come in and collect her. She must rest here for another ten minutes before walking down the stairs. And then get out—both of you."

In the car she lay back in the corner and slept, all the way home. No, she wasn't in any pain, she had assured me. How was I to smuggle her into her bedroom without anyone seeing? Bill might be home already. Nina certainly was. The car stopped in front of her gate.

"Anabel, listen, if we meet Bill or Nina, we'll say you suddenly got a bad migraine in my dressing room, and that's why I'm taking you home myself. Do you hear me?"

"Yes."

I rummaged in her purse and found two different keys.

"Anabel, which is your house key? This one or the other one?"

She opened her eyes, looked at me distractedly, then at the two keys I was holding out to her. She snatched one of them forcibly out of my hand and crammed it back in her purse.

"So it's the other one," I said, opening the car door. The chauffeur and I helped her across the front garden and carried her up the few stairs to the door. No light in the entrance hall. Thank God! I whispered to the chauffeur to go and keep the engine running—I'd be right back. In the darkness my watch glowed seven-thirty-five. Christ! But I couldn't just dump her on the floor. Without switching on the light, I groped my way along the wall to her bedroom, half pushing, half lifting her. From the library came the sound of a rapid radio commentary, some boxing match— Bill was home. I opened the bedroom door. She fell from my arms onto the bed. I switched on the bedside lamp—and turned at a noise. Nina was standing in the doorway. For a second she looked at her mother, then at me, questioning but indifferent.

"Look after your mother, Nina," I said hastily. "She can do with it. She was sick with an awful migraine in my dressing room. Put her to bed and bring her a hot-water bottle."

"A hot-water bottle? For a headache?"

"Yes, yes! Her feet are cold. Hurry up, Nina, I've got to get back to the theater. Why don't you help me!"

"I'm always glad to help *you*," said Nina and began to undress her mother. The last thing I saw was Anabel's white face, her eyes tightly closed, before I ran out of the house.

The car raced through the wet streets. A red light—another one—my teeth were chattering. "Please drive fast or I won't make it." Ten to eight . . . six minutes to . . . three minutes to . . . and the car stopped at the stage door. The stage manager, Maudie and the doorkeeper were all standing outside in the rain, waving excitedly.

"Thank God!" moaned the stage manager. "I thought I was going to have to make an announcement . . ."

"Thank God!" whispered Maudie, rushing along the passageway and down the stairs behind me, unzipping me as she went.

Everywhere the dressing-room doors stood open and a chorus of "Thank God!" and "Whatever happened to you?" and "Why, you're made up already!" echoed in our wake. Maudie threw the nightgown over my head, I shook off my shoes, squirmed out of my stockings and ran barefoot back the length of the passageway leading to the stage, Maudie following with brush and comb. The bed, already turned down, was waiting. I jumped in, hissed, "Get the hell away from me, Maudie darling," as the stage lights dimmed and went out. I got into position under the bedclothes. Then came a familiar, ever-new and exhilarating rushing sound. The curtain was going up.

17

Next morning at the studio, during a break in the shooting, I hurried to the telephone. I had to know how she was. I wasn't allowed to leave the set, however, and was forced to make out, over the turmoil and the hammering around me, whether she was telling me the truth when she said she was still in bed, but everything was fine.

"Well, it's all over now," I shouted, struggling to sound buoyant.

Her voice was faint as though it were coming through a sieve. "What did you say?"

"I said, it's all over now," I yelled as hard as I could.

"Yes, all over," she repeated almost inaudibly. Perhaps she was in pain after all.

"I'll drop in on my way to the theater. Just for a few minutes."

•

She was lying flat on her back when I opened her bedroom door. Everything was white, her face, her nightgown, the pillows, those forlorn hands, except her hair and her eyes, now circled by dark shadows.

Without taking off my coat I sat down on the bed, turning the clock on the bedside table toward me. Ten minutes. First the essentials. Any pain? No. Had Bill noticed anything? No. And Nina? Neither. She hadn't asked any questions, just brought a hot-water bottle and left.

Pause. What else could I ask? I couldn't think of anything. But that sudden drought in my brain came directly from her, from those vacant eyes, from that arid voice. She didn't seem to give a damn.

Then suddenly her face relaxed as if she had caught hold of a train of thought and her eyes came to life again. She clasped her hands over the sheet—white on white.

"Listen to me carefully, and don't interrupt," she said, paused, and spelled out every word of the next sentence. "I can't come with you to the Gurnemantzes'."

Although she spoke so slowly, the words came tense and inflexible. In spite of her injunction, I flared up. "Anabel—please—we've already got the tickets and the sleeping car is reserved! You need a vacation more than ever. Think of the swimming in the warm sea . . ." The black eyes stared stonily at the covers. "The peaches—remember? Aesculapius! Our suppers on the terrace—you said yourself you'd never had such a marvelous time." I shriveled up; there was no sign of a reaction from her. One last time I tried. "But why? Why on earth can't you?"

"Because Ferencsi's coming. He'll be here for a whole month."

Oh. That, of course, was a different matter. All the same, I found it hard to swallow the bitter pill. I very nearly burst out, exactly as I did when I was a child and a cherished plan of mine was thwarted, "But I was looking forward to it so much!" To which the inevitable impassive grown-up answer had been: "Then you'll just have to unlook."

I began to unlook. I got up and walked toward the door—had to flail about once more: "I hate the fellow. What does he give you except unhappiness?"

"Not all the time."

"What's the good of that? That's no way to live."

"It's better than nothing."

"Oh, for God's sake," I muttered and left.

.

Diary, June 1939:

Just got rid of her. It wasn't easy but I was prepared for it. "Ferencsi" got me out of the jam. She said: "Oh, for God's sake!" and left.

When I invented Ferencsi, sitting among the Christmas wrappings, I hadn't the faintest notion that I was handing myself a marvelous defensive weapon, a permanent alibi, an ever-valid excuse, a cast-iron immunity.

Funny how he gets more real all the time. I've now invented a wife for him, French, red-haired, a bit short in the leg. Maybe that's how writers work, the fiction factory just grows and grows with a life of its own. Pity L. never asked about the children, for I was prepared for that, too. I was prepared for anything—except for J.'s child.

Last night I heard every single hour strike. One always claims that, but last night it was true. I was counting them, didn't really want to sleep. Could have taken the stuff Dr. Lauter gave me to help me "spend a decent night." Of course he saw through the whole thing, never for one moment believed in Miss Shelling, the kindergarten teacher. When I entered the consulting room, he was standing by the window, looking down at the street. "Is that your car?" he said. I nodded. "Good," he said. "At least you'll get home comfortably."

I thought I'd better say something to him—if not an explanation, at least a few words to thank him. "Doctor," I began—but he raised both hands. "Don't tell me anything. Don't make any confessions to me. I'm going to do it and it isn't the first time. But I can't stand any more confessions."

I liked him. I liked him very much. Unfortunately he clamped the ether mask over my nose and thus wiped himself out. I only have a vague memory of what happened after that. Didn't come to properly until much later. In bed. Nina. Hot-water bottle. Didn't have the strength to put it on my belly. It stayed where she placed it, burning my feet. Heard the church clock strike eleven. Alone. Good. Silence and darkness and plenty of time to sort things out.

It was a boxing match. I was in one corner—and at the same time in the opposite one. The gong sounded and I went right in and punched myself. Right away a murderous jab on the chin: Give J. up! That was quite enough for a start, and I fell clean through the ropes. Climbed back into the ring. Went on the defensive, dancing around. Why give J. up? He doesn't know, L. doesn't know. So why give him up, what's changed? At that a terrific punch caught me on the head: Do you really believe you can continue indefinitely—waiting, waiting, waiting in the apartment, listening for the sound of his key in the lock . . . ?

The key! There'd been something about a key. Whatever was it? Then I saw it—in L.'s hand! Had I dreamed that? No! There she sat, next to me in the car, as large as life—holding our doorkey in her hand.

Almost a K.O. The gong saved me just in time. Rubbed myself with a towel and administered a pep talk: What's the panic? She hadn't noticed anything, nothing had happened, so shut up, for God's sake. Second round. A merciless uppercut right smack in the face: You're going to give up the apartment! No, I yelled, flailing and punching in all directions and missing every time. I grabbed hold of my opponent and hung on with all my strength so that he was unable to hit me again. Then I fell down. Flat on my back. The referee was bending over me, counting: "One: Give up the Gurnemantz vacation. Two: Give up the apartment and take a trip around the world. Three: Give up J. Four: Give up L."

Give up—give up! I gave up. K.O.

The next day she had written:

It's enough . . . I was about to write: It's enough to drive anyone insane—but now it occurs to me that perhaps it's all for the best. It might even help. It *will* help, I know it, though at the moment the pain makes me breathless and I feel I'm suffocating.

He called early this morning. I was awake, forcing myself to make plans for a trip around the world. With Bill, of course. Maybe with Nina too. Stay away for months and months. After we come back, refuse to see J. and L. Give no reason. Just refuse. Then the telephone rang.

He doesn't know what happened yesterday. Am certain L. hasn't told him, she swore she wouldn't. But he senses something's up, he feels the tension, wonders what the hell is going on—and wants out. Typical. That's his only method of dealing with things: to get out. I understand only too well. Am no hero myself. He spoke hurriedly, in a way I'd never heard him talk before, as if he were being chased by something. Said he was leaving. Today. For Paris. He couldn't stand it any longer. (What did he mean by that?) He'd meet us there. "Us" being L. and me. Then we could go on to the Gurnemantzes' together. I didn't answer. Let L. tell him I'm not coming. Maybe he'll be glad! That thought almost choked me. I could hardly speak, barely managed to answer. I feel as if the slightest breath of air could blow me to smithereens.

PART TWO

18

Already three fifteen-minute poses this morning. Even during the coffee breaks the painter didn't utter a single word because she wanted to remain "charged." She was plain stingy in that respect, for she was never quite sure how long her fuel would last and she hoarded every bit of it. "I'm getting to be short of breath," she said, and by "breath" she meant the sparks flying from her paintbrush.

For the third time that morning she returned from the kitchen with her tray, but now there was a dish on top of it containing something warm, two plates and a pair of poultry shears.

"Lunch break," she said, setting a plate in front of me. "I bought a chicken. Ready-cooked."

She cut it in half and began to eat her half neatly with her fingers. I hesitated.

"It can fly," she said with her mouth full. "For anything that flies, fingers are okay."

We ate in silence. From time to time she wiped her hands on her smock. I used my poncho. Suddenly, brandishing a chicken bone like a club, she glared at me as if she'd just remembered something disgraceful.

"How did it come to an end between your Jerome and Anabel?"

"Someone broke it up."

"Anabel's husband?"

"No. Another woman."

She replaced the bone on her plate, picked as clean as if a dog had been at it, brooded for a moment and then seized it again and tapped her teeth with it.

"Another woman?"

"Jerome met someone else. In Paris. We were about to leave for our vacation again, our Gurnemantz vacation in the south of France, to pick peaches. He'd left ahead of time for Paris, where we were going to meet. I couldn't go with him, I was in a play in London with two more weeks to run."

"And Anabel?"

"She stayed in London. She was sick."

"Sick."

She played with her chicken bone, looking covetously at my plate. I had eaten all the dark meat and left the spongy white stuff.

"Aren't you going to eat that?"

"I don't like it. It never tastes of anything."

She pushed her plate aside and took mine.

"You've never been hungry, have you?"

"Not really, but pretty close to it."

"That doesn't count."

"I know."

"It would have done you good."

"I know."

"But in other respects you seem to have been through the

mill, all right. Well, come on, tell me the rest. And don't just fend me off with chapter headings. Why did your Jerome go off on his own? Was he sick of Anabel?"

"He was sick of everything. He hadn't sold a painting in two years. Just a drawing now and again. He earned his living from book jackets. The pay wasn't bad, but it was making him ill."

She wiped her mouth on her sleeve with finality, groped without looking for her Gauloises and nodded.

"I once had to paint Christmas cards."

"And so one day he blew his top. 'I'm leaving for Paris today. I've got to have a show there somehow, even if it's only at the flea market.' He took half a dozen canvases with him and showed them around. That's how he met her—the other woman."

"A painter?"

"No, her husband owned the gallery."

"A gallery owner? Who was it? I know every single one in Paris."

"Dujardin, Rue St. Honoré."

She leaned across the table, forcing me to look at her.

"Jeannine Dujardin?"

I took a deep breath. She knew Anabel—she knew everyone.

She let herself fall back in her chair, smiling to herself.

"I never met her. That sort of woman wasn't my cup of tea. But quite a number of painters in Paris were keen on her. She started out as a model, you know. I only knew her husband, Dujardin. Showed twice at his gallery. That was before he married Jeannine. He was quite a guy, that man. I never understood how he and that nitwit ever got together. So your Jerome fell for her? How did she manage that?"

"I don't know. I wasn't there."

Actually I knew very well. Babs had told me all the details.

The painter frowned; she'd obviously expected more for the price of her half-chicken. She looked at her watch.

"Can we have another go." It was a statement, not a question, and she got up, her eyes already full of colors, lines and shapes, trotted over to her stool in front of the canvas without waiting for an answer, and sat down as if she had taken root.

I held the pose. Thought of the entrance to the Dujardin Gallery in the Rue St. Honoré. I'd passed through that entrance once—later on. A heavy Spanish door with an ancient wrought-iron lock. And through that entrance door, early in the morning, Jerome had lugged his six canvases in the hope that Dujardin might see him before the rush of clients and visitors began. But Dujardin wasn't there. Out of town, said his assistant, he didn't know where. When would he be back? No idea. Jerome insisted. "Surely somebody must know. Hasn't he got a wife or something?" From an adjoining room came a voice: "Yes, he's got a wife or something but she doesn't know either."

Babs had described it all exactly the way it had happened; she knew her well. Jeannine had appeared in the door to the private office and had looked Jerome up and down as he unpacked his canvases. The secretary had tried to stop him. "Madame, don't forget that we're booked solid until next spring." But Jeannine said she was always interested in new talent and told Jerome to bring his pictures into the office.

I'd been inside that office too. Later. I'd taken a good look at it, a man's office of course, a man's workroom. Wood paneling, a large desk and a black leather reclining chair. That's where she must have been sitting, I thought. Or reclining à la Récamier. Jerome had stood his pictures against the wall and then—said Babs—she had offered him a sherry.

After which they'd looked at the paintings together. Jeannine had taken her time, sticking out her thumb at arm's length like an expert and closing one eye to "test the proportions." After all, she knew the trade. She'd been standing next to paintings and lying next to painters for so long that she believed she knew something about it.

Jerome was an extremely talented young painter, she said, though, unfortunately, that alone was not enough. You needed some kind of trick, some gimmick, to make your work stand out. Like the young painter she had discovered recently, she said, who simply painted one broad black stroke vertically across a plain gray canvas, or two red ones. The title of the black one was *Moses* and of the red one *Abraham Lincoln*. Now he was doing blue and green ones too and they were selling like hotcakes.

Probably Jerome had liked her at first sight—Babs said men fell like ninepins for her—or was it the possibility of an exhibition at the Dujardin gallery? He must have smelled an opportunity in spite of *Moses* and *Lincoln*. And at that point —one mustn't forget that—at that point he was prepared to do anything at all. Later on she got under his skin, more than he'd bargained for.

At any rate they had lunch together at a bistro on the Left Bank, an old haunt of Jerome's. Cheap, of course, frequented by taxi drivers, and Paris taxi drivers know where to find good food. Babs told me that as soon as she heard about that, she knew it was serious, because Jeannine avoided what she called "dirty little holes in the wall" like the plague, her past having been too full of them. And after lunch they went to the Hotel de la Muette.

•

"That's enough for today," said the painter. "No, don't go yet, I'll make coffee."

I went into the bathroom. It smelled of turpentine once more; she had fired the nice Spanish cleaning woman. I took off my poncho and hung it on the door, contemplated the greasy chicken stains.

"Ready!" came her voice from the studio.

We drank in silence, as usual. Now, after her illness, she seemed drained every time we took a break, and she would gulp the coffee down with her eyes closed, waiting for it to take effect. She obviously needed something to wind her up again, something to grease the wheels. Why not a drink? There was no liquor in the studio, not even a bottle of rum.

Slowly she opened her eyes.

"How old were you then?"

"Early twenties. But in those days when you were in your early twenties you were a lot younger."

"And Jerome?"

"A few years older."

"Mere children."

I got up and wandered over to the window. The studio was on the sixth floor, with a vast view of the city, not a pretty one, but familiar, London roofs, London chimneys. I could see the dark, blurred reflection of my face in the window, and behind and merging into it, the whitish-blue, almost sunny sky. When I first arrived in London, there had been far more sunny days, I thought. I never seemed to need a coat; children and young people hate coats and warm underwear. "Take your coat," my mother would call after me, and I would only laugh, waving to her and running for the bus. Running, always running. I could even eat while running. Cherries, for instance, spitting the stones out at tree trunks along the road as I streaked past them. The painter was right. We were mere children, Jerome and I, and whenever I stepped out of the house I felt in my bones that I was the youngest person on the street. Grown-up, though, the youngest grown-up.

"I know what you're thinking," I said, standing on tiptoe to get a better view of some treetops in the distance to find out if they belonged to a section of Hyde Park, our Hyde Park.

She made no answer.

"It certainly does seem strange," I said. "That is—it doesn't seem strange to me because I can't imagine it any other way, but it must seem strange to an outsider that I was so easy to cheat, and for so long. And also I imagine you're asking yourself, 'Well now, didn't *she* ever play the field a bit? And if not, why not?'"

"I don't ask myself stupid questions," she said, pouring herself a second cup and feeling for her Gauloises. "What's more, it's clear as daylight."

"It wasn't virtue. I can't stand virtue. Maudie, my dresser, used to say, 'Virtue is when there's no bid.' I remember there was of course a certain amount of bidding, but I never gave myself the chance to get interested, I simply didn't have the time. I kept one eye firmly on the clock, always on the run, always rushing . . ."

"Compulsive," she said calmly, examined her fingers, picked up the jar of lanolin cream that was always within reach and rubbed some on her hands. "Compulsive," she repeated without turning around to look at me. "And under pressure from inside and from outside, plain as plain. But don't fool yourself, you'd have found the time—had you wanted to."

"But I didn't want to. Do you mind if I open the window?" She shook her head, buttoning her smock tightly around her neck. I pushed up the window and breathed the cold, still air. The smell of greasy roast chicken and turpentine and swirls of smoke drifted past me.

"Why would I have wanted to look at other men? To prove something to myself? What, for instance? After all, I had Jerome, didn't I, and that was sufficient proof, wasn't it? At least I believed I had him, and that was all that mattered to me. For three long years I believed I had him and I'm glad I didn't know any different."

"Ostrich! A wise bird, happy as long as he keeps his head in the sand? What happened when you dug your way out of the sand? How did you find out about Jeannine?"

"I arrived in Paris—and Jerome wasn't at the station. I drove to our hotel, the Hotel de la Muette, and registered as his wife, as I always did. I was informed he already had a wife. The concierge—I knew him from way back—a bald-headed, bristly old walrus, said she wasn't staying at the hotel but she came every day. He showed me the slip: 'M. et Mme. Lorrimer.'"

The painter massaged the lanolin violently into her fingers.

"What did you do?"

"I sat down in the lobby next to my suitcase and waited. It wasn't long before he appeared. Alone. He saw me sitting there and stopped in his tracks. I could see that he'd forgotten. Forgotten I was coming, forgotten me altogether. The walrus was watching us from behind his counter. I walked over and said, 'I'd like a single room, please.' I signed with my own name. Jerome stood next to me, saying nothing, while the walrus looked at him meaningfully. I went up in the elevator alone. They sent up my suitcase. Then Jerome came up."

"Did he tell you?"

"Yes."

"How did you take it?"

Now it was getting cold. I closed the window and returned

to my chair, putting out a tentative hand toward her Gauloises.

"But you don't smoke!"

"I do—occasionally. At the dentist, for instance."

She lighted it for me. I often had to smoke professionally, sometimes daily on stage, at a fixed hour, but it never took hold of me, never did anything for me. Maybe Gauloises were something special.

"I asked how you took it."

"I heard you, but I don't know how to answer properly. If I'd try to describe it—crying all night, black days, watching the river rush by from the top of the Pont d'Alexandre for hours on end—none of that brings back the way it really was. But when I think of the taxi driver, then it all comes back to me. Then I can feel it all over again."

She looked at me attentively, even stubbed out her cigarette.

"The next day I took a taxi—I can't remember why—a long ride. In front of me the taxi driver's powerful, shapeless back, a thick neck with a deep horizontal wrinkle, and neatly trimmed gray hair underneath his cap. He didn't talk to me, he just drove. Soon he would stop for lunch, maybe at his regular bistro, where he'd meet his friends—or he'd drive to his wife. All of a sudden I envied that taxi driver with such a soul-sickening intensity that I couldn't remember ever having felt anything like it before. I'd have given anything to change places with him, never mind if he had to spend ten hours a day chained to his steering wheel in the maddening turmoil of the Paris traffic, never mind if he was approaching the end of his life and I was just beginning mine. He knew where he belonged—and I didn't. He had firm ground under his feet—I was adrift. He breathed slowly and with dignity—I kept convulsively snatching deep breaths because my lungs felt empty, as if they were about to collapse. I longed so desperately to transform myself into that man that I seriously believed I might bring it off by the end of the ride, if I just concentrated hard enough. Suddenly he slowed down and stopped. I got out, paid, and held out my hand to him. He gave me his, surprised, and I hung on it as long as I dared. Then he drove off. I had failed. The pain fell upon me once again and worse than before."

The painter got up and walked over to an old desk, standing in a corner of the room, covered with dust and so oppressed by canvases piled up against it from all sides that it was almost invisible. She opened the top drawer, rummaged in it and returned with a newspaper clipping.

"I cut this out. I thought it might give me a few guidelines when you weren't posing. But it didn't. Did you ever look like that?"

It was a reproduction of an old studio photograph, and I couldn't help laughing at the flat, smooth moon face, the helpless round eyes under thin penciled eyebrows and the sterile, professional smile on the lips.

"Yes, that's what I looked like. I even remember that photograph. I thought at the time it was marvelous."

She took it from me, studied my face and then the piece of newspaper again and shook her head.

"If your name wasn't printed underneath, I'd never have recognized you. There's absolutely no connection between your present face and this one. It's a different person. Your voice is probably different too."

"I don't know. My voice always gives me a shock when I hear it from the screen—I always imagine something quite else. My idea of myself is also quite different from what I see on the screen. That's a shock too, at the beginning of every film. Afterward you get used to it. You get used to yourself."

I leaned forward and touched my cigarette to the newspaper clipping. It flared up and the painter quickly threw it in the ashtray.

I got up. "I'd like to go home now. I'm tired."

•

I wasn't tired, but I wanted to go home. Though first I intended to make a little detour to those trees I'd glimpsed from the window. The sky was still clear; it was cold but the air was dry and there was no wind. After sitting so long, it felt good to walk along the streets. I walked fast. I didn't run anymore the way I once used to, but I still couldn't saunter or stroll or tarry.

Down Oxford Street to Marble Arch, still standing up, undamaged by the war. But Lyon's Corner House, where I'd first met Jerome, had disappeared in favor of a huge movie theater. I crossed the street, just as we'd done eleven years before, and entered Hyde Park by the same gate walking toward the same out-of-the-way corner with the deck chairs that didn't even cost sixpence. No deck chairs now, in winter.

This had been the beginning, here, under these very trees. And the end had set in on that day in Paris, at the Hotel de la Muette. The following afternoon, when we went to see Babs, it had edged a little closer.

Jerome hadn't told me "Madame Lorrimer's" name. All I knew was that her husband owned a gallery; I didn't give a damn which one. In Babs's sitting room sat a girl in a bright-yellow summer dress. "Madame Dujardin."

The girl gave me a friendly smile. To Jerome she nodded and said, "*Ça va, aujourd'hui?*"

Babs sat down next to her on the sofa and explained, "Madame Dujardin's husband is the owner of the gallery in the Rue St. Honoré."

Aha! *"Ça va, aujourd'hui?"* She didn't yet know how he was today. Yesterday she had known, though.

She was perhaps a couple of years older than I, no more. A provocative and aggressively turned-up nose, very beautiful amber eyes, fair hair. Sitting there on the sofa, she looked like a Brimstone butterfly. She studied me lazily, relaxed and not at all unfriendly, wanted to know if I'd had a good journey and if I was tired, Jerome having told her my play had just closed. No one bothered to explain to me that Jerome and this girl knew each other. Or why.

If he knew that she was going to be there, at Babs's that afternoon, he showed no sign of it, looked neither surprised nor pleased. He sat next to me, listening to Robert Siodmak talking about his new film and occasionally making monosyllabic comments. He didn't speak to Jeannine or to me.

The two women on the sofa, one in black and white, the other in lemon-yellow, did most of the talking. They were apparently good friends—at least they had plenty to talk and laugh about. In French, of course. I fancied that they were talking and laughing about me, although I heard them discussing someone else. Were they asking each other whether I "knew"? I could see that Babs "knew."

I was holding a drink with a lot of ice in it. My fingers got cold too, and the chill was slowly creeping up my hand and my arm.

"You've got goose pimples," said Robert Siodmak, examining my bare arm. "Are you cold? In this heat?"

He, obviously, didn't "know." The chill was penetrating my body, soon my teeth would start chattering. Help!

Help? Why hadn't I thought of that yesterday—why had I let a whole unbearable day go by—why had I let myself sink into this awful quicksand instead of striking out for dry land, picking up the telephone and shouting: "Anabel! Help!"

I'd been standing for too long on the exact spot under the

trees where our deck chairs had once stood. Then the sun had been shining. The dogs with their masters and the nannies with their baby carriages were still there, but now they were all walking briskly homeward, because it was beginning to grow dark. I found a taxi and returned to the hotel.

19

Diary, July 2, 1939:

When I got home, I found a note on my bedside table. L. had called. Wanted me to call her back at once at the Hotel de la Muette. It was late, two a.m., we'd been to a concert and then out to supper. Just Bill and I. First time for ages. Did my best to talk to him. More difficult than ever. But I really tried. Don't want to call L. What if J. answers? He knows now I'm not coming to the Gurnemantzes'. I write those words as if they meant nothing—yet as I spell them out, I'm writhing with the pain of it, writhing like a worm. Must, *must* remain firm. Won't call her back. It's only one last attempt of hers to make me change my mind. If she only knew how easy that would be! One word from J.—and I'd be off to the station in a flash!

So that was why she hadn't called back!
I had left the Siodmaks' as soon as I decently could and returned to the hotel on the pretext that I was about to catch a cold. Jerome stayed on—I didn't care, help was on the way. Anabel! She'd know what to do, she'd tell me. I laughed on

the way sitting in the taxi—I actually heard myself laugh—
because Popeye the Sailorman had come to my mind, eating
his spinach. Anabel, my spinach.

For the rest of the day I sat in my room, waiting. Nina
had answered the telephone. "Nina, I must urgently speak to
your mother." She'd gone to a concert. All right, I'd wait up
until she came home.

I waited. Midnight and then one o'clock, two o'clock. At
three I asked the night clerk for something to make me sleep
and he brought me a white pill. I had never taken a sleeping
pill before. It made short shrift of me, made me quickly go
under in a deep, dreamless sleep.

I woke up late and immediately reached for the telephone.
Anabel! The maid said she'd gone out. I left another message for her to call me. Urgent!

I waited. Probably she'd left early in the morning to meet
Ferencsi, a thought that obliged me to try to be happy for
her. I spent the entire day in my room. Silence.

·

A note from Jerome had been slipped under the door. It said
that he had lots of things to do and would be having lunch
with a gallery owner. (A gallery owner? Well, sort of.) He'd
be back at the hotel to pack in the afternoon, and our train
would leave for Marseilles at eight that evening.

At six he poked his head around the door. I was standing
at the window; I hadn't even dared to sit out on the balcony
in case I missed the telephone. He didn't ask what I'd been
doing all day, seemed distraught and irritable. I heard him
giving the chambermaid hell—something I'd never heard
him do before. We drove to the station in silence.

This time we had been extravagant and taken a two-berth
second-class sleeping compartment. Last year Anabel had
shared our third-class one, containing three beds. Jerome

had slept on top, I'd slept in the middle, Anabel in the bottom berth. First we'd had dinner in the dining car and they had shared a bottle of red wine and then we had made our way back through car after car, endlessly it seemed, laughing and squealing and lurching and swaying with the motion of the train, until we finally reached our compartment. Blissfully exhausted, we collapsed on Anabel's bed, all three of us, until we'd recovered sufficiently to take turns at undressing discreetly in the tiny toilet compartment. Jerome, the last, climbed the ladder to his bunk and turned out the light. In the darkness we called out to each other: "Sleep well! Happy dreams! Good night! Sleep well!"

The memory assaulted me and proved so lethal that when Jerome said he was tired and didn't want any dinner, I quickly turned out the light over my berth to hide my tears. Fully dressed, I lay on my blanket until I had calmed down enough to get up and unpack my nightgown and brush my teeth by the light that shone in from houses rushing by along the tracks. Above me Jerome was snoring gently.

20

The train wormed itself booming and moaning into the station in Marseilles at seven o'clock in the morning. Slowly it glided past hundreds of people packed on the platform despite the early hour, all craning their necks upward, everyone's eyes eagerly searching each passing train window for the object of their early-morning pilgrimage.

Jerome shoved our suitcases along the corridor while I, leaning out of the window, scanned the sea of faces for the Gurnemantz threesome. There they were—but it was only a twosome. Peter and Eva, tanned, laughing and waving, fought their way through the crowd, Peter catching the suitcases Jerome tossed out to him, while Eva stood under my window, beaming up at me and asking the questions one always asks at railway stations, expecting no answer beyond a nod of the head. Yes we'd had a good journey, yes we'd had a good breakfast, yes it was a glorious day.

"Where's Ursula?"

"At home. It's a good three hours from Grasse to Marseilles—and the car's not getting any younger, you know."

This was quite evident a few minutes later when we

watched Peter patiently using the starting handle to crank the old cart into action.

So Ursula still wasn't well. By now an entire year had passed since she'd told us. Could it possibly be something sinister? In the ten months between our visits to the Gurnemantzes, we never exchanged letters. "If anything's wrong, you'll hear about it soon enough," we said when we kissed each other goodbye. All the same, last Christmas I had written and asked for news about Ursula's health, but in place of information I received a card with a drawing of Aesculapius, carrying a Christmas tree on his back, with the entire family assembled in front of him, their arms full of peaches. *"Joyeux Nöel!* Peter, Ursula, Eva, Jean-Pierre," it said. Happy Xmas.

•

They were standing at the garden gate, waving, when we roared up, the boy, now ten years old, with close-cropped stubbly blond hair, tanned and naked except for his swimming trunks, and his mother next to him, looking not the least bit ill—on the contrary, she had gained weight, her freckled face was fuller than it had ever been before, her strong arms were as muscular as a man's.

"Something's up again," I said to Jerome when we were alone in our room. He nodded. "Poor Peter."

It wasn't only with me that Jerome was taciturn. I watched him later through the window as he sat on the terrace wall with Gurnemantz. Neither of them spoke; both were looking into the far distance with the vacantly concentrated expression of dogs when they seem to be listening for a bell inside themselves.

During lunch we all made an effort, as if by agreement. Sometimes three people would start talking at once, trying to avoid a silence. Eva, who was sitting next to Jean-Pierre, tied his napkin around his neck for him and rearranged his fingers when they gripped a knife too close to the blade. Ursula looked on.

Peter and Eva, who had gotten up at the crack of dawn to meet us, dispensed with their coffee in order to get some sleep. Jerome, on the other hand, declared he didn't need a siesta and would go for a walk. At this, Jean-Pierre eagerly asked if he could come along—and was refused. He was sorry, said Jerome, but it would distract him, since he was on the lookout for subjects to paint. In the nick of time I remembered that I had brought an airplane kit for the child, who, quickly comforted, disappeared with it into his room. Ursula and I were left alone on the terrace, watching the wasps buzz about the remains of our lunch. "Oh, just leave it," said Ursula when I got up to carry the plates back to the kitchen.

We stretched out side by side under an old umbrella pine. Peter had laid out the terrace in such a way that at noon half of its ground was shaded by the tree to protect one from the burning rays of sun, though it was powerless against the heat, which only Aesculapius, gray and invulnerable, could withstand without having to lie down. All the dogs were stretched out against the cool terrace wall, panting in short, convulsive gasps, unable to bark, wag their tails or show any other sign of life.

I, too, would have liked to collapse and close my eyes, but Ursula, lying right next to me, was humming the same song again and again, and off key to boot. I sat up and looked at her, stretched out in her old kitchen apron, freckled arms crossed behind her head, her excessively long legs with the schoolboy knees and angular feet in sandals. She always wore sandals because she didn't want to appear taller than Peter.

"You're well again, aren't you?"

"I could uproot a tree—preferably a peach tree," she said and laughed noisily upward into the dark parasol of the pine tree. Turning her mop of short, curly brown hair toward me, she added, "But *you* don't look too good to me. Was your play exhausting?"

"Eight performances a week."

"Go and sleep," she said. "I'll wake you up at six when we start picking."

I wasn't sorry to go, nor did I want to know why her laughter had sounded so joyless. Could be that she sensed it wasn't only the eight performances a week that had made me look 'not too good'—and could be that she, too, wasn't up to sharing other people's troubles.

•

At six o'clock we assembled at the orchard gate, each arriving from a different direction though all with the same expression of determinedly eager, slightly forced cheerfulness on our faces, all except perhaps Eva, who yawned unashamedly while helping Jean-Pierre strap the baskets on Aesculapius. Jerome appeared from nowhere and went ahead with Peter. I hung back as we passed the water cistern to splash cold water on my face.

Everyone chose his own row of trees. Jerome selected the bottom one and set off down the steep grassy terraces with his baskets; two rows below me Ursula hummed her tuneless song; I could hear Eva's bursts of laughter and from time to time Peter's deep bass voice. Occasionally somebody whistled for Aesculapius. The smell of the hot pine bark, foliage and fruit was soothing as ever—everything was as it had always been, yet everything was quite different.

I wasn't working properly; my arms seemed to be aching. I kept moving around, trying to keep an eye on Jerome, who was picking five hundred yards or so below me. Sometimes I caught sight of his hand or a tuft of his black mane, but mostly I could only tell which tree he was working on from the movement of the branches.

Then, suddenly, I couldn't see either head or hand any longer, and the trees in the bottom rows stood motionless. I climbed laboriously up on the strongest branch—it bent under my weight—and balanced perilously on one knee, just in time to see Jerome's blue shirt disappearing among the olive trees that covered the lower slope of the hillside.

The branch began to creak ominously. I hastily jumped down and inspected the damage: a crack in the cleft! Full of remorse, I shamelessly clamped a leaf into it—Peter made a tour of inspection every evening—and sneaked to the next tree. Where had Jerome gone? The lower gate of the orchard led only to the olive grove which served as boundary to the neighboring farm—one couldn't get to the street that way. Was he tired of picking? Was he again looking for subjects to paint? At seven o'clock in the evening? My basket was filling up with peaches—until I suddenly realized I hadn't checked a single one for quality. I discovered I'd picked a lot of hard ones, which I hastily threw into the bushes. One rolled downhill and landed at the feet of Ursula, who picked it up in surprise.

"This one's still green!"

"It broke off by accident. Sorry!"

She looked up at me for a moment, then went on picking.

I didn't take my eye off the olive grove. For a full half-hour there was no sign of life, then the blue shirt emerged again, and a few minutes later the branches in the bottom row of trees began to shake as if a tornado were passing through or as if the picker was fighting a duel with the recalcitrant fruit. And all this to the accompaniment of loud and cheerful whistling from that direction. What could have happened to put him in such an exuberant mood that he was giving Aesculapius a kiss on the nose?

•

Supper on the terrace, then Pernod and almonds—as usual. Memories of last year and of Anabel got stuck in my head. Why hadn't she called back?

Suddenly I knew why: Something had happened with Ferencsi! That was the reason. I'd have to call her immediately.

"Did you get your telephone installed?"

"No," said Peter, "and we never will. I've given up. We can manage without one, and if there's something urgent we go next door to Madame Raquin's. She has one."

Tomorrow morning then: Madame Raquin.

•

Later that evening the old routine: The girls lay down, dressed, on their beds and slept, were called at three o'clock and staggered in the darkness, still half asleep, to the truck.

Suddenly a wide-awake little voice called through an open window, "I can hear you! Next year I'll be coming with you."

Ursula, who was walking a few steps ahead of me, stopped.

"Who told you that?"

"Eva promised me."

I can't be certain of what happened next because I was groping my way along the wall with the others, but there was a sudden scuffle of feet, then something that sounded like a slap, and a half-smothered cry from Eva: "Are you crazy?" Then silence, except for the sound of our footsteps. A moment later the lights of the car went on and we climbed in, Eva beside Peter, who was driving, then Jerome, then I.

Ursula was the last to jump in, after slamming the garden gate shut.

.

When I woke up, the other bed was empty. Jerome must have dressed without making a sound, or I had been too deeply asleep to hear him, for we hadn't gotten home from our early-morning swim in Nice until six o'clock. For the sake of everybody's safety, I had had to decline my fifteen-minute stint at the wheel and had slept shamelessly all the was home, either on Jerome's shoulder or on Ursula's. I couldn't remember how I'd ended up in my nightgown and in bed.

Already one o'clock. Madame Raquin! I threw on my clothes and ducked out the front door to avoid Jean-Pierre. On the days following our market excursions he would keep himself quietly occupied all morning so that we could sleep, but around noon he would be tired of his toys and ready for company. I saw his cropped blond head bent over the air-plane kit outside the garage and tiptoed toward the orchard gate—in vain; children have keen ears. "Wait! I'm coming with you," he yelled, catching up with me in a couple of leaps.

"I'm only going to Madame Raquin's to make a phone call."

"You too? Jerome's just gone there. He wouldn't take me with him."

I stood with my hand on the open orchard gate, pressing the latch up and down, and looked into the blue eyes looking up at me expectantly. So Jerome had gone to make a phone call—to the "gallery owner" in Paris . . .

"But I can come with *you*, can't I?" He must have noticed that I wasn't listening because he boldly put his hand on my arm and shook it. Then—instinctively?—he spoke the magic words: "I know a short cut, but you'll have to wade the stream."

Barefooted, he ran along the first row of trees without looking back, certain that I would follow, then jumped down to the next terrace like a rabbit. I slithered after him, clutching at boughs and branches, and saw him crawling under some bushes before leaping down a couple more terraces. I blessed my espadrilles, which kept me from slipping until the herd instinct and the instantaneous coordination acquired in my girl-scout days shifted into gear, and I made it.

Swerving suddenly sideways and downward, he reached the foot of the hill and stopped at a certain place in the tall wire fence which surrounded the orchard. I panted up. He knelt on the ground and triumphantly showed me a spot where the wire was slack enough for someone to slip underneath it, lifted it a few inches and wriggled through like a dog. From the other side he looked at me with contempt as I leaned against the fence, trying to catch my breath. He didn't know why I wanted to get to Madame Raquin's as quickly as possible, but he didn't care—the whole thing was a game, a race, we were going to beat Jerome! And there stood this stupid woman who gasped for air, wasting valuable time!

"Come on!"

Obediently I flung myself flat on my stomach and wormed my feet through the eight-inch gap. Jean-Pierre grabbed them, pulling and twisting mercilessly and with all his strength until he had my stomach, chest and shoulders safely on the other side. But what about my head? The aluminum links dug into my neck—like the blade of the guillotine, I thought, as I ground my nose in the dirt.

"Shut your eyes and take a deep breath. Now!" he commanded, pressing down on the back of my head with both hands. I was just about to suffocate—he grabbed my hair and pulled me through in the nick of time. As I got up, spitting dirt out of my mouth and blindly trying to get the sand and grit out of my nose and eyes, he burst out laughing. "You've certainly got a thick head!" he said. "The stream's just down there, you can wash your face in it."

He jumped up and disappeared under oleander bushes. I hobbled painfully after him, drained and parched, longing for a drink of cold spring water. He was waiting for me, up to his knees in the stream, kindly offering to splash me.

"Don't you dare!"

Whereupon he climbed up the bank on the other side and disappeared over the hill. I held my face under the water as long as I could, then proceeded to rinse amazing quantities of sand out of my ears while discovering some sizable scratches on my neck. Suddenly I couldn't keep on my feet any longer and collapsed on the nearest rock. After all, what was the hurry? I knew now why Jerome was from time to time off looking for "subjects to paint." What was the point of getting to Madame Raquin's before him?

Jean-Pierre reappeared on the far bank.

"You've lost," he shouted across the water. "Jerome's there already. Do you give in?"

"Yes. But I still have to use the phone."

"I'll show you the way," he cried magnanimously. "And I'll wait for you or you won't find your way back."

I stopped in midstream.

"Do you think I'm going to crawl back through that hole?"

"Sure!" He caught sight of my face. "Uh—you haven't got any guts."

Two bends farther up the stream stood Madame Raquin's house, shaded by tall willow trees. Jean-Pierre ran ahead, for even though the race was over, he couldn't slow his pace down to mine. He was soon back, however, with the news that Madame Raquin had invited me to a glass of wine—her own, of course, "the best in the entire region."

The last few hundred yards took me through a carefully manicured vineyard, its grapes and leaves sprayed a mottled green-white. Twice more Jean-Pierre ran back and forth to the house. He had told Madame Raquin I was an actress, he confided in whispers, and it turned out that she'd never seen an actress before in her life. He tilted his head sideways, gave me a critical look, and added, "But she'll be disappointed— the way you look now." He fished a handkerchief out of his shorts. "Spit!" he said. I spat and with a surprisingly gentle touch he rubbed the last bits of dirt out of my hair line.

The house was a two-story cube, painted yellow with brown shutters. It had no balcony and no terrace, but right next to the front door was another, smaller cube, a grape arbor. The six posts erected years ago around which the climbing tendrils of the vine had cautiously wound themselves were now completely covered up. Branches as thick as an arm had intertwined affectionately and braided themselves like pigtails into a square roof, whose green leaves and still-unripe grapes cast a gentle greenish sheen on the people and objects below.

Hand in hand we entered the arbor. If Madame Raquin was disappointed at the sight of me, she didn't show it, but lifted herself an inch or two from her chair to greet me. She was enthroned in lonely stateliness behind a garden table, a bottle of wine and a half-filled glass within reach. Her broad face was framed by white hair—light-green in the glare that filtered through the vine leaves—like tangled knitting wool. Her sly little foxy eyes encased in little cushions of fat smiled at me amiably. A set of yellow teeth, grandly bared in welcome, added to the impression of benevolent neighborliness.

"*Bonjour*, Mademoiselle."

"*Bonjour*, Madame Raquin. I hope I'm not disturbing you."

"Not at all, I'm always glad to see visitors. Jean-Pierre, bring two glasses."

"Two?" His blue eyes opened wide and stared at her incredulously, not daring to hope.

"Yes, one for you too." He was gone in a flash. "If you teach children early enough to appreciate good wine, they'll never be drunks later on."

I thought of Monsieur Raquin, who was said to have drunk himself into an early grave on his own wine. He'd obviously been taught too late to appreciate it. I wondered if Jerome was still on the phone to Paris. Right through my misery, I was suddenly struck by the prosaic thought that we really couldn't afford any of this.

"Madame—may I use your telephone?"

"*Mais oui,* as soon as the young man has finished. He always talks for a long time. Do you know him? I believe he's staying up at the Gurnemantz house too." (She pronounced it *"Gürman."*)

Jean-Pierre reappeared with two glasses.

"You pour," said Madame. "If you're going to drink, you must be able to pour. Hold the bottle at the top—careful! Don't spill a single drop."

The child clutched the bottle with both hands, biting his lips in concentration and effort as the wine gurgled slowly into the glasses. Breathing heavily, he set the bottle down.

"Bravo!" said Madame. "Well then—your good health."

We clinked glasses and drank.

"Wonderful!" I said. Jean-Pierre wanted to say something too but he was fighting for breath and his eyes were streaming. His first taste of wine. (Peter had always vetoed it.) He must have been expecting something quite else than this pungent, slightly sour beverage.

"Madame?" That was Jerome's voice from inside the house.

"Won't you join us, Monsieur?" called the old woman over her shoulder. "Come and have a glass of wine—I have a visitor."

I sat there like a piece of stone. I couldn't imagine what he'd say—or what I would say, or why I had come charging over here at all. What on earth had I intended to do? Snatch the receiver out of his hand?

"I really haven't time, Madame." Through the arbor's wall of leaves I could vaguely make him out as he was standing in the doorway. "They're expecting me for lunch. I'll be back this evening, though, and then we'll have one together. Would you find out what I owe you?"

"Coming." She heaved herself out of the chair and waddled on huge shapeless legs out of the arbor and through the open door of the house.

Saved.

Jean-Pierre raised his glass and clinked it once more against mine.

"Cheers!" Again the blue eyes filled at once with tears but he swallowed bravely. "She's fat, isn't she?" He leaned forward and whispered in my ear. "But she's not going to have a baby."

"Are you sure?"

He nodded reassuringly.

"She's always this fat. Once, long ago, she had some children, two at a time—"

"Twins?"

"One of them takes care of the vines here. The other is . . ." He tapped his forehead.

"Crazy?"

"He can't eat by himself, she has to feed him. You know something? Maybe she has another one in her stomach. I asked her, but she says no. I think she doesn't want to admit it, because it's probably like that too"—he tapped his forehead again—"if it's been sitting inside there for so long, don't you think?"

"Could be."

"Do you know why she wheezes like that?" He whispered again. "She has amsta."

"Amsta? What's that?"

He puffed and gasped like a locomotive. "That's called amsta, don't you know that?"

"Amsta? You mean asthma!"

He stared at me, puzzled and vexed—but was rescued from the dilemma by the return of Madame.

"You can have the phone now. Did you like your wine?"

I hurriedly drank up but prevented the child from following suit.

"Run on home and tell your mother I'll be right back. And say thank you for the wine."

"*Merci*, Madame." He made his little bow, adding, with the expression of a connoisseur, "An excellent wine."

Madame Raquin laughed and shuffled ahead of me into the house. The telephone, an old-fashioned box with a handle to crank it up, hung on the wall in the dining room. Through a window in the hallway I had seen Jerome's blue shirt making for the olive grove, while Jean-Pierre's blond crew-cut bobbed along on the other side through the vineyard.

It was nice and cool in the dining room because the shutters were closed, and Madame showed no intention of switching on the ceiling light. She groped her way along the wall, lifted off the receiver and cranked the machine vigorously.

"What number do you want?"

"I want to make a call to England."

"Person to person?"

"Not necessary."

She cranked again.

"She's having lunch, that lazy good-for-nothing operator, so it may take a while. For the young man I always make it person-to-person. Always to the same number in Saint-Tropez. He has a girl friend there, a married woman—*Allo,* Mademoiselle—ah, there you are at last."

She handed me the receiver and groped her way out of the room, closing the door behind her.

Mechanically I gave Anabel's number. I'd have known that number in my sleep, and just as well, for my brain was completely emptied by what Madame had just said. Jeannine Dujardin in Saint-Tropez! Practically next door! So that's why he'd said he wanted to ride the Michelin electric train along the coast and maybe spend a few days looking for subjects to paint . . .

I leaned against the wall, pressing my forehead against the cool stone, wishing desperately that I hadn't drunk the wine, trying to sort out the jumble of thoughts that came racing back into my head. Saint-Tropez . . . next door . . . therefore cheaper telephone calls . . . soon he'll go there by train and never come back . . . and then, suddenly, Anabel's voice.

"Hello?"

"Anabel?"

I knew I was screaming. I couldn't speak, all I could do was to howl into the receiver without restraint.

It was a while before I could hear anything except my own sobbing. She had probably made several attempts to interrupt me or calm me down, because now she called out severely, "Pull yourself together and tell me what's happened."

I told her. Starting with the single room at the Hotel de la Muette, then the afternoon at the Siodmaks', Jerome's solitary walks in search of subjects to paint, and now Saint-Tropez and the Michelin electric train. I didn't know whether she'd got it all or even whether she was still on the line, because, when I finally stopped speaking, there was nothing but a dead silence.

"Anabel? Are you there? Did you hear what I said?"

"Yes, I heard."

"Anabel, what am I to do? Anabel! Say something!"

"I'll come."

"What?"

I had shouted so loudly that I clapped my hand over my mouth.

"Stop crying. Don't let him notice anything—don't tell him anything—don't tell anybody anything. I'll be there."

She had hung up.

I called her name again several times, but there was no sound from the black box. I hung up the receiver and leaned my head against the wall. She was coming. She was leaving Ferencsi, the man she loved—leaving him in the lurch—to come to me. Was there anyone else like her in the whole world? Was there ever such a friend? I rolled my temples, my forehead and my burning face back and forth against the cold, damp wall, as if I could drink the soothing coolness. Anabel was coming. Anabel knew. Everything was all right again.

The black box squawked and buzzed like a swarm of bees, bringing Madame back into the room. Just as well that it was too dark for her to see my face. She took the receiver from my hand. "*Merci*, Mademoiselle, I'll see to it." Neighborly friendship was one thing—but the exact amount of how much my call had cost was another. After all, this was a call to London. A pretty penny!

No, I thought, as I counted out the money, cheap! Dirt cheap! Money? How could money come into it when all of my life was at stake?

21

I made my way back through the olive grove, taking my time, thinking, sorting things out, planning, giving my red, swollen eyes time to recover. Late for lunch? Never mind, let them wait or eat without me. All the same I took in the fact that the garden gate was open. Jerome, usually so meticulous, must have charged through, as absorbed as I was in plans and deliberations. Aesculapius might easily have escaped!

I closed the big gate and slowly climbed the orchard terraces. "Don't tell him anything." Of course I wouldn't. God knows if he'd even be here when she arrived. The Michelin train! Which hotel would "she" be staying at? Maybe I could find out from Madame Raquin, who set up the person-to-person calls for him. "Don't tell anybody anything." That one was more difficult, since I'd invented convincing reasons for Anabel's sudden cancellation, a long and complicated story about some sort of mysterious malady. The whole family had been genuinely disappointed that she hadn't come with us; her room had been prepared for her, flowers on the bedside table . . .

I climbed the last steps—and found myself facing Ursula, watching for me at the upper gate of the orchard.

"The spaghetti's being kept warm on the stove. Jean-Pierre told me where you were. By the way, he smelled of wine. Did Madame Raquin—?"

"Yes, she did."

She laughed.

"She's been trying for ages—the old witch! She's obsessed with the idea that the child needs to be 'immunized.' Do you know what time it is? After three! What's going on today? Everybody dribbling in, first Jean-Pierre, then Jerome—and now you. Eva's about to blow her top in the kitchen."

"Ursula, I'm not hungry—please!"

She looked at me for a moment, nodded, turned and went back to the house, calling something through the open kitchen window.

I wanted to continue my "sorting out" and looked forward to the cool silence of our bedroom. Alone! I made sure that Jerome was out on the terrace, under the pine tree, reading a small booklet. Perhaps a railway guide.

I closed the shutters and crept into my unmade bed. In London Anabel's travel arrangements would be well under way by now, reservations for the Dover-Calais boat and for a berth in the Paris-Marseilles sleeping car. What would she tell Bill and Nina? Above all, what would she tell Ferencsi? Suddenly deeply ashamed of my wild, selfish screaming for help, I pressed my face into the pillow—at the same time hugging it gratefully as if it were Anabel.

How soon could she get here? When would I get news from her saying, "I'm in Paris," or, better still, "I'm at the station in Marseilles"? Three or four days at the earliest. I would have to live through them calmly and quietly.

But—oh God! Suppose she couldn't get reservations? After all, it was the holiday season!

·

In the late afternoon, freshly bathed, I made my appearance on the terrace. No one in sight. I climbed up on the wall and looked around, eager to try out my newly acquired equanimity. Not a living soul. Only Aesculapius, on his day off, grazing way down at the bottom of the slope.

Silence. An unnatural, desolate silence, most unusual in the Gurnemantz ménage. Last year they'd all been members of the same orchestra, but now everybody seemed to be a soloist. They still "played" together but each simmered and stewed somewhere on his own. Earlier on, on my way to my siesta in the "thigh," I had quickly glanced around: Peter was tinkering with the truck, Ursula had started to take down the washing from the clothesline, Eva was banging around in the kitchen, no one was paying attention to anyone else or lending a hand or boosting moral by just standing close by, chatting and laughing. There was no life left in the team, although the individual limbs were still twitching like those of a galvanized frog.

I sat on the wall and looked down. Everybody who stepped out onto the terrace and sat on the wall looked down. Way down below, willow branches breaking through the olive trees marked the course of the stream—and somewhere down there, among those very willows, was Madame Raquin's little yellow cube with the old black telephone box. In the green arbor Jerome would be taking a glass of wine with Madame . . .

How had Jerome reacted to the news that Anabel had decided not to come? How very strange that I had to make an effort to pin down the exact moment when I'd told him!

He must have suspected it the instant he saw me sitting alone in the lobby of the hotel. But we'd hardly said a word to each other there, for my appearance as the second Madame Lorrimer had eclipsed everything else. So I must have told him later, upstairs in my "single." Yes, that's how it had come about—he had asked and I naturally told him the truth: that Ferencsi was in London. I remember his looking surprised for a moment—and then definitely relieved. He still didn't like Anabel! But only because he didn't really know her. Now, when she suddenly showed up here, at least he'd be forced to realize what sort of a person she truly was, a woman who was capable of jeopardizing her love in order to help her friend! For he would of course immediately realize that Anabel was coming to help me stand up to the "gallery owner." He would have to respect her for it—and hate her all the more. But Anabel wouldn't give a damn about that. She didn't really like him either.

.

During supper Jerome remarked casually that he would be leaving by the Michelin train tomorrow. I managed to continue winding my warmed-up spaghetti around my fork. Tomorrow!

"When will you be back?" asked Ursula, the housewife.

"In two or three days. I'm going to stop off in Saint-Tropez. There's a gallery there."

"The Nouveaux Artistes Gallery," said Peter. "I know it. Not bad. But they take one-third of the sales price."

"They can take half as far as I'm concerned. All I want is to see the damn things hanging on a wall—and people looking at them."

He pushed his chair back, got up and sat on the terrace wall. Peter turned his wary, slanting eyes toward him.

"It's about time, too. By the way, if they want a deposit to cover expenses—catalogue and all that—we can advance you something."

Ursula nodded, although she hadn't been asked.

Jerome didn't answer, just stared down the slope.

"I'll drive you to the station," Eva piped up. "What time does your train leave?"

"One-thirty."

"I'll make you a sandwich," said Ursula.

"I'll write you a note to the Nouveaux Artistes," said Peter.

They're playing chamber music together again, I thought.

•

Jerome was up early the next morning. He had slept badly. Once I had waked up to see him standing by the window looking out into the night before creeping noiselessly back to bed. A little while later it sounded as though he was sitting up, bending over me. I kept my eyes tightly closed, but I felt that he was watching me. Then he lay down again.

While he was packing, I dressed. I was making for the door when he grabbed my arm and forced me to look him in the face.

"Let me go—it's only for a few days."

"I'm not stopping you."

"You're spoiling it for me, your face is spoiling it."

I had promised myself not to probe, not to demand an explanation, to wait quietly until Anabel arrived. But in spite of my firm resolutions, I heard myself asking him the question that had been haunting me ever since the Hotel de la Muette. "Could you—could you live without me?"

He immediately let go of me and turned away. I'd ruined it.

He went to the closet, took out a shirt, folded it and said

matter-of-factly, "I can live without anyone—if I have to. You know that."

No, I didn't know that. I'd thought I had a special place in his life. "But I don't have to, do I?" he added—and there was that old defensive smile again. "I'll be back in a few days."

He placed the shirt carefully in the suitcase.

I left the room.

It was only eight o'clock, but the hot breath of the sirocco hit me in the face. What was I to do now? Eat, drink, pick peaches, sleep—until Anabel arrived. In three days at the earliest . . .

I remained standing in the guest-room doorway, trying to get up enough energy to walk across to the terrace. Something bright-red was catching the light over there. Ursula and Eva were surely still asleep. A visitor? For a moment I was tempted to go back into our room and throw myself down on the bed—but Jerome was in there, packing.

I set myself in motion, took a step forward, then another . . . the red spot grew bigger . . . my sandals grated on the sand . . . the spot took shape and turned around . . . Anabel.

She called—and I ran, collapsed sobbing beside her on the terrace wall.

How was it possible? How had she managed it? Yesterday noon she'd still been in London. Had she taken a plane?

"I simply got into the car, the little Alfa—there it is, by the garage—and drove off. Direction: south. Got to Dover at six, got a place on the eight-o'clock ferry. And kept driving."

"You didn't stop over in Paris?"

"I wouldn't be here if I had."

Of course she wouldn't, stupid question.

"So you drove all night?"

"Yes. Just got here."

I searched her face for signs of exhaustion and found none. On the contrary she looked wide-awake, full of energy, almost electrified.

"But I wouldn't mind some breakfast. I haven't eaten anything since lunchtime yesterday."

I shook myself like a wet dog to get some coherent thoughts into my brain.

"Stay here and relax. I'll get it for you."

She laughed and got to her feet.

"I know what kind of a cook you are! But you can get the tray ready."

She followed me into the kitchen. No word, no sign, no questioning glance. She behaved as if she had planned her visit this way all along, because she enjoyed driving fast and nonstop in her Alfa.

She put water on to boil, sliced some bread, stuffing a dry piece in her mouth, found the coffee, milk and sugar while I watched, holding the empty tray. I couldn't think of a single word to say.

Bending over the stove and absorbed in the gradual heating of the water in the pot, she asked casually over her shoulder, "Is he still here?"

I pointed to the window: Jerome was walking slowly toward the terrace. He jumped up on the wall and looked down into the valley. My heart began to pound. I sat on a kitchen chair while Anabel walked over to the window and looked at him, standing there with his back to us, a lonely silhouette on the long wall. Then she said calmly, "Watch the water, don't let it boil over. Pour it over the coffee— there, in the glass filter. I'm going out on the terrace to speak to him. Get the tray ready, breakfast for three—but don't bring it out until I call."

At the door, she turned around to add, "And don't forget to turn off the gas."

I went over to the window, following her with my eyes. Jerome heard her footsteps, looked over his shoulder—and remained motionless. She walked slowly toward him, picking up a chair on her way, turned it around, and sat down facing him. I could see nothing but his face and her back, once again only a spot of red.

I didn't dare make a noise by opening the window, but I watched his face like a hawk, trying to guess what she was saying to him. He turned toward her, put his hands on his hips, remained standing on the wall in this posture, challenging—and dangerous. She made a gesture as if asking him to sit down, but he stayed where he was.

As far as I could tell, he still hadn't spoken a word. His head was lowered; he reminded me of a young black bull I had seen in the arena in Madrid. Was Anabel still speaking? He seemed to be listening to something.

From behind me came a hissing sound—the water was boiling over. I ran and looked for a potholder—I'd never been any good at handling hot pans—finally grabbed the hand towel, picked up the pot with both hands and carried it over to the coffee machine as if I were holding the Holy Grail. I poured the water on the coffee. It splashed over and I jumped aside, swore, wiped the floor with the hand towel, gave up and rushed back to the window.

Anabel turned her head and called out, "How's breakfast coming along?"

Frantically I threw open one cabinet after another in search of cups and plates, savagely pulled all the drawers out to look for knives and spoons, and piled everything on the tray. No room for that coffee-filter thing—oh well, I'd get that later. Opening the door with my elbow, I stepped out on the terrace.

Jerome jumped down from the wall and took the tray

from my hands without so much as a look at me. Anabel's face gave nothing away.

"The coffee," I stammered. "Just a moment . . ."

I turned and raced back to the kitchen, grabbed the coffee machine—and set it down again. What was going on out on the terrace? What had she said to him?

The door opened and Eva's sleepy face appeared. She looked around, stunned.

"What's happened? Have we had vandals in here? Good Lord—it stinks of gas!" She ran to the stove and turned off the gas. Only then did she see my face. "Don't you feel well? Why didn't you wake me up if you're hungry?"

I shook my head and pointed to the window.

"No!" she shouted in amazement. "Anabel! Is she all right again?"

Picking up the coffee machine in her strong, capable hands, she walked out on the terrace, laughing and calling. Through the window I saw Peter and Jean-Pierre approaching, then Ursula—greetings, embraces—nothing to be afraid of anymore, the tornado had passed. But I stayed in the kitchen for a little while before I joined them on the terrace.

22

What had she said to him out there on the terrace when she sat on the chair with her back to me? I leafed through the diary, although I knew she never took it with her to Grasse, but perhaps she'd written about it later.

Nothing.

There weren't that many entries left, and those I skipped for the time being. I didn't feel up to them as yet, I was too caught up in my own journey through the past. Right now I was on the point of reliving those days in Grasse with such detailed precision it was as if I had myself written a diary at that time, and was now reading it again. Every face, every word, even the light and the time of day—morning, noon or night—everything had been faithfully recorded and came flooding back. Not hectically and randomly, as it had at first, but more systematically, and more thoroughly.

I now actively enjoyed posing in the studio, getting lost in my thoughts. The familiar room with its smell of paint, the music, the presence of the silent, shapeless form in front of the easel—all created a balmy emptiness in my mind, so that the bygone course of events could unfold at leisure. I was so absorbed and far away that it often came as a shock when the fifteen minutes were over.

The painter praised me. "You sit there now as if you really belong. Almost like a professional model. I can't work properly unless my model cooperates, and you're so lost in your memories that your face now matches my poncho. Indians sit for hours like that, chewing coca, or not even chewing, just thinking about something that feeds them inside. Exactly like you, now. Anabel's a hard nut to crack, isn't she?"

She laughed. She had given up asking me questions.

One day, out of the blue, I said, "You mentioned some time ago that you knew Dujardin. What kind of man was he? What did he look like? Tell me about him."

She gave me a puzzled look, surprised at the urgency in my voice, leaned her head back to stare at the ceiling, took off her glasses and thought.

"Dujardin? When I knew him he was about forty. Short, but well put together. He held himself very erect but not stiff. He had a definite—presence, authority. Thinning hair—dark. Dark eyes too. A strong face—good face—large. Eyes, nose, mouth—all large. Very decisive. Good voice. Hands—yes, good hands too. Actually he wasn't much interested in the gallery, he only bought it to give himself something to do. His father had plenty of money and let him do what he wanted. Once he showed me his Sanskrit manuscripts and medieval illuminated books. That was more than just a hobby; he was an expert, the Louvre used to consult him at times. What you want to know is, of course, how Jeannine fitted into all this. Nobody could understand it. She was his second wife—the first one had died. He was said to have been happy in his first marriage and—well, you know the old story, one tries again and can't repeat the trick. While I was having my second show with him, he suddenly

disappeared from one day to the next. No one had any idea
where he was. Clients came—people like Leger or Van
Dongen—wanting to speak to him, and I was particularly
angry because I couldn't very well do the dealing and haggling over my pictures myself and his secretary was a half-
wit. One day she told me all the dirt—he fired her later when
he found out. Jeannine, she said, was in Barcelona with a
bullfighter, living quite openly with him in his apartment,
sitting in the president's box whenever he appeared in the
arena. One afternoon he was awarded both ears and the tail,
and the French newsreels picked it up. I didn't see it but I
heard about it. Apparently you could recognize Jeannine
quite clearly in the box, bending down to embrace him,
while the audience cheered. That was the day before Dujardin disappeared. A week later—the last week of my exhibition—he showed up again. Without Jeannine, said the
secretary. I must say, he looked as if he'd been crucified. All
kinds of wild rumors were going around—he had beaten
Jeannine up or she had beaten him up. It finally turned out
that he had beaten up the bullfighter, who wasn't able to
fight for a while. Apparently Jeannine nursed him, and I
suppose that gave them time to get to know and bore each
other. Anyhow all of a sudden she was back, though she
didn't show her face in the gallery. Now then—if you're
ready . . ."

I was ready. I had a lot of new material to work on, new
angles had just evolved: Dujardin. According to Anabel, he
had been the key.

Now then—take it easy, don't rush, go back to the scene
on the terrace, at breakfast, the day Anabel fell out of the
sky. Extraordinary, the aplomb with which she caught on to
Eva's cry: "Are you well again?" and the innocuous explanation of her "miraculous recovery." She took care, of
course, not to go into details—after all, she still didn't know

what was supposed to have been wrong with her—but changed the subject elegantly and nonchalantly to the effect that one didn't bore one's friends with one's ailments.

Did Jerome believe her? His face seemed to me pale under his tan, his narrow eyes unfathomable, though he ate with concentration and appetite. Suddenly he looked up and said to Eva, and apparently to no one else, "You needn't drive me to the station. I'm staying here." Astonishment and consternation among the entire Gurnemantz clan.

Peter protested. "But you must go! It's important for you. Here's the note for the gallery. Anabel won't mind if you're away for a few days, we'll take good care of her, won't we, Anabel?"

She smiled disarmingly and nodded, noncommittally. The others didn't notice anything, kept urging Jerome to go, wanted me to persuade him—I remained neutral and silent—and didn't give up until he said, "After all, it doesn't have to be today. I can go another time."

Soon after that Anabel excused herself and went off to the second guest room. She wanted to "rest a little." She hadn't mentioned that she'd been driving all night—it wouldn't have made sense and would have sounded suspicious, coming on top of all those stories about her illness and quick recovery.

Wise Anabel, equal to anything. She would now take the reins, take over, teach me.

The terrace gradually emptied as the Gurnemantz family dissolved in all directions to go about their individual business. Jerome and I remained. I, because I didn't know what else to do, he, because he had something to say to me.

"Well? Are you satisfied?"

He took my hand and stroked it, almost the way he used to.

"Yes."

It was true. I certainly ought to be "satisfied" now that he'd given up Saint-Tropez—for the time being at least. That I owed to Anabel.

He seemed to be thinking along the same lines.

"Quite a coincidence that she should arrive this morning, isn't it?"

He knew, then. Had she told him? Not that it mattered. Better—and simpler—to tell him the truth.

"She's here because I asked her to come." He didn't answer, but since he did not relinquish my hand, I felt this might be a good moment to tell him the truth. "She dropped everything, imagine! She dropped her lover, left him high and dry in London, sitting there all by himself."

He let go of my hand as if it had burned him, and jumped up on the wall, turning his back on me. I watched him, feeling relieved and gratified. Without a doubt, my story had considerably impressed him. A flood of love and gratitude for Anabel overwhelmed me—but he suddenly turned to face me and rudely cut off any further account of her self-sacrifice.

"So you think she's helping you?"

"Well, you're not going to see—you're not going to Saint-Tropez today. That's a help."

I looked up at him. He squatted down, stretched out his hands and cradled my face in them, looking urgently, almost beseechingly, into my eyes.

· "You should let things take their course. Unfinished business rots and torments. Do you understand what I mean?"

I shook my head. To me the only thing that mattered was that this "business" had been nipped in the bud. Out of sight, out of mind.

Jerome let go of me, said he was going to Madame Raquin's to call Saint-Tropez and cancel his visit.

He left and I remained alone on the terrace, alone and

suddenly assailed by gnawing doubts. "Let things take their course . . ." What had he meant by that?

•

Market day. Peach-picking day. I was glad to have something to do, since Anabel hadn't reappeared as yet.

"The journey must have been very tiring for her," said Ursula, who was working next to me to make sure I didn't pick any more unripe peaches. No danger of that, I was on my toes today. "She mustn't come with us to Nice tonight."

That was quite all right with Anabel. She didn't show up until we were out on the terrace by candlelight, drinking our Pernod and eating almonds. Leaning against the pine tree in something long and white, she said she wasn't hungry but she'd like some coffee. Shortly afterward, when I looked back at the pine tree, she was gone.

I felt somehow let down. I had hardly exchanged a word with her, yet there was so much to tell, so many questions to ask, especially about what Jerome had said that morning about letting things take their course. How long would she be staying? Probably only a few days; she'd want to get back to Ferencsi, surely.

Peter and Jerome were changing a tire on the truck, Eva offered to put Jean-Pierre to bed, Ursula and I were left alone in the dark.

"How do you like Madame Raquin?"

"I like her."

"Could you imagine her as my mother-in-law?"

Mother-in-law? I didn't know what to reply, and Ursula wasn't expecting me to.

"She knows what's going on here," she continued. "Probably the whole neighborhood knows. You've seen for yourself how Eva's acting. Any moment now she'll be claiming

that Jean-Pierre's really *her* child. Madame Raquin has a
son who's a widower—no, not the retarded one, the other
one. She'd like us to get married. I think it's really Jean-
Pierre she's after—she's taken a great fancy to him. She has
visions of him taking care of our peaches and her vineyards.
Not a bad idea at that."

"Ursula, I don't know what's going on here. I can see that
something's wrong, but—"

"Remember our council meeting last year? I've been
completely well again for months, but Eva says that Peter is
her whole life. *Basta.*"

"And what does Peter say?"

"Why don't you ask what *I* say?"

"I think I know."

"Do you?"

"You wish that council meeting had never been held."

She walked across the terrace and sat down on the wall. "I
was sitting right here, wasn't I, exactly a year ago. Well, if I
could turn back the clock . . ." She broke off.

"What would you do?"

"The same thing. There was no other solution. And now
you can ask me what Peter says. Peter says nothing at all. He
hopes we can keep everything flexible—adaptable. He still
sees people the way a sculptor sees them. As long as we're
still clay, still malleable, there's hope. What he'd really like
to do is wrap us in wet cloth at night to keep us soft until the
next day."

"You mean he can't decide between the two of you?"

She didn't answer.

•

When we got home at five o'clock the next morning, I found
a note on my bedside table. "Slept enough. Gone to Cannes
to visit friends. Plaza Hotel. Back this evening. Anabel."

Not a word of it was true, I knew that even before I'd finished reading it. But where was she?

In spite of my disappointment and a feeling of having been abandoned, I fell into bed, dead tired as usual. Toward noon a rustling sound at the door woke me up. Someone— probably Jean-Pierre—was trying to slip a piece of paper under the door.

Jerome was still asleep. I got up without making a sound. A telegram. For me. "Call me Hotel Albi Saint-Tropez Anabel."

This time I was lucky, for Jean-Pierre and his fishing gear were immersed in the water cistern and I was able to escape into the orchard without his seeing me. Downhill I went once again, through the lower gate and the olive grove to the square little yellow house. An old Renault was standing at the door and a young man with fair hair was carrying crates of empty bottles out of the house. Probably the widower; the fine curly hair reminded me of his mother. He nodded and glanced at me curiously. The actress! His mother was in the kitchen, he'd fetch her. A glass of wine? No, thank you, no time!

Madame Raquin waddled up, arms spread wide, yellow teeth bared, and kissed me on both cheeks. Another telephone call to England? No, this time to the Hotel Albi in Saint-Tropez, please.

"The Albi? Oh, yes, I have that number," said Madame. "That's the one the young man always calls. Person to person?"

Anabel at Jeannine Dujardin's hotel! What could she possibly be doing there? While Madame turned the crank, shouted and laboriously spelled out "Maclean," I thought about the Brimstone butterfly sitting on Babs's sofa, gently flicking her toes in her sandals, as befits a butterfly. . . .

"*Voilà*, Mademoiselle."

She handed me the receiver and wheezed out of the room.

"Anabel? What in God's name . . ."

"Listen. I've been waiting for hours for you to call. I'd like to get back tonight, but I don't know if I'll make it. If I'm not back by eight, don't worry, it means I'll be staying here and I'll be back tomorrow morning. Tell the others I'm visiting friends at the Plaza Hotel in Cannes. Jerome mustn't know I'm here. Okay?"

"What are you doing there? Are you talking to Jeannine?"

"No, to her husband. He's the key."

She hung up, as abruptly as usual. She never said goodbye. When she was through, she simply hung up, leaving you holding the receiver. A tiny protest pimple sprouted on the so far unblemished skin of my gratitude. She was turning me into a child. Deliberately.

Outside, Madame was waiting. She insisted that I take a glass of wine in the arbor. While she waited for the operator to tell her the charge, I racked my brains over Anabel's puzzling words: "He's the key." Monsieur Dujardin. What was he doing in Saint-Tropez? Had he returned to Paris unexpectedly, found his wife gone, and set off to find her?

Madame came snorting through the leafy arbor entrance, her forehead and upper lip covered with drops of sweat. She plucked a vine leaf and wiped her face, but it crumpled up and little scraps of it stuck to her chin.

"Clean," she said collapsing into her chair. "Nothing's as clean as wine. Even its leaves. Your good health!"

But before I could raise my glass, the foliage parted for the second time and Ursula's head appeared, with Jean-Pierre's yellow crew-cut a foot or so below it.

"Come in, come in," called Madame, overjoyed. "Jean-Pierre, bring some glasses—and let my son know!"

She made several unsuccessful efforts to get to her feet, in order to embrace that long beanstalk which was Ursula, gave up, wheezed, thumped her chest and turned a bluish color.

"The sirocco," said Ursula. "Shall I bring your drops?"

Madame gasped for air like a codfish on dry land, shook her head, grabbed Ursula's hand in place of a cold compress and held it to the top of her heaving chest. Ursula, embarrassed and bent double, drew her hand away and stood up straight.

"Here," she said, picking up Madame's glass. "The cure-all."

The old lady pushed it aside. Her eyes were still popping out of her head but her breathing was easier.

"It's not the sirocco," she gasped in my direction as if asking me to be her witness. "It's the constant worry. I'm not going to last much longer and what's going to happen here then?"

Ursula frowned; she knew this was directed at her.

Jean-Pierre returned, followed by Marcel Raquin, whom Madame formally introduced. Four glasses were ceremoniously filled. Jean-Pierre glanced at his mother—the fifth remained empty.

"To the boy's health!" wheezed Madame, who had intercepted the glance. We all drank and looked at the blushing towhead, who reached up to Madame Raquin to hide his embarrassment.

"You've got something on your chin," he said, carefully scratching off the specks of green while Madame closed her eyes in bliss.

Suddenly she opened them again and said firmly, "Marcel, show Madame Gürman the new irrigation system. She could do with something like that at her place."

Marcel, who was considerably shorter than Ursula,

looked up at her yearningly. Ursula's lips trembled, and she abruptly turned to me, ignoring the others.

"When we bought the hill five years ago, we had no money for that kind of thing, you know. Peter racked his brains and finally came up with a crazy idea. He'd read in the papers that the fleet had docked at Toulon, so he went there and inspected their old pipes. He guessed they would have no use for them, and sure enough, they were just lying around, so they practically gave them away, glad to get rid of them. He hauled them up here—poor old Aesculapius had a hard time, I can tell you—and for months on end it looked as if giant worms were wriggling around the house. One by one, he patched them together, and that's still the only irrigation system we have. It works pretty well though, doesn't it? Anyway, we're proud of it, but maybe it's time to make some changes. So, I'd be interested to see yours, Monsieur Marcel."

"So would I," exclaimed Jean-Pierre, running after them —much to Madame's displeasure.

"A fine young couple!" she declared emphatically, parting the vine to gaze after them. Marcel's head reached just to Ursula's shoulder. "I'm against divorce, I'm a Catholic," she added severely, raising her voice as though her father confessor were in hearing distance. "But in this case . . ."

She pounded the table with her fist, gave me a challenging look, bent forward and hissed, "It's not true that I used to beat up my late husband, people only say that because he was puny and I'm fat. I'd have liked to but I couldn't, he had the strength of a giant when he was drunk. I hated him, all right, because I had one stillbirth after another—all full-term, *that* was the reason, Mademoiselle! They'd lay them down on the sheet, not breathing, all of them full of alcohol —or that's what they looked like to me. And that's why I was happy to see him buried. I didn't shed a tear at his

funeral, and people never forgave me, for you're supposed
to cry at the funeral, that's the custom here. But when the
priest said, 'And now our beloved brother is gone from us
forever,' I said aloud, 'Amen!' Just look at the two that survived, Mademoiselle! Upstairs there's one who can't even
speak, and out there in the vineyard, Marcel—well, he's all
right, thank God, and he's a good son, but the doctor says he
can't have any children. Now you see . . . " Her voice grew
faint, as if she were repeating something she said to herself a
hundred times a day, sitting here in the green arbor. "You
see—if we could have Jean-Pierre, there would be no problem. Do you understand me, Mademoiselle?"

I understood but I didn't feel like admitting it, so I got
up.

"Nobody but the child's on my side!" exclaimed Madame
in despair.

"Jean-Pierre? You mean to say he'd like to change fathers?"

Madame made a slapping gesture, as if my question had
been a mosquito.

"*Mais non, mais non*! He wouldn't have to change fathers.
His father's right next door and he could go and visit him
every day." She drew a deep breath and her voice took on a
threatening tone. "But he'd only have one mother—his own
mother, Madame Gürman!" She looked at me significantly,
bared her teeth in a flash and added, "*And* a grandmother."

·

"That's it for today," exclaimed the painter, grinning. "Do
you realize you've been posing for half an hour? You were
so wrapped up in yourself that I didn't stop. Didn't you
notice?"

I hadn't noticed anything, I was still in the green arbor.

As I opened the studio door to leave, she called after me, "I've just remembered something else about Dujardin. He's supposed to have lived for a long time in India, before the war. He was keen on yogi or yoga—or whatever you call it."

23

When Anabel finally returned from Saint-Tropez at lunch-time the next day, she revealed only what my urgent questioning managed to dig out of her. I had to be patient until after lunch, when she at last beckoned to me and we wandered toward the olive grove in order to avoid the others.

But it was too hot to walk, even under the shade of the trees. We marched side by side in silence until we found some large flat rocks down by the stream where we could sit and dangle our feet in the water.

"Well?" All I knew so far was that she had spent the first night sitting on the beach—while we were at the market in Nice just a few miles away—and that the next morning she had made the rounds of the hotels until she had finally found Madame Dujardin registered at the Albi.

"And then—what?" The water was cooling my feet but not my impatience.

She was sitting very straight, dressed in a blouse and shorts, letting her long white legs float in the water. She never exposed herself to the sun if she could help it, never got a tan.

"Then the desk clerk called her room. No answer." She broke off a willow branch and waved away the gnats.

"But—what was it that you wanted from her?"

"I wanted to look at her, maybe—speak to her, maybe not. I had no particular plan in mind, I was playing it by ear. You wouldn't understand, you have no ear for that kind of thing."

Another protest pimple was about to sprout—but I decided not to stand up for my ear.

"And then?"

She put down the willow branch and smiled.

"The desk clerk said Madame Dujardin had a friend with her. Perhaps she would know."

"Who's the friend?"

"A Madame Siodmak."

She picked up the willow branch again and swished it methodically in a semicircle around her head. Long slender willow leaves fluttered anxiously through the air, landing hesitantly on the surface of the water as if they knew what was in store for them: the swirling, tossing rush downstream and the final drowning.

So Babs had accompanied Jeannine to Saint-Tropez—or the other way around. Did Anabel know about Babs's earlier connection with Jerome? Had I ever told her about it? I couldn't remember.

She threw the naked willow branch after its departed leaves and watched them, absorbed, on their course downstream, getting stuck here and there—until they finally disappeared around the riverbend.

I put my hand on her arm to call her attention back to me, to my anguish, to my ordeal—to *me*! After all, she'd come all this way to help me, hadn't she? Yet, since her return from Saint-Tropez I had the extraordinary feeling that she'd forgotten me.

"Anabel—did I ever mention to you that I know Mrs. Siodmak?"

"She told me. She told me about Jerome too." She looked at me and laughed. What was so funny about that? Puzzled and unamused, I watched her in silence, but she paid no attention to me, stared again into the water, thinking aloud.

"I liked her—she seems to have a lot of fun—does only what she likes—or maybe she makes herself like what she does. Anyway, I can't imagine her worrying about anything as long as there's a deck of cards at hand."

"It looks as if you've become fast friends."

"At first sight. She told the desk clerk to ask me to come up—maybe she thought it was you, using a false name! I opened the door and there she was, in bed, her hair tied on top, looking like a black-and-white Easter egg, playing solitaire on her breakfast tray. Those hands! I've never seen such useless hands. The cards stuck to her fingers like postage stamps. Can she ever really take hold of anything? She was amazed that I knew Jeannine was there, and asked what I wanted of her. I said I was visiting the Gurnemantzes with you and Jerome—and at that she almost upset the tray."

Anabel stopped for a moment, lifted her feet out of the water, let them drop back in, dipped them in and out, smiling to herself. The splashing got on my nerves.

"And then?"

"We talked about you and about you and Jerome—and then, luckily, before I was forced to explain my visit, the telephone rang. The desk clerk. Had Jeannine come back? When was she expected? There was a gentleman downstairs asking for her. Mrs. Siodmak put her hand over the receiver and whispered excitedly, 'Jerome's here.' But, to make sure, she said into the telephone, 'Ask the gentleman's name.' And then . . ."

Anabel stopped smiling, drew her legs out of the water

and, hugging her knees, frowned and stared ahead. She spoke so quietly that I could hardly hear her above the babbling of the stream.

"And then—her face just fell apart, and I was afraid her jaw would drop on the lace of her bed jacket. I thought, who on earth is she speaking to? What's happening? Why is she so flabbergasted? It couldn't be Jerome, so who could it be? She made a visible effort, gained control of her chin and said to the desk clerk with studied calm, 'Monsieur Dujardin? Yes, of course I'll speak to him.' She'd completely forgotten me, stared at the cards on the tray, obviously waiting for this man to get on the telephone. I watched her preparing herself, considering possibilities, rejecting them again—and then she said hoarsely and all in one breath, 'Jean? Well, well, how are you? What are you doing here?' She listened for a moment, then went on with a slightly forced laugh. 'Oh, I see, Robert told you! How nice! Of course. Why not? After all, it's no secret. Jeannine's down on the beach already, I'll tell her as soon as she gets back. What's your room number? 52? Let me write it down.' She quickly added that she hoped they could get together for a drink, but I knew from the sound of the telephone that he had hung up. All the same she said, 'Well, goodbye, Jean,' into thin air before replacing the receiver."

•

Six years later, after the war, Babs told me her version of the scene. Once again I was sitting by the water, but this time not on rocks under a willow tree but in a padded lounge chair beside a bright-blue Hollywood swimming pool. Robert Siodmak had made it in Hollywood, directing first-class films which everyone except Babs admired. "I can't stand your pictures," she used to say, which made him laugh, but she now ran an imposing establishment, a combination of Americanized comfort and European coziness, and a permanent haven for European refugees, successful ones as well as lame ducks.

But in spite of her new mink coat and a garden full of orange trees, Babs missed her stronghold, the café. Cafés didn't exist in Hollywood, because there were no pedestrians— everyone rode around in cars—and you can't have a café without passersby to comment on. "Where's my Paradise?" she would sigh. "My café! The place where you can get away from home without having to be in the fresh air!"

Glumly, she would sit beside her pool, lower herself reluctantly down the ladder into the water and "swim," not horizontally, but standing erect, her head held high, hair piled on top.

I can't remember how the subject of Saint-Tropez came up. Perhaps we'd been talking about Jerome . . .

"God, what a day that was! It started early in the morning when that girl friend of yours suddenly burst in on me! When the desk clerk said a lady was asking for Jeannine, I thought of course it was you! And then that woman showed up—with those eyes! She gave me such a shock that I laid out my solitaire all wrong and of course it didn't come out and messed up the entire day. I knew at once she was there to spy on us for some reason—and just at that moment Jean Dujardin called. He was an old friend of mine, he'd just come back from India and wanted to join Jeannine and me for a few days. So touching! He always was such a very warm, loving person. While I was talking to him, I noticed that that woman—what's her name again?"

"Anabel Maclean."

"Yes—that she ate me up with those black eyes of hers. What on earth is she after, I asked myself, what's she doing here? I bet she's up to something! So I said to her, 'Maybe we'll come over to visit you all, Jeannine and I. After all, I knew the Gurnemantzes from way back in Paris!' At that she had the nerve to say, 'Don't you do anything of the sort—you've caused enough trouble already!' And she flounced out of the room. I wanted to run after her and ask her what she meant by 'making trouble.' I'd only come to Saint-Tropez with Jeannine so she wouldn't be alone—she and I often used to spend a few days there 'together—but my cards had got all mixed up and I had to straighten them out first. I looked for her all day in the hotel but she'd gone. Was she really a friend of yours?"

•

But Anabel wasn't gone. She stayed in the hotel, that day and the following night too. As Babs suspected, she was up to something. Something in Room 52.

"I knocked. No one called 'Come in!' but the door wasn't locked. As I walked in, an extraordinary feeling came over me. The huge living room was empty—the door to the balcony stood open. I crossed the room on tiptoe—I don't know why. Did I want to catch him unawares? He was sitting on a chair in the shade, facing me, and he didn't look at all surprised to see me standing at the balcony door. He was waiting for Jeannine, of course, yet I felt certain he was waiting for me."

She thought a while before continuing.

"I can't describe the way I felt. I'd known plenty of men before I met Bill, and I thought I was pretty good at classifying them at first sight. I always knew right away who was a possibility and who wasn't and which ones might become dangerous. But this man was something else again, much more disturbing than anybody I'd ever met, he was a magnet—and at the same time unapproachable, and right there in the balcony doorway I'd blundered into his magnetic field. I can't even describe to you what he looked like, although I sat opposite him for several hours. His arms were resting on the arms of the chair, his hands hanging loose—that much I remember. He gave you the impression of having no life in him—and yet some kind of current was crackling around him or passing back and forth between us, as if I were hooked up to some electrical machine.

"'Welcome!' he said, without moving. I stepped outside into the sun and sat down on the other chair. Everything I did required an effort and yet I was compelled to do it. Something commanded me. 'My name's Anabel Maclean,' I said. He nodded. 'I've come to speak to your wife.' He nodded again. And that was all I had to say, my head was empty. I remember thinking, it's a good thing I told him my name because right now I don't even know it anymore. What am I called? Who am I? I couldn't for the life of me remember. I sat up straight in my chair, I saw him without really taking him in, I saw the sea without seeing it. Have you ever been given an anesthetic? It was like the last few seconds before you're extinguished—you know everything that's happening, you can still feel everything, but you can't make use of it. No, that's not quite correct, for there *was* one thing I did know, one thing I did feel: I wanted to hear his voice! He had only spoken that one word: 'Welcome!' I have no idea how long I sat there or how long the silence lasted."

She turned and looked at me as though I had just said something uncanny. "Hypnosis? Have you ever been hypnotized?"

"No. I'm scared of that sort of thing. Once at the house of some friends I met a man who was hypnotizing people. But I stayed out of it, I was afraid I might fall asleep forever."

She turned away and stared into the stream again. I stared too. The tangled reflection of willows and sky, constantly moving yet remaining the same, had a slightly hypnotic effect of its own. One couldn't sit there and look at some-thing else, one's eyes were irresistibly drawn to the water, held by it.

"Then he spoke, but I can't tell you exactly what he said. I'm not keeping things back, I simply don't know. Ever since, I've been trying to nail down exactly what it was. Something to the effect that he wanted to talk to me but not right then. Later. I said that it was imperative for him to know that Jeannine—that Jerome—that you—but I stut-tered and lost track of what I was saying, and in the end I didn't even know what I'd come for anymore. Something made me get up, walk through the balcony door across the big living room and out into the hallway. I'd already re-served a room. I lay down on the bed. There was only one clear thought in my mind: He wants to see me again this afternoon at five, on the balcony. That is, he'd commanded me to be there. Until then I could sleep."

·

Beside the pool in Hollywood, six years later, Babs leaned back against the white cushions and filled me in about Jeannine's return from the beach that morning, while Anabel was sleeping. Jeannine's bedroom was next to Babs's, the door between the two rooms was ajar, and there was the Brim-stone butterfly, laughing, sweaty, with sand sticking to her legs, her yellow hair like wet straw.

"Jean's here," said Babs. Jeannine stopped laughing and leaned against the door, looking cross.

"That's all I needed," she muttered. "Couldn't he have stayed a few days longer in—in wherever the hell he was? He's been gone three months, I was beginning to wonder if something had happened to him. Now, who let the cat out of the bag about Jerome? Probably Roger, that sneaky secre-tary of his, the dirty little swine!" She laughed again.

"Maybe there'll be another cockfight like that time in Madrid. You'd better warn Jerome, Jean's left-handed, with a mean uppercut. He gave Rodriguez a cauliflower ear to remember him by. Oh well, I'd better go and see him. Let's get it over with." Babs could hear her in the bathroom whistling the "Toreador" song from *Carmen*.

Half an hour later she reappeared in the doorway, bathed and her hair done.

"Room 52? Okay. I think I'll tell him to go to hell. What does he mean, showing up like this out of the blue, making trouble—"

"Be careful," said Babs. "My solitaire didn't come out."

"*Merde* on your solitaire!" said Jeannine, and Babs could hear her whistling as she walked down the hallway. Only then did it occur to her that she ought to have told Jeannine about the visit of that extraordinary woman. . . .

Sighing, she had put the cards away for the day, had dressed and had gone to the hotel beauty shop to have her hair washed. When she came back, Jeannine was in her room.

"Well—how did it go?" Babs asked.

Jeannine turned a white, fragile little face toward her, her mouth open, her eyes terror-stricken. Instead of the radiant Brimstone butterfly, there hovered a plain cabbage white, utterly defeated, facing the end of its short life span.

"What happened?" exclaimed Babs, aghast. "Did he hit you?"

Jeannine shook her head.

"That would have been better," she whispered. "Even a cauliflower ear would have been better—you can hide that under your hair."

"For God's sake—what did he do?"

"He didn't *do* anything." She went over to the bed and collapsed on top of it as if she had just run several miles.

"You know Jean, don't you? But you'd never recognize him, he's completely changed, he's . . . " Her voice trailed away.

Babs, wide-eyed, sat down beside her on the bed.

"I know what you mean. This morning on the telephone, it was Jean—and it wasn't Jean. He sounded most peculiar."

Jeannine was slowly recovering, and the color was coming back to her cheeks. She clutched Babs's hand, the Botticelli hand, as if it were made of steel.

She had marched into Room 52, Jeannine said, whistling away. There was no one in the living room—but something had caught her by the throat, made her cough and choke, and snuffed out the whistling. At first she thought she'd swum out too far that morning, because her legs suddenly seemed to be made of lead. It took all her strength to walk across to the balcony door. Jean was sitting there in the shade, and the shade was so deep that she hardly recognized him, and yet it was broad daylight, noontime. He hadn't uttered a word of greeting, although he hadn't seen her for three months, nor did he invite her to sit down, but she managed to make it as far as the empty chair in the sun. It was probably the heat that made her breathless and parched, so much so that it cost her a real effort to say, "Hello, Jean." She had intended to add, "What are you doing here?" but the words stuck in her throat.

At this point in her story Babs stood up and paced back and forth beside the swimming pool. The very memory was too disturbing for her to sit still. At last she came to a stop in front of me.

"Do you believe in that sort of thing?"

"What sort of thing?"

"You know—extrasensory perception or whatever it's called."

"No. Even bona-fide, old-established ghosts take off when I enter a haunted house."

"I'm not talking about ghosts! I'm talking about those powers, powers one is supposed to be able to acquire—"

"Like voodoo in Haiti?"

"Or Indian fakirs."

"Well, that's different, you have to believe in them because you can see them with your own eyes, sitting there for weeks at a time with their arms raised up like withered branches—"

"Exactly," said Babs. "It seems, out there, on that balcony, there was the same sort of atmosphere as looking at a fakir—although Jeannine knew all the time it was only Jean and nobody else and she even remembered how he'd always bored her—and she couldn't understand herself, because he was really quite fascinating—at least that's what she thought for a moment. She wanted to say something nice to him, but she never got the chance. He spoke, apparently only a few sentences, she couldn't remember the exact words, but she got the message all right: He never wanted to see her again except once—that very evening, and only for a few minutes. She was to say yes or no. In any case she was to take the early-morning train back to Paris, pack her things and leave the apartment. Roger would be there. Divorce. If she accepted his one condition, she could take her jewelry out of the safe. She would receive three thousand francs a month, enough to live on. No more. If she didn't agree to the condition, she would have no claim to anything."

"What was the condition?"

Jeannine had sat up, said Babs, staring ahead with eyes full of hatred.

"I don't understand it," she kept repeating. "If he never wants to see me again, then what does it matter to him?"

"What does what matter to him?" Babs had cried and freed her hand from Jeannine's iron grip. Jeannine didn't need support anymore, she looked perfectly all right, she was even laughing—full of hatred and a bit mad—but she was laughing.

"He's only a little man, after all. However much he may have learned in India, he hasn't grown an inch! He always was a humorless son of a bitch." She buried her hands in her hair, shaking with laughter. "His one condition—the little man's revenge—his one condition—"

Now she was screaming, couldn't stop. Babs ran into the bathroom, got a glass of water and threw it in her face. She made no protest, stopped screaming, dried her face, giggling to herself.

"His condition: that I never see Jerome again!" Babs had remained silent, she had expected worse. "It's okay with me!" shouted Jeannine, as though Dujardin could still hear her. "I don't give a damn. Jerome's not that important to me. It's a pity, of course—there's something about him that I like very much. Oh well, I'll get over it. However, come to think of it, I can only speak for myself in this business. After all, Jerome has some say in this too, hasn't he? Jean can't order *him* around, can he? Maybe Jerome doesn't want to give me up—I can't help that, can I? And Jerome doesn't care whether I have any money or not. *I* care though, I must admit! I was poor too long."

•

The shade was growing deeper inside the stream, the water was almost too cold. Only the rocks we were sitting on still glowed with heat. Anabel had her eyes closed as if she were lying on her bed at the Hotel Albi, sleeping, as Monsieur Dujardin had ordered her to do.

"Just before five I woke up and went to Room 52. Now the living room and the entire balcony were in the shade. He was still sitting in the same place—in fact, I had the impression that he hadn't moved since I'd left that morning. Again that strange feeling of something tugging at me and propelling me forward—I felt it as soon as I entered the room, and on the balcony it was even stronger, as if I were being pulled forward by the hair, though it didn't hurt, in fact it was rather pleasant, like letting yourself be blown along by the wind on the seashore. The chair I'd sat on that morning was now standing next to his, and something steered me irresistibly toward that chair. I sat down and he smiled. How can I describe that smile to you? I felt more secure, more tranquil, than I've felt for a long, long time."

She stopped, lifted her head as if somebody had just called her name. "It's still with me—not quite the velvety feeling I had at the time, but I still know exactly what it was like. I was twelve when my mother died, that's how far back I have to go to remember anything similar. Then he made me speak. I say 'made me speak' because that's just the way it was. Like in the Bible. The Lord said: 'Speak!' and whoever had the honor—spoke.

"I told him about Jerome—but he raised his hand. Again I was reminded of the Bible: He knew! There was no need to tell him anything. I believed him, although I couldn't explain it to myself. Perhaps he'd seen Jeannine in between! He guessed what I was thinking and nodded, yes, he'd seen her. Aha, that explains it, I thought and was at the same time surprised that I still needed explanations! He looked at me and smiled again. This time it was as if someone were gently massaging my back, stroking my spine until every nerve responded. That's why I was able to tell him about you. He listened. I've never seen anyone listen like that—everything I said seemed to drop into a deep well, sending an echo to the surface. Things came to my mind that I really knew nothing about and yet I heard myself telling them. A lot of things became clear, others were confused—and remained confused. He never said a word, didn't even nod, but I knew he understood everything."

"Did you tell him about Ferencsi?"

Had she heard me?

"Ferencsi!" I repeated. "Did you tell him?"

Her face, up to now wide open, vulnerable, became guarded. "Yes, I told him."

"What did he say?"

She let her straight eyelashes descend over her eyes the way a jeweler drops his iron shutter to protect his property from burglars. She was about to lie and I had no wish to listen.

"He made no comment, no suggestions. Then he talked about Jerome." I hung on her lips once again. "He's had a look at the three pictures Jerome left at the gallery in Paris and he thinks they're good. He's willing to give him a show."

I jumped to my feet, grabbed her by her shoulders, forgot everything she had said, took in one thing alone: Jerome would have a show at Dujardin's! I shook her furiously, ecstatically. "Why didn't you tell me at once? Don't you understand, this is going to be—"

"Wait. There's a snag."

She freed herself from my grip, turned her face away.

"What? What?"

"Jerome can have a show at Dujardin's—quite soon, too, in October—if he undertakes never to see Jeannine again and not to get in touch with her."

That was what she called a snag? An exhibition—*and* Jeannine out of the way! I threw myself at her, shouted, cried, sobbed—suddenly felt apprehensive. Had I misunderstood anything? Or was she holding something back?

"Anabel—what's the snag?"

"What—do you think—is Jerome going to say?"

212 · Lilli Palmer

I sat down again, thought it over, putting the question to him in my mind.

"He'll—accept."

"And—you are willing to tell him?"

I didn't answer. So that was the snag.

"Can't Dujardin tell him?"

She shook her head.

I got up again, walked a few steps, stared into the water, saw nothing but the snag.

Then I heard her voice, her arid voice: *"I'll* tell him."

24

The question was: When was she going to tell him? How long was she going to keep me on tenterhooks?

I didn't dare to ask. Our easy, volatile intimacy of old was now extinct. Difficult to remember that only a few weeks ago in London I'd been sitting opposite that yellow wing chair, unloading my troubles without having to think twice, without the smallest doubt that she would understand, sympathize and help. She was still "on my side"—but surrounded by an atmosphere of silence, or rather of withdrawal, far away from me, from all of us.

·

When we emerged from the olive grove and walked up the hill in the late afternoon we found Jerome and the three Gurnemantzes on the terrace, sitting stiffly on chairs in a semicircle. Opposite them sat a young man with glasses and a receding chin and next to him a woman, also with glasses and a receding chin, in skirt and stockings despite the heat, a Monsieur Vallé and his sister, partners in an art gallery in Nice whom Peter had invited to show Jerome's work.

As we approached, however, there was no mention of his canvases; the topic was "political commitment in the visual arts." No opening there for olive trees, gypsies and foreign legionnaires.

Eva was talking eagerly, Peter was doing his best, Ursula wasn't, Jerome never said a word, kept staring at his three neglected "children" propped against the pine tree. Just you wait, I thought, those three are going to hang in one of the biggest galleries in Paris, beautifully framed and lighted, and people will stand in front of them, lost in admiration—just you wait!

The chinless couple were by now holding forth about the sociological impact of painting while we all sat speechless and halfwitted, wondering how we'd survive supper in their company.

Eva disappeared into the kitchen, and Aesculapius and Jean-Pierre were introduced as conversational reinforcements. On the pretext of helping Eva, I went after her and piled plates and glasses on the tray, never taking my eyes off the terrace. Anabel was sitting next to Jerome—but they weren't talking. Nor did they when the meal was over. The Gurnemantz trio accompanied the guests down to the road to make sure they really left. I went along so that Jerome and Anabel were left alone on the terrace. In vain. Looking back from the garden gate I thought I saw a white silhouette entering the house, and when we returned, Jerome was alone.

One last glass of Pernod for the men. We lay on the mattresses, exhausted.

"Perhaps I should give up," said Jerome. "Start something else, the way you did. Aesculapius is getting old. I could carry the baskets back and forth."

"Aesculapius is in the prime of life. You don't know the first thing about donkeys, though you may be one yourself.

You must never give up. Your work's good. I've sent off that note to the Nouveaux Artistes. Get on with it, go to Saint-Tropez, they'll be expecting you."

Saint-Tropez! It wasn't only the gallery that was expecting Jerome. The Hotel Albi was expecting him too—Jeannine in her room, and Dujardin on his balcony . . .

"Anabel!" I screamed soundlessly. "For God's sake, hurry!"

•

Next morning Jerome left our bedroom very early and without explanation. From the window I watched him walk to the terrace and sit down on the wall, waiting. Before long, somebody was bound to see him there and get breakfast.

I made the beds, hung up clothes and cleaned up the bathroom. When I looked out again, a female figure was approaching the terrace. Anabel. She stopped in front of him, evidently saying something, whereupon he nodded and stood up. At last! Relieved and cowardly, I remained behind my window, watching. Anabel knew what to do, Anabel would pull it off. This was the right moment to tell him— though surely not on the terrace! Surely they would go somewhere where they'd be undisturbed! Correct. They were leaving. I retreated hastily from the window, because they were walking in my direction—was she going to talk to him in her own room? No, they walked past the guest rooms, looking straight ahead, not speaking, past the house, toward the orchard gate and along the straight shady path, several hundred yards long, framed by olive trees.

By now they were obviously talking. Jerome stopped and said something while Anabel walked on. He caught up with her—she stopped, turned toward him and spoke. I only knew she was talking from the movements of her hands, because, already halfway to the gate, they had turned into small figures without face or features. Now it looked as if she was asking him to go on further, but Jerome leaned against an olive tree—I could hardly make him out in its deep shade—while Anabel, in her light blouse, remained standing in the middle of the path, clearly recognizable in the light filtering through the branches. She was still speaking—urgently, it seemed to me. Now she took a step backward, as if fending off what he was saying. He stepped out of the shadows, walked up to her, raised his hand and slapped her in the face. She fell sideways to one knee and collapsed on the ground.

I ran out of the room. Halfway along the path, Jerome was coming toward me. He grabbed me by the arm.

"Let go of me!" I screamed, pushing him away, but he held me tight by the wrists. I tried to break free but he held on, his face and his burning, stricken eyes close to mine.

"Don't listen to what she's saying," he whispered. "Don't listen to her—she's trying to break us up—don't listen—don't believe her—"

He couldn't hold me any longer. I tore myself free—or perhaps he let me go—and I ran toward Anabel, who was still lying on the ground, though not in the way she had fallen. She had put herself on her back, her arms extended sideways, as if crucified. I bent over her, but she made no move, just lay there, eyes open, staring up into the branches. I looked for marks on her face but there weren't any. There were tears, though, running sideways past her temples into her hair.

I knelt down beside her, begging her to get up, to tell me why Jerome had hit her.

"You know why," she said quietly.

I jumped up and ran back to the house. When I opened the door to our room, he was lying on the bed, hands clasped behind his head. I closed the door and leaned against it, didn't want to get any closer to him.

"You've hit her in the face—I saw you. How could you hit her? You can't do that—"

"Do what?"

"Hit a woman—a woman who has nothing to do with you—"

"Anabel hasn't anything to do with me?"

"Of course she hasn't. You can hit your own wife if you have to, but—"

"If you have to, you can also hit a woman who has nothing to do with you." He spoke quite quietly. A different person.

"Why did you have to? She hasn't done you any harm. She only told you about Dujardin's offer. You know very well that she only went to Saint-Tropez to help me."

He gave me a long, sad, searching look.

"Yes, I know. I'm sorry. I shouldn't have done it."

"You should tell *her* that, not me." He nodded slowly. "Will you tell her?" He nodded again and smiled. "Well then—come."

He sat up, put his feet on the floor, rested his elbows on his knees and let his head fall on his hands. I waited at the door. I should have felt relieved, the "snag" was now a thing of the past. She had told him—and so he'd hit her. Understandable enough. What was worrying me then?

What was worrying me was that it *wasn't* understandable that he should have hit her. He was still sitting on the bed, his face buried in his hands. And what about the exhibition at Dujardin's? Maybe he hadn't taken it in—or was he more involved with Jeannine than I wanted to admit? Was that what was worrying me? No. It was a weird feeling, as if I didn't know him at all. Or Anabel either.

He raised his head and got up. Together, we left the house and walked along the path. She was sitting in the grass under an olive tree, calmly watching us approach and stop beside her. She didn't look at me, only at Jerome. He repeated the words he had spoken in the bedroom as though he had learned them by heart: "I'm sorry. I shouldn't have done that."

She made no answer, just kept looking at him. He gave her a little nod as if to say, "Okay?" And I thought for a second, but they're playing a game! There was no need for him to apologize—she's not a woman who has nothing to do with him, she's an ally, she's Jerome's ally, not mine!

He gave the same little nod to me as though asking, "Will that do?" Then he left.

I sat down on the ground beside Anabel, tearing up blades of grass around me.

She followed Jerome with her eyes until he disappeared on the terrace. Then she leaned back against the tree trunk.

"I haven't told you why I stayed over in Saint-Tropez last night."

I had never even given it a thought! Of course. Hadn't she said she was going to see Dujardin again at five?

"That was again an extraordinary thing." She was relaxed and spoke slowly and thoughtfully, as though nothing had happened on this beautiful morning to disturb her peace of mind. Jerome hadn't hit her, Jerome didn't exist, I didn't exist, she had erased us. She wasn't talking to anyone in particular; I had the uncomfortable feeling that if I hadn't been sitting beside her, she would have spoken aloud in exactly the same way. "That afternoon, when I was sitting on the balcony with him, I saw him close his eyes, as though his eyelids had suddenly become too heavy. Before I had time to stand up, he said, with his eyes closed and without the least attempt at an apology, 'Please go now, I'll expect you at ten o'clock.' And I left. It didn't seem at all impolite that he didn't get up to see me out. I had the feeling that he couldn't because he wasn't on the balcony anymore, he was somewhere else, somewhere far away. I slept until shortly before ten. Very soundly.

"This time he was standing by the balcony railing, looking out at the dark sea. The table was laid. There was a bottle of wine in a cooler but only one wine glass. For me. He drank only water. We ate, almost without talking. There was only a lantern on the table—one could hardly see one's plate. The waiter went to and fro without a sound, like a shadow, as if he were barefooted. Later I noticed that he *was* barefooted. His face was dark above his white jacket—an Indian. The concierge told me afterward• that Monsieur Dujardin had brought him and installed him in an adjoining room. Only the Indian was allowed to wait on him.

"The night air was completely still. Somehow the food disappeared and then the table. Only the lantern was left on the floor between our two chairs. Later on he extinguished it and we sat in the dark, but I had no trouble seeing him, perhaps because I could hear his voice so clearly."

She chewed thoughtfully at her upper lip.

"Now, in broad daylight, it's hard to describe what they were like, those hours up there on the balcony. He would talk for a long time, then remain silent for a long time. I said very little. I had the feeling that he knew all about me. He told me what it was that had originally taken him to India: copies of Sanskrit manuscripts in the Delhi museum. And there, in Delhi, he had met the guru, the man who had opened the door to a new existence by teaching him that it's possible to gain complete mastery of the body and the mind. Right at the start, he said, he was amazed and fascinated by one of the guru's teachings: 'It's a mistake to believe that we've achieved everything when we've learned to love our fellow men. The most important thing is to understand our enemy. Our friends have nothing to teach us. We *learn* only from our enemies.' Jeannine, his wife, was his enemy. For the first time in his married life he gave up all attempts to change her or dominate her; instead he tried to understand her—and learn from her. And so, after spending two months in India, he believed he was already well on the way to salvation and inviolable harmony, but when he returned to Paris, his peace of mind slowly ebbed away and he found himself more vulnerable and more emasculated than ever before. At the same time some sort of calamity occurred—I didn't quite understand what it was and didn't want to ask, something physical, a fight or perhaps a duel—anyway, it had to do with his wife, that much I understood. It made him decide to go back to India and study seriously and for as long as it would take to extricate and redeem himself once and for all. Soon he would go back there again, he said; one needed the landscape and the "brothers" from time to time, and the austere life in the cool, low, rambling house. 'How does one learn?' I asked. 'How do you go about it?' 'There are lots of ways,' he said, 'but they all lead to the same goal. Every teacher has his own methods. Mine was a young man, the only young man among many old ones. I chose him because I thought his mind might still be flexible, more tolerant in dealing with my European foolishness. I was wrong there. He was the most uncompromising one of them all.'

"I interrupted him. 'How did you start?' I had to know that, I absolutely had to know the point of departure.

" 'He led me into a white room, empty except for a table and a chair. The table was covered with a green cloth, completely smoothed out, not a wrinkle or a seam to catch the eye or divert the brain. For that's the whole point: The brain has to be starved into surrender. Only then does it learn to obey and become subordinate to the will. I sat down on the chair and he placed a matchstick on the green cloth. "Look at the match on the cloth. Think only of it, the match, the cloth, nothing else. *Think*: the match. *Think*: the cloth." That's all. The moment your thoughts wander, the moment you begin to think: "I'm sitting uncomfortably" or "I'm bored" or "What am I doing here?" the exercise is over. Then you start all over again.'

" 'How long did you manage it?'

" 'Seven seconds the first time. Later ten minutes. Now as long as I like.'

"The matchstick, the cloth, the white room, the brothers, the landscape—seven seconds—I wondered if I could do it too.

" 'Of course you can,' he said, and it no longer surprised me that he always knew what I was thinking. Then he began to speak again, for the first and only time in an urgent tone—and at once his shape and his face darkened and seemed to melt away until I couldn't see him anymore. Even his voice came from far away and I couldn't understand everything, however hard I tried. I mustn't go back to London, he said, that would be dangerous for me, I must stay here or go to Paris—or to India. There I'd be safe. I said—or perhaps I only thought—'But I must go back to London! Bill—Nina—'

"He said, 'Your husband and your daughter are better off without you than with you,' and those words I heard again quite clearly because I knew he was right. They were singing in my ear, those words, as though he were repeating them over and over: 'Your husband and your daughter are better off without you than with you.'

"I made no attempt to contradict him. Why should I? I'd always known it—but always accompanied by hatred. Now I saw it without hatred, crystal-clear. That's what made it so awful.

"Again he said something about danger in London, re-peated that I mustn't go back there on any account. But I could hear no echo inside myself, I was empty, the connection had been cut off. The matchstick on the green cloth . . ." She turned her face toward me and laughed. "It's funny—wherever I look now, right at this moment for instance, there's his face and there's the matchstick on the green cloth. Over there is the terrace—and in front of it I see the matchstick and the cloth—"

I followed her glance and saw figures moving, waving, then a shout: "Where are you? Come and get it!"

We got up.

·

Breakfast. The huge coffee pot was passed from hand to hand, milk, sugar, the long, thin, golden-brown loaf of French bread from which everyone tore off a hunk, honey to spread on it, yogurt for Jean-Pierre, a bucket of carrots for Aesculapius, an egg for me—"because you're a spoiled brat."

"I'm going to Saint-Tropez today," said Jerome to Eva. "Can you drive me to the station?"

"I'll take you," said Peter.

Anabel broke off a piece of bread and smiled at me. Had she heard what Jerome had just said?

"If you pack fast, you can catch the eleven-twenty," said Peter.

"I don't need to pack," said Jerome. "I'm not staying over. Today is market day, isn't it? I'll take a late train back and meet you all at the market."

They got up. Jerome bent down, kissed me quickly on the cheek, waved to the others and followed Peter to the garage.

I ate my egg, drank my coffee and sat on for a while.

Even after the table had been cleared, I still couldn't move.

"It's a good thing he's going," said Anabel. "In fact, it's necessary."

Was she still my friend? Jerome had gone and here she was using words like "good" and "necessary." I gave her a hostile look. She smiled.

"You've forgotten. Jeannine's left by now."

I closed my eyes. What was the matter with me? Of course, Dujardin had ordered her to leave. Still, just in case: "Are you sure she's gone?"

"I was standing yesterday morning by the desk in the lobby when I heard the doorman say, 'A taxi for Madame Dujardin.' Then came a lot of luggage and then came Jeannine. Alone. The doorman said, 'I hope we'll see you again soon, Madame,' and she walked right past him. Bellboys jumped to attention, the porter loaded her luggage—the taxi driver had to help him—she got in, no tips, not a word of thanks, and banged the door. The doorman, the bellboys and the porter stood outside watching the taxi drive away."

Exit the Brimstone butterfly. Beautiful, bright-yellow, sporting in the sunshine—but short-lived.

"What will Jerome do when he gets to the Albi and they tell him she's left? Will he go on to the Nouveaux Artistes?"

"Perhaps. But there are other possibilities at the Albi."

•

"At first I was really happy to hear Jerome's voice when he called," said Babs, reliving those fateful days at Saint-Tropez as she swam the prescribed ten lengths slowly and with dignity in her Hollywood pool. Every one of her movements was an order to the water: "You to the right—and you to the left." Everybody in Hollywood swam, some full of vigor and body-building ambition, spanking and flogging the water, others, like Babs, because in California it was the thing to do. "He (or she) swims every day" was a solid character reference.

"I thought of returning to Paris with Jeannine, but Robert said on the telephone it was so hot there that the asphalt had started to melt and people's shoes got stuck in it, so I decided to stay on for a few days. And the very next day, out of the clear blue sky—Jerome."

Babs grabbed the ladder, declined a helping hand, climbed panting out of the pool, gave the gleaming blue water a last dirty look and sighed.

"When I think how well I felt in the old unhealthy days . . ."

She stretched out on the cushioned chaise lounge, covered her face with Nivea cream and closed her eyes.

"You know, Jerome and I had always been able to laugh together—but not this time. I had to tell him the whole story, about Dujardin and Jeannine, every detail of it. He wanted to call Paris immediately and talk to her. I said, 'Do you want to ruin her life? Can you keep her?' Whereupon he sat at my desk and started to write her a letter. I said, 'Jerome, *no one* writes to Jeannine, don't you know that? One takes her out, one goes to bed with her—but one doesn't *write* to her!' And so he just sat there, his head in his hands—I'd never known him like that before. And yet I don't think it was anything to do with love, that's not Jerome's cup of tea at all—though half-finished affairs can be dangerous, but that wasn't it, either. He was in a fix, he was at Dujardin's mercy twice over. That was it. Finally he said—and I believed him—'I could kill that man!' "

•

Nonetheless he went to see him. That very day. For when he came down to the lobby after seeing Babs, the Indian was waiting for him. Jerome told me about it later. The man had suddenly appeared, blocking Jerome's way. "What do you want?" Instead of an answer, the Indian pointed to the elevator. The bell captain intervened.

"This is Monsieur Dujardin's valet."

Jerome's stored-up hatred exploded into the dark face. "You can tell your master to go to hell."

But the man didn't move.

"He doesn't understand French, or English either, Monsieur," said the bell captain.

Jerome had the feeling that the Indian understood every word, although the dark liquid eyes stared blankly ahead. The man turned and walked toward the elevator. Jerome followed.

The elevator was crowded; Jerome and the dark-skinned man stood chest to chest. Jerome's narrow nomad's eyes glared malevolently into the shiny black ones close to him, but they were met and deflected by an impenetrable wall of tranquillity. The Indian just stood there, calm and gentle, his shoulders relaxed. Silently he glided along the hallway in front of Jerome, stopped outside a door and opened it without knocking.

Dujardin was sitting at the desk in the living room as if he were in his office. Brochures, weighty tomes and catalogues were stacked neatly in front of him. Dark suit, white shirt, glasses, the French businessman. He stood up courteously and held out his hand across the desk.

"Dujardin."

Jerome thought it unnecessary to introduce himself. This man had sent his servant to fetch him. All right then. He ignored Dujardin's hand and his gesture to sit down, and remained standing in front of the desk.

Dujardin sat down and began to speak, curtly, in short spasms. He had a pen in his hand with which he checked off items on a sheet of paper. Not that he exactly avoided looking at Jerome, but it was the paper that claimed his attention.

"Mr. Lorrimer—I saw three of your paintings in Paris. Unfortunately only three."

"I have three more here," said Jerome involuntarily—and bit his lip.

"Good. Send them to me in Paris. I already appreciated their quality from the first three. I like your themes too. I need a figural exhibition after the last abstract ones. At the moment I'm showing primitive Asiatic art, Persian and Indian miniatures. I can offer you October first, that is, the first three weeks of October, a good date for sales."

Jerome listened quietly.

"My proposal: The gallery will retain twenty-five percent of the proceeds and will assume all costs, including framing. How many paintings would you have available?"

Jerome opened his mouth—but remained silent. Dujardin continued as if he had received an answer.

"Twenty-five is a good number. No sense in hanging them too close. In my gallery every painting has room to breathe and is individually lighted by a wall spotlight."

Jerome moistened his dry lips with his tongue.

"I think you'll be satisfied with the frames—our man works for the Louvre. Of course it would do no harm to let us have another five canvases to hold in reserve, because we may easily sell out. Now, about the catalogue: a color reproduction on the cover and four black-and-whites inside. I'd like you to leave the choice to me; I know my clients and their taste. We'll send out over two thousand catalogues. I hope you will attend the vernissage. That is always important."

Jerome stared at him, bracing himself against the desk with both hands, leaning forward, trying to force Dujardin to look at him. Dujardin lifted his face, the eyes behind the glasses questioning, neutral, courteously interested.

"What about Jeannine?" snarled Jerome.

Dujardin took off his glasses and polished them carefully with his handkerchief.

I've got you! thought Jerome.

Dujardin put his glasses back on.

"I also need a short curriculum vitae and a photograph. For the back of the catalogue."

Jerome leaned over the desk and grabbed at his collar, at his neck, shaking him, choking him. Dujardin offered no resistance. His glasses fell off, revealing myopic eyes which looked at him unseeingly. Jerome let go, stood still for a moment, shaking. Then he bent down and picked up the glasses. The bridge was broken. Someone took them out of his hand; the Indian was standing behind him.

Jerome walked slowly toward the door. As he reached it, he heard Dujardin's voice: "Mr. Lorrimer, I'll expect your three paintings in Paris toward the end of the week. Our transport agent will collect the others in London. Please leave your address with the desk clerk."

•

Jerome took off his shoes, rolled up his trousers and walked slowly along the beach, letting the water wash over his feet. At this time of day, siesta time, Saint-Tropez was dead.

He wasn't hungry. Nobody is hungry after losing a battle. He kicked at the water with his feet. His troops were decimated, his ammunition spent. Bound hand and foot, he had accepted the victor's terms—the fulfillment of all his, Jerome's, dreams. The irony of it! *Vae victis.*

He sat down under a deserted beach umbrella and watched a couple of fishing boats riding at anchor, their green paint, striped with red, reflected in the rippling water. Van Gogh, he thought. He'd have liked that. Automatically he felt in his pocket for a pencil. No sketchbook, damn it.

Jeannine. He forced himself to think of her. She was in a mess and it was all because of him. My fault, as usual, he thought without bitterness or remorse. On second thought he decided that for once it *wasn't* his fault if she was left high and dry; after all, he hadn't exactly found her in church, she knew what she was doing! Nor would she remain on her own for long; Jeannine was a born survivor. And as far as her connection with the man upstairs at the Albi was concerned, that had been ruptured long ago. He had ignored Jerome's question—"What about Jeannine?"—not because he was bleeding from a wound too painful to touch upon but because he didn't seem to remember who it was Jerome was talking about. That was what had enraged Jerome to the point of knocking his glasses off his nose, and the man had sat there, naked, at his mercy—if only for a moment. But that moment was worth it.

He stood up and looked at his watch. Soon the shops would be raising their shutters and reopening their doors. He waded through the sand back to the sea wall.

When he entered the Nouveaux Artistes gallery, his trousers were still rolled up and he was carrying his shoes.

The gallery was empty.

"My paintings, please."

The man in the office, who looked like an Italian, heavyset, sturdy, hair parted in the middle, looked at him in surprise. Wasn't this the young man who had knocked so modestly at his door in the morning?

"I haven't had time to look at them yet. Why don't you come back in a few days' time—"

"No, thanks, I'll take them along now."

"Just a moment, please—"

The heavy man was unexpectedly quick on his feet and went over to the canvases, still standing with their faces to the wall, where the young man had respectfully placed them that morning. What had happened in the meantime? Had his competitors, the Saint-Tropez Artists Gallery, shown signs of interest?

"Wait a minute—I might have time right now—let's take a look at them."

But the young man shook his head and marched to the door, his canvases under his arm. "Bye," he muttered, closing the door gently behind him.

One has one's little triumphs, thought Jerome, stopping outside on the pavement to tie the string around his three "children."

.

Nice. Four o'clock in the morning on the marketplace. Still too hot to wait in the truck. Ursula, Eva, Anabel and I got out and sat down on the running board.

"There's Marcel," cried Ursula suddenly and got up.

"Marcel?" Anabel followed her with her eyes as she pushed her way past the stalls and through the hammering, shouting crowd to the Renault, from which a young man was unloading crates and large glass balloons encased in wickerwork.

"Our neighbor's son," Eva yelled in her ear. "Marcel Raquin. He grows wine."

We all watched as Ursula greeted the young man, who looked up at her in surprise and adoration. He didn't even stop to close the doors of his car, but escorted her a few steps away to a café, where empty tables and chairs stood waiting for the market to end. They sat down. We made no comment, just watched them in silence. Eva smiled.

A dark figure carrying a large package planted itself in

front of us, saluted and stowed the canvases inside the truck. "Where's Peter?" asked Jerome.

We pointed vaguely to the heart of the turmoil and he plunged into it.

The canvases! So the Nouveaux Artistes hadn't kept his paintings! And—had he seen Dujardin? Dark as it was, I had tried to read something in his face, but it told me nothing. I wanted to jump up and run after him—but I caught a look from Anabel in time. She nodded reassuringly. She seemed satisfied.

•

Later, in the sea, I watched her swim farther out than usual, turn on her back and drift with the current, which carried her slowly away from us. I swam over to her. Her white face rested on the water like a lotus blossom.

"I'm leaving tomorrow. Or maybe right away, as soon as we get home."

I had no right to plead and implore. Ferencsi's arms were waiting for her in London.

"Won't you sleep for a few hours first?"

"I'm not tired. On the contrary. But don't tell the others. Don't tell anyone. I'll leave a note for Ursula, thanking her and all that. And—don't be unhappy, everything is going to be all right. You'll see."

•

When I woke up at midday and saw a note slipped under the door, I felt orphaned and cried.

25

The painter telephoned.

"No sitting tomorrow. I'm going to Paris." Astonishment on my part. "I've been offered a show." Congratulations on my part. "But I want to take a look at the place first. All new people since the war. I'll be back on Friday. I'm under pressure now—I'd like to include your portrait. Twelve o'clock on Saturday as usual."

Three days without work and without compass.

I reached for the diary. I hadn't opened it for an entire week. I knew it was of no use to me at this moment, for it wouldn't have contained any reference to those July days in 1939 in Grasse, those days that I had decided to relive once again on my own, in slow motion, hour by hour, up to the morning when Anabel left for London. That accomplished, she could take over again.

Diary, July 1939:

Drove home, slowly this time. Spent two nights on the way— but not in Paris. Made a detour around. Had the feeling that Jean would find me in town wherever I'd be staying. Jean. I

now think of him as Jean. Perhaps he was still in Saint-Tropez.
More likely, in fact. First, because he wanted to talk to
Jerome about his exhibition—he'd already done that, though,
I could tell by Jerome's face that night at the market in Nice.
Second, and more important, he would want to wait for
Jeannine to get out of the Paris apartment. "I'll have to air the
place," he'd said. "Thoroughly. Chatterjii"—the servant—
"will melt aromatic candlewax to a thick paste, dip his naked
feet in it and walk through all the rooms, climbing over the
chairs, the sofas and the beds, leaving his footprints behind.
When the wax hardens, he'll scratch it off and the air will be
clean again." He was standing at the balcony railing as he
spoke, and he laughed. It suddenly occurred to me to tell him
about the footprints Edmonde had left on me. To tell him, for
instance, that even now I can't smell turpentine without getting
sick.

I laid the book down on the table. Edmonde! So that was
the painter's name, her Christian name. No one knew her
real name. She signed her work "E.T." and had become
famous under her nickname, "Madame Eté."

That was the first time I'd ever been able to talk about it. No
one listens the way Jean does. I had hardly mentioned my dear
stepmother—and he already knew what Edmonde had meant
to me. When I told him that even today I can't have my
clothes dry-cleaned, that they either have to be washed or
given away when there's a spot on them because the very
thought of turpentine turns my stomach, he interrupted me. "It
will never make you sick again. As of now you'll actually
enjoy the smell of turpentine or benzine. Like fresh pine
needles."

It's true! On the way home I had to stop three times to fill
up. Usually I have to get out of the car and move a

considerable distance away, but I forgot all about that, sat where I was, paid, drove off again—suddenly remembered and actually thought I noticed a smell of treebark or resin or pine needles inside the car. How easily one can fool oneself if one trusts somebody! A tricky thing . . .

He told me, quite casually, that he knew Edmonde, that she'd had two shows at his gallery. No further comment.

We stood side by side on the balcony for a long time. Most of the lights were out. Only a lighthouse in the far distance turned slowly around, and for a split second one could distinguish the sea from the sky and remember where one was standing. I would have liked to stop that beacon. Only in complete darkness, without horizon, without familiar shapes, could I tell him everything. Everything. Even about the apartment in St. James's Street. That was the only time he reacted. He reached for my hand and pressed it so hard that it hurt. He said I must give up the apartment at once, in fact never set foot there again, give notice by telephone and mail them a check. He was so insistent that I think I promised. Of course I can't keep my promise, I still have my things there. So does Jerome. Have to pay Mrs. Cook too.

At twelve o'clock on Saturday I was sitting in the studio holding my old pose. The portrait was finished, but when I said so, the painter just muttered, mixing her paints.

During our coffee break she chortled into her cup.

"I've got a bit of news for you."

"About your exhibition? Have you accepted?"

"It's all arranged. Decent people. A bit young but well mannered. No, I mean a bit of news for *you*. I went to the Dujardin Gallery. It isn't there anymore—that is, Dujardin isn't there anymore. He's gone off to India or Tibet or somewhere for good. Nobody knows where he is. It's now run by other people, mediocrities, uninteresting. But I made

234 · Lilli Palmer

some inquiries. Jeannine's still around. Do you know what she did during the war? Joined the resistance fighters!"

"There's an old Jewish saying, 'Before I'm surprised—I don't believe it.'"

She laughed. "She really fought. In her way, of course. She had a couple of German army officers for lovers. Pure patriotism. And so, during the occupation she had plenty of nylons and champagne for herself and plenty of military information for a fine young chap in the resistance. After the war she married him. The people at the gallery had her address, and I didn't want to pass up the opportunity—for your sake." She grinned. "Now you're sitting there with your ears pricked up like a dog's. Well, her husband is an instructor at the local driving school. He's younger than she is. They live in Neuilly, in a little house with a garden. God-awful! Roses around the door, a swing for the kiddies. Two of them. A fat woman opened the door—I wasn't sure at first whether this could be Jeannine or not. A living room with crocheted mats all over the place, and a mother-in-law who lives with them. Didn't leave us alone for a minute, either, but Jeannine didn't seem to mind. She showed me a print in their bedroom—abstract—the only souvenir of her Dujardin days. Mother-in-law stood in the doorway watching us suspiciously, an old dragon with her mouth turned down and a mustache like a hussar. Jeannine remembered my name. I pretended I'd come for Jean Dujardin's address, but of course she didn't know it. Then I left. The children were playing in the sandbox in the garden. Pretty funny, eh? Hold it! There's an expression on your face just now—I'd like to get that on the canvas! Keep thinking the same thing. Let's get back to work."

It was easy to keep thinking the same thing, to run the film backward, back from the fat wife of the driving instructor to the German army officer and to the Hotel Albi in Saint-Tropez.

•

At the Gurnemantzes' the hot days had dragged on after Anabel's departure. Outwardly everything was just the same. Only Jerome was now excused from picking, for he would set out with his easel in the morning and return only when the light began to fade. He painted doggedly, joylessly. Even in the evening, when we stood the wet canvases against the trunk of the pine tree and admired them, the corners of his mouth turned up into the old defensive smile. He wasn't fooling himself. He didn't allow himself to forget the reason why on October 1 posters would appear all over Paris saying: LORRIMER. FIRST EXHIBITION. DUJARDIN GALLERY.

Ursula spent some time every day at Madame Raquin's— on account of the asthma. She always took Jean-Pierre with her. Peter didn't say anything, Eva did three people's work and could be heard singing in the kitchen. Aesculapius showed up on the terrace more frequently, as if he sensed something, trotting from one person to another, nodding his head vigorously, and was paid off in carrots. Once, when I was drying dishes, he poked his big donkey's head through the kitchen window. I had the feeling I could lift off his head—and there would be Bottom standing outside like in *A Midsummer Night's Dream*.

Once, while I was filling his baskets in the orchard, Peter appeared with a bottle of disinfectant to get rid of the ticks which liked to settle in the long donkey ears. I held on to the wildly twitching gray felt tubes while Peter painted away.

"Peter," I finally said into the silence, "why don't you talk to me? Nobody talks to anybody anymore. Everyone's stewing in his own juice. Couldn't we have another council meeting?"

He shook his head and kept on painting.

"The weather's changed. We're all frozen. The great ice age is coming."

"Don't you mind Ursula spending so much time at the Raquins'?"

"I have no right to mind. If she's going to marry Raquin, the boy has to make friends with him."

"And suppose she comes back to you?"

"Then Eva will kill herself. That's what she says."

I released Aesculapius's ear and he made his escape, protesting loudly.

"Take the chance! I don't think she'd do it, she's always singing so happily in the kitchen—"

Peter packed up his pharmacy, took out his pipe, filled it, and thought it over.

"I have an idea that the ones who sing in the kitchen are apt to cave in when the going is rough."

•

When I got back to the house, a telegram was waiting for me. From my agent. "Return soonest stop Leading role excellent script *Captain's Lamp* with Oskar Homolka stop Rehearsals begin July 20." I ran to Eva, to Ursula, explained to Jean-Pierre, kissed Aesculapius, whirling in ecstasy like a spinning top. All the pressure of the last weeks had lifted—at least for a few glorious minutes.

Where was Jerome? Somewhere under the umbrella pines on the adjoining hillside. Clutching my telegram and trying to stay in the shade, I raced down our hillside and up the next one. I could see him in the distance, crouched on his folding chair, absorbed and paying no attention to my shouts announcing my arrival.

"Jerome!" I waved the telegram under his nose. He disengaged himself from something a long way off and made an effort to focus on the piece of blue paper.

"Well, what are you going to do?"

"How can you ask?" I cried. "There's a train at eight-thirty for Paris. If we can't get a sleeper, we'll simply have to sit up."

He stuck his brush in the jam jar dug next to him into the sandy ground. Then he said with slow deliberation, pointing to the half-finished canvas on the easel, "I can't come with you. You can see for yourself why I can't."

I sat down in the sand. Why was I always charging ahead like a horse with blinkers thinking only of myself? To hell with my London job—it was Jerome's turn now at long last. Of course he couldn't come with me, he now had to look after his own interests. My excitement and ecstasy melted away. Ahead of me lay nothing but the long railway trip back to London, rehearsals—alone.

Not completely alone, though. Anabel! But could I impose on her again? I'd really have to let her spend all her time with Ferencsi—if he was still in London.

Jerome would stand on the platform tonight and wave to me. Separation. Weeks and weeks of separation. And just at the time when it was so important to reconstruct our life together again. We were rid of Jeannine, root and branch, but that didn't mean that we two had grown back together again. We'd have to go about that slowly and cautiously—and casually. No demands, no searching looks, no "proving our love," just being together . . .

All *kaput* for the time being. Should I turn down the part? Could I afford to?

Jerome too had been staring thoughtfully into the pine trees. Perhaps he had been thinking along the same lines. I hoped so. Now he started squeezing paint out of tubes and picking up his brushes again.

"You could do me a favor though: Take my finished paintings with you and deliver them to the Dujardin Gallery, rue Faubourg St. Honoré."

•

I sat up all night, slept for a few hours, and when I woke up we were at the Gare de Lyons. Taxi to the Hotel de la Muette, and in answer to the porter's fond inquiry, "No, Monsieur's not with me this time," a quick shower and off to the Dujardin Gallery with the paintings.

The secretary had been duly briefed and took charge of the package; Monsieur Dujardin wasn't around. Disappointment! I had looked forward to meeting him. The secretary showed me into the office, unpacked the canvases and stood them against the wall—just as Jerome must have done when he came for the first time while Jeannine was lying on that leather sofa over there! The secretary nodded approvingly; Monsieur Dujardin would be pleased . . .

I took the bus back to the hotel. Economize! Who knew whether the new play would be a success? The heat wave was finally over and it was pouring rain. Paris in a summer rain. The pavement glistened, the Arc de Triomphe was reflected on the Champs-Elysées. My bus took me past the Café Colisée. Babs! Should I call her up? Certainly not.

After sleeping for a couple of hours at the hotel, I called her and we met at the Colisée. Her faithful followers didn't bother us; most of them had left Paris, if possible for America, and she herself, she told me, would be leaving soon for Hollywood. Robert had had a couple of offers.

I looked around and thought that Paris smelled of war. People were hurrying through the street, nobody strolled about windowshopping, the cafés were half-empty. I had never seen the Champs-Elysées so hushed. Only Babs doggedly radiated high spirits in her usual black-and-white elegance. Obviously, the little mishap at the Hotel Albi lay way behind her.

"Why isn't Jerome here?"

I explained. She stared at me open-mouthed.

"An exhibition at Dujardin's? How did he manage that?"

I shrugged my shoulders, looking ignorant and clean. She sensed something, couldn't puzzle it out.

"And where's your girl friend—what's her name?"

"Maclean. In London."

"And Jerome's staying on in Grasse?"

I nodded, managed to keep up the innocuous expression on my face. She gave me a thoughtful look.

"You know, you're not quite so germ-free and wholesome as you used to be. You're catching up!"

"I'm learning. Soon I'll be allowed to stay up late and talk to the grown-ups," I said, paying for my own coffee and for hers.

Back to the hotel. There was still some time left before my train. I stood by the window, looking at the trees, whipped by the rain. The Calais-Dover crossing would be awful. Telephone. A voice I didn't recognize.

"Jean Dujardin."

"Yes?"

"I'd like to talk to you about Anabel."

"Yes?"

"Tell her I'm waiting for her here in Paris. But not for long. I'm going back to India."

"But she can't just drop everything and—"

"Before long, millions of people are going to have to drop everything."

He seemed to be speaking of a *fait accompli*. War. An alarm bell started ringing in my brain: What would become of *The Captain's Lamp*?

"Very soon individual destinies won't count anymore,"

said the voice. "Your friend has only a few weeks' time. She must hurry. I'm waiting."

He hung up. I remained sitting on the bed, trying to find my way out of this labyrinth. What did this man want of Anabel? He knew all about Bill and Nina—and about Ferencsi. Why was he interfering? And so authoritatively, as if he had a right to, as if he were her guardian or guardian angel. He hadn't mentioned the "danger" that was supposed to be threatening her in London. All the same, his voice left me resentful and troubled.

•

Diary, July 1939:

> L. back from Grasse. Quite unexpectedly. Alone! Rehearsals for a new play. Jean called her in Paris—
> No echo inside me. Every day pushes him farther away. On the balcony at the Albi I seriously considered—only for a second but quite seriously—going to India. Getting away, making my escape, stripping off my life like an old dress and burning it. Putting on another one, start again. Absurd. I'm Bill's so-called wife, Nina's bad mother, I run the house, I'm brailling a new book for the blind. From morning to night I have only one thought in my head: When will J. be back?

•

Rehearsals had started. A good part, an insolent young woman who goes through "terrible sufferings," grows up and is "purified" in the process, the way these things happen in scripts.

A telegram from Jerome: "Tomorrow Simon's sixtieth birthday stop Take bottle red wine stop Four canvases finished stop Love Jerome."

Dilemma. Tomorrow I would have rehearsals all day and an

evening script session at the director's home. I called Anabel, although I felt guilty, having seen her only once and
very briefly since I had gotten back. On top of it I had
actually forgotten to ask her if Ferencsi was still in London
or whether her trip to Grasse had ruined everything. What
kind of a friend was I? One couldn't excuse everything on
the grounds of pressure of rehearsals.

But on the telephone Anabel was her usual self, didn't
seem to feel at all neglected. Yes, of course she'd get the
wine and take it to Simon. In case he wasn't home—there
was no *r* in August—she'd leave the package at the door.

She called me that evening. Simon, she reported, hadn't
been home.

•

Diary, August 1939:

Visited Simon. His birthday. Brought him wine from J. and L.
and cognac from me. Received an appropriate welcome. Had
firmly resolved not to drink with him. Refused the first glass
but kept him company on the next four. Felt wonderful. Told
him—I'm afraid—all about my trip to Grasse. Except for
Jean. I didn't leave him out on purpose—after the fourth drink
I didn't have any control over my purposes—but because Jean
just didn't show up. He remained invisible, out of reach.

Simon enjoyed it all immensely. He needed cheering up just
as much as I did: His axolotl is dead. Assassinated. He left his
cleaning woman to look after it while he went to the seaside on
vacation. She fell ill and sent her sister over to clean up. The
sister had never seen an axolotl and when she saw it floating
there motionless, she thought it was dead and flushed it down
the toilet.

We were both in mourning. He for his love, I for mine.
Simon, whom I hate, is the only person I can drink with. And

only then can I stand him. What's more—it almost doesn't stop there! I don't fool myself. Ever since Edmonde I've tried my damnedest to suppress it but it's still there. Edmonde couldn't take alcohol, she'd fall into a kind of stupor, sitting or lying on the floor, her eyes and mouth wide open, looking surprised and moronic. I used to die laughing at her. Once—strange, now I actually feel ashamed, whereas I used to get a kind of kick out of this memory—once we were drinking in the studio when what's his name, that pianist, knocked at the door. Can't even remember his name, only that he was crazy about me. Edmonde was half gone already, so I poured another whiskey down her throat and she passed out, stiff as a ramrod. And then I made the pianist—what the devil was his name? Richard something—I made him sleep with her instead of with me. I remember we both thought it was terribly funny. Between us, we carried her into the bedroom—and then I went back to the studio and kept on drinking until Richard came back from the bedroom. Suddenly, the whole thing seemed to me extremely squalid and I threw him out. Never saw him again. Edmonde didn't wake up until the next morning. She knew nothing, thought she'd had a nightmare. After that she never touched another drop of alcohol—although I never told her! I was afraid she might kill me. And today, twenty years later, I got really drunk again. And with Simon, who's responsible for the whole mess, for Jerome's his work after all. He'll never be able to shake his father off, for Simon's the stronger of the two. There's no chink in his armor. The more I insulted him, the more happily he agreed with me.

When I began to flag, he went over to the attack. Said he hoped I wasn't trying to kid myself that I wanted to save J. for L.'s sake. Nothing but my own vanity and my own jealousy had made me race across France all night like an avenging angel, he said. The hell with L.! I, Anabel, was the one who had lost J., I'd been beaten with my own weapons.

What is truth anyhow? Everyone has his own. I denied it, told him I'd broken off with J. beforehand, swore a sacred oath on "my daughter's life"—at this he nearly choked with laughter inside his wobbly double chin and congratulated me on my sense of humor. When it was all over, I found myself at a dead end, disarmed. I staggered down the five flights of stairs, holding on to the handrail. Never in my life have I felt such hatred, such impotent hatred. Sat at the wheel for ages before I drove away. Wasn't sure I could find my way home.

•

After an interval of one week there was another entry, the last one. August 1939:

Jean's trying to reach me. Person-to-person calls from Paris. I always pick up the receiver—after all, it might be J.—and tell the operator that I don't know where to get in touch with Mrs. Maclean. Which happens to be true. I'm not in touch with her.

I had a letter from him today—where did he get my address?— he was sailing this week, I must hurry, he had reserved two cabins—

None of this concerns me. I'm not reachable. I'm on another ship, traveling in another direction.

J.'s been back in London for several days, so L. told me. Not a word from him. I didn't expect anything else and yet I'm incapable of taking any action. I sit at my desk and look at the telephone. In front of me is the brailling machine and the book I'm working on, in case Nina comes into the room. She does so quite often nowadays, unfortunately. Tells me about her exams. As though she were trying to include me in her life. Too late. No interest. My loss. But—how can a child replace the man you love?

L. senses something, although I do my damnedest to keep

her from suspecting anything. She calls me from rehearsals, driving me crazy because I think each time: J. at last! She wants to know how I am, apologizes for the hundredth time for not coming to see me. I'm glad she can't come. How could I explain the way I look? My clothes are flapping about me, I look like a scarecrow. I'd have to resurrect Ferencsi and blame it all on him—and that thought makes me puke now.

Jean wrote that war would break out within the next three weeks. As if I cared. Other people care, though; it's the only subject of conversation all around. Total strangers babble away at each other on the street, seeking reassurance. Bill's organizing a branch office in Scotland—he's expecting his call-up any moment because he's a reserve officer. He's in high spirits, as if he were looking forward to it.

L.'s rehearsals are in hot water. Yesterday on the telephone she said in a shaky voice, "We may not even open."

J. would have remained in Grasse if war were not just around the corner. I wonder if his exhibition will still take place? L. says J.'s not very hopeful but is neither disappointed nor depressed. I know why. He's probably even relieved. He's rid of Jeannine, of the Dujardin "charity" exhibition, and he's rid of me. In fact, he's rid of all the counterfeit currency in his life.

Those were her last words. Except for the letter—still unopened.

26

"Where were you in the autumn of 1939?" I asked the painter.

"In Paris. Where else?"

She was giving the canvas a coat of temporary varnish. She leaned back and narrowed her eyes. "The raw umber on the shoulder has sunk right into the canvas. English paints! French umber never does that. I'll have to go over it again. Pose, please."

I pulled the poncho over my head, sat down in my chair and submerged myself into the nightmare days of those last few weeks of peace in 1939.

In the middle of August they had called a meeting on stage. The director, looking pale, remained standing in the wings, staring at the floor. We knew what was coming. For the last week *The Captain's Lamp* had been barely flickering— two members of the cast had already been called up—and today it would be extinguished.

The producer saw to that. Rehearsals were suspended as of today, he said, that is—well, they would be temporarily interrupted. He hadn't given up hope but in the present political situation—one could only pray that things would soon settle down—one never knew—anyway, for the present there was nothing one could do except listen to the radio, read the papers and wait.

We melted away. Everyone silently picked up an envelope containing half a week's rehearsal pay at the stage door. The doorkeeper waved to us, knocked at his wooden leg. "Got that the last time around. Only have one more to give."

I found my little car at the parking lot and caressed the wheel. It would have to be sold at once. Misery. How about ambulance driving? Good idea, I'd sign on today.

But my mother was waiting by the window with a huge smile on her face: My film company had called! Could I come to the studio immediately; an American actress had preferred to go home while the going was still good, and the film had to be finished, with retakes of all her scenes. Hallelujah! That very afternoon I stood in front of the camera and worked every day—until the morning of September 3.

"That's it," said the painter. "I'll have to wait and see how it looks when it's dry."

While she was making coffee—for the last time?—I wandered about the studio, saying goodbye. Of course I'd be back sometime, but only as a guest; I wouldn't belong anymore. I came to a stop in front of the bookcase. There, exactly at eye level, stood the little bronze head.

I picked it up and placed it on the table. Throughout those long weeks, while I had relived my life with Anabel, I had to make the same effort every time I entered the studio, to remind myself that she had once led another existence, a ragtag, dunghill one, with Edmonde, the painter.

She entered with the tray from the kitchen, sat down, poured the coffee. Anabel's head stood exactly midway between us. We drank in silence, our eyes meeting on Anabel's profile.

September 3! An easy date to remember. I raised my eyes to the painter's blunt face.

"Do you remember what you were doing on September 3, when the declaration of war was broadcast? Here in London it was eleven o'clock in the morning."

"I was in Paris, sitting in my bathtub. And you?"

"I was in a film studio, lying on a few square yards of artificial grass."

She stretched out her hand and pulled the little bronze closer, taking off her glasses. "And Anabel? What was she doing?"

"I don't know."

She gave me a severe look, had one last go at cross-examining me.

"Weren't you friends anymore?"

"Oh yes, we were friends."

She looked at me for a long time, sighed, gave up, pushed the head aside.

"Pose, please. Just a last check. I think we can finish today."

I picked up the little sculpture, carried it over to the mantelpiece and put it down where I had first seen it, half hidden by the vase.

Took up the pose. Looked in the direction of Anabel's head.

•

I knew very well what Anabel had been doing on September 3. I had been told. In detail. By two eyewitnesses, Nina and Mrs. Cook.

Nina had had lunch with her mother and heard her say she was going to the library for the blind. She wanted to find out what they were going to do with all those books, she had said. There might soon be a great many more blind people . . .

She had put on her red coat and left. But she didn't go to the library for the blind. She went to St. James's Street.

Mrs. Cook was working in the living room when she heard a sound at the front door. She switched off the vacuum cleaner and called, "Anyone there?"

"It's me, Mrs. Cook."

"Oh, Madam!"

Anabel was hugged and kissed. Thank God she was back! Just in time, too—Mrs. Cook had been so worried—and where's the young gentleman? Called up already? Not yet. Oh well, there was plenty of time for that, after all, one still wasn't quite sure . . . perhaps Mr. Chamberlain hadn't really meant what he'd said that morning, perhaps he was just trying to show old Hitler . . . what did Madam think?

Anabel was not given time to answer. She was stripped of her coat and forced to accompany Mrs. Cook on a tour of inspection. Big summer housecleaning, everything neat and shiny.

The old girl thought Anabel looked a bit thin. And pale! What about a nice cup of tea with lemon? Mrs. Cook shuffled off to the kitchen, leaving the door open, talking away while the kettle boiled.

Receiving no answer from the living room, she stuck her head around the door and saw Anabel sitting very straight on the sofa, like a visitor, looking around the room as if she were seeing it for the first time.

Mrs. Cook ambled into the room with the tray, collapsed into a chair, poured out two cups, murmuring a belated "If Madam doesn't mind . . ."

Anabel stirred her tea.

"Mrs. Cook, I—we'll have to give up the apartment."

Oh Lord, oh Lord! That was just what Mrs. Cook had been afraid of, everybody was giving everything up! She made one last try: "But Madam, the apartment's so convenient! When the young gentleman comes on leave . . ."

Anabel didn't answer, kept on stirring her tea.

Something began to dawn on Mrs. Cook. She hesitated, then took the plunge. Really, the young gentleman was—if Madam would excuse her—he was a bit too young. That never worked out, she could tell her a thing or two herself, her own late lamented had been too young too, six months younger than she was, that made quite a difference, a man ought to be older, ought to be able to protect one . . .

Anabel nodded absently. Encouraged, the old woman laid a hard, wrinkled hand on her arm. Madam was still young, there were other fish in the sea! She herself hadn't believed it in her first grief, but later on . . .

Anabel gently freed her hand in order to open her handbag, took out her purse and laid some pound notes on the table. Three months' wages.

Mrs. Cook made a half-hearted protest, pocketed the money and staggered to her swollen feet. She must finish vacuuming, she said, or she wouldn't be able to sleep that night. Just five minutes more, if Anabel didn't mind.

Anabel didn't mind. She remained sitting, even with the machine buzzing around the sofa, lifting her feet obligingly so that nothing should be overlooked. The roar didn't seem to bother her.

Later, she got up and sat down at the desk, took a pad of notepaper and an envelope out of the drawer, rummaged in her purse but couldn't find what she was looking for. Turning to Mrs. Cook, she made a writing movement with her hand. Mrs. Cook understood, took a pencil out of her apron pocket and held it up questioningly. Anabel nodded and Mrs. Cook vacuumed over to the desk and handed it to her.

She wrote very briefly—just a few lines, as far as Mrs.

Cook could tell—tore the sheet roughly off the pad, put it in the envelope and sealed it.

"Shall I post it for you, Madam?"

Not necessary, thank you. She put the letter in her handbag. Tore off another half-sheet and wrote something on it. Without putting it in an envelope, she stuffed that in her purse too.

"I've almost finished, Madam."

She smiled at Mrs. Cook. No hurry.

At last the vacuum cleaner stopped raging and was wheeled back to the kitchen. Anabel remained sitting at the desk, her head resting on her hand, waiting patiently. Probably for the young gentleman! Oh well, this wasn't the first time Mrs. Cook had seen her sitting about, waiting, though all the other times she'd been restless, impatient to get rid of her. This time she was quite different. Mrs. Cook untied her apron and hung it on the kitchen door. Then she returned to the living room.

"The key, Madam."

No reply.

"Madam?"

"Oh, yes. Thank you, Mrs. Cook."

The old woman looked at the motionless figure at the desk and realized that Anabel wasn't even aware of her presence anymore. She felt hurt.

"Well then—goodbye, Madam. Many thanks . . ."

"Goodbye, Mrs. Cook."

·

A few minutes later she put on her red coat, slipped the long strap of her handbag over her shoulder and stepped out on the balcony.

27

On the late afternoon of the same day a police car stopped outside No. 104A, Cheyne Walk. Two officers got out, looked up at the sky for a moment—the first drops of rain were beginning to fall—and disappeared inside the house.

Shortly afterward they knocked at Simon's door.

Simon got up, distinctly annoyed at the disturbance. He had just set up a new sheet of graph paper and was waiting for Jerome; the refrigerator was empty. This morning the declaration of war—and already the authorities were knocking at his door! What did they want? Gas masks? Ration cards? No? Well, what then?

They'd like him to come along. Out of the question! What was this all about? Alien registration?

The men in uniform hesitated.

"Sir—it's a question of identifying a body—"

Simon stared at them in bewilderment. "There must be a mistake somewhere—"

One of the men took a piece of paper out of his pocket and spelled out, " 'Contact Mr. Simon Lorrimer, 104A Cheyne Walk.' Is that you, sir?" And since the fat man made no move, just stared at him with wide-open eyes, he held the piece of paper in front of his face. "Recognize the handwriting, sir?"

Simon, with shaking hands, put his glasses on. "No."

The policemen looked as if they didn't believe him. The body was that of a woman, they explained. Thrown herself from the balcony. In St. James's Street. Nobody knew her—that is, nobody knew her name.

For a split second Simon thought it was me, as he later confided to Jerome, but when the policeman spoke of black hair and a red coat—

"Anabel!" he whispered hoarsely.

"Sir? Then you do know her, don't you? What is her name, please?"

Simon silently cursed his bad memory, his lack of interest. Jerome had in fact mentioned her name—some Scottish-sounding name. "Macmillan or Maclaren or something like that . . ."

"Sir, you'd better come with us, please."

Simon retreated hastily behind his desk. Absolutely not! The whole thing had nothing whatever to do with him!

The policemen were full of solicitude. "It's only a question of a few minutes, sir—the City morgue isn't that far from here, we'll take you in our car."

"No!" Simon yelled at the top of his lungs. "I mustn't leave the flat!"

"Why not, sir? You'll be back in a jiffy—"

They advanced a step. Simon barricaded himself, picking up his chair threateningly.

"Impossible! I can't—there's an *r* in the month—"

"How's that again?"

"An *r*! September has an *r* in it—I can't go out in the street—"

The officers exchanged glances, then moved to encircle him, one of them closing in from the left, the other from the right.

"And it's raining!" Simon screamed. "I haven't got a raincoat—"

A few minutes later they were dragging him toward the police car, a woolen blanket thrown over his head.

•

They drove him rapidly to the City of London morgue. Although it was still pouring rain, a few people stopped under their umbrellas to watch a fat elderly man being forcibly hustled out of a police car and through the entrance.

In the outer office Simon regained his composure. He broke away from the policemen's grip with a surprisingly deft movement, wiped his wet forehead and said imperiously, "Where's my blanket?"

It was brought in from the car while he stood erect, like a bear about to pounce. He snatched the blanket from the policeman's hand and began to fold it, matching the corners with extreme care, taking his time. His guards did not interfere.

"And now?" he asked curtly.

The two policemen beckoned to him to follow them down the long dark corridor. There was a strong smell of Lysol and of something else—Simon didn't know what it was but he had to stand still for a minute, gasping for breath.

The policemen stopped outside a door, waited politely for him to catch up with them, and opened it. The room was no bigger than a large waiting room. Tiled floor, tiled walls, about a dozen stone slabs, some empty, some occupied and covered with sheets.

One of the policemen remained at the door. The other

walked across and raised one of the sheets, dropped it again, went on to the next slab, raised the sheet, and beckoned to Simon.

Simon took a step forward, turned and retreated to the man at the door, whispering hoarsely, "I can't do it—don't you understand—"

The policeman took off his helmet, passed his hand over his sparse hair, and looked at the figure in front of him, at the limp shoulders and the helpless, gaping mouth.

"Come on, man," he said slowly. "Show some guts."

"Come on!" called the other one.

Simon took a deep breath. Just a few steps—

Her head was turned to one side. All he could see was the black hair, matted with blood, and part of the forehead. He fled back to the door, sweating profusely. "Anabel," he groaned, leaning against the door frame.

Outside in the hall was a bench, probably placed there for good reason. Simon just made it. He put his head down between his knees. When he was able to sit up again, one of the policemen was holding a glass of brandy out to him. He gulped it down—suddenly clutched his forehead.

"My son! My son knows her name."

"Where is your son? What's his name?"

"Jerome. Jerome Lorrimer. He may be at his apartment."

They helped him walk down the long corridor to the office. He knew the telephone number by heart; he'd always been able to remember figures. The policeman dialed and handed him the receiver. It rang and rang. No answer. No one at home.

"Is there anyone who would know where your son might be?"

Yes, I might. But Simon didn't know where I lived, in fact he may only have known my first name.

"Wait outside," said the policeman. "We'll call the number every ten minutes and let you know."

There were more benches in the corridor. Simon chose one under the window and managed to open it, but the rain came streaming in. He shivered and wrapped himself in the blanket.

Gradually it grew dark. At one time, one of the policemen came out of the office and looked at the motionless figure under the blanket, then returned, closing the door. A short time later they called him in. The number had answered.

"Jerome?" whispered Simon. "It's me—Simon. No, I'm not sick. Jerome, what's Anabel's last name? Quick, Jerome, tell me, what was her name? Maclean?" He turned to the watching faces. "Maclean! Anabel Maclean. I told you it was a Scottish name."

A policeman took the receiver from him.

"Excuse me, sir, but do you perhaps know the address too? Yes, sir, something has happened. Sorry, sir—she fell from a balcony. No. Killed instantly. Do you happen to know whether there are any relatives? Hello? Are you there?" He reached for a pencil. "William Maclean, 32 Queen's Gate, S.W.2. Is that her husband or her father? Aha. Thank you, sir. Just a moment, please—" He turned to Simon. "Your son wants to come and pick you up here—is that all right? Yes, sir, City of London morgue."

•

Simon went back to his bench. The policemen left for Anabel's house to inform her husband. A good thing they hadn't tried to saddle him with that too. What the hell did it have to do with him, anyhow? Why had Anabel asked that he be notified and not her husband? And if she was trying to get her own back on somebody, why not on Jerome?

The last time she had been to see him—how long ago was it? A week at the most—she had stood by the door, holding on to the handle because she'd had too much to drink, reciting poetry, a passage from John Donne, the famous one, which even he had recognized: "No man is an island, entire of itself . . . Any man's death diminishes me . . . Therefore never send to know for whom the bell tolls—" At that point he had joined in and they had declaimed in unison, "It tolls for thee!" And they had burst out laughing. She had been laughing too, he could swear to that, she had laughed just as loudly as he had, repeating, "It tolls for thee!" and pointing at him.

Had she said anything after that? Simon racked his brain. No. She had left. He had heard her going downstairs, still laughing.

He pulled his head in like a snail and wrapped himself up in the blanket as if it could make him invisible.

·

The next time he looked up, Jerome was standing in front of him. Behind him, an official.

"This gentleman would like to see the body of Mrs. Maclean—"

"No!"

Simon shook off the blanket, jumped up and grabbed his son.

"No, you mustn't! Out of the question."

Jerome was pale under his tan, haggard, his lips pressed tightly together, the dark eyes flickering dangerously.

"I must see her."

But Simon held him firmly, pressing him against his great chest, feeling his son's body against his own—for the first time.

The official watched with neutral eyes.

"Is the gentleman a relative?"

"No!" shouted Simon.

"Only the family may give permission for the body to be viewed."

Jerome pushed against Simon's shoulders with his fists and broke loose.

"I'm a friend—an intimate friend—"

"Sorry, sir," said the official. "But why don't you wait here? They'll be here before long. They've already been notified."

Jerome clasped and unclasped his hands.

"Come," said Simon quietly. "Come. Or do you want to meet them?"

Jerome looked along the dimly lit corridor and considered for a moment if he shouldn't simply run down the length of it and throw open every one of the doors—but the official intercepted his glance and lifted a warning hand without saying a word.

Simon folded up his blanket again.

"Come on," he repeated calmly.

It was dark outside. The rain was falling less heavily, a steady warm late-summer rain.

"Let's go to my place," said Simon.

Jerome shook his head.

"I can't. I've got to go back to our apartment. She might be there already, waiting for me. She's been on her feet at the studio all day. I always get our supper ready."

They were still standing in the shelter of the portico. Simon looked uneasily around, but there was as yet no car in sight bringing "the family."

"Let's walk a few steps until you find a taxi." They wandered down the dark street in silence. Tonight, the evening after the declaration of war, most people were staying at home, listening to the radio, arguing, speculating, making plans.

Jerome paused.

"What were you doing there? How did you know?"

"She had a note in her purse asking that I be notified."

"You? Why you?"

Simon lowered his head, hesitated.

"She wanted to punish me."

"Punish you? She didn't even know you."

"Yes, she did, she came to see me. Twice. I never told you. I liked her, I liked her a lot. That's why it was so terrible to see her lying there—"

Jerome stepped up very close to his father, peering through the darkness into a face that involuntarily drew back.

"What did you do to her?"

"Nothing."

"What did you say to her?"

"Nothing except the sort of thing you and I always say. Nothing else. You must believe me. I was just joking—"

Jerome raised his trembling fists and held them close to his father's eyes. "I know your jokes!"

Horrified, Simon watched the tears rolling down his son's cheeks, watched him shiver in the warm air, turn and run blindly across the street.

"Jerome!" shouted Simon. But he didn't turn around.

•

When I opened our apartment door that evening, he was sitting on the bed.

"Good Lord!" I cried. "You're all wet."

He ran his hand over his wet hair, his dripping coat. Only then did I see his face. He made an effort to stand up, but I quickly sat down beside him and took his hand. Ice-cold.

"Jerome, what is it?"

He looked at me with stricken eyes, looked away, tore his hand out of mine and sat motionless for a moment. When he turned back to me, the eyes were guarded, and his voice was firm.

"Anabel's dead. She jumped from the balcony."

He gave me time, waited until I could speak.

"Where?" The Macleans' house had no balcony.

Without taking his eyes off me, Jerome said in a quiet, steady voice, "In St. James's Street. She had an apartment there. *We* had an apartment there, she and I."

He's lying, I thought. I don't know why he does it, but he's lying.

"Ferencsi? Did she have an apartment with Ferencsi?"

"I am Ferencsi."

His eyes held mine until I was able to stand up and walk over to the window. I felt an acute pain in my stomach and remember opening the window and noticing that it had stopped raining. There was a pleasant smell of wet leaves. War had been declared that morning. Anabel was dead. What Jerome had just said was thrown out by my mind with extraordinary rapidity, was not allowed to register. Not yet. First the other hurdles. Don't rush me, Jerome, or I'll collapse.

"When did it happen?"

"This afternoon."

"Does Bill know?" No answer. I turned toward him, saw him nod slowly. My feet took me to the telephone at the other side of the bed. I sat down beside it, picked up the receiver, put it down again.

"Why did she do it?"

"I didn't want to see her anymore."

"Because of Jeannine?"

"No. I just didn't want to anymore. Hadn't for a long time."

We sat there on the bed, our bed, each on his own side, back to back. He got up, walked around the bed and stood in front of me.

"I told her that I'd like to die in your arms."

"That's easy," I said. "The hard part's living together *until* you die."

"Don't you want to anymore?"

I took his hand, still cold as ice.

"I don't think so. If I still feel tomorrow morning the way I feel now—then no."

•

That was the last time I saw him.

I heard later that he had been drafted soon afterward.

•

I spent the whole of the next day filming. Got through it somehow. That evening I went straight from the studio to the Macleans'. Saw Bill. Saw Nina.

Bill very pale, his lips pressed tightly together. Already in uniform, with a black armband. He was sitting stiffly in a chair in his library, looking at the empty fireplace. I took another chair and sat down next to him. He gave me a hostile look.

"Did you know?" he asked in a dry voice.

"No."

A long silence. I think he believed me.

"How can one live for twenty years next to a woman and know nothing about her?"

"You knew she wasn't happy."

"But all the rest! I had no idea. Why didn't *you* know? Women are supposed to have a better instinct for that sort of thing."

"I was too busy."

He turned his head and looked at me out of somber eyes.

"I asked you a serious question."

"I gave you a serious answer."

•

Nina was waiting for me in her room. She wasn't wearing black. I put my arms around her and we stood holding each other. Now, for the first time, I was able to cry. She wasn't. She did not cry. She whispered into my neck, "Do you know now—about St. James's Street?"

"Yes."

"I've known for more than a year. I saw her coming out of the house—him too. At times I wanted to tell you, then I'd think: better not. I'd suspected something for a long time. Hadn't you?"

"No."

"I don't understand that."

"I was too busy."

She pulled back to look at my face, wiping away my tears with her hard little hand.

"What will you do now?"

"Go on living."

She disengaged herself from my arms and stood in front of me, very straight, her shoulders no longer hunched, her face serious, not sad, grown up.

"I'm going to volunteer for the Land Army. It said on the radio that they need sturdy girls. I'm sturdy."

•

Bill called me after the funeral. He said he had something to give me. I drove over, parked at my usual spot next to the garden gate. Every step I took reminded me that this was the last time.

Bill was waiting for me in the library. I took my time crossing the living room, but I never paused, not even by the yellow wing chair.

He was sitting at his desk with a cardboard box in front of him.

"This is for you," he said. "It has your name on it. I found it in her safe." He hesitated, smoothed his fair, wavy hair. "And—the police gave me this letter. It's marked 'For L.' It was in her purse. They opened it but it contains nothing of any interest to them. I resealed it but—I read it too. Sorry. But I thought, perhaps—anyway, it's for you."

He pushed the box and the letter over to me and got up.

"I'm glad about the war," he said. "I hope they'll send me over to France."

Some ten months later, he was there, trapped at Calais with his regiment. He fought his way out, survived Dunkirk and D-day plus 3, went through a campaign in the Vosges as major in a commando unit. Survived.

Simon didn't. A bomb got him in his apartment in December 1941. He never went to the air-raid shelter during the months with an *r* in them.

Peter Gurnemantz also died in the war. He had volunteered for the foreign infantry regiment and was among the first to be killed. After the liberation of France in the autumn of 1944, I had a letter from Grasse. Ursula wrote that Eva had had a breakdown after Peter's death and had spent several years in a sanatorium. She was better now, however, and the two sisters were living once again together on the Gurnemantz farm—Jean-Pierre was now sixteen! New peach trees had been planted and were doing fine. But Aesculapius was dead. . . .

•

All that was left was the letter. The diary, locked up again with its golden key, had returned to its old cardboard box. There was really no need to carry it around with me anymore. Perhaps I ought to get rid of it, throw it in the Thames.

I opened the envelope.

One page crudely torn off. No salutation.

I feel an enormous relief. I'm completely free. No one has any power over me anymore. I don't love anybody—or else I love you all equally. It amounts to the same thing.

Do you remember the last time we went swimming at Nice? The current was carrying me out to sea, I was very happy letting myself drift along—but then you came swimming up, looking at me so anxiously—

Now you don't need to worry about me anymore.

A.

28

The painter was on the telephone.

"I'm just packing my canvases for Paris. Maybe you'd like to see your portrait before the crates are nailed up."

In the studio was a huge shipping crate, six feet high and almost as wide. The canvases were stacked one on top of the other, separated by slabs of cork. On the very top was my portrait.

She took it out, put it into a plain, makeshift frame and stood it against the wall, looked back at me and scrutinized my face once again.

"I can still see a couple of things I'd like to change, but I suppose I'd better leave it as it is. A portrait's never finished, anyway. You know, you look quite different now from the way you looked at our first sitting."

I felt quite different too. It's not true that one grows up slowly but surely; one marks time for years—and then one suddenly takes a leap forward.

The painter knelt in front of the canvas, took off her glasses and peered closely at it.

"What do *you* see when you look at yourself in this picture?"

"A half-finished woman."

She nodded slowly.

"That's what I was after. Your face still has quite a few possibilities."

She got up and passed her hand over my forehead, my cheeks, my chin, as if she were blind and wanted to "see" me. "Don't ruin it," she growled, almost threateningly.

Ruin what? My face? No, she meant my entire keyboard, the white as well as the black keys. So that I wouldn't wind up in the end looking like a double-crossed clown . . .

That was her goodbye. Suddenly she was in a hurry to get rid of me, as if she could hardly wait to be off, bag and baggage. For Peru. For how long? A few years, perhaps forever. She flew off like a bird, free as a bird.

One day somebody would find her, all shriveled and rolled up in a ball like one of Simon's flies, and dried out like her Indian mummy, the Doge's cap still on top of her head.